W9-BVN-168

DAMIAN

A NOVEL BY

Melissa Mather

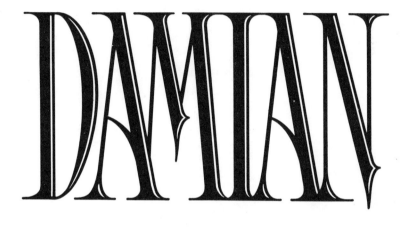

DAMIAN

Franklin Watts New York Toronto 1986

Library of Congress Cataloging in Publication Data

Mather, Melissa.
Damian.
I. Title.
PS3563.A8354D36   1986   813'.54   85-29390
ISBN 0-531-15005-4

The reader more conversant with the Greek language may judge some of the transliterations in the text overly simplified and indeed unnecessary; I ask him to consider the bewilderment the non-Greek-speaking reader faced, let us say, with *mparmpouni* instead of *barbouni*, and be compassionate.

I would like to thank Chrysanthi Bien, under whom it was my good fortune to study and whose text, *Demotic Greek*, has been my prop and my guide and for her kind help in going over the Greek used herein. Where Mrs. Bien's beautiful native tongue is used correctly, the credit is entirely hers; where my variations may strike the knowledgeable reader as worse than unfortunate, indeed impertinent, I plead my obtuseness as a student.

Melissa Mather
Hartland, Vermont

Athens is real, Lesbos is real, but the village of Pyrgotafos is, I regret to say, purely a product of my daydreams. It follows that its inhabitants and what happens to them are dreamed up also. Sorry.

also by
Melissa Mather

Rough Road Home
One Summer in Between
Emelie

to my daughter
Mary

DAMIAN

CHAPTER

1

The promise of dawn has vanished, the paling stars blotted away. Beyond the thick glass there is only blackness, utter and absolute. I think: *We're suspended in a void.* I think: *They say hell is nothingness. I am in hell.*

Beside me the wine salesman slumps farther across the armrest. I shrink against the window. One fifteen . . . but that's New York time. I should have set my watch ahead before takeoff. Might as well wait until Athens now . . . Glyfada, that is.

"The airport is over near the sea, in Glyfada," Mike informed me in that remote tone he's affected lately. (As if he can't quite place who I am.) "Half an hour by cab should see you to your hotel. I expect to wind things up in London in time to catch Tuesday's early flight to Rome, where with any luck I'll make the one o'clock plane out. We'll be going on to Damian's on Wednesday—I'll want at least one day to get acquainted before his birthday—which gives you a day for the Parthenon, a museum or two, and all those seductive shops, free as a bird, no husband in tow—how lucky can you get?"

So tomorrow we'll be done with these damnable "you go your way, I'll go mine" flight plans. Tomorrow Mike and I will be together. Good title for an abstract: *Converse between Strangers, Diverging.*

"You know very well I'm not ecstatic about going," I said. "Going by myself just makes it worse. For one thing, I don't speak a word of Greek. Well, of course neither do you—"

"No problem. Everybody speaks English, at least around Athens, so don't worry about being a woman alone, and all that. In Greece the traveler is sacred. If I remember correctly, he and/or she is under the protection of Zeus." There was that familiar chill in his blue, blue eyes. "As for what you call my 'side trip' to London, it seems the least I can do. The Three Bees are picking up the tab for both of us, remember, which is damned generous of Bingy, if you ask me."

Well, of course it is. Oh, my, yes. I can just hear Joshua Bingham, founder and president of Bingham, Bugle, and Bligh, being very, very generous. "Kay still moping and grieving, eh? Enough's enough, my boy! Certain amount healthy. Therapeutic—yes, indeed. But it's a year now, isn't it? Long enough, Cunningham! Yes, indeed, long enough!" He'd suggested Mike take two or three weeks, as soon as he's cleared his desk—"Good God, my boy, you've earned it!"—and hop over to Europe, relax and enjoy. "And take Kay along—our expense, of course. Women! They're the very devil, Cunningham! Brooding, always brooding!"

Maybe it hadn't been exactly like that, but it's probably close enough. Because Bingham would have been right: I *am* always brooding. Had Mike said anything? Dropped a hint or two, remarked worriedly that I just don't seem to be snapping out of it? Maybe I do need to get away—maybe I need to even more than he does—but I do *not* need Greece! I do *not* need Damian!

Whatever he's like.

Even so, I find it hard to believe Mike would divulge to anyone how I've put away my pencils and my chalks and haven't sketched a child since. How I've taken to keeping the blinds drawn on either side of the house, so as not to see the neighbors' walks booby-trapped with baseball bats and trikes. How I keep the windows closed, too, when in the long summer evenings . . . in the long summer evenings when the children's voices flute through the fading light like birdsong . . .

Perhaps Mike didn't have to say anything. Perhaps the observant Mr. Bingham observed I no longer turn up at the clambakes and the boat rides and the museum forays and the theater parties he schedules with such tireless enthusiasm for the families of his copywriters, his media planners, his account men. Mike may have had to make some excuse. Though anyone reasonably intuitive could have drawn the obvious conclusion: Kay Cunningham—"*Can you blame her? Wouldn't you feel the same?*"—can't bear the sight of other people's children; Kay Cunningham has turned her face away from all children everywhere.

If only I dared snatch some sleep! Sweet oblivion, the poet says . . . except that mine is never mercifully blank. I dream . . . I dream he's calling me, that once again David calls me, and this time I say I'm coming, this time I go . . .

Stop it, Kay! Think about something else. Anything else. These accursed flight plans: think about them. Whose idea were they—Bingham's? He'd have no reason to know how I dread flying alone. But then, does Mike? When for years we've always flown separately as a matter of course? Parental flight insurance, Mike called it. And naturally Mr. B. would consider costs, and send me the cheapest, i.e., most direct, route. No doubt he left the details to Mike, and Mike, in turn, to his secretary. "Get me to London and my wife to Athens . . ." Reflex action. Habit. Mike may even have thought that I wouldn't want to hack around by myself where we'd honeymooned, ten light-years ago.

Well, he should have thought again! He should have realized it's *cheating* me to have a stranger sprawled beside me in what could at any moment be the last seconds of my life! Trapped in this thin skin of aluminum, buoyed by nothing but a whim of physics above the hungry waters, I have a right to have my own husband beside me, should the life-pulse of the engines falter and die, or this round of glass be sucked out, and I after it, and these nameless, faceless forms dozing in the dim light come streaming after me, down and down, our thin screams lost in the heaving sea—

"Care for a cuppa?" I gape at the discreetly striped tie, the oily hair plastered with care across the gleaming scalp. "Goblins gonna getcha." The wine salesman grins ingratiatingly. "Have some coffee. Only way to survive seven aye emma, take my word."

It's hopeless: he's as persistently friendly as a poorly trained puppy. No sooner were we airborne last evening than he tried to erode my New England "standoffishness" (Mike's word) with a continual drip of confidences. He'd just been home for the first time in a month. Missed their anniversary by a measly day, how about that? Here, take a look at last week's schedule: Madrid on the ninth, Zurich the tenth to the twelfth, touch base in Karlsruhe, then home. Now he's off again. Rome. Athens. Back to Karlsruhe. I tried to appear interested; I felt it was the least I could do after he insisted I share one of his sample bottles. (The Riesling was surprisingly good.) Just the same, I wish there were some way I could rebuff strangers without seeming rude. I certainly didn't want to know his name—"Raphael Sanzio, no cracks, now," he'd said with a wink. Naturally I didn't tell him mine. Once anyone knows your name, there's a break through the wall you can't ever entirely close.

We finish our coffee, and now—oh, God! I might have known!—now he's bringing out snapshots. A boy, soft and plump; a girl, thin and scowling. Quite ordinary-looking, both of them, but alive: I have to give him that.

"You got children?"

The carpet of cloud has rolled back and I can see a ship, a minuscule black bug on the silvering waters.

"No," I say, without turning my head. "No, I have no children."

"I dunno but what you're lucky," he says with transparent insincerity. "What it costs to raise 'em these days you wouldn't believe."

I tip back in my seat and close my eyes. I ought never to have said I'd come. This whole trip is pointless. Worse than pointless, even for Mike. Go to Greece and look up that child he's gotten interested in? Crazy! What can he hope to get out of it but more heartbreak? Strange how some men seem born to be fathers. It comes as naturally to them, it's as imperative for them, as motherhood is for most women. Maybe they picture human existence as a kind of bridge, a fragile span of rope strung across an abyss. And this bridge, if a man is to pass over it safely, must be firmly anchored at both ends: as he must have parents, so must he have a child; the biological continuity is essential . . .

I pull my seat up and squint at wisps of cloud, at a glimpse of the sea, everything unbearably bright. Nonsense—Mike isn't that cerebral. One of his more endearing yet exasperating traits is the way his emotions infiltrate his intellect. (Like the blue streaks in a good Roquefort, I told him once.) Exasperating because it makes reasoning with him so difficult. I've never been able to change his mind by pointing out mere facts; facts alone, unsupported by feelings, strike him as irrelevant.

Not that I didn't, this time, do my damnedest.

"We'd be snooping, Mike! Poking and prying and—and making like social workers, but without the excuse! Because *no way* am I going to consider adoption, you hear? *No* way, not now, not ever!"

"You don't seem to get the point, Kay. I've *got* to have these three weeks when I don't have to get myself past that goddam tree! Is that asking so much? As for Damian—you say I'm trying to promote some kid I've never seen to take our son's place. *Nobody* can do that—I know that! It's just—well—" and he looked at me, for a moment it was the way he used to look at me, and my insides turned over. Then: *David, David,* I thought again, and I steadied.

"Remember how before David was born I was

— 6 —

glad we didn't have a choice?" Mike went on. "Boy or girl, either would be exactly what I want? I meant it: it was true. It was only after David came I couldn't imagine the world without him. I couldn't really remember how it had been, before. It was sort of as if he always was. God help me, I thought he always would be—at least as long as I was. David was born, and the world was changed for all time, and so was I. Now he doesn't exist anymore, but I can't change back. I . . . still expect to see him. I listen for him to come in . . . to slam the door. I used to tell him . . . I used to ask him nicely . . . damn it, I used to yell at him not to slam the goddam door—"

"Gosh, Dad, I didn't—my friend Jimmy let it slam, honest! I remind him and remind him, but he keeps forgetting."

David's friend Jimmy drew with crayons on the wall in the upstairs hall. David's friend Jimmy broke the window. *("He's a lousy catcher, Dad.")* Once when I found the light on after ten o'clock, David said apologetically that Jimmy was afraid of the dark.

For a while Jimmy was so accepted a member of the family that Mike and I would use his name in a kind of code. "David, what's the matter with Jimmy that he can't close the refrigerator door?" "The grass is sopping wet, David. Do you suppose Jimmy has sense enough to wear boots?" And when the time came that Jimmy didn't seem to be around anymore, we both missed him.

"Whatever happened to Jimmy?" Mike wanted to know, when David admitted it was he who had "borrowed" the hammer and left it outside.

"He moved away."

"Does he ever write to you?"

"*He was kind of dumb, Dad.*" Affectionately. "*He never learned how.*"

"Do you miss him?"

"*Kind of, Mom. But I kept getting older, and he didn't.*"

I stare into the radiant east, and the voices in my head go on and on, and I can't shut them up.

Maybe Mike set up these his-and-hers flights on purpose, because he wants a day or two to himself, to think things out. About us: to think about us. He said he didn't blame me, but he must. I do! Oh, God, I blame me! Everybody . . . I read it in everybody's eyes. Even in yours, Mike. You don't know it's there, maybe, but it is. It is!

"Breakfast, *madame?*"

The coffee has a foreign accent, not unpleasant. I poke at the resilient omelet, nibble at the durable brioche, and try to appear unaware of the sly side-wise glances with which the wine salesman is favoring me. As if he's plotting an opening bid.

"You know Paris pretty well? You work there, maybe?"

I say with chill reserve, "I'm not stopping in Paris."

"Okay, so I lose." He makes a clown's grimace. "I got this game I play, see. Helps pass the time, know what I mean? Match the tourist to the city. You and Paris—a natural, I'd've bet."

"No, I'm going to Greece," I say with (I can't help it) a trace more warmth. He does well enough at peddling his wine, I gather; his clothes, though hardly elegant, clearly cost money. Funny he should try to poor-mouth. Sketch him in charcoal? No: ink, with a

— 8 —

wash. Plump oily face, jowls shadowed by a day's beard. Thirty-five, maybe forty. Mike, thank God, has kept his trim. Imagine having to admit such a man as this to your bed . . . Imagine clasping a soft, marshmallowy waist, feeling a pillowy belly . . . Imagine having to identify him in the morgue: *"Are you quite certain that is your husband, madame?"* *"Yes, yes, I could hardly be mistaken . . ."*

Trim fields, clipped trees, travel-poster houses tip and tilt, tumbling past. We're down. Down safely. I draw in a breath, release it slowly.

My seatmate yawns. "I sure hope they hurry with the local papers. I like to get the feel of a place right off, know what I mean? Don't worry if you don't *parlez la belle française,*" he adds paternally. "They have 'em in English, too. *Tribune,* anyway."

"Thank you, I have a book I'm determined to finish." And I make quite a business of opening my Herodotus. *". . . Croesus asked Solon who was the happiest person he had seen . . ."*

"You staying at the Grande Bretagne?"

I pretend not to have heard. *" 'Two young men of Argos,' was the sage's reply. 'Cleobis and Biton . . .' "*

"It's smack dab in the center of Athens. Handier than the Hilton, maybe, but gimme that good ol' American know-how."

"We're staying at the Caledonia," I say dismissively, my eyes on my page. "My husband always prefers something indigenous to the country."

"The Caledonia, huh? Yeah, I guess he'll find that the genuine home-grown product, that's for sure. None of that 'where the hell am I?' stuff when you wake up." He shakes with amusement.

Speed-reading past the deaths of the young men—

my God, is everything I touch booby-trapped?—I skip to the next page. " 'Look to the end . . . Not infrequently God gives a man a glimpse of happiness, then ruins him utterly . . .' " I gaze blindly across the tarmac. They were right, of course, those ancient Greeks. Who can know the end of anything? Before there was any Mike in my life, before there was David, I longed to live in Paris, that enchanted city where the trees are forever in leaf, rustling in the golden dusk. I dreamed of letting its magic transform my slight talent until— who knows?—I might paint like an angel possessed. An enchanted age, twenty, I reflect now with the desolate wisdom of a dozen years later. At twenty anything is possible: at twenty we are immortal.

Before there was David . . . Mike had called me his moon-goddess. "Rising rounder and fuller as the days roll by." Tenderly.

To which I'd replied in typical downbeat *Kay*-dence. "Not roll, Mike—plod. Or crawl. I swear I think time has gone into gridlock and I'm going to be swollen up like a prize pumpkin forever!"

"Nothing lasts forever, Kay. Not even human gestation. It only seems to."

As it turned out, so did childbirth—my style. Mike had done his level best to be sustaining, hour after exhausting hour, holding my hands, wiping my face, moistening my lips, never for a moment leaving my side. It was only briefly, toward the end, he'd let slip his mask of confident reassurance and had burst out: "Damn it, Kay, you haven't done anything to anybody! Why should you be punished this way?"

I tried to tell him nobody suffers because they deserve to, it just happens.

That's how much I knew—then.

But at last there was David, pale peach-fuzz hair, eyes blue as Mike's, fingers and toes all accounted for. And he'd thrived, and we'd been happy. Six years: six radiant years. Almost seven. And then . . . and then it was David who was siphoned off into the void, into nothingness, and I was the one who plunged after him. I am the one who is falling still, silently screaming . . .

I'm falling alone, I see with stinging clarity. Mike somehow—and this is surprising, because anyone who knows him would say he'd be the one more shattered, being the more emotional—he somehow caught hold of something. Faith, perhaps . . . I don't know. I reached for him as I plummeted past, but he wasn't there, he'd caught hold of something and was safe. And he was impatient with me—now and again he still is, though in all decency he tries to hide it. Does he think I choose to fall past the handholds that might save me? Can't he understand that when I reach for them they aren't there? They were there for him, but they're not there for me. There's nothing . . . nothing I can grab on to . . .

When the plane rises again and straightens, aiming for Rome, I find I'm on the wrong side to see Paris even in the distance.

CHAPTER

2

"I see they're sendin' that fellow from Genoa home piecemeal," Mr. Sanzio remarks chattily, refolding his newspaper. TERRORISTS THREATEN . . . I can't catch the rest. "Funny thing, whole world gets its idea of law from the Italians—okay, the Romans—and here their descendants got less than anybody, 'cept maybe the Greeks." He chuckles. "Musta exported it all."

"Is that supposed to be funny?"

"Yeah, well, it's not worth a million laughs, I gotta admit, trottin' round to identify your husband's finger, say, or his ear."

"I don't see how you could . . . I mean, and be sure."

"Why would they fake it? Either they got him or they don't. They're not gonna have some spare parts around like a lousy *body* shop, are they? Fresh enough to pass off as recently his, know what I mean?" I swear if there weren't the armrest between us, he would poke me in the ribs with his elbow. "She's lucky to have a chance to get him back, at that. Usually they don't, not if they've gone to the police. She better hurry and pay up, or they'll be askin' her to identify somethin' essential next. His fuel pump, maybe, or his generator." He shakes with appreciation of his own wit. "Of course that would put *finito* on their chances of makin' any solid profit this deal."

"Maybe she doesn't have any money." Coldly.

"Don't you believe it! They only snatch guys who are loaded. Well, it's not a nice way to make a livin', I gotta admit. I never said it was."

What would the widow do then? Give away everything her husband owned? Close his house and move away . . . pretend he never existed? Maybe it's different when it's your husband, not your son. Maybe it's easier. Women replace their husbands every day . . . happens all the time. Sometimes they don't even wait until he's gone. But no one thinks of replacing a child. Except you, Mike.

"Magazine, *madame?*"

I shake my head. Groping for my shoulder bag, I pull out the fat envelope emblazoned with the Three Bees' logo. It bulges with a year's exchange of letters: on the first of each month, from the Greek boy to Mike; on the fifteenth or thereabouts, Mike's—carbons of Mike's—to the Greek. All of which I've been shamed into reading. Promising to read, anyway.

"Look, Kay, I know you don't want to go—you've made that plain enough—but at least you're going. Now don't arrive not knowing a damn thing about anybody, as if you couldn't care less!"

What did he expect? When the very first time he brought those letters home had been less than one week after David's death! Even now, more than a year later, remembering, I go cold with anger.

"How *could* you be so callous? For God's sake, Mike, how could you bring such things into this house? Into *this* house!"

As if he'd upended a sack of snakes in the living room.

"I didn't ask for this job, Kay. It's another of those extracurricular chores that Bingy dreams up. This one rotates from one second-echelon guy to another, and it just so happens it's my turn. I'll be damned if I'll bitch about the timing!"

"Don't tell me Bleeding-heart Bingy actually thinks writing to a clutch of children would be good therapy for you!"

"For me *and* for you, Kay. He made quite a point of it. 'Ask your good wife's advice, my boy,' said he. 'Get her involved. Women, poor creatures, tend to put their personal tragedies at the center of the universe.' "

I could scarcely speak. "And what did you tell him?"

"That I thought everybody did," Mike said carefully, "not just women. 'Grief, sir,' I said, 'isn't at the center, it *is* the whole goddam universe.' Whereupon he handed me the children's names and told me to get cracking."

"You must have said more than that!"

"What should I have said? That you've swept the house bare of any sign our son ever existed? His toys to the children's shelter, his bed, his bureau, his clothes to that family that was burned out—you think I told Bingy that? And his books—all his books—"

Everything except that folder of sketches. I didn't know what to do with them. I still don't. They're still there, like an undefused bomb, in the cupboard behind Mike's desk. David at one year, bemedaled with Band-Aids, charging across the lawn in gleeful dog-trot. David the three-year-old clown—*"See my new hat?"*—a huge blanket pin balanced on his head. David poised like a gymnast on his tricycle: he would stand on the seat, his irrepressible hair still fairer than Mike's; he would perch there, crowing, blue eyes dancing. Then he would leap off . . .

The sun on the sheet of clouds is blinding.

I think: I've got to stop this. I think: I'm not going to scream, or weep or wail or tear my hair. Nobody does that sort of thing anymore. No black veil, no black armband: not good form. And if possible no tears—at least no noisy tears. *Very well, Katharine, you may go to your room until you can control yourself.*

The surface of the sky is hammered fire.

"Oh, all right," I told Mike finally. "You have to answer the children's letters. I accept that. But how often? And—forget the therapy angle—whatever *for?"*

"Deductions for charity, mostly. The firm is supporting a dozen kids through the Helping Hand—that's some do-good outfit based in Delaware. I'm assigned the four in Java, Bali, Greece, and Brazil. They write once a month, and I reply in the name of the firm. I'm stuck with the job for a year—everybody is. Continuity, Bingy says. 'Cast your mind's eye over the arrival of our letters, my boy. A hamlet of eighty, possibly a hundred souls—how often does any humble dweller therein get any mail?' " Mike's mimicry of his employer was tempered as always by a strong infusion of exasperated affection. " 'Why, the mayor might even post them in the village square! So use our best rag stock with the full-color letterhead. No sense in stinting!' "

"This whole thing is idiotic beyond belief," I said crossly. "Who in that hamlet—I believe that was Mr. Bingham's word—is going to be able to read anything in English? Or are you suddenly fluent in Portuguese or Greek?"

"The folks at Helping Hand have already thought of that. They've hired interpreters, and a translation goes right along with the original. I'm to enclose an extra sheet of letterhead, Bingy said—might as well get as much exposure for the firm as possible. Just think, Kay"—dryly—"even now 'We Blaze the Trail, You Make the Sale' may well be infiltrating from Southeast Asia to the Aegean!"

I said stubbornly, "If those letters are company business, why can't they be done on company time and in company territory?"

"Because nobody else has used office time, that's why. It didn't occur to me you'd want me to plead special circumstances." Mike looked at me, his blue eyes remote. When I said nothing: "The problem is, I can't think of anything to say that doesn't sound either asinine or unreal. Except for the Greek boy, *they* seem unreal." He sorted through the letters. "Here's what I mean—no, wait, Kay, I really do need your input, at least until I get this off the ground. Listen to this—"

Flipping back a sheet covered with script like delicate Islamic decoration, he read from the translation stapled beneath. " 'Dear Sirs: I write this letter with the help of my neighbor. I would so much like to have a remembrance from you, dear Sirs.' That's it for Kamar in Java. Francesca in Brazil reports that she is, and I quote, 'grateful for the sunglasses which my grandmother need very much. They lessen her headache when she walk in the street.' And Sang Kook in Bali wants us to know that 'every day when I come home from school, my mother being ill I look after my younger brothers, but I Sang Kook am always glad to do it.' Now what the hell should I answer? 'Dear Coerced Kamar—'? It'd never get past Bingy—he signs our replies himself, worse luck. 'Dear Francesca, I'm thirty-two years old and I've never been hungry a day in my life'? That would be honest, at least. 'Dear Sang Kook: The twenty dollars we send you wouldn't begin to cover my lunch check today'?" He tossed the letters down. "Know how they seem to me, these kids? Like shadows on the other side of an abyss."

I said reluctantly, "That barely subliminal whine could be all the fault of the interpreter."

"You may be right. Because listen to this—it's from Damian, the Greek boy—he writes in English himself, all on his own, as he never lets you forget." And in a warm and affectionate voice—oh, God! as if the letter were from David!—Mike read:

" 'Dear American friends: I greet you and hope you are well. I am well. My uncle Georgios is well. My aunt Berek is not well, but it passes. Erasmios the burro is well.

" 'As always I write this letter with no help from any man. I tangle my tongue with the English words. Like new fisherman with bad nets! Greek is much easier language than is English, here even the babies can speak it.

" 'My aunt says enough. Now I say good-bye.' "

Mike refolded the letter, the shadow of a smile on his lips. "He repeats that every time he writes, that bit about it being all his own work, I mean. I take it the light under the bushel is not a concept of strong appeal to the Greek mind."

"Hey, Dad! Look where I am! . . . Hey, Mom, want to see me jump from here? . . . Hey, Dad, I'll race you off the dock! . . . Watch this, Mom—"

The clouds are bits of cotton wool blowing past the wing.

Of course Mike would find it easy to write to that little Greek. That *wily* little Greek. Of course Mike would know what to say. Would look forward to hearing from him. Would want to go see him. Would be tempted to consider adoption.

Pushing David out . . . No, not deliberately. Easing, maybe. Easing David out.

Gingerly, I explore inside the Three Bees envelope and fish out a single sheet of cheap, brittle paper. Along penciled guidelines the carefully drawn letters march neatly.

Dear Sir and Lady Foster Parents Cunningham:

I greet you and hope you are well. I am well. My uncle Georgios is well. My aunt Berek is again well. Erasmios the burro is always well.

If I make error, please forgive, but also scold so I can learn. With these letters no one tells me how.

Last week we had great storm and one fishing boats broke on rocks. Kyriakos the friend of my uncle prayed to Poseidon and came safe to shore. His boat lost a sail. My uncle Georgios is angry, Poseidon is pagan god now we have trouble in village. I am glad Kyriakos not drown.

My uncle Kostas come back from foreign
land. No more work for Greeks. In Germany.
My uncle Kostas looks for taxi to buy cheap.
He hopes get rich from tourists.

My uncle Georgios say my letters too
short, not worthy the money for postage.

My uncle Kostas, my uncle Georgios,
my aunt Berek send greetings for the New
Year.

My friend Kyriakos send greetings for the
New Year.

My godfather Nikos send greetings for the
New Year . . .

No mention of the box of clothing Mike sent well before Thanksgiving. Not a word about Mike's check.
Yet the boy must know—witness the salutation—that
his benefactor no longer is the Three Bees, but Mike.
(Mike and I, that is; Mike has been scrupulous to include me.) The Helping Hand was phasing Greece
out, he told me. That spunky country could make it
on its own now, they said, so they were "deactivat-
ing" it. Therefore Bingham, Bugle, and Bligh no
longer would be concerned with the welfare of one
Damian Mikhaïl, orphan, age ten, son of Mikhaïl,
unaccounted for since 1972, grandson of Damianos,
officially dead during the reign of the Colonels.
There'd be no tax advantage, Mike said dryly, if gifts
to charity weren't funneled through a legit organi-
zation.

"I can't just drop the boy, Kay, with a 'So long,
kid, you're on your own.' Hell, I wouldn't do that to
a dog—just boot it out and drive off. What's a lousy
twenty bucks a month? We'll never miss it, but he

would. Besides, I'd miss his letters. So would you, if you'd ever condescend to look at them." Bitterly.

If I'd read those letters then, it would have been disloyal. Why couldn't Mike see that? Disloyal to David, I mean. It's bad enough to be reading them now, but at least I'm not enjoying them . . . As I return the one I've finished to the fat envelope with the azure and bronze logo (Mediterranean colors: the sea is a carpet of crushed sapphire), the envelope slides off my lap and would disappear under the seat ahead if the wine salesman, with surprising speed for one of his bulk, didn't block it with his foot.

He waves aside my thanks. "You in advertising?"

"Not at the moment." (Well, that's true enough.)

"You work for BBB but you're on vacation—that it?"

Here we go again, I think wearily. "That's my husband's firm. I'm—actually, I guess you could say I'm a housewife." I'll be *damned* if I'll tell this rotund little creep I'm an artist. An illustrator. (Try to be.) Whoever notices who does the illustrations? Only a reviewer, maybe. "Kay Cunningham's little sketches have a certain simple charm . . ."

Mr. Sanzio is rambling on. "Your husband oughta be proud. 'Wicheta Wine from the Heart of the Vine'—remember that one? I tell you *we* didn't like it! Wicheta was anglin' to cut into our market, and it was a near thing." He chuckles. "Yeah, your husband's got a good shop there in that Three Bees."

"I'll tell him," I say pleasantly, and make rather a business of pulling out another letter, and of smoothing it flat.

Dear Damian . . .

Not one from Mike! I can spare myself that, at least. I refold it hastily, yet words leap from the page:

Dear Damian:
   Today is the first day of spring, and it's snowing. Have you ever seen snow, I wonder? Do you . . .

I can hardly believe it! Mike was writing to that little Greek on March twenty-first! On David's birthday! Writing to that—that *intruder* who is brazenly thrusting himself between us, who isn't connected to either of us in any way whatsoever: not by blood, language, or religion, nor by any degree of shared experience or common history. And to this totally alien child, whom he has not so much as laid eyes on, Mike chose to send this communiqué, this dispatch to the enemy. On what should have been David's birthday—his eighth birthday—and was in actual fact the first anniversary of his death.
   "Have you ever seen snow . . ." Mike must have written it on the way home, then. I remember there was another of those crazy, unseasonal, murderous snow squalls in the late afternoon. Mike would be sitting by himself, withdrawn, gazing out at the no-man's-land sliding past the train window, at the desolation of frost-blighted grass and black pools of tidal water, of shapeless sprawls of landfill where isolated factories glow and steam like vents in a volcano: a godforsaken view now concealed, now revealed by that wet, pasty, can't-see-ten-feet-ahead

lethal snow; and sitting there, coming home to a non-celebration of a non-birthday, he was inspired to write a chatty, chummy letter to what is already, in his mind, his dead son's prospective replacement!

Because: "What would a Greek child make of it, do you think?" he'd said, swirling the ice in his before-dinner drink. And when I, like a fool (if ever there was a moment for saying nothing, it was then), quite naturally said, "Make of what?", he'd plunged ahead. "The Meadows in winter. Well, any time of year, actually. Say you were to pluck a Greek child from his village all steeped in sunlight and thrust him down here without any 'combat training'—would that patch of commuters' paradise look to him, as it does to me, like the threshold of hell?"

By *God*, I'll read that damned letter! Now, before I . . . I lose my courage!

Dear Damian:
Today is the first day of spring, and it's snowing. Have you ever seen snow, I wonder? Have you ever seen how it quiets the world and hides everything ugly? You go to bed and the world is all frowsy and brown, cluttered with a lot of stuff nobody wants anymore, and when you wake up everything is clean and white and beautifully smooth, and so still you can hear the slightest sound from far, far away. It's as if God changed his mind and started over . . .

I refold the letter with painstaking care. *He'd have written such a letter to David, if David had lived . . .* I feel empty, and frightened, and faintly sick.

— 22 —

This time I am careful to choose one safely from the Greek.

Dear Sir and Lady American Parents:
Good morning to you. Thank you for yourself writing to me. Here all is good. All the trees are green . . .

In February? You wouldn't much like it where we live, my little infiltrator of affections! Our February is cold, cold, cold, as I shall not fail to mention.

My uncle Georgios is pleased with the rains. He prays this year we have fine harvest. I like to shake the trees and send the olives falling like green rain.

I am doing fine with my studies. I go regularly to my English lessons 3 hours every week. I pay 30 δρακμέχ for one hour. I study with Mrs. Meade (you pronounce it like Mηδ) English lady who live in Petra. Mrs. M. say you have right to know how I spend money you send. At this time I do not spend all because I ride to school with my uncle Kosta. Money I do not spend I save, so I can buy ship. Kyriakos say okay get rich and own ship but no good sail the wide seas myself—no, this not for Greeks unless the gods punish him. I do not think the same. For me great good fortune is to be free as the sunlight that shines all the world round. Go see the whole world, why not?

Kyriakos is strange man though he is my friend. All time say the sea is enemy, it swal-

lowed almost all Greece it will swallow you
and me like big fish eat small. But always
when we slide out of harbor and the wind
catch the sail he starts to sing. "Oh my lovely
lovely bird," he sings. "Α, Πουλάκι μου,
Πουλάκι μου." Forgive me Sir and Lady, it
sound better in Greek . . .

Do you too think you are immortal, Greek boy? That noth-
ing as capricious as death can happen to you? Not true,
Damian whoever-you-are. You, too, are mortal, even as
David . . . even as I.

"He wanted me to time him," I said, when they'd
taken him away, and they'd gone, too, all those people with hungry eyes, with avid, staring, guilty eyes:
the police and the ambulance crew and the passers-
by and that priest somebody called, I suppose because of my name. At long last Mike and I were alone
in the silent house. "He wanted me to come see how
fast your sled would go. He wanted me to time him
from the big elm to the road."

In the silence we could hear the heating pipes
expand in a progression of muffled thumps.

"Why didn't you?"

"I don't know . . . I don't know *I don't know*."

The plane is dropping for Rome, its shadow a
great gull skimming the dazzling waters. I hug my
ribs. Empty . . . I am always empty now. Will always be so. Can be nothing else.

"Don't grieve, my darling." Mike's voice, his eyes,
his touch overflowed with tenderness (I wonder
if he remembers?) when in spite of everything David
was safely born, and I on that first waking must be
told he would be our last as well as our first. "Don't

grieve—we can love one child as much as we could five."

Of course we could. And did. And I still do.

"Family of Five Die in Fire—" and there's the grief-distorted face of the mother full on camera, her crime (like mine) that for a few fatal minutes she did not watch over her children, she "only stepped out a moment," and now the rest of her life is her punishment. What a curse, to be a woman and a mother! To have the power to bring life but not to keep it! What difference do numbers make? No one can multiply or divide pain. Pain is absolute. Loss is absolute. Grief is absolute.

The plane touches down, rebounds once, twice. As it rolls to a stop in the bright Roman sun, passengers burst into laughter, into quick applause.

CHAPTER

3

Mike says airports are basically so much alike you can't ever feel very far from home. Not true of Rome: not today, anyway, with soldiers strolling two by two everywhere I look, each with a rifle tucked under his arm like a newspaper. Otherwise the terminal is the usual city-in-itself that always seems so fake, like an overly clever stage set. As I prowl the futuristic complex of tunnels and walkways and escalators echoing with multilingual announcements from ubiquitous loudspeakers, I console myself that somewhere there is a real city, of fountains and streets of steps and baroque churches; for all I see of it, Rome—the real Rome—could be a myth. Modern version of Tantalus' torment, air travel.

I exchange ten dollars for a clutch of paper *lire*, browse in a bookshop where I find Vasari's *Lives of the Painters* in English, and on impulse stop at a candy counter and spend the rest of my *lire* on a huge slab of chocolate in truly dazzling metallic paper; perhaps it will do for a peace offering to Damian. Then, setting my watch by a clock that boasts the time from Seattle to Singapore, I accept my boarding pass and take a seat in the holding area. If it please my plane to be prompt, I have only an hour to wait.

A slender young woman stops to ask a question of the official at the departure gate. She carries a large flat basket painted robin's egg blue; a small girl clings to her skirt. Now she crosses in front of me, sets the basket on the floor practically at my feet, and, lifting the little girl on the chair next to mine, sinks onto the one beyond.

I stare stoically at the page before me. Did they have to be so obsessed with painting babies, those Italians? *Madonna and Child . . . The Adoration . . . The Slaughter of the Innocents.* No use to change my seat: wherever I sit, there will be the young woman in full view, there will be her children.

From beneath the embroidered quilt a faint cry emerges. The young woman addresses the little girl in an urgent undertone in (I think) French. She scrabbles in her bag. Now she cuts through my line of vision carrying a nursing bottle. The child on the seat beside me lets out a piercing wail. Hurrying back, the young woman lifts her down and tries to soothe her in a shaking voice. The child clings to her, sobbing. A quick glance at my luggage tags, and then: "Please, *madame*, to watch my baby while I heat the milk?"

I barely glance up, glance away, and nod.

I don't have to look at it. I can just sit here and make sure nobody snatches it. She must be insane to leave it with a stranger this way! My God, if I were a real kook I'd make off with it and she'd never see it again . . .

The young woman is back. Gathering up the baby, now fretting in earnest, she says, "Oh, I do thank you, *madame*! I go here, I go there, nobody tell me

— 27 —

nothing! At last the woman in the W.C. say to hold it in the basin, in the hot water." Her face is almost as white as the kerchief covering her hair.

Concealed by the quilt, the baby is guzzling noisily.

I have to say something. "Have you come far?"

"From South Africa, *madame*. I go to my husband's parents in Belgium."

"A long way." Politely. "Will you be going on soon?"

To my distress, she bursts into tears. "No one knows! I ask one, I ask second, each say different! Now *that* one"—she tilts her head toward the gate— *"he* say I have wait of six hours, and they do not know if there will be space for me!"

I can't just go on reading . . . "How old is your baby?"

She wipes her cheeks. "One month, *madame*."

One month! Why isn't anyone with her? My God, I hope she isn't widowed. Maybe they travel separately, out of prudence, as Mike and I have done. But the children are with her; the father might as well be, too . . .

"Thirteen-oh-five flight to Athens now boarding—"

I collect my gear. On impulse I put the chocolate by the young woman's handbag. "Here—please take this." Brusquely.

"Oh, thank you, *madame!* My little girl and I thank you—"

The infant is directly in my line of vision. There is its hand like a starfish, kneading the silk of its mother's blouse; there is its hair like thistledown.

My throat closes. Without a word I snatch up my bag and escape.

It's a relief to be rid of Sanzio. This time my seat-mate, a stocky man in a dark suit, never raises his eyes from the newspaper he's frowning over; I might be invisible, I think gratefully, though not entirely so, perhaps, as he seems to be taking care not to claim any of the armrest or to encroach on an inch of my leg space. Nor will the headlines in his paper disturb me, being literally Greek to me.

"—flying at twenty-nine thousand feet. We land at Glyfada at fifteen hours five minutes, Athens time—"

We're over the spine of Italy. In the clear air the mountains are a contour map, their spiky peaks pulled from Play-Doh. A frill of surf outlines the shore sliding far beneath us. I wish I had a map of some kind, so that I could identify the land masses that dot the waters below. Perhaps then I could control my thoughts, corral them, keep them from twisting out of my grasp and dodging back, always back . . .

"Damn it, Kay, must we spend the rest of our lives rattling around in this overdone anachronism of a house? It's plain crazy for the two of us!"

It had seemed such a good idea, when we were first married, to live there where I'd been happy when a child. Perhaps it is absurd to stay there now, Mike and I alone. It was (I admit it) an absurdly impractical inheritance: three stories, six bedrooms, seven fireplaces, plus porches and cupolas and dormers patched on wherever it struck the builder's fancy. God knows the upkeep is appalling and the heating bills astronomical. But move away? No! I couldn't . . . I can't.

"It wouldn't be any better anywhere else, Mike. Oh, the bills would be smaller, but that's not it, is it? In every other way it would be worse, because it would all be . . . strange." I groped for words. "Empty, I mean. With nothing to—to link today to yesterday. As if our yesterdays didn't exist. As if *David* never existed."

For a long moment Mike said nothing. Then: "I hope you have some faint glimmer, Kay, of what the hell you're asking, and not only of me. Of yourself, too."

"Of *my*self?" I said. "All I'm asking *you* is that I not be expected to pretend we never had David!"

Mike didn't say any more, then or later, so for quite a while I assumed he'd accepted the fact that I couldn't leave where David had been . . . where he still is. And then on David's birthday (should-have-been birthday) he was barely in the house, hadn't even waited for dinner, just fixed himself a drink, and then, coolly and without preamble:

"It'll be the middle of May before I can get away, but that still gets us to Greece before the worst of the heat. I want you with me, Kay, because I'm going to look up Damian. You've a right to be in on this from the beginning, to speak your piece while our plans are still at the talk stage—"

"*Our* plans! *Oh*, no—yours, Mike! All yours!" I couldn't help it, my voice rose. "You told me once you wanted everything in this marriage to be ours— remember? *Our* money, you said, no matter who earned it. *Our* car—*our* house—oh, it sounded mighty fine! 'His and hers' marriages, you said, lead to his and her divorce. And now you're planning this pilgrimage to meet this little pen pal of yours—don't talk to me about *our* plans!" I shivered suddenly. "You want to adopt him, don't you?"

"I don't know," Mike said quietly. "How can I, until I've seen him? Maybe I won't know then. These things don't happen overnight. Maybe he won't want me for a father—"

"That's not true! You've already made up your mind—why don't you admit it? Sight unseen, you're planning to adopt that child! *That's* why you're going—you won't say so in so many words, but I *know!* You stand there and expect me to—to *connive* at replacing—at choosing a replacement—"

With one part of my mind I listened to this tirade with righteous approval, almost exultation: how *could* he? How could *any* father? With another, I heard it with growing horror. *Shut up, you fool!* But I didn't . . . does anyone?

"Kay, will you *listen* to me? I *know* David is dead! I know no one can 'replace' him, as you put it. I know, too, you and I can never have another David, not of our own making. I accept that as fact, as the way it is, and I've never blamed you—"

"Oh, yes, you have!" I cried. "When you talk of tripping off to Greece to check out a—a likely replacement—that's what he'll be, this Greek boy, whatever you choose to call him—when you expect me to tag along on this shopping expedition, you most certainly *are* blaming me!" My eyes burned, but no tears came. Tears are easy. What do they heal? Nothing. *"I'm* to blame for David's death—that's what you think, isn't it? You asked me where I was when it happened—you asked me what I'd been doing! Before we even had him buried, you asked me that!"

Why didn't I go? Why didn't I? When David called me to come see what he'd made for his new sled, why didn't I put down my brush, put on my jacket,

— 31 —

and go? How long would it have taken—five minutes? Later, I said. Later . . . So I didn't know he'd built that jump. I didn't know he was sailing right out into the road. What was I doing that was so much more important?

Another island slides by, an abrupt little island like a toy boat, steep-sided and solitary. And now I can see the opposite shore, and the treeless land rising like crumpled brown paper. A barren, desolate land, I think. Perhaps I won't feel as strange here as I expected.

"It's grounds for divorce in the more civilized of these fifty states to live apart for six months." Mike had drained his glass, and now his blue eyes caught and held my shocked gaze. "They're speaking of the body, you understand, not the heart. We've been living apart this whole year, Kay. How seldom or how often our bodies join has nothing to do with it. You can't call what we've been doing 'making love'—you can't say there's been any joy in it. Coupling, that's all it's been. Hell, freight cars couple—that doesn't mean anything . . ."

Down in the valleys there are roads, and something moving. Trucks, perhaps. Now more water, but with ships. And land again, more golden than brown.

"I've had it with sitting in this house, the silence between us like double-thick glass." Mike's voice shook. "Me: 'I see Congress has voted itself another raise.' You: 'How nice for them.' Me: 'I see the Cypriots are getting very tense with all that Turkish troop buildup.' You: 'Really?' You may not call that silence, Katharine my Kay, but I sure as hell do."

Katharine my Kay . . . sometimes in the night when a burst of rain has wakened us. *Katharine my*

Kay when we listen to the wind in the bare and frozen elms behind the house. Unfair, unfair to use those words when what he's saying is: "So I'm going to Greece and I'm asking you to come, too. If you won't—well, I'm not issuing an ultimatum—I've not reached that point yet—but it certainly ought to be clear to us both you've made a choice, and it's one that doesn't include me. As for what I said that night—I don't even *know* what I said that night! But, Kay—my God, don't you see? *You* haven't buried David yet!"

How can I bury him when I still can hear him call? "Hey, Mom—come and see!" And, "Right away!" I say. Or sometimes, "Okay, just a minute—I'm coming!" And he waits for me. He does, Mike. He laughs at my fears, but he doesn't go down. He listens to me, his mother. Who loves him. Who always made time for him. Who always put him first.

Warning lights are on; we're circling for Piraeus. Set my watch ahead: the sun rises an hour earlier in Athens than in Rome. If it rises at all, I think in dismay as we slip down into an opaque yellow-gray overcast like a dirty smear.

Until death do us part . . . The trouble is, the vows don't spell out whose.

CHAPTER

4

Like descending into a kiln, I think as I trail across the baking tarmac to the terminal. Here, out of the sun, the heat no longer blisters, it steams. I set down my suitcase (the merry-go-round has given it an early ride) and shed my linen jacket; my silk T-shirt is already damp. Beneath the corrugated roof the tourists' voices reverberate in a jangle of unfamiliar tongues. Which way to the taxis? The signs—good Lord, the signs are all in Greek!

A line is forming before a wire enclosure: the money exchange, no doubt. Better now than later; for all I know, the tip-money packet Mike bought me in New York won't even get me to my hotel. I'm counting the drachmas I receive for my traveler's check—singularly cheerful-looking bills with the likenesses of mustachioed heroes crisply printed in chrome green, Prussian blue, raw ochre, and crimson lake—when I become aware there is something vaguely familiar about a phrase someone is calling . . . that that little man in the wrinkled brown suit is chanting.

"Mah-dahm Kew-neeng-huhm! Mah-dahm Kew-neeng-hahm!"

"Are you looking for me? My name is Cunningham."

He narrows his eyes. "Mrs. Michael?" I admit it. "A pleasure to welcome you, mah-dahm." His smile blinks on, blinks off. "And your luggage, mah-dahm?"

"Over there, by that pillar."

He clicks in disapproval. "Not safe. There are many foreigners about. It is the time of tourists, you understand."

As if we're the annual plague of locusts.

"Are you from the hotel?"

"No, no—American Express, mah-dahm. Your husband telephone this morning. He fears the strike may make for you the difficulties." Seizing my suitcase and carry-on bag and using them as buffers, he scurries off through the crowd.

I hurry after him. "What strike—what do you mean?"

"This morning everything stops." He scoots through the revolving door and I follow. "What we call the general strike."

"Will there be a taxi?"

"Certainly a taxi. I have hired for you a taxi. Through here, mah-dahm, if you please."

Outside, the heat is a clenched fist.

"Are you to meet my husband's plane tomorrow?"

"I do not know, mah-dahm. I am told to meet you, I meet you." He flips his hand and a cab parked beyond the line of buses shoots diagonally through traffic and screeches to a halt. "This taxi is already paid, do not let him tell you otherwise. If you wish to tip, that is your affair." He sets my bags on the front seat, hands me in, and rattles off what I assume to be directions to the driver.

The taxi leaps forward. We turn onto an avenue bordered by beds of dusty spikes of flowers. For all that the air is hot and gritty and noticeably chemical in odor, I welcome the breeze from the open windows. The crucifix dangling from the driver's mirror swings jauntily; a portable radio on the dashboard emits a plaintive yet melodic chant, repetitive, insidious, Eastern.

The driver is looking at me in his mirror.

"English? Lady is English lady?"

"American." I gaze fixedly at the road ahead.

"American. Good." We overtake a truck packed with helmeted soldiers. The soldiers wave. "Tour?"

"I've come to see Greece, yes." If this is a sample of the English the Greeks speak—

"Tour?" Impatiently. "American lady in *tour?*"

"Oh—no, I'm by myself." I collect my wits. "I mean, I'm meeting my husband."

He shoots me an incredulous glance over his shoulder. "Husband at Hotel Caledonia? Not meet plane?"

I say shortly, "He had to stop in London on business."

Why on earth do I answer his questions? Do I really care that this Greek cabdriver not think me, an American, snobbish or aloof? Oddly enough, I *do* care. Didn't the passport bureau, in one of its friendly little pamphlets, go out of its way to remind me that I,

— 36 —

the American Tourist Abroad, am the unofficial am-
bassador of my country? Well, then . . .

"Like swimming?"

"Swimming?" I am genuinely bewildered.

"In ocean. Swimming in ocean. You like?"

"Of course." At least he doesn't ask me how I
like Greece: that's a plus.

"Good. Fine. I take you swimming. This afternoon, six o'clock. You like?"

I gape at his face in the mirror. It seems a remarkably ordinary face, homely, possibly honest,
certainly Greek. "Oh—uh, n-no—no, thank you, I
really couldn't. My—my husband will be coming—"

"Plenty of time. One hour to ocean, swim, eat,
swim some more. One hour back again, meet husband. What you say?"

"Thank you, I really can't." I start to laugh,
swallow it. (What do you say, Mike? This is Nico-
demus Papadopoulos, my cabdriver from the airport
who took me swimming this afternoon—the Greeks
are such a hospitable people!)

A line of sawhorses barricades the avenue; soldiers cluster at either end. Without slackening speed
the cab makes a sharp turn and lurches onto a side
street.

When I can trust my voice: "What's all this about
a strike?"

He lifts his shoulders. "Workers asking and government saying no. Students shouting and government saying be quiet."

"I wasn't sure there'd be any taxis."

"Many taxis." He turns to speak to me directly,
and my heart quails. "Half taxis working, half on

strike. Half buses running, half not." He grins, revealing irregular teeth blotched with brown. "Strike very Greek."

We stop at a red light and in the relative quiet the music throbs and wails. The driver beats intricate time on the steering wheel. He is watching me in the mirror again.

"You like? You like music? Dance?"

"Yes, of course." Do I want him to think Americans are tone-deaf killjoys? "My husband and I are very fond of—of music." I do not add, "and of dancing." It has occurred to me there is something so foreign, so "very Greek" about his questions (cabdrivers in New York tend more to pronouncement and denouncement than to interrogation) that I'd better adhere strictly to the truth. Lying to this man— this Greek—on his home territory may somehow anger his gods, those Greek gods who are forever mingling with us mortals and meddling in our affairs. Furthermore, a frank "I'm very fond of dancing, but unfortunately my husband—" might look like a kind of fishing.

I land my catch anyway.

"Good. Fine. I take you to Plaka—very old, but music—much music. Tonight, yes? Eight o'clock. Okay, yes?"

"*No.*" This is getting ridiculous. "My husband will be coming," I say in some desperation. "He'll be tired from his journey, but I—we thank you anyway."

So much for the truth and placating his gods. On second thought, how can they take offense? Aren't they themselves always lying? Befuddling mortals for the fun of it . . . deceiving them . . . seducing them?

"Tired. Okay," the driver says with a laugh and a wink.

I gaze frostily ahead. At the bottom of the slope a small van is double-parked, blocking the intersection. Three feet from its fender we skid to a stop. My driver leans on the horn. He shouts. After a moment, he gets out, stalks over to the van, and beats a brisk tattoo on its horn.

In the doorway of a shop across the way a man appears, telephone in hand. My driver shouts. Brandishing the phone, the other hollers back. My driver raises a clenched fist, shouts, smites the van with the flat of his hand, and spits. Then, abruptly, he strolls back. He has a graceful walk.

"American men same like English, tired in the evenings," he remarks conversationally as he slides behind the wheel.

I say nothing.

Flinging his phone aside to dangle on its wire, the other man snarls the van's motor into life and jerks the vehicle forward a bare two yards. We inch past. "Bandit!" my driver shouts as we turn the corner. "*Anarkhikós!*"

"I agree," I say.

He peers at me in the mirror and makes a comment in Greek. When I do not reply: "You no speak Greek?"

"We have the same word—'anarchist.' "

He nods. "Very Greek," he says.

The lobby of the Hotel Caledonia is crowded, dark, noisy, and very, very shiny with glossy black pseudo-marble on walls, ceiling, floor, even on the massive columns that rise like rectangular tree trunks among ebony armchairs. Smoke from dozens of cigarettes hangs motionless in the heat. I make my way through the crowd to the reception desk, where slick-haired young men in sweat-stained linen jackets field a barrage of anxious questions. Catching the eye of the one nearest, I give my name.

He makes a brief search. "I regret, madam, there is no one here by that name."

I say patiently, "*I* am Mrs. Cunningham. I believe you have a room booked for me. For my husband and me."

"For today?"

"Yes, certainly for today. Monday, May sixteenth."

"*Cuh*-ningham?" He checks swiftly through another file. "No, madam, not here. I regret. Perhaps you mistake the hotel?"

Where can I go? After all, it's "the time of tourists"—every hotel will be full. And how will Mike ever find me?

"This *is* the Hotel Caledonia, is it not?"

"Certainly, madam. But I regret, we are fully taken."

"I have here"—I search my bag—"I have your letter confirming our reservation—"

"Cuh-ningham does not begin with *kappa*—what you call *kay?*" He examines the envelope with an air of incredulity, then, shrugging, rechecks his files. "But certainly: Mr. and Mrs. Cuh-ningham. If your husband will sign the register, please, and I will require your passports."

"I will sign," I say pleasantly. "My husband comes later."

The elevator is so full surely not one more . . .
The bellhop gets on. I get on. The crowd compacts
and the door snakes shut. Groan to the mezzanine,
shudder to a stop. RESTAURANTE; at this hour the area
is deserted. On to the second floor, the third—and
out, thank God. There has been a notice, in German,
a language in which I am far from fluent, but the essential statistic, the maximum safe number of occupants, was only too clear: 16. There must have been
half again as many, I think as I follow the bellhop
down one hall, down another, yet another, and into
a room. *His wife was killed in an overloaded elevator in a
Greek hotel.*

I tip the bellhop and he smiles his way out. Re-
closing the window (he has clearly expected me to
be delighted by my choice location over the zestful
street life below), I turn on the air conditioner to
drown out the din, sink down on the bed, and fight
back a tidal wave of . . . not homesickness, exactly.
Displacement. Uprootedness. Exile.

Question: what on earth am I doing here? Answer: trying to keep my marriage together. And just
how "together" is it now? I here, Mike elsewhere,
oceans and continents between us, and that's the way
it will be, it will be no different, we'll be no closer
though we're in the same room, the same bed . . .

*What else could I do, Mike, but try to erase all trace
of him from our lives?* In truth the house is full of him
still, especially when it's emptiest. Seven-forty in the
morning and no thunder of feet on the stairs. Three-
ten in the afternoon and no door flung open, no shout
of "I'm home!" Of course everything had to go, Mike,
and at once, and the door of his room shut fast, closing off the worst emptiness. Surely that's less mor-

bid than if I kept everything as he left it: pajamas on the floor, crayons spilled across the window seat . . .

Stop it! Shower. Get some sleep, some food. Put your world back in orbit, Kay. (Go through the motions, anyway.)

The water is a blessing, washing off the miles, the unreadable language. I stretch out on the bed—what bliss to be horizontal!

When the phone wakes me, the room is in shadow, and for a moment I can't think where I am. Then I snatch up the receiver.

"Mike! Oh, *Mike,* hello—" He's lonely, too! He's calling! "Oh, Mike, where are you? I—I miss you, you know?"

Silence, thick and . . . listening.

"Mike? Is that you, Mike? *Hello*—"

A voice comes on, quite near. "Hallo?" A Greek voice.

"My phone rang." I can hardly bring the words out.

"A mistake, madam. Please excuse."

Six-thirty . . . Four-thirty in London. No telling where he is. But he'll call back. He won't leave me in limbo.

At seven I phone the desk. Have I had a call from London?

"Sorry, madam, we do not keep record of calls coming, only of going."

No point in tears, though I'm tempted. Food, that's what puts starch in the troops, as Mike would say. Somehow I overlooked lunch; no wonder my morale is sagging. I phone room service.

The desk regrets. "Because of the strike, you understand, madam. Many of our peoples do not attend. Very sorry for inconvenience. Unless madam is ill?" I am happy to say I am not ill. "Hotel has *estiatório*—"

"I will dine there, thanks. And if I have any calls between seven-thirty and nine, would the desk transfer them there, please?"

"Pardon?"

Hurriedly, I spell my name, stressing the C, and hang up. If, because of the strike or for any other reason, the hotel cannot transfer calls to the restaurant, I don't want to know it. This way at least I can hope.

The elevator, a long time in coming, is too full to shoehorn in another soul. I make for the stairs. Two flights down, I emerge into purgatory. The entire area between the elevators and the entrance to the restaurant is crammed with slack-suited women and sport-shirted men wailing and lamenting in French. I ease my way to the doorway. Perhaps it is my height, perhaps that I am the only female in sight in a skirt, but the maître d' comes over at once.

"*Chat?*" He points to the one empty place at a table for eight.

"Chat?" Blankly. "I'm sorry, I—"

"*Chat* tour, *Chat* tour!"

"Oh—no, I'm—" But a short woman in a bright rose pants suit has pushed past and flung herself into the chair. There is no other vacancy anywhere.

It is like swimming upstream to reach the elevator, which is nearly empty on the plunge to the lobby. I grope my way through the gloom—surely the very same people aren't still watching over the very same piles of luggage?—and manage to catch the eye of the one clerk on duty.

"*Neh*, madam," he smiles, pointing. "*Kaffeh? Neh*, madam!"

I must get a good Greek-English phrase book. It's moronic not to know even "yes," "no," or "thank you."

The coffee shop is an afterthought at the end of a narrow hallway. It, too, has shiny black walls and a shiny black floor, but it is brilliantly lit, and its five or six tables, all of which are empty, cheer the eye with bright blue oilcloths. Along one wall a serving counter displays cakes and other edibles. A young man with polished black hair and a rather soiled white jacket lounges against the work space behind the counter.

Speaking slowly and enunciating clearly, I say, "May I have some coffee, please—*kaffay*—and also some cake?" And I point to a saffron-colored slab studded with currants.

The young man pulls himself upright. "The first thing we decide," he says, almost imperceptibly weaving back and forth, "is—what kind of coffee shall it be? Greek? American? Or espresso?" He has no accent whatsoever; we could be in a snack bar off Harvard Square.

"Greek," I say.

He nods solemnly. "When in Greece drink Greek. So. The next thing we have to decide"—his eyes slide over me—"is—sweet? Or medium?"

"Medium."

"Not Greek." He shrugs. "But the lady has courage. Greek coffee, she says. She is also polite. She does not say Turkish coffee. Please, you sit. I bring everything."

I sip the thick liquid in the tiny cup and nibble at

the cake, which is dry and curiously tasteless. The waiter stations himself where he has a good view of my legs and says, "I speak good English, you think so?"

"Very good," I say truthfully.

"I am four years in the United States. In Connecticut one year, in New Jersey one year, in California two years. You know these places?"

"I've never been to California."

"I had an American wife for a while. Now I am divorced."

"Oh . . . I am sorry."

"Why you are sorry? Is much better this way. No good to be married to a woman a man is tired of. I am glad to be back, here people are more alive. You are married?"

I break off another morsel of cake. "Yes," I say.

"You are happy?"

What a question! Do all Greeks plunge at once into intimacy? Or is it just that people do seem to say the most extraordinary things when it isn't their native language . . . as if they've become someone else, someone not afraid to be more open, more free.

I say dismissively, "Certainly I'm happy." (Liar!) I stir the coffee; if it weren't so hot I could finish it at a gulp. Confound it, I'm going to drink every drop of the granular syrup, I'm going to eat every crumb of this mummified cake!

"You like the Greek coffee?"

"Very good." Another lie. It's getting to be a habit.

"You are alone?"

"I told you, I'm married."

"But you travel by yourself. American women all travel by themselves. Husbands too busy, too busy making money." He laughs, as if the notion pleases him.

"May I have the check?" I say coldly.

He makes a gesture of distaste. "Please—I am not a rich man, but I like to buy your coffee."

"Don't be absurd." I open my purse. "How much?"

A shrug. "Forty drachmas."

I take out a fifty-drachma note, which he accepts absently. Then he smiles. "Tomorrow same time?"

"I doubt it." I, too, smile, but not warmly. "Good-bye."

"Good-bye, beautiful lady." Softly. "Good-bye until tomorrow."

He probably makes a bit on the side, I think as I go back to the desk. A steady trade, I've heard. Perhaps the cabdriver, too . . . Yes, of course. Grow up, Kay.

There have been no calls. No, none for Cunningham with a C.

Not now, Mike, don't phone now: as the elevator creeps upward. *Not now, not yet, Mike:* as I hurry through the interminable halls. *Only a minute more:* as I try to turn the key—

I can hear the phone through the door.

"Damn it! Open up!"

I'm in. "Mike? Hello, Mike? Hello—" There is only an empty hum. "Hello," I repeat stupidly. *"Hello—"*

The hum reverts to the dial tone. Frantically, I signal the desk.

"Please—this is room two-fifteen—Cunningham, Mrs. Michael Cunningham with a C—oh, good evening, Mr.—uh—Mr. Efstratiou." I swallow my impatience. "I just received a call, but we were cut off.

— 46 —

I think it may have been from London, and I wondered—you're sure?" I sink onto the bed. "No, that's quite all right, I'm not—not distressed. Thank you."

Face it, Kay, it couldn't have been Mike. Even though no record is kept of incoming calls, they are relayed through the switchboard. And Mr. Efstratiou is not sure, he is busy, you understand, but he does not recall anyone asking in English . . . Oh, yes, a man's voice, yes, certainly, but speaking Greek, madam. Oh, yes, Greek, he is quite, quite sure. With an accent, it is true, but what does that signify? Greece is a country with many, many peoples, all different, *proud* to be different . . .

If this were a dumb thriller, I think as I detach myself with some difficulty, it would be somebody checking up on me for some reason. Have I arrived, is anybody with me . . . that sort of thing. AMERICAN HOUSEWIFE HELD HOSTAGE IN ATHENS: spicy reading in the *Paris Tribune*. " *'Funny thing,' wine-salesman Sanzio said to his wife and kiddies, 'I sat next to her on the plane to Rome. Yeah, that dame who got herself abducted right out of her indigenous hotel. I wouldn't have said she was the type . . .' "*

Lights are on up and down the avenue. The level of noise is astonishing: are mufflers illegal here? I close the draperies and turn the air conditioner up a notch. At least the strike hasn't cut off the electricity, whatever it may be doing to the phones. No—what ails you, Kay?—those aborted calls weren't from Mike, remember? And they weren't anything sinister, either, you idiot. They were routine wrong numbers, and when you answered in English, whoever it was simply hung up. As you would have done yourself, Kay, if you were home and somebody answered in Greek.

Shivering with cold, I move restlessly about the room. Mike should be here on the three o'clock plane tomorrow. Three-thirty to the hotel . . . four o'clock at the latest. Which gives me the morning and half the afternoon. First, the Archaeological Museum for the *Mask of Agamemnon* and the *Poseidon;* after that, the Parthenon. Then no matter what happens—no matter how things stand between us later—I won't have come to Greece and gone away again without seeing Schliemann's greatest find, or the bronze they say is the most beautiful male body ever, or the stones that are music and poetry and radiance and light . . .

But meanwhile: meanwhile I'd better get on with those letters. Damn it, I said I'd read them, so I'll read them! And this evening is really my last chance; over breakfast tomorrow would be cutting it too close. I'll get into bed, and then I'll speed-read them, bolt 'em down like a dose of medicine. And then I'll put through a call to London. Forget all those things I said: just put the call through, Kay . . .

Bathed, brushed, and in my coolest nightgown, I prop myself on the spacious bed (this whole evening is a his-and-hers waste of Olympic proportions) and reach resolutely in my shoulder bag for the letters.

And can't find them.

Because they aren't there.

CHAPTER

5

They *have* to be! I distinctly remember shoving the envelope into that deep pocket and then tucking the flap over. They can't have fallen out: I'd have had to turn my bag upside down and shake it, to lose anything from in there.

Well, they *aren't* there. Everything else is: makeup, tissues, aspirin, flashlight, change of clothing—compulsively I sort through the clutter, as if somehow the letters will materialize. And of course they don't. Then where *are* they? Somebody must have taken them! Oh, come off it, Kay—why on earth would anybody do that? Who would want them?

Now calm down. You were reading them on the plane to Rome, and you hadn't had much sleep—you hallucinate when you've skipped sleep, everybody does—so maybe you put them inside, in one of those sections that zip.

But I've already looked in there! My passport is still with the police, or wherever they send it, but my wallet, my health card, my traveler's checks are all right where they belong, but no large envelope with the bronze and blue logo.

Oh, God! Mike will think I deliberately lost them

so I wouldn't have to read them—that I'd do anything not to have to read them, including contriving
to lose them and then lying about it.

I wouldn't do that! When I think how he treasures them—they're the letters David never wrote,
that he was never old enough to write—Mike *must*
know I wouldn't lose them on purpose!

He'll believe I did. Why wouldn't he believe it?
Didn't I lose his son?

I do not put through a call to London.

I wake suffering from nothing so modern as jet lag
or so ancient as remorse: it's old-fashioned hunger
that consumes me. I haven't really eaten since—let's
see, not since dinner on the plane, and that was day
before yesterday.

The dining room is much improved overnight.
Sunlight streams through the window wall, a number of tables are empty—the tours must already have
departed—and the decibel level is tolerable.

Smiling, immaculate in pale linen sports jacket,
the headwaiter leads me to a table for four and with
a flourish pulls out a chair. The table is already occupied by a youngish couple, in sport shirt/slack suit
uniform, and I hesitate.

"Sit down, sit down!" A friendly grin. "We're not
nuts, we don't expect to find privacy anywhere in
Greece."

Brooklyn, I think, pleased, and sit.

A hunched-over stork of a waiter plunks a plate
of rolls and a small pot of tea in the general vicinity
of the couple. Food! I think happily, and say, "I'll
have coffee, please, and—" but he is already out of
earshot.

"Ben and Edie Posen, the Bronx."

"Kay Cunningham, last stop on the Erie, New Jersey." For once I feel no reluctance.

"You on the tour, Kay?"

I shake my head. "Are you?"

"Heck, no. We drew up our own. Seven days on the *Orion*—we're going to Istanbul and the islands." They beam at each other and laugh with delight. "We've been planning this for a whole year—Mykonos, Rhodes, Corfu—the works!"

The waiter sloshes a cup of coffee before me.

"I'd like some orange juice, please, and—"

"*Juice?* No juice! No! Impossible!" And he rushes off. I confess I gape after him.

"Hey—" Ben Posen signals the headwaiter. "Could we have some hot water here? And this lady doesn't have any rolls."

"The rolls are for everybody," the headwaiter says, smiling.

"Okay, but she wants some juice, too."

"I'll call your waiter." Smiling.

"She already asked him," Edie says. "When she said 'juice' he had a nervous breakdown. Maybe he's gone off into a corner to cry." She looks at her husband and giggles.

I study my coffee. Language gap . . . She doesn't know how she sounds. I don't know, really, how I do.

"Very tired," the headwaiter says, smiling. "Seven hundred for dinner last night, half the waiters on strike. Very tiring." Still smiling, he moves away.

"Ben, give Kay the paper. We're through with it."

He hands me an *Athens Times*. "It's in English, how about that? We swiped it in the coffee shop of the Grande Bretagne yesterday." He grins. "They offer it free to their guests."

"At eighty bucks a day they can afford it," Edie shrugs.

"Lookin' it over makes us glad we're gonna be out of reach for a week," Ben remarks. "One bright spot, though. That Dutch fellow, what was he in? Publishing?"

"Textbooks, I think," Edie says.

"Yeah, well, they got him back alive, which makes a nice change." Ben adds more sugar to his tea. "This kidnapping is gettin' like an international cartel—a real growth industry! They'll be sellin' shares on the Big Board next. Two million his family paid to get him back—dollars yet! After fifty-six days with his head in a grain sack, can you feature that?"

Edie shudders. "I'd have gone out of my living mind. Like what they did to Patty Hearst in that closet. I'd have gone stark raving, and it wouldn't have taken fifty-six *minutes.*"

"Cheer up, it won't happen to you, I'm a poor man, and your daddy is broke, not to say bankrupt."

"They could make a mistake. Nobody's perfect. They could take me for somebody else."

"I dunno but given my druthers, I'd rather be snatched than shot, any day," Ben says moodily. "You'd get a chance to argue. Think of those Eyetalian tycoons steppin' out to lunch all suave and elegant, and the next thing they know some character with a grievance is pluggin' 'em in the kneecap." He drains his cup. "Well, them's the breaks, no pun intended. See you around, Kay."

Given my druthers, I'd rather be snatched than

shot, myself . . . Say they did smash your knee, you'd never be able to move easily again, without pain, with grace and power . . . but crablike, propped on canes . . .

My coffee is cold. ITALY WON'T TALK WITH TER-RORISTS . . . *see page four.* I smooth the paper open. " *'Italy refused to barter for the lives of three kidnapping victims,' said a high government official . . . 'No negoti-ations would be tolerable that would place Marxist terror-ists on the level of interlocutors and judges of the demo-cratic system . . .' "* What on earth is meant by that? Though the rest is clear enough, God knows. *"In spite of the fact that forty-seven days after his abduction the ter-rorists killed a chemical executive, the government remains adamant: no bargaining."*

Seven weeks of terror and despair, with his own government disdaining to intercede for his safety! Too weak to protect its citizens, yet too proud to lift a finger to save them! *Here's the corpse, signora; would you care for a State funeral? Please, signora, try to con-trol yourself. Remember he died for the dignity of the State . . .*

I turn back to page one. STUDENTS SET OIL AFIRE . . . and there they are, caught in a freeze frame: surprisingly formal for rioters in their white shirts and dark trousers, dark ties flapping, they crouch before the overturned barrels; black stains leap to flame be-fore the Archaeological Museum. So much for the *Poseidon.* Some other time, perhaps, though more likely not. But surely the Parthenon will be, in every sense, well above the current unrest.

I stop by the desk to check my box. No message. Did I really expect one? Or just hope? Whichever, my pang of disappointment is real enough, and painful.

Outside, the heat pours over me like a coat of paint. The strike seems not to have affected the traffic, which is raucous, pugnacious, and dauntingly swift. There are no cabs, empty or filled; ignorant as I am of the language, to get on a bus would be madness. I'll have to walk, which is the best way to see the city, anyway. Afoot, at three miles an hour.

I buy a map from a vendor who by osmosis seems to understand what I need to know. Opening the map—it's in English as well as Greek—he taps it forcefully: that's where I am now, see? And the way to the Acropolis is clear enough, I find: down Panepistimiou to Constitution Square, on past the National Gardens, turn left at Hadrian's Gate . . . I can hardly get lost.

Athens proves a city of contrasts. Not two blocks from my hotel, across the facade of the university is stretched a banner splashed with angry letters like daubs of blood; the forecourt seethes with several dozen young men milling about restlessly. Yet farther along, in a huge sunken area dotted with bright awnings and crisscrossed by walks lined with goldenfruited trees, men in dark suits sit reading, talking, sipping coffee, or simply staring thoughtfully at each other; Greeks, not tourists, I decide—who else would wear black in this heat?

Stop for a confection of honey and walnuts from a pushcart. Try a shortcut through the public gardens (and turn back almost at once: too many lovers, arms about each other's waist; too many children, darting like dragonflies). On past Hadrian's Gate— and there against the sky the Parthenon floats like a mirage. For the first time I am glad I have come.

I cross a wide and empty avenue to where a gate

stands open, its admission booth unattended. As I follow the path up, its steep incline slippery with needles from the pines hanging motionless in the heat, I meet no one, see no one. It's almost eerily silent; not even a bird stirs. I climb higher, and now I can see the roofs of Athens, fading from copper to rose to gray, stretching to the sea.

I round the last turn and soon find myself in a cobblestoned court clogged with tourists. Toiling up from the buses that wait like patient nannies below, many appear to be completely on their own, wandering about bemusedly; others come in large disciplined clusters under the hawk eye ("Follow always my blue unbrella!") of a strong-lunged guide.

From here the stones leading to Athena's house are worn smooth as a river. I climb past a clump of ivory camomile clinging to a crack, past a file of pale apricot poppies scarcely a hand-span high, their petals scraps of crumpled tissue paper . . .

And then: *Here I am. There it is.*

Somehow I have always thought of ancient peoples as smaller than myself, and their accomplishments correspondingly diminished in scale. This temple—perhaps because of the light, the air and sky and wind, space all around, swimming in space and the city lapping at its base like a polluted sea—this temple with its great soaring columns seems magnified, glorified, larger than life.

Beyond the rope barrier there's a sign forbidding anyone to approach the portico or even to set foot on the great steps. It's the first I've seen that's in English—English, French, and German, actually—as well as in Greek: obviously it means business.

"Not only we treat the marbles against air pollution," a guide is explaining, waving his hand at the haze settling like a pall over the city, "which makes the marble to crumble. Also we protect from thousands upon thousands of feet, tramp tramp tramp like giant army every day without ceasing."

The sun saturates the air, it drenches the tourists, it pours without stint over tumbled columns, soaring temple, ropes and guards and warning signs. I am backing off to get a better angle through my viewfinder when I am swept up by a gaggle of tourists being herded to one corner of the temple. "Base looks to the eye completely straight, I am right?" the guide says crisply. "This is trick of optics. Base curves out and also up—not much, very little bit—but enough so if one puts a hat at other end, then stoops down, so"—demonstrating—"one can see the rise is sufficient to hide the hat. Ancient Greek architects were very skilled. They knew without this slight curve base would not look straight. So, imagine, please, at far end a soldier's helmet, or a gentleman's top hat. Now—"

When they have moved on, I go over to take a look for myself. It proves easy enough to imagine a hat—a nice round derby, say—sinking out of sight as I stoop lower, for I can clearly see the swelling in the stylobate rising as my eye level sinks; obviously the curve is sufficient to hide that imaginary headgear . . . or head. For as I straighten, there *is* a head—a man's head—directly in my line of sight. Like John the Baptist's on a platter, I think, my heart pounding. Gazing fixedly at me from behind dark glasses. Hatless, which is foolish in this sun. Scalp shining with sweat between the skimpy strands plastered across—

I stand erect so hurriedly my head swims. A moment later my sight clears, but Sanzio (I am sure it was he) is nowhere in sight. I'm more puzzled than alarmed: didn't he say he was going first to Rome and then to Athens?

I retreat out of the sun. The museum proves a cool oasis for humans and a sanctuary for the few statues rejected, or overlooked, by Lord Elgin. Ivory melding into palest almond, veined in salmon and cobalt: the marble is unexpectedly beautiful, and so lifelike I can almost imagine the blood coursing beneath. That rider looking back to gauge how far ahead his mount has sped him: how exultant he is! And the other—a young boy—riding bareback: his leg hangs limp, I swear it! As if it's alive, warm to the touch . . .

Where are my pencils, my chalks? . . . And at this moment, when I am aware—I can't believe it!—I miss my tools—that the time may come when once again I may actually use them—at this very private moment I am for a fraction of a second conscious of someone in the doorway; out of the corner of my eye I see someone familiar—or do I?

I'm not quick enough. The doorway is empty. And now a Japanese couple enters, followed by three perspiring women fanning themselves, declaring they're close to collapse. I slip past into the next room. No sign of him, of course: of Sanzio. There are four or five plump, balding, dark-haired men, but Sanzio is not one of them. I must have been mistaken.

Suppose I wasn't? Suppose it really *was* Sanzio. Whatever can he be up to? He wasn't on my plane yesterday, I'm sure of that, though of course there must be later ones. Can he possibly be following me? Not necessarily: the Acropolis is a magnet for every tourist in Greece. But Sanzio isn't your ordinary tourist; he comes here often, or so he implied. If he isn't trailing me, why does he keep ducking out of sight? I should think it would be much more like him to push forward and claim old acquaintance. *What about those phone calls?* Maybe they weren't normal lousy phone service—maybe they were Sanzio, checking up on me. Whatever for? Wait—if he's got the letters—and he *must* have—maybe it's Mike he wants to know about . . .

You, Kay, are being ridiculous! Two days' solo travel and you're getting paranoid. Nobody stole those letters, you lost them. Nobody is listening, all silent and sinister, at the other end of the phone. No chubby little wine salesman is changing his schedule in order to tail you around Athens. What on earth *for?*

Nevertheless, I hurry outside to look around. He's nowhere in sight. What would I say if I found him? "May I trouble you for my letters?" Come off it, Kay.

A little boy has ducked under the guard ropes and goes leaping up the great steps. Beneath his navy blue schoolboy shorts his skinny legs are pale. Turning, he grins down at his father and strikes a pose by one of the towering pillars: *Here I am.*

A guard lets loose several angry blasts on his whistle. Neither the boy nor his father pays the slightest heed. Obviously a Greek (I think) in his dark business suit and highly polished shoes, the father fusses over his camera, adjusting the focus, checking the light meter. The boy moves nearer the sign. He dusts it lightly with his hand. He leans against it with truly enviable nonchalance. David would do that . . . David, or his friend Jimmy.

"Jimmy dared me, Dad, so I dared him right back . . ."

I blunder past the grinning guard, scramble down the path to the forecourt, plunge the rest of the way . . . and well before three I'm back in the Caledonia. Home free. Sanctuary.

Tourists five-deep make it impossible to reach the desk. I can't even see if there's a message; I'll have to phone from my room. The telephone is the ultimate interrupter, taking precedence over everything but making love or dying. Even then I suppose some flakes would answer . . .

"Neh?" Muted bedlam. "One moment—"

The receiver is replaced, not gently. I dial again. No answer. I'll have to go down, after all . . . No, better stay where I am. It would be just my luck to be in the down elevator when he's coming up, or to miss him entirely in the smoky murk of the lobby.

I shower and dress, choosing the navy silk knit that Mike especially likes: age-old tactics of a woman with something to confess. "I'm terribly sorry, I know how much those letters meant to you . . ."

Four o'clock, and no Mike. Four-thirty. It *can't* take him this long from the airport. *My God, maybe the plane—* No, I'd have heard—*how?* How would I? Who'd phone me? I can't even read the goddam headlines in the newspapers . . . He's missed his plane, you hear? *Missed his plane.* There'll be a message . . .

The tourists at the desk have dwindled to a single line. The clerk flicks a glance at the boxes. No, nothing for 215.

I can't believe it. It isn't at all like Mike, no matter how desolate the territory between us. Would the clerk know about any planes down? I can't ask: to ask would make it true. "I was . . . was expecting word from my husband."

My unspoken obsessive dread gives my voice an extra dimension I don't intend, and the clerk sighs. "Very well, I look in the *poste restante,* madam. Sometimes there may be mislayings." He slips an elastic band off a clutch of envelopes and sorts through them with practiced speed. "How you spell?"

"With a *C.*" Absurdly, I sketch it in the air.

He begins again. "Aha—a message. A cable, madam."

It is from Mike. He is delayed. *Thank you, God. Thank you.* I'm to get out of Athens at once before the strike turns violent. Specifically, I'm to take the eleven o'clock plane for Mytilene ("Proceed Mytilene . . .") where I'll be met. Then wait at Damian's, he'll follow as soon as he can—for sure by Friday.

Rather different, I think bleakly, from the droll but endearing "I love you I love you I love you, ask Jimmy if I don't!" of two years ago. This time not a word about why he's delayed. Not even a hint that he's sorry. Perhaps he's not sorry. Perhaps there in London, walking those streets where ten years ago our future embraced and enchanted us—meeting himself ten years younger, ten years happier, ten years more filled with hope—perhaps he's realized he does not love me, does not miss me, does not need me. And why should he? What do we have in common?

Only a grave . . . only a child's headstone, not yet softened by wind or frost.

CHAPTER

6

I work my way over to the doorway where the light
is better and reread the cable. Filed last evening at
sixteen hours—four o'clock London time, six o'clock
here. So the plane I'm supposed to be on must have
left this morning, obviously: eleven o'clock this
morning, well over five hours ago. No place in Greece
can be five hours by air from Athens, so for a couple
of hours at least—more, probably—somebody has
been rattling around in this Mytilene place, wondering where I am. Not very nice, they'll be thinking,
not to show up and not to send word.

Speaking of which, why *didn't* Mike phone?
Though maybe he did try. No: those calls last evening were after six; he'd already filed this cable by
then. He cabled by choice. *Go to Damian's, he'll follow. Delayed.* The hell he's delayed! He's planned it
this way—I'm sure of it! Planned it so that I'll have
to meet that boy on my own, no buffer or shield.
That's why he didn't phone! Because he knows I'd
argue. Right from the beginning he's mapped it out
like this, and if there had been no strike he would
have come up with some other excuse to send me

out of Athens ahead of him, to—where? Where on earth is Mytilene? As for Damian, what the devil *is* his last name? Where's his village? I haven't any idea. And when I didn't turn up today, whoever was to meet me must have thought I'd changed my mind and decided not to come at all, so nobody will meet tomorrow's plane—why should they?

Get out of Athens at once. Take the eleven o'clock plane. If Mike was going to be that wordy, couldn't he have added to whom and where? Though I suppose it's all in the letters. I could always call him and ask. If he's still in London, that is. But then I'd have to admit I lost them, and I'd rather postpone my *mea culpa* as long as possible.

American Express! They'd know where Mytilene is, and get me that far. If I'm not met, time enough to phone Mike from there.

I study my map of the city. Nothing, not a clue. No use to ask at the desk; they've changed shifts and now it's that same fellow who could barely direct me to the coffee shop. What I need is someone who speaks English like a native, like that fluent Lothario in the café. If he doesn't happen to know where Am Ex is, he can look it up in the phone book. Which I haven't a doubt is in Greek.

He greets me like royalty—royalty with whom he is on exceedingly good terms.

"The beautiful American lady is back! Please, sit down!" He polishes a chair with a napkin. "What you want today? Another coffee medium?"

"Very sweet, please." The sugar may hold off starvation, at least for a while. "Also I need advice."

"Advice!" At once he is solemn. "You take me

for scholar? Never! I am man of action! I have no desire to be your teacher, beautiful lady—unless you
wish for me to teach you the arts of love?"

"Thank you, no." I give an obligatory smile, to
show that I know—and I know he knows I know—
this offer is routine courtesy, so to speak. "I have to
buy a plane ticket to a city called Mytilene—have you
ever heard of it?—so I have to find the American Express—"

"American Express? Aieee—" He appeals to
heaven. "Look—look at my face!" I look. "Do I not
have an honest face?"

"I guess so," I say cautiously.

"Yes, certainly, very honest. I have a very honest face. Would I, very honest man, take you to
American Express to buy *Greek* plane ticket? Never! I
look after you better than that, beautiful lady! I take
you to *Greek* travel agency—agency of my sister's
husband's brother. He thinks only of being big success, and to be big success you have to give best
possible service, is this not right? Aha! Philosophy!"

We set out. He has changed his waiter's coat for
a bright blue sports jacket, and as he steers me
through the crowds, he gives my arm a squeeze.
"Come on, baby!" he cries, and I hope he didn't take
the letters; it would be idiotic to be trusting the thief.
But he was never near my bag, I'm sure of it, and
anyway, what can happen to me surrounded by all
Athens out for a stroll?

"My name is Alexandros," he says, taking his
hand from my arm and putting it in comradely fashion on my far shoulder. "What's your name, baby?"

I remove his hand. "Cunningham," I say briefly.

"Cunningham? I never heard this name before. In America my friends call me Alex. What do your friends call you, Cunningham?"

I struggle not to laugh. "They call me the whole thing."

"So." He smiles tolerantly. "A name is a name."

We pass the university, and I ask what the banners say. He shrugs. "Students are angry because they are always angry. Do not let it concern you, beautiful Cunningham. Come, we cross the avenue—now!" We dash to the other side. "Now we sit here. Very famous café, Florio's. Travel agency is not open at this hour. Baby, you feel okay? You don't look so good."

There are odd dancing lights on the tabletop. "I'm fine—it's just that I'm awfully hungry. I can't remember when I ate—"

"You have no money?" In horror.

"Oh, I have money. I just—this is stupid, but I just didn't bother . . ." It seems too much to explain.

He snaps his fingers at a waiter and says something in staccato Greek. Then he leans across the dime-sized table and gazes at me with tender solicitude. "You will see that I take care of you, the best possible care in the world!" His knee presses mine.

I move my leg. "Thank you," I say distantly, and wonder if it would be possible to remove myself gracefully from his escort. I decide to postpone withdrawal tactics until I've eaten.

The waiter sets before me a salad of such dazzling proportions its platter nearly covers the tabletop: tomatoes, peppers, cucumbers, olives, anchovies, chunks of white cheese—never, I think, have I eaten anything more delicious! We share a basket of crusty bread; he has a small glass of some clear liquor, which clouds when he adds water, I, a glass of lemonade, cool but not iced.

"Ouzo." Alex touches my glass with his. "For you, Cunningham, better the lemonade. On not much to eat, ouzo is dynamite."

The waiter brings the check, which Alex allows me to pay as a matter of course. Or habit. I'm feeling vastly better; thank God my blood no longer fizzes like carbonated water.

"If you'll just point out where the travel agency is, I can easily find my way back tomorrow."

"Why not go now, Cunningham? Today is Tuesday, everything opens at five."

His sister's husband's brother's travel agency is on one of the streets angling off Constitution Square. We go up in an elevator like an ornate bird cage and get off at the eighth floor. On a frosted glass door are a few words in Greek, with SARRIS AGENCY, TRAVEL beneath.

Mr. Sarris, a heavy-set man in an elegant brown linen suit, scowls at his brother's brother-in-law, who smiles winningly.

"Andreas, you will be pleased to meet my friend, Mrs. Cunningham—" Alex turns to me. "I am sorry, you do not tell me your last name, I cannot make proper introduction."

"Cunningham is my last name," I say sweetly.

"Your *last* name?" He draws a sharp breath. "All this time I think we are friends, you give me your last name! You have been laughing at me!"

"No, honestly I haven't—"

Mr. Sarris delivers himself of a swift thrust of

Greek, of which, naturally, I can catch only one word: Alexandros.

Alex says with dignity, "Mrs. Cunningham, beautiful American lady, wishes to buy plane ticket. I tell her you are Greek travel agency and in business of selling plane tickets. So—enough. I leave you." He gazes at me ardently. "Farewell, beautiful Cunningham with hair like sunlight on field of wheat. I shall never forget you." And he strolls gracefully out.

Mr. Sarris clears his throat. "Please be seated, madam." I sit. Mr. Sarris sits. He pushes a button on his desk. "You will have a coffee, surely?"

A young woman with improbable auburn hair and exceedingly high heels taps in from a room beyond. While Mr. Sarris is speaking to her, she permits herself a sidewise look at me. Why am I an object of curiosity? Because this is a Greek tourist agency? Catering to Greeks, I mean. Or is she wondering how it happens that Alex brought me here?

Clearly Mr. Sarris is wondering the same thing.

"Alexandros is a good friend of yours, madam?"

"Barely an acquaintance." Feeling something more than this may be called for, I add: "He speaks excellent English and I have no Greek. He has been most kind to direct me here."

"And where would you like to go, madam?"

"To Mytileen."

When he looks blank, I spell it.

"Ah, yes. And when, madam?"

"As soon as possible. I should have gone this morning."

The young woman returns bringing two thimblefuls of coffee, very sweet. I sip. Mr. Sarris studies me further.

"Madam, you are for the first time in Greece?"

"Since yesterday afternoon."

He leans forward. "Madam, you are a guest in my country, I must warn you. I who am Greek am ashamed to say it, but there are those young men— they hover about the cafés like wasps looking for ripe fruit—who think only of money and how to get it. Only of money! Beware of them, madam. Forgive me."

"I assure you, Mr. Sarris, I appreciate why you have spoken." Ye gods, I think, I sound so stilted. "But Alex—Alexandros—has been nothing but—uh— friendly and helpful. Truly."

Mr. Sarris nods, and taps the button again. This time it's a young man who enters, a thin young man with sunken cheeks, jacket hanging loosely from bony shoulders. He, too, glances at me with guarded curiosity.

"This is Mr. Paradellis, Madam Cunningham. He will make arrangements for your flight to Myitilini."

"Madam Cunningham?" the young man says incredulously. "Madam *Michael* Cunningham of Beta Beta Beta?"

"Why, yes!" I say in amazement.

"Welcome, *kyría* Cunningham! Welcome to Greece!" he cries warmly, his homely face lighting up with a smile. He bows. "I am honored to greet the American mother of Damianós Mikhaïl!"

CHAPTER

7

We sit beneath an awning in the Platéia Syntágma-
tos, as he calls Constitution Square, our chairs facing
the wide steps that lead to Panepistimiou Street. A
self-absorbed fellow who could be a holdover from
the sixties reclines on the lowest step; bearded, san-
daled, and forehead-banded, he strums aimlessly on
his guitar.

"Hippie," says Nikolas Paradellis disdainfully.
"Foreign hippie."

Nikolas had further introduced himself as we de-
scended in the bird-cage elevator. "Damian writes you
about me, no doubt. Why are you surprised we
should meet? Is coincidence, but life is concidence,
kyría mou, whenever the gods choose to meddle. In
my life I think the gods meddle very much." He
smiled briefly. "Does not Damian tell you I work in
Athens? Oh, yes, surely he writes about his *koumbáros*—his godfather? Ah, that is it! He calls me always uncle Níko—now you know me, yes?"

"Yes, of course," I had answered lamely. Why
can't I come right out and admit I don't know anything about anybody? That I haven't read those let-

ters which must have cost Damian so much effort to write, so much postage to mail? Because not to have read them is worse than losing them, that's why. It's deliberate rejection: the ultimate put-down.

Nikolas Paradellis has made a hotel reservation for me—for Mike and me—by phoning direct to Molibos. "More comfortable for you there, Mrs. Michael. Hotel Silver Bird is right on the sea, hotelier speaks English. Hotel in Petrá too Greek, and nothing in Pyrgotáfos, it is very small village, of course."

If I just keep still and listen, he may fill me in on all I need to know. Drumming restlessly with nicotine-stained fingers on the metal table that holds our tiny cups of coffee, he gazes at me with disconcerting intensity. New Yorkers, I reflect, look through you, as if you don't exist. Keeps them from getting involved, and all that. But the Greeks seem to scorn such gambits. They look *at* you, they *look* at you . . . Though this man's scrutiny holds no hint of sexual challenge, which is a pleasant change.

I say, "You don't like hippies?"

"They are beggars. Parasites. They beg from their parents, who are so foolish as to send them money. They beg from us Greeks, who are much poorer than they, who have to work to stay alive. Why do they think they have the right to sun themselves like lizards and not work? The rich should not beg from the poor."

"Perhaps they aren't all rich."

"That one is American. He wears the uniform. He is rich."

How ugly Nikos's face is . . . as if he starved as a child, and the bones never grew properly.

"Do you know of an art supply shop anywhere

near here? I want to get some pencils—" And am dumbfounded at what I've said. As if a paralyzed limb, leaden and dead, at long last feels a tingling.

"But certainly, a very good one almost directly on our path to the Hotel Kakofonia." He grins. "Who booked you there, kyría—American travel agent?"

"I suppose so. My husband's firm arranged everything."

He nods. "Very sad. Many foreign people come to these beehives. What they learn of Greece I hate to think." He summons the waiter and pays for both coffees. When I protest: "My pleasure," he says dismissively. "Please, no more."

I allow myself to be escorted back to the hotel. It is a pleasant walk. Nikolas Paradellis does not attempt to hold my hand or put an arm around my shoulder; he does not call me "baby." True, he keeps using that phrase that sounds like an endearment—kyría mou—but no doubt it's just a politeness.

The next morning I am checked out and waiting by the curb when, as promised, precisely at nine-thirty A.M. a cab swoops up and Nikolas Paradellis gets out.

"I wish you a safe journey, kyría Cunningham." He closes the cab door after me as if he were shutting a castle gate. The sunlight mercilessly highlights the seamed and pitted planes of his face. "Give always my best wishes stón kýrio Cunningham."

"You may see him before I do. He spoke of reaching Athens this afternoon. I'm going to look for him tomorrow in—Molibos, is it?—on the chance."

"Molivos," he corrects me politely. "Beta is pronounced vuh in dimotikí—very confusing if you know classical. But your husband—you would like that I have him met?"

"He'll probably arrange with American Express. Thanks anyway."

"I shall of course phone him and extend to him a welcome. You have your plane tickets safe?"

Solemnly, I assure him I have. He gives brief instructions to the driver and waves me off.

I reach the airport shortly after ten, which gives me more than enough time to provide myself with a small sack of pistachios and some almond rolls. Nikolas Paradellis has warned me there's no meal on the plane, for it's only about an hour flight; however, the hotel bus takes two hours to cross the island, arriving always after the dining room is closed.

"If by any chance you are not met," he adds, "be very sure to settle what you pay the taxi before you get in. On Lesvos as many other places, taximen are bandits. Not all, you understand, *kyría mou*, but always the one you have."

So Mytilene is on Lesvos—spelled, no doubt, with a *b*—and Lesvos is an island. Any connection with Lesbian? The one derived from the other, I mean. Well, obviously. Might be something about it in my Herodotus. (Which I've packed out of reach, of course.) And where *is* Lesvos, anyway?

Baggage inspection is no more than a glance in my shoulder bag, a poke at my carry-on. The plane itself looks about as airworthy as a secondhand school bus. Ignore the worn cleats on the ramp, Kay. Ignore the frayed rope holding the door open. Focus your mind on the fact that this crate goes every day to Mytilene and every day returns. Safely.

Three ear-splitting blasts and we take off. The plane bucks and rocks, climbs and sinks. My fellow passengers are as unperturbed as if they're commuting to work. (As perhaps they are.) Thirty-three indigenous commuters and one uneasy American tourist. Plus the stewardess in her rough-weave smock embroidered so colorfully at throat and wrist—charming, charming! The man across the aisle works a crossword in Greek. The black-clad woman next to the window clutches an oddly mobile wicker basket. My ears complain the cabin isn't pressurized. We can't be very high: whenever the plane's wing dips I catch a glimpse of waves, tidy, well disciplined, and brilliant blue, with little boats like toys on a pond. Someone is speaking German. And someone else something that doesn't sound Greek. I hear no English, that I do know.

The airport at Mytilene is not much larger than a sandlot ball park. We pick our way across the broken pavement, the wind snatching at skirts and ties and sending umbels of dry fennel tumbling past. Beyond the lineup of vehicles waiting—there's no sign of a bus—our luggage is dumped in a heap by the entrance to the terminal, a chunky cement-block building with all the charm of a chicken hatchery. I help myself to my bag and go inside to inquire if the bus is nonexistent or merely delayed.

The terminal consists of a single room painted a sickly green and meagerly furnished with a few battered chairs along one wall. There are, however, two signs, both comfortingly bilingual: [something] TICKETS, and [something] RESERVATIONS. Tickets speaks no English. Reservations, yawning over a newspaper, knows nothing of any bus from any hotel, nor can he suggest alternate transportation, except, of course, the taxis. Telephone? In booth outside, lady missus.

I find the phone around the corner from the entrance. It obligingly swallows any coin offered, but after that, nothing. No matter how I spin the dial, I can rouse no human anywhere. Instructions posted in English read as if they've been penned under water. I go back inside. English-speaking Reservations has disappeared. There seems to be nothing for it, then, but the taxis. Once again—and I profoundly hope it's for the last time—I lug myself and my gear outside.

Jabbering animatedly in German, a cluster of tourists is filing into a minibus; everyone else has left. I approach the three taxis remaining and attempt to open negotiations.

"How much to Molibos? How much to the Hotel Silver Bird?"

The drivers stare at me thoughtfully. They are hard-bitten men with tired faces, and when they grin at me, revealing tobacco-stained, neglected teeth, they look like starveling hounds hoping for a bone. My heart sinks.

"Molibos—how much?" I mouth the words exaggeratedly.

"Hah-ooo muh-ch," Number Three says loudly, and traces with a calloused finger in the dust on the hood: 25.

Twenty-five dollars . . . Well, I can't walk, and I can't stay here. Reluctantly, I'm about to get in when behind me a man speaks.

"Haben wir Raum für eine Amerikane?"

Blond, bespectacled, and with considerable photographic equipment slung about his neck, he wears leather shorts with embroidered suspenders and knee-high socks with tassels. All exposed skin is sun-burned a salmon pink.

"*Ja! Ja!*" Fifteen faces gaze at me, beaming. "*Gasthof Silbervogel, hier wir kommen alles!*"

"*Ich bin Professor Furchtwanger.*" He makes me a little bow and reaches for my luggage. "*Hermann Furchtwanger, von Nürnberg.*"

"*Vielen Dank',*" I say with heartfelt sincerity. "Kay Cunningham, U.S.A."

We climb aboard.

My companions are an exceedingly cheerful lot and very friendly. Though my German is nowhere near as fluent as Mike's, the babble around me sounds so blessedly familiar I feel I could burst into speech any time I wish, and I begin almost to enjoy myself.

Inland, the terrain proves mountainous. Pasture roses spill over the roadsides, and olive trees lean against the terraced slopes like warriors exhausted by battle, some so crippled by age I marvel they are still standing, for their trunks are mere shells. In the dappled shade brightened by spikes of yellow broom now and again a goat is tethered. The road twists like a mountain brook, the driver sounding his horn at every curve; this continual honking becomes a kind of background music, at once exhilarating and soothing. We swoop past sturdy three-wheeled ve-hicles that look for all the world like mechanized wheelbarrows. We bully our way through a herd of rambunctious donkeys. Occasionally we pass a house, and always it is a small square structure with stuc-coed walls painted rose, or aqua, or lemon yellow. And everywhere and always the poppies blow, large as saucers, scarlet in sunlight, glowing blood-red in shade.

The guide switches on his loudspeaker. "Hopefully our guest interests herself in archaeology?" he says in German.

"Oh—yes!" I answer in some bewilderment.

"Good! We, too, take pleasure in the study of what remains of ancient civilizations. We plan to view a Roman aqueduct, today or tomorrow. But here we have a democracy. Now we must decide: who is for today? And who is for tomorrow?"

The *Heute* won, and the bus is slowing to turn onto an unpaved road when a bright yellow vehicle with TAXI upright on its roof zips past and squeals to a halt directly in front. A man and a boy spill out. They race back to the bus, where the man begins pounding on the door and shouting.

"*Kyría* Cunningham! *Kyría* Mee-*kay*-lee Cunningham!"

"*Wir sind* hijacked," the professor says, and his flock laughs.

"Please—*bitte*—*sie sind meine Freunde!*" Catching up my bag and suitcase, I stagger down the aisle. "Please, Herr Professor—*öffnen Sie die Tür, bitte schön!*"

Framed in the doorway, the young man (he might be in his late twenties) does indeed look like a bandit: he has a very brown face, very black hair, very black mustache; his white shirt is open to the waist over a very brown and beautiful chest; all he needs is a cutlass thrust through his belt. He gives me a rapid once-over, followed by a wide smile of welcome.

"So we rescue you, dear lady Cunningham!" His teeth are very white. Then, with a lightning change of expression: "*Freunde—wir sind Freunde!*" he snaps angrily at Professor Furchtwanger, who is asking me in a low voice, *"Sind Sie sür, gnädige Frau?"*

Belatedly cautious, "Who are you?" I ask in English.

"I am Kostas, of course! And here is Damianos Mikhail—at last you meet! This road they turn on, it is not for Molivos—no good to go on detours with strangers, you are too trusting! Come with us and we keep you safe. Now, where are your luggages?"

I make a brief speech of thanks to my hosts, which is very well received and roundly applauded. Amidst Valkyrie cries of *Auf Wiedersehen!*, the tour bus crunches on down the graveled side road and disappears from sight.

Silence, sudden and acute. Beyond where the taxi stopped there is an immense olive tree. It looks as if it has cracked in half, just simply split, as if it grew too large for its skin. A man could easily take refuge in there, from the weather, or from a pursuer . . .

I have to look at him. I can't stand here forever watching the dust sifting down . . .

"Damian makes great sacrifice," Kostas says, laughing. He tosses my bags onto the back seat. "He has made absent from school in order to bring you from Mytilene! But we are not lucky—two ladies from hotel wish to take plane to Athens, and after fashion of ladies they are not ready, so we are late. You forgive?" His teeth are really dazzlingly white and even.

"Yes, of course," Stiffly. "There is nothing to forgive."

I feel as if I were about to meet my husband's mistress: defensive, insecure, resentful—and overwhelmed with curiosity.

I turn my head.

CHAPTER

8

The boy looks at me measuringly. His face, as close
to expressionless as is possible for a child of his years,
is very adult in its dignity and control. Adult, and
hostile. I am taken aback. For some reason I've been
expecting—dreading, really—that he would fawn over
me. No way did I anticipate this . . . remoteness.

"How do you do, Damian?" I say distantly.

He is beautiful, of that there can be no doubt. His
eyes are large and dark, his brows level, his mouth,
though unsmiling, as beautifully modeled as the lips
on the statues in the Acropolis museum. His resem-
blance to his uncle is extraordinary. Like the faces of
the riders in the frieze, I think: variations on a single
theme.

"How do I do? I do well." Damian's tone is such
an accurate echo of my own that for a moment I think
he's mocking me. No: he's simply taking his cue from
me. Perhaps he's as defensive, as insecure, as resentful as I am myself.

What does one say to such a child? It's no use to
imagine, as Mike must, that he is David grown older.
David, no matter how long he lived, would never

have been as old as this boy. He would never in all his life have turned on me this . . . archaic gaze.

"Come, get in, plenty of room for three together when all are friends," Kostas says cheerily. "In Mytilene they tell me your husband is not with you. Does he not come?"

"He had business in London. I expect he'll be coming tomorrow—for sure by your birthday on Friday, Damian."

"Yes, he writes me he will be here. But I do not understand. Why is day I am born important to my American father?"

"Don't you celebrate it?"

"What means this word?"

"Celebrate? Oh . . . make a family party."

"No. Is not important. Name day is important."

"You must have two, then." I try to smile; my face feels stiff. "One for Saint Damon, one for Saint Michael."

"*Damianós. Mikhaïl.* My name's Greek, not English. Not American." He keeps his eyes on the road ahead, his back very straight. He sits between us, his knees drawn up a bit because of the hump in the floor. Both knees are scarred, I see. I'm reassured to observe these blemishes, which I take as proof the child is mortal, and not a . . . a bored and naughty god in human guise, amusing himself by dabbling in my life . . . in mine and Mike's.

Mike will love him on sight. He'll never see this isn't David three years older. Of course this Greek is as dark as David was fair, but that's mere surface variation. What Mike is sure to see is that Damian, as was David, is . . . is the first brush stroke, laid right. Is the opening phrase of a song, sung pure and true. Is the sun rising, the clear morning light . . .

"What is your saint's name, *kyría* Cunningham?" Kostas skids the taxi expertly around a graveled curve. The road is one hairpin turn after another and there are no guardrails.

"Kay," I say reluctantly. If he starts calling me "baby"—

Kostas looks puzzled. "*K?* Is to say *kappa?*"

"It's short for Katharine, only nobody calls me that."

"Kath-a-rin. I like Kath-a-rin. Very pretty name. Much more pretty than Kay. In Greek is Katerina." He pronounces it *Kah-ter-eén-uh;* it sounds like music.

Damian looks at his uncle out of the corner of his eye. "I shall be glad to meet my American father," he states flatly.

"Yes." I swallow hard. "He looks forward very much to meeting you, Damian."

"I very much, too," Damian repeats. We gaze fixedly ahead.

The air is hazy in the distance, the tips of the mountains hidden. We drive through a village where pomegranates ripen in the dooryards and TV aerials perch like storks on the Venetian red roofs. Children run to stare as we pass. Nowhere in Greece is one safe from them, it seems; they are always out of doors, always on the periphery of adults' activities, observing, imitating . . .

"I'm sorry if you were looking for me yesterday," I say stiffly. "My husband sent a cable, but I didn't get it in time."

"We hear nothing about yesterday neither," Kostas assures me. "Hotel say you come today."

The road has dipped almost to sea level. As we skirt a marsh where dikes trap the water in shallow rectangles, I ask about the strange white piles on the far side. Could they be unusually pure and white sand?

"Salt." Kostas waves a hand. "Very simple way to have enough: use the sea. Greece a poor country, must use all she has. I am guide for tourists, I know everything about island of Lesvos. Everything. You have questions, I tell you all." He leans forward to look at me past Damian's aloof profile; his smile with the flash of even teeth against his brown skin would sell ten million tubes of toothpaste.

"Those olive trees—the ones that are all hollow—how old would you say they are?"

He shrugs. "Is question for university professor."

Damian: "Eight hundred years."

"I have scholar for nephew! No charge, Professor Demetríou—*kyría* Katerina is almost family!"

No, I am not, nor will I be, not to any degree whatsoever!

"My uncle Yeoryios has some he say is older than that."

"Your uncle Yeoryios fills you with fairy stories. Believe always what I tell you," Kostas says lightly, and again Damian gives him that sidewise look.

Now we are climbing again. The land grows barren, the steep and rock-strewn hillsides baking in the sun. Only along the roadsides do any such plants as mullein and aloe and thistles find roothold. In all that bleak and empty landscape there is almost nothing moving. Once we pass a flock of sheep, drab gray and black, grazing on God knows what among the rocks. And once we pass a burro with a man astride; a barefoot woman in shapeless black trudges along behind. (I think it tactless to ask questions about that, and refrain.) And now there is the sea again, stretching to the northern horizon. All along the coast the edge of the shore is an irregular band of green, the only true green in sight, as if the soil has had to absorb its moisture from the sea. In the distance a fortress broods on a spit of land; around its base houses spill like toys.

"Molivos," Damian says abruptly.

"We do not go so far," Kostas remarks. "Hotel is here." And we turn into a courtyard and draw up before a flight of steps. Geraniums splash from terra-cotta planters on either side, and above the door is a handsome sign—in Greek.

"In English is 'Silver Bird,'" Damian says kindly.

Kostas totes my bags into the lobby and I follow. Light, bright, fresh and clean, with red-tiled floor and a view of the water beyond a wide terrace—the Silver Bird is very *Greek* Greek, I think with satisfaction.

The young woman behind the desk takes a quick puff on her cigarette and sets it carefully in a saucer. "Oh, yes, Mrs. Cunningham, Mr. Paradellis phoned about you." She flicks a glance at Kostas. "I am very sorry, we have no room until Friday. A tour comes, you understand, with three more than expected. We are entirely full. I am sorry."

An irrational sense of desolation, of being abandoned, sweeps over me, and I feel my face freeze into that coldness I have learned, this past year, to don like armor.

Kostas is incredulous. "You have nothing? Telephone calls from Athens are like dead goats—worthless?"

"Perhaps there is room in the village, madam." The young woman picks up her cigarette and inspects its glowing tip.

"No, never! *Kyría* Cunningham is American mother of my dead brother's son! We beg her not disgrace us, not go to hotel"—Kostas doesn't actually spit, but the gesture is so implicit in his tone the young woman flinches—"but no! she wishes make us no trouble. Now you, Voula, want shame my family more, you tell her go beg shelter in village!" He seizes my bags as if they're filled with feathers. "I rejoice you have no room! Come, *kyría* Katerina, accept shelter of my brother's house. Not worthy so great a lady, but what we have is yours!"

Damian leaps to hold the door, his uncle strides out, and I meekly follow.

There is little so likely to break the ice between strangers than to be, if not ejected, then rejected, and that through no fault of one's own. With a distinctly heightened sense of camaraderie we set off down the coast road. It runs between patches of garden, now, where old men stoop over rows of cabbages, past orchards not yet bearing fruit, past burros almost hidden beneath baskets of beets and lettuce or bales of hay, past a man riding sidesaddle, five-gallon cans as cargo. We skirt Molibos with the sea to our left, the road hugging the harbor where a scattering of workaday boats, small, sturdy, one-masted, drowse in the afternoon sun. On our right the village climbs the hill in a series of stone embankments surmounted by the sprawling ruins of the fortress.

A line of opaque cloud marks the eastern horizon. Kostas tosses a look like a javelin across the intervening water. "Tourkía." He nods toward the north. "That way is Troy, maybe thirty kilometers. Very famous—you have heard of this Troy? Very old. Some say soldiers from Greek army came to Lesvos to rest. Why not? Lesvos is lovely, you think so? More lovely then. Venice cut off trees. Like a great fire, Venice."

"Con-fla-gra-tion." says Damian. He preens himself. "I learn in school. Is from the Latin. Venice a conflagration."

"Your uncle speaks of events that occurred—how long ago? two thousand years?—as if they were yesterday. Time is so elastic here, one's measurers get all out of whack."

"Out of whack," Damian repeats with satisfaction. "Is very good. Out of *whack*. I like."

North and east of Molibos the road snakes within a stone's throw of the shore. Every few hundred yards we pass soldiers strolling two by two. Like in the airport in Rome: is the entire Mediterranean ringed by armies watching, waiting, weapons at the ready— for what? The strand of rusted barbed wire that sags from one flimsy metal post to another along the edge of the road wouldn't hold back a lamb. And those modest cement structures perched on the rocky hillside every mile or so—can they be a species of bantam fort? I suppose so: there's always a soldier or two lounging in full view. It would all seem more ominous if the music drifting down the barren slopes— music clearly audible above the wind of our passing—weren't so melodic and lighthearted.

Abruptly, we are in another village. There is the

harbor with fishing boats at anchor. There is the town square, and tables set about an open area by the water. There is the school with a shout of children.

"Is that yours, Damian?"

He gives me a strange look.

"No, is kindergarten," Kostas says with a laugh. "Damian is big boy, he goes *stó dimotikó* in Petra. He does not write you?"

"Of course," I say. "Faithfully." I am burdened by the weight of my duplicity. "But where are we now?"

"Pyrgotafos. Not to mistake for Petra, which is big city of one thousand people."

"And Molivos?"

"Very big," Damian says solemnly. "Twice as big as Petra."

"And ten times as big as Pyrgotafos," Kostas adds, equally solemn. "Which is town of two hundred peoples—you see why needs such big, big name!" Again that thousand-watt smile. I wonder if he's aware of its voltage. Well, of course he must be.

The road through the village is mule-steep and so narrow that anyone on foot—the black-robed, bearded priest and the small boy with the long loaf of bread (unwrapped) under his arm—has to dodge into a doorway to let us pass. Luckily we meet no vehicle and are soon safely through and into the countryside beyond.

Here the soil is evidently less impoverished, for on either side olive trees silver the slopes in the fitful wind. We make one more turn, go a few hundred yards down an unpaved lane, and stop before an open gate leading to a modest cube of a house, lemon-colored, its red-tiled roof surmounted by an elaborate dovecote. Kostas turns off the engine. "My brother's house." His voice is flat, neutral. I can't read his face.

An outside staircase leads to a porch running the full width of the upper story. Geraniums in oilcan planters are ranged up the staircase like footmen at a fancy-dress ball. There are two doors, one opening onto the porch, one in the shadows below. A wreath of—dried herbs? flowers? I can't tell from here—hangs above the upper door. In the silence and the heat I can hear doves calling.

Kostas sets his thumb on the horn. The upper door opens and a woman appears, wiping her hands on her apron.

"My brother's wife," says Kostas, his face bronze marble.

"My aunt Verek," says Damian under his breath.

We get out, and still the woman stands motionless, gazing down at us impassively. As we cross the courtyard I feel very much the intruder. Weren't Mike and I invited? My God, did we invite ourselves?

Kostas addresses her in Greek, and she comes forward reluctantly. She could be forty years old, perhaps forty-five. Her hair is drawn back severely; her face is tired, secretive, stoic. Her shabby black dress with sleeves rolled above the elbow, her faded black apron, her rope-soled shoes detract not a whit from her formidable dignity. She speaks unsmilingly in a flat voice, and I am convinced she doesn't want me here any more than I wanted to come. *Damn* it, Mike! Did you have any idea it would be like this? Is *that* why you're not here?

Kostas translates. "She asks that the American mother of her husband's brother's son please to come in." He looks directly into my eyes, and his smile reassures me. He, at least, is glad I'm here; perhaps I've just imagined the rest.

The house is a fortress against the sun. On every window slatted blinds are shut fast, as if the very daylight were a danger. Through the door on my left I can see an old-fashioned gas range, one of those that stand on spindly legs with the oven to one side. The room is painfully neat, almost bare, and everything is immaculate, the freshly mopped terrazzo floor still damp.

The frosted glass door at the end of the hall leads to the bedrooms, Kostas tells me. "My brother's house is big, though he is not rich. Four bedrooms—my father hoped for many sons." He laughs. "So there is always one for renting to tourists, and when I am not here there is mine also."

The woman Verek ushers me into the room across from the kitchen. The parlor (if that's what it is) offers little by way of comfort or distraction. There are no curtains at the windows or carpet on the floor; the only pictures are icons—Byzantine faces in sepias and deep blues. There is nothing in the room to read: not a single book, not so much as a newspaper.

The woman returns bringing a painted tray with three tiny glasses of clear liquid, a pitcher of water, and a small dish of figs in syrup.

"My brother's wife bids you welcome. Please—eat, drink. *Glykó* for being guest, ouzo for homesickness." Kostas's smile is muted, as if in Verek's presence a warmer degree of friendliness would be out of place.

Everyone watches as I sip the ouzo. It is like liquid sunshine; warmth rolls on my tongue and strokes my throat. From her position near the door, her hands folded across her apron, Verek gazes at me unblinkingly. Taking me in inch by inch, I think, and am therefore the more disconcerted to find myself smiling at her conciliatingly.

She addresses a brief remark to her brother-in-law, who shrugs.

"What does she say?"

"Nothing of interest."

"She asks how old you are," Damian says.

Kostas snaps at him, and Damian is on his feet with one swift fluid motion. "I go tell my uncle Yeoryio you are here, American mother."

I take another swallow of ouzo. "I'm thirty-two," I say.

Kostas translates, accurately, I assume, for the woman looks at me resentfully and again delivers herself of a sentence or two. Her voice is acid.

"What does she say? Please—I must know!"

"She says she, also, has thirty-two years, but that Greek years and American years are not the same, not for a woman."

"I know . . . I'm sorry."

"Not your fault, Katerina. Do not be sorry. I am not sorry."

Kostas sips his ouzo, swirling the liquid in the tiny glass. I barely touch mine; it seems foolhardy to take more than a drop at a time. The woman remains silent, impassively waiting. Somewhere beyond the shuttered windows I can hear bells, intermittent and melancholy, lighter than cowbells, less substantial. Only the *zazz* of a motorcycle from far off seems real.

There is a heavy stride of boots in the hallway and Yeoryios Demetriou comes in, Damian slipping in after him like a shadow. Heavier than his brother, cleanshaven, with bushy brows and a mop of unruly black hair that hangs nearly to his shoulders, he has obviously just come from work, for his shirt, open at the throat to a tangle of black hair, is wet with sweat, and his trousers, stuffed into knee-high boots, are stained with soil.

"I bid welcome to the American mother of my brother's son." His black eyes regard me with courteous reserve. "You do honor to my house. Please forgive I am not here at your arrival. Not know the hour."

His wife brings him a glass and a small squarish bottle. Yeoryios refreshes mine and his brother's, then fills his own.

"To friends." With one swallow, he drains his glass. "It is my hope you have a good journey."

"Very good, thank you."

"And your husband, American father of Damian, is he not with you? We are not to have the pleasure?"

I explain about London, and the strike, and Mike's concern.

"*Kyría* Katerina is promised room at Silver Bird," Kostas puts in smoothly, "but hotel says sorry, too many Germans come, no room. I bring her here, I know you rejoice to have American mother of Damian as guest."

"Very good, yes, hokay. I am proud you make us visit."

"If you're sure it won't be an inconvenience—"

"No such word in Greek for visit of friend."

The woman Verek speaks. He transfers his heavy

gaze to her and regards her in silence. Flushing, she repeats her remark.

Kostas says with an enigmatic smile, "My brother's wife wishes to know why you do not wait for him, your husband."

"In Athens? But I explained why—"

"Not Athens. In London. Why you do not wait in London."

"My wife is stupid woman!" Yeoryios says harshly. "Asks questions like *dáskalos*—like school-teacher!"

"I didn't go to London. My husband and I always take—" Wrong tense. "We always took separate planes, because of our son." My voice shakes. "It was . . . safer. Not to have both parents in the one plane, you understand. We felt a child needs— must have—at least one parent . . ." I can't look at Damian.

"You have a son, *kyría mou?*" Yeoryios frowns at his nephew and snaps something in Greek. Damian looks abashed. "Why am I not told this? I am shamed that American parents of my brother's son do not feel free to bring their son to my house. My country very old, has much that will make child to think mankind is precious, is jewel—"

"Please!" I struggle to steady my voice. "My son is dead. We—my husband and I—took separate planes out of—of habit."

I hope.

"This is not long ago, *kyría mou?* Your grief is young?"

"A year now."

He nods. "Like yesterday."

Again his wife puts a question to him, and he replies with one word. She sucks in her breath. When she speaks once more, her husband gestures to her to be silent. She speaks again, this time with a stubborn edge to her voice.

Yeoryios says with obvious reluctance, "You have other children, *kyría mou?* A daughter, perhaps, to fill your arms?"

I say with difficulty, "I could have only the one child."

And now Verek turns on Kostas and spits out a comment. Both men answer her, but she is not to be dissuaded. That her remarks have to do with me I have no doubt: she keeps tipping her head or flicking her hand in my direction. Her voice rises, becomes shrill.

Damian touches my arm. "Please come, American mother." Softly, "I make you to know Erasmios. You like? Come—" And he leads me outside.

I follow the child through the courtyard gate and along the wall toward the rear of the house, where a vegetable garden as precise as a checked tablecloth extends to a row of sheds. Beyond this, in the shade of a fig tree, an ancient burro is tethered. When it lifts its head at our approach, the bell dangling from its necklace of blue beads makes a mournful note.

"My friend Erasmios." Damian scratches the beast's neck affectionately. "Before my uncle Kostas comes home bringing much money and buying taxi, every day after goats are milked Erasmios and I take it to Mr. Voufounos the cheesemaker, and then we go to school. While I work hard with my books, Erasmios waits in the shade of the plane tree, and I envy him."

Damian turns on me a smile of such sweetness I can scarcely bear it. That open, trusting, *sharing* smile . . . *Oh God oh God. Mike, why did you drag me here? To punish me further?*

Kostas comes looking for us. "So, we go to the house of Paradellis the poet," he says cheerfully. "Very advanced thinker, Nikolas Paradellis. Not superstitious. Maybe atheist, but you not care. He is good man, though what kind of poet is not for me to judge—good, bad, terrible—who can say?"

"I . . . met him in Athens."

"He works in travel agency," Kostas nods. "A poet must eat. Is problem they have, always hungry. I am sorry, *kyría* Katerina, you cannot stay at my brother's house. My brother's wife very superstitious."

In the silence we retrace our steps past the ruler-straight rows of cabbages, past the lemon-yellow stuccoed wall, to where Yeoryios stands by the courtyard gate, stiff as a sentry.

"*Kyría* Cunningham, I ask your forgiveness. You do me honor to be my guest, you are welcome in my house, to eat but not to sleep. My wife is afraid. Is bad luck to have childless man and wife to sleep overnight. Please, do not be angry. On some things my wife cannot think like human being."

"It's all right," I say awkwardly. "I quite understand."

Verek is wiser than they know. Anyone childless for the reason I am childless would indeed be a contamination.

Damian flings himself into the back seat, and we set out for the village. Evidently Kostas chooses to return by a different route, for we follow a steep track that leads past tilled fields and turn onto the coast road about a hundred yards beyond an ancient tower. As we head back down the Molibos road into Pyrgotafos, I see we have come full circle.

"Uncle Nikos has no television," Damian says abruptly.

"Never mind," I tell him. "It would all be in Greek, wouldn't it? Fat lot of good that would do me."

"Fat lot," says Damian happily. *"Fat* lot, fat *lot*. I like!"

"Why you not want to learn Greek?" Kostas says in surprise. "Is beautiful language."

"I'm sure it is. But I'll be here only a few days. How much could I learn in that time?"

"I teach you. Not today—today is holiday. Tomorrow is school day."

At this Damian bursts out in Greek. Kostas cuts him short. "Speak always English before *kyría* Katerina. Is very rude speak unknown language before a guest."

"I say is very *rude* go to school when my American mother comes many thousand miles to visit me!"

"Never fear, little one, I take good care of American mother." Again Kostas flashes me that smile. "Maybe you like go on fishing boat, Katerina? Since you are artist. Very beautiful, the sea at dawn."

Mike must have written quite a bit about us, I think uneasily. "Perhaps later, when my husband comes."

"Sea very beautiful Friday, morning of my birthday, when I *not* go to school. Why we not take my American mother in Kyriakos's boat on that day? My American father is here then, surely."

"*Not* surely," Kostas says in annoyance. "If he comes tomorrow, fine, hokay. But maybe he comes Friday. If he is in Mytilene only by midday, how he goes fishing at dawn?"

"Plenty of time *before* we go for to meet him!"

I decide it behooves me to weigh in on Damian's side. "My husband wants the whole day to be something special, Kostas, so let's plan it for early Friday, no matter what."

"Hokay, I tell Kyriako clean up *Pouláki Mou*, throw out dead fish." And Kostas laughs, at some private joke, I suppose. "When husband comes we have festival. My brother Yeoryios plans for Friday evening some music, some singing and dancing and eating and drinking. Tomorrow, Thursday, you want go meet your husband?" We pull over to one side of the square. "Maybe you like better go swimming, take little rest when day is hot."

I think of the long miles to Mytilene, the heat and the dust. Surely Mike wouldn't expect me to . . .

"On Friday, my birthday, *after* we go fishing," Damian says pointedly, "is time for walks, for swim. Tomorrow, when I go to school"—his sigh implies the prospect is woefully dreary—"I hope my American mother will visit. Talk to my teachers. They will praise me and she will be proud. I study hard and I do good work. Besides, my classmates will envy me, and I will like that."

"No need drag American mother to school, show her off like new donkey! *Kyría* Katerina's beauty will be legend in village of Pyrgotafos, in Molivos, in Petra—"

"I thank you for those kind words, gentlemen,"

I say with a laugh, "but I think I would like to see Damian's school, Kostas. It's one of the things a mother should do—"

Without warning, a wave of anguish breaks over me. I gaze blindly across where some workmen are mixing concrete; they appear to be mixing it directly on the ground, how odd . . . I struggle to breathe evenly. *There* at least I did my duty. Again and again I went to talk to David's teachers, to confer about his faults, to listen as modestly as I could to their infrequent praise. How smug I'd been! To praise the child is to praise the parent, as any parent knows. *"Come see my slide! Come see!" "Not now, I'm busy, . . ."* I ought to be grateful God doesn't issue report cards on parents. (Oh, doesn't he, though?)

Kostas reaches across and squeezes my hand. "It comes and goes, goes and comes like the tides—I am right? Do not lose heart, Katerina. You will be victor over this grief, but it is too soon."

I cannot speak.

"You stay here for one little minute. I go tell Niko's mother we are come."

He lopes off up a narrow cobbled lane so steep it is more a flight of shallow steps than a road. Above it the houses lean toward each other like gossips.

Damian climbs over the seat back and wriggles into position behind the wheel. He touches it lightly with his fingertips.

"Someday I have boat like Kyriakos. You come visit me, I take you and my American father in my boat. You like?"

Breathe in, slowly, slowly. "That will be . . . very nice."

"You like boats or taxis best?"

"I don't really know much about boats."

"I neither, but I learn. My friend Kyriakos teach me."

Easier now. "I suppose there is a lot to learn."

"Very much." Damian nods. "I must carry map in my head, where are the rocks, where the deep water, how the winds change. All about the ropes and the sails—oh, there is very, very much."

"And the tides," I say. "You must learn the tides."

Damian makes a gesture with his hand. "Here no tides." He turns to look at me, his eyes dark and wide, deep as the sky on a starless night. "My uncle Kostas no sailor. This about tides, it is not so, not here. We have just"—he moves his hand up and down three or four inches—"pretend tides."

"Your uncle was talking about something else," I say, my voice steady.

"Yes," Damian says. "I know." He continues to gaze at me, frowning with effort as he sorts over his words. "Here no such tides," he says slowly. "We have streams—how you say for rivers in the sea?"

"Currents?"

"Yes, currents—very dangerous. But not tides. You will see, American mother. Not by our shore. Not here, in Pyrgotafos." He smiles, again that smile of piercing sweetness. It creeps from his lips to his eyes. "You will see," he repeats confidently.

My heart turns over. *No,* I think in panic. *No, I can't—not again. I won't.*

But I have: I know I have. In less than half a day—a handful of hours—the child has captivated me, apparently without effort. Without, I suspect, either of us wanting it.

CHAPTER

9

I wake to find the room taking shape in gray morning light. Somewhere doves are fluting their mournful calls, over and over, loudly, insistently. Clearly they are Greek doves, I think with a smile, for it's plain they share the national yen for noise.

Last evening, too—and this I did not expect—was really quite enjoyable, being very Greek, which is to say pleasantly noisy and zestful. It began with Zoë Paradellis welcoming me as if I were a daughter returned from a pilgrimage. She gave me her own room as a matter of course and moved in with her daughters; she made up the bed with embroidered linens from a great chest of cedarwood; she plied me with honey cakes and the inevitable ouzo. Calling her daughters to begin preparing supper, she insisted that Damian and Kostas share it, too.

"I go tell my brother we stay here for eating," Kostas said. "I leave Damian for interpreter."

Neither Zoë nor her daughters speak English. In no way does this dampen Zoë's zest for conversation. All the while she was chopping tomatoes or pounding away at some long streamers of seafood, she chattered as ceaselessly as the doves. A plump little woman with bright snapping eyes and a round, soft figure, now and again she would pause, her head cocked expectantly; when I could only smile helplessly, she would nod and smile, too, as if my nonreply were exactly right.

Apparently Damian felt her conversation was chiefly for her own pleasure, for he offered only occasional abridgments of her remarks. "She hopes you like *oktapóthi*," he said once. "I tell her you crazy about all things Greek." Again: "She wants know how old you are. I tell her my aunt Verek ask too." Here Zoë laughed, nodding approval. "She say you must be rich, only very rich women look twenty-two when they thirty-two."

The house is halfway up the steep-stepped lane. There's a patch of courtyard scarcely large enough for the row of oilcan planters filled with herbs and the ramshackle pen confining six white hens and a black rooster. The windows have solid shutters on the outside and louvered ones within; these are painted turquoise, or apple green, or tomato, or powder blue, following no particular plan or design that I can see but rather as if gifts of leftover paint have been gratefully received. On the ground floor are two rooms: next to the courtyard, the one Zoë has given me, and behind it, the one she now shares with her daughters. Cooking, eating, and what I suppose might be called communal life all take place in the single room on the upper floor, which can be reached only from outside, up the flight of stone and concrete steps from the courtyard. A faded wreath of herbs hangs above this upper entrance, and inside, under the lintel, a blurred and wavering cross is traced in smoke.

It was nearly two hours before Kostas returned. "My brother very sorry he cannot come," he remarked cheerfully, unburdening himself of two bottles of wine and a basket of strawberries as big as plums. "I think he like come very much, but his wife is ashamed and therefore angry. He not want to make her more angry. But my friend Kyriakos comes. He is by Spyros Armenis the ropemaker when I come through Molivos. I tell him you are here and he happy to come."

"There's no need for your brother's wife to feel ashamed," I said, troubled.

"You don't ask what I find out at hotel."

"Was there a message?"

"Yes, certainly a message! Your husband phones. You not here, says hotel. I am angry, Katerina. This is truth but not *all* truth, I say. What I tell *kyría* Cunningham, where is her husband? 'How I should know?' says this woman who smokes like a man—" and he mimed blowing smoke from his nostrils. " 'I do not ask where husband is,' she says. 'Not my business!' "

"Well, thanks for going all the way to Molivos just for me."

"I not go special. Every day same time, six o'clock, I ask who needs taxi tomorrow. Who comes, who goes. This chimney of a Voula tells me four tourists want to take drive to Eressos, see grave of Sappho. I can earn two thousand *drachmés* in one day if I drive them. But maybe I must meet *tón kýrion* Cunningham, I say. Why she not ask when he comes?

'Not my business,' she say again. 'Reservation is for Friday. He wants come sooner, not my business, not my problem.' I tell her she is stupid, has head like empty wine cask! 'I am not stupid!' she says. 'Husband say Hotel Caledonia tell him wife goes to Silver Bird in Molivos. Do I say no, she is not here, she goes with Kostas Demetriou, and if you are here, Mr. Husband, you would sharpen your knife, you would sharpen two knives? No, I do not say that!' she says. 'I tell him wife is with friends, that is all, no more. If you, Kostas Demetriou, wish to know when husband comes, telephone hotel in Athens and ask—ha! ha!' I see she has head like hollow cave and tongue like scorpion. So—I telephone Athens. Person to person to Hotel Caledonia, is not that good thinking? If your husband is there"—he shrugged—"I am out much money. I am in luck. He is not there. Has reservation for Thursday, says hotel. Very good. Tomorrow I go to Eressos, get rich from tourists. Friday I go to Mytilene, meet *tón kýrion* Cunningham, and for now we let that Voula cook her brains, hokay?"

It occurred to me I might have reason to be grateful to Verek, after all. Though Mike has never been subject to fits of jealousy, being, I suppose, too confident of his own virility and of my (some would say archaic) fidelity to be troubled by such doubts, still, a man needn't be as superstitious as Verek to suspect that dazzler Kostas of being bait in a trap set by some bored and prankish god . . . or of being that bored and prankish god himself.

"O Kyriakos comes!" Kostas cried. "Now the good time begins!"

Kyriakos Karandonellis has a weatherbeaten face,

a falcon's nose, a pirate's mustache, very white teeth (one broken), and a rolling gait. It seemed to me he was very much aware of the Paradellis girls, plain, sturdy-looking young women in their late teens. He kept staring at them appraisingly, as if they were exotic creatures of doubtful utility but undeniable attraction unhappily priced beyond his means.

"And your husband, *kyría mou?* He comes, too?"

I told him Mike would be on Friday's plane.

Kyriakos nodded sagely. "American men work very hard, too hard. And how old is your husband?" When I said Mike is also thirty-two (nice of me: saved him asking), he nodded again. "Does he also look ten years younger? In Greece he would look forty, maybe fifty. Rich men work very hard, worry much. Poor men work hard, too, also worry, but very strange, the gods are kind. You see my friend Kosta? He is poor man, but is he not young and beautiful? Me, I am not so young and not so beautiful, but I am not old either." His smile was a faun's leer.

With no railing to obstruct the view of the sea, the flat roof over the second bedroom forms a kind of stage, and there we ate a veritable feast. The octopus, though chewy and a bit strange in spite of its sauce of garlic and tomato, proved delicious, as did the fish Kyriakos brought, a delicate fish with pinkish flesh. And there was a salad with olives and cheese, and crusty fresh-baked bread, the strawberries, and the wine. As we ate, the sky and the water deepened from pearl to slate, the afterglow faded, and the stars hung low.

I cannot remember another such supper in all my life, so full of warmth, I mean, that overflowed irresistibly, bubbling up and boiling over, like a brook in spring. There was a great deal of talk, in English and in Greek, and laughter, and now and again singing. When we had finished all but the wine, which seemed inexhaustible, Melita, the eldest daughter, shyly brought out her dulcimer, or *santouri*, and Kyriakos sang a ditty which Damian found hilarious, something about a drunken sailor named Stefanos Stathakos who couldn't find his way to Akra Korakas. (Big joke.) Then Kyriakos and Kostas persuaded Damian to join them in an exclusively male dance as formal, as graceful, as ritualized as a minuet: charming to watch. After this they all insisted I sing— everyone must do something, they said, it was not fair to listen only—and so, in my uncertain contralto, I wavered bravely through "Shenandoah"— only to feel a sudden, intense stab of loneliness. *Surrounded by strangers . . . far from my own people . . . how did I ever get myself into this?* But this fit of hunger for home soon passed, and by the time we bade each other good night, I could smile my way through "Kah-lee-neek-tah, Zoë," to which she replied a laughing, "Good nigh-eet, Katerina!"

Mike would have loved every minute of it, I think now, listening to the rooster rousing his harem in the cool dawn. If Mike were here by me now . . . here in this narrow bed . . . "Listen to that lunatic bird, Kay," he'd say. Softly, his lips to my ear, his breath stirring my hair. "Kind of comforting, isn't it, that for a thousand years—five thousand—there's been a cock crowing before sunrise. Very sane. Shows the world's still in orbit."

"Very Greek," I'd say sleepily. Or maybe I'd have enough sense not to say anything. *Oh, God! it's been so long, so long . . .*

The daylight grows stronger, warming from rose to gold. Now I can hear sparrows in the vine overhanging the window, and somewhere a sheep bleating. I grope for my watch: five-thirty. That early? I get up quietly and reach for my clothes. If Mike were here . . . "It was weird, didn't you think, when those Germans joined in?" I'd say in a low voice, very low, so as not to wake anybody in the next room. "Not the joining in, I don't mean that," I'd explain, still in a whisper. "I mean Kyriako's reaction." " 'Weird' is hardly the word," Mike would mutter. "I'd opt for 'venomous' myself, especially as applied to your charming friend Kostas."

We'd been caroling away at a folk tune Damian learned at school when five or six of the German tourists came strolling down the lane: Professor Furchtwanger, and the peppy lady archaeologist, and the enthusiastic scholar like an elderly gnome, and two or three others. They'd been inspired to respond to our song with one of their own. When the last notes of their *"Schönheit der Schönheit meiner Traüme gleichen"* had floated away to silence and been duly applauded, Herr Furchtwanger called up to me that they'd been to see the tomb. Most delightful was the walk and most interesting the tomb, but somehow a misturn on their way back to the harbor where waits their minibus they have taken—down this lane, is it not so, *gnädige Frau? Nicht!* Kostas said harshly. A guide who cannot guide is no guide! Back! Go back! First turn to left, go down. *Gehst Du immer nieder.*

Clearly it would be all right with Kostas if they continued their downward journey until they wound up in hell.

Kyriakos said nothing. He had not moved, had not so much as stirred, while the gentle *Gemütlichkeit* of their ballad drifted through the dusk. He did not applaud, though Zoë and I clapped generously. Only when the little band had trudged on up the lane and out of sight beyond the turn did he come to life. Then he rose, stalked to the roof edge, hawked, and spat. Returning, he snatched up the *santouri*, stroked it once, and broke into song. A faintly mocking song, I thought, though I couldn't have said why. Kostas was grinning, Zoë regarded the singer soberly, and nobody translated, not even Damian.

I gather up my sketchbook and pencils, easing the door closed behind me. The light is much stronger now, every detail of courtyard and gate standing forth in sharp focus. At least Kostas didn't misdirect the Germans, I see, however hostile his words; twenty yards up the lane I take the first turn to the left, and there is the attenuated staircase, as promised, plunging to the harbor half a mile away. And everything, everywhere I look, cries out for paint on paper. In the distance the waters are a wash of apricot, turquoise, and silver. Where the lane is steepest a locust tree is shaking out its lavender tassels over a retaining wall, like a girl drying her hair. By the time I do several quick studies, the sun is a vermilion disk well above the rim of Turkey.

I turn onto the shore road. Two women, all in black and carrying market baskets, are hurrying toward the village. As they catch sight of me I am startled to see them cross themselves: has my reputation as an accursed childless woman spread from Pyrgotafos to Molibos? It's only after they've passed me with a smiling *"Kaliméra!"* that I notice the ram-shackle building across the way, not much larger than a toolshed, with a truly do-it-yourself cross atop its sagging roof: a cross of rusted wire whose curlicues look as if they've been fashioned from coat hangers. I'm casting about for the best angle when I notice the time. Quarter past seven already! The tumbledown chapel with its antic cross will have to wait.

As I start to retrace my steps, I see I've managed to attract the notice of two very lean and hungry cats. For some reason—well, for obvious reasons—I'm reminded of Verek. Poor Verek . . . and poor Yeoryios. My God, yes, poor Yeoryios!

His defiant song finished, Kyriakos had given me a savage grin. "It is good that Damian's uncle Yeoryios is not among us. He does not welcome the barbarians from the north, that Yeoryios. But you have not met him, *kyría?*"

Somewhat at a loss—hadn't Kostas told him why I was Zoë's guest?—I stammered an embarrassed yes, I had. Kyriakos shot a glance at Kostas, who slid into rapid Greek. Kyriakos shook his head, muttered, and sighed. Whereupon Damian was inspired to revert to his role of translator.

"My friend Kyriakos say it is great pity my aunt Verek has no child and not much husband."

Kostas threatened to cuff Damian. Zoë intervened. Kostas, whose meaning couldn't have been plainer if he put it into basic English, gave her to understand that someone ought to shut Damian's mouth. Zoë had then spoken softly to the boy, who flushed painfully.

"I not know such talk not fit for ladies' ears,

American mother. Is everyday talk in Pyrgotafos. I
not know is dirty talk."

Poor Yeoryios, I think, shooing the cats out of my
path. Poor Verek, too . . .

I don't know which I pity more.

CHAPTER

10

Kostas is lounging against his taxi. Damian, in shorts and bright green T-shirt, briefcase at his side, is in the back seat, his expression as resigned as a commuter's.

"Five minutes only!" Kostas cries. "Hokay Damian be late to school, American mother makes excuse, but Melita must be to mayor's house by eight o'clock or she gets scolding!"

I toss my sketchbook on the bed and snatch my shoulder bag, race upstairs to gulp coffee, and in less than four minutes I'm back outside. It is five of eight when Melita waves good-bye in Molibos; by eight o'clock we've picked up four tourists—"Two Frenches and two Germans," Kostas says, as if describing livestock—and are on our way to Petrá, packed three to the front seat, three to the rear, with Damian demoted to the floor.

"I vass not avair vee muss share this taxi," says the German husband coldly to the back of Kostas's head.

His wife, next to me in the front seat, nods vigorously. "Yes, yes, you ask two t'ousand drachmas, fife hundert for each, now here are two more for free?"

"My nephew goes to school in Petrá every day," Kostas says pleasantly. "Is the law."

One of the French women leans forward and says imperiously, "And *madame?* I do not believe I have had the pleasure."

Kostas flicks a glance at her in the mirror. "I not either," he says, smiling.

"Don't worry, I'm not going all the way to Eressos," I say hurriedly. "I get out in Petrá, too."

"You vish to go to Eressos, you are velcome, madam," the German leans forward to assure me. "Ve can vunce again divide the fee—fife into two t'ousant is four hundert—vich is to say, you giff to each vun hundert drachmas—"

"*Kyría* Cunningham rides in this taxi to the *moon* and back for free!" Kostas says, suddenly savage. "Who pays what is not for you to say! Is my taxi! I am like captain of ship, you understand? *I* say, you *do!*"

It is a long ten minutes to Petrá.

At last Damian and I are deposited across from the schoolyard gate and the taxi darts off in a swirl of dust. Beyond the open gate the yard swarms with children: children leaping, children running, children jumping rope, children wrestling. The air reverberates with their cries. And I—I am stricken as much with guilt as with grief. I can't go in, go past . . . I can't even go near. "*—the sort of thing a mother would do—*" Oh, no, it's not! It's betrayal—deliberate, voluntary betrayal.

"Perhaps—perhaps later, Damian," I stammer. "Not just now—"

"Much better in afternoon," Damian agrees. "In mornings is always the dull lessons. One hour past midday, American mother—you come then. When you tired, we go. Early." And he grins.

A bell rings. The girls swinging on the gate hop off and begin rolling down the sleeves of their navy blue dresses. Slowly, Damian pulls on his navy blue shirt; it, too, has long sleeves.

"Mrs. Meade in hotel here—you like meet her? Very nice teacher. Speaks very good English."

I watch him cross the road and climb the steps to the schoolyard. The children are forming lines, boys in one, girls in the other. A group of men and women stands facing them—teachers, I presume. After an interval of congealing quiet, adults and children make the sign of the cross, once, twice, three times. All chant something. Again the sign of the cross. And now the children enter the building, not in a docile or orderly fashion, I'm relieved to see, but noisily, chattering and twittering like sparrows, hopping impatiently, shoving. I can't tell which is Damian.

Eight-thirty: too early to go calling; I'll have to kill an hour or two. And so I wander along the unpaved lanes and gape at a clump of bamboo by a stream, at bedding draped from an upper window. I gaze into a butcher shop where lambs' carcasses (skinned, but identifiable by their faces) hang upside down, into a tailor's shop, old-fashioned treadle machine against the window, into a leatherworking shop. And everywhere the mourning doves lament from the TV aerials, and everywhere the scent of honeysuckle weighs on the air as heavily sweet as in a funeral parlor.

I think: *This is where he lives.* I think: *This is where*

he must spend the rest of his life—doing what? Ferrying foreigners about, like Kostas? Smiling and smiling through "the time of tourists"?

Perched on the top of a rocky knoll is a golden-domed church, blindingly white in the morning sun. With the vague notion of familiarizing myself with the setting (if nothing more) of Damian's religion, I toil up the steep path and step into a golden jungle.

Golden lamps like the pendulous flowers of some luxuriant vine hang in clusters in the shadows overhead. Gold-fringed banners droop from blood-red poles, gold-twined. Crowding every flat surface of pillar and wall are dozens upon dozens of icons, gold-haloed. Icons form a veritable multitude on the great gilded altar screen that stretches across the eastern end of the church. In the center, the largest and most elaborate depicts of life-sized Christ with the Virgin Mary, both with Byzantine faces: long, slender ovals with large melancholy almond-shaped eyes brooding heavy-lidded over the griefs and sins of mankind.

You see, Mike? He doesn't even worship the same god.

A tray of candles has prices posted next to a slot for the money: 10-5-3-2-1 dr. I make short work of any incipient Protestant objection (so what if it doesn't work? besides, you never know) and choose two of the five-drachma size. I light one candle for Mike and me, for our marriage, and the other I light for Damian, for his plans to be a sailor. A man should be what he wants to be.

It isn't until I'm halfway down the hill that I realize *I lit the candles for the living* . . . I never thought of what David wanted to be. He'd never said, had he? So I couldn't have, even if I'd remembered. But

I didn't remember. My God, I never thought of David at all.

The hotel is a plain barrackslike structure of peeling white paint and narrow tall windows behind ribbons of verandas. A picket fence encloses the sparse lawn where dusty bushes droop for lack of water and a scattering of locust trees offers only meager shade. An elderly woman sits enthroned on a skimpy metal chair, her back regally erect. A serving woman has just balanced a cup before her on a footed tray.

"Are you by any chance Damian's foster mother?" She zings the question at me as if it were an arrow.

I wince. "You must be Mrs. Meade, his English tutor."

"I'm Clementine Meade, yes. Do join me in a cup of coffee." She signals imperiously. "Don't be apprehensive. I've trained them how to brew a potable cup."

Thin but wiry, her bushy white hair of so ragged a cut I suspect she does it herself, she looks like an autocratic gnome. Her skin, of which a great deal is in evidence—her sleeveless sundress stops several inches above her knee—is deeply tanned and has the ripply texture of the weathered skin of the very old. Her eyes, a faded blue, are startlingly light in her brown face.

"And what do you think of him?"

"Of Damian?"

"Of course of Damian! Does he please you? Does he please your husband? Will you be wanting to adopt him?" She extends her cigarette case, raises her eyebrows a fraction when I refuse, and lights up.

"My husband hasn't met him yet." Instant interrogation must be endemic to the soil, I think wryly. "As for adoption, I'm not even considering it."

"Well, *that* will be a great relief to him! Have you told him so? What did he say?"

"The subject hasn't come up." And I add, somewhat to my own surprise, "I wasn't aware he's been dreading making such a choice."

"Not he—*his* mind is thoroughly made up: against! No, what Damian dreads is that you and your husband will pressure his uncle into forcing him to become an American."

What in God's name had Mike written the child? What had he "promised"?

"Would that be such a terrible fate?" I manage to laugh, though there's an edge to my voice. "And how could we make the child *or* his uncle do anything they don't want to do?"

"Offer the man money. Which he desperately wants. Or his wife does. *He* may know it would be useless, but she, I imagine, still cherishes the notion that some surgeon somewhere can repair the effects of the interrogators with their bludgeons and their rubber hoses. Which is possible, of course, but unlikely." She inhales deeply. "The—what shall I call them? 'Inquisitors'? Yes, an excellent word—the Colonels' Inquisitors were regrettably thorough. Do I shock you? One forgets how innocent Americans are." Twin jets of smoke punctuate her remarks.

"Not so much innocent as inexperienced," I remark sweetly. "But what had he done? Yeoryios, I mean."

"Distributed a pamphlet, chalked a slogan—you know the sort of things students do: harmless, futile gestures, though sometimes disruptive. He was at the

university at the time. However, Gheorghios Demetriou—I prefer, and use, the hard *gamma* of classical
Greek; I can't abide the modern *yuh yuh—Gheorghios*
was the brother of Mikhail Demetriou, Damian's
father, who being a member of the Center Union
Party was rounded up along with thousands of others during that autumn of 'sixty-nine and, like them,
simply vanished. He had just been married, alas.
Damian was born the following spring, and his
mother did not survive the birth. A common story,
perhaps, but I confess I find it affecting."

"I'm trying to remember exactly what happened.
Some sort of revolution, wasn't it? That quite recently got put down?" The Ignorant American, I think
ruefully. But good grief, in 1969 . . . in 1969 my horizons didn't extend much beyond the next skiing
weekend, and as for Mike—well, he was extending
his to protest the draft, of course, and the whole
Vietnam scene. But nobody was rounding Mike up,
or beating him with rubber hoses. He didn't just not
turn up one day, and I never hear . . .

"Revolution? You could call it that, I suppose.
Fascist revolution. You haven't read Greek history?"

"Nothing more recent than Herodotus."

"Indeed. Perhaps a brief précis of those lament-
able years might not be amiss, if you are to have the
slightest hope of understanding Damian and his
family. Where shall I start? With the twenty years after
the war—World War II, you understand: *my* war—
twenty years during which no less than forty-four
governments rose and collapsed? No, too tedious—
but to some extent those years do explain why the
Colonels, that archconservative group that backed
Papadópoulos, could move in: nature abhors a vac-

uum, and all that. Anyway, in 1967 one hundred and fifty years of Greek democracy jolted to a stop. The Junta—backed by your CIA, my dear, and a steady flow of American dollars and American weapons—proceeded to turn back the clock. The enemy, as the Colonels saw it, was literacy—a man who reads is a dangerous man!—so practically the first thing the Junta did was to reduce compulsory education from nine years to five, and I *despised* them for that. As for the rest, it was the usual dictatorship with all the familiar dreary trappings. No free speech, no free elections. Censorship of the press. The knock on the door at dawn. Arrests and questionings, exile to the islands if you were lucky, torture and death if you were not."

I say hotly, "I can't believe my country supported any such monsters! Why would we do such a thing?"

"My dear, I never said your *country* did—only your government. In return for military bases, of course—the usual excuse."

"How did they get rid of them, then? The Greeks, I mean. If the Colonels were backed by the Goliath of Washington, I should think they'd still be here!"

"Sheer bungling stupidity, my dear. Or failure to read their own history. They made the mistake of plotting a coup against Archbishop Makarios of Cyprus, and the Turks chose the occasion to move in—surely you read about that? I believe even the *New York Times* mentioned it." Dryly. "And in the general mess resulting, Papadópoulos found himself promising an election, which he lost." She smokes placidly, her pale glittering eyes on my face. "Just about then, you remember, the United States chose to change its own political shirt. That was when you rid yourselves of your Greek vice president, wasn't it—that fellow who was so loud with his praise of the 'morality' of the Colonels. Evidence of which Gheorghios and Berek Demetriou live with yet, day in and day out. As does Damian: let's not forget the children."

Broken bodies, broken hopes, broken lives . . .

"No wonder he can't think of leaving them," I say lamely. "They're the only parents he's ever known."

"Such as they are." Mrs. Meade scowls into her empty cup. "I suppose Greek parents are no worse, really, than English or American, but I confess I find their methods shocking. Male children are appallingly spoiled. They're so pampered, so indulged, it's no wonder they grow up to be—well, what they are. Of which Damian's uncle Kostas is a prime example." She beckons to the serving woman. "Now if you wanted to adopt a girl child, it would be hopeless. Girls are useful about the house, and therefore easily placed. But boys—boys are going begging. No Greek wants to adopt a male child, not formally, anyway. Give his name to one who hasn't his blood? Never! That would be worse than *plastós*—'bastard,' you know—having the blood but not the name."

I know what a bastard is, I think, nettled. Schoolteachers! They never change. "But in a way Damian does have Yeoryio's blood. Not directly, of course, but from the grandfather. I should think Yeoryios could feel that in a way the boy *is* his own."

"The situation is a bit more complicated than that." She nods her thanks as our cups are filled. "As I understand it, Mikhaïl Demetriou inherited the land

and the olive trees, not in the English way, legally and properly from father to eldest son, but in the Greek, or argumentative: he who shouts loudest gets most." For the first time, a glint of humor warms her eyes. "At Mikhail's presumed death—his body never turned up, but one must be realistic: he was not among those released from the prisons or returned from the islands—the orchard could go to the next eldest brother, or the land could be divided. However, there really isn't much Demetriou land, and if the olives were divided, neither brother could support a family on his share—Gheorghios barely scratches out a living as it is. How he settled all this between himself and Kostas I don't know—by the usual bullying and barter, I suppose. For Damian there is nothing—there never was."

"His father didn't have time to make a will?"

"It's possible he never knew about Damian, and in any case he wouldn't have left his land and his trees other than to his own brothers, not when his son was an infant."

"What if Damian's mother had lived? He didn't make any provision for her either?"

"The notion would never have occurred to him. He knew his brothers would care for his widow as for their own sister; it's the Greek way."

Still, there should have been something for Damian . . . "The money Mike sends is such a small sum. What's the tuition at school, do you know?"

"Now there you've touched on one way—the *only* way, I may add—that Greece is truly an advanced country. Tuition is free right through the university. A child can continue in school as far as his talent will take him. Provided, of course, his wages aren't needed. Few families can afford to dispense with the earnings of children, who turn everything over to the father as a matter of course." She glares at me accusingly. "The salaries are one-tenth of yours, and what you consider necessities are often to the Greeks luxuries priced hopelessly out of reach. The cheapest car, for example, a flimsy little one-pedal affair, costs three thousand pounds!" (Is that my fault?) "But enough!" She stubs out her cigarette. "I know a place where they make an excellent fish stew. It's not too early for lunch. I don't keep Greek hours—never could! But the *tavérna* knows my ways."

As we take our places at one of the tables clustered under a bamboo awning, a boy not much older than Damian scampers up with battered tableware. We are the only women in sight, a fact of which Mrs. Meade appears oblivious, as well as of the men staring at us over their mugs of coffee and games of chance.

"How does it happen your husband hasn't met Damian?"

I explain about Mike stopping in London, and my coming on ahead.

"What a bore for you." She offers me the bread. "I wish I could give you luncheon in the house I'm buying, but it's nowhere near ready yet. You cannot *imagine* the delays! And every transaction must be for cash. Peasants—they're all peasants, even in Athens. If they can't have gold, to clink on the counter or nip between their teeth, then it must be folding money: something to count, to feel. None of your bank drafts, if you please! Though there they have my sympathy. Money cabled from home has a way of disappearing, as it were, into the Minotaur's maze, not to surface for weeks!" She lights a cigarette. "Would you care for a sweet?"

I glance at my watch. "I've only got time for another coffee, thank you. I must be at the school by one. Damian hopes to be excused early, so we can walk back. It's not all that far, I suppose—five miles or so."

"To an Englishwoman that distance is but an afternoon's stroll, but frankly I did not know Americans ever walked!"

"We don't, we run," I say, and show my teeth in a smile.

"Excellent! Then you won't go bloated into middle age." She waves her cigarette at the occupants of nearby tables. "There's nothing so beautiful as a young Greek, is there? Then—well, like flowers they bloom, they fade. They slump, they thicken, they *coarsen*." She puffs smoke, gazing critically from one impassive face to another; I profoundly hope no one near understands English. "No wonder the Greeks still think that to die young is a gift of the gods."

Mr. Sarris, with his liver-spotted hands. The cabdrivers in Mytilene, teeth like old dogs'. Nikolas Paradellis . . . well, he was born with an old man's face. But Kostas, one day? Damian?

I say woodenly, "You mean Kleovis and Viton?"

She regards me with surprise, almost approval. "I understood the ancient myths are seldom taught anymore—a mistake, for we have much to learn from them. They are, after all, history told in parable. Unfortunately Damian's school texts show a most regrettable emphasis on the state religion and on war, glorifying both to such a degree the children are conditioned not to think for themselves."

I am impelled to remark that Damian seems to be a reasonably independent thinker.

"Yes, and I take much of the credit," Mrs. Meade remarks complacently. "I am continually challenging him: 'Is that really true or have you merely read it somewhere?' Very healthy for his mental development, though it may make trouble for him in school."

It may make trouble for him in life, I reflect. Kostas thinks himself a lucky man because he owns a taxi. When Damian is Kostas' age, will he think himself blessed with good fortune if he has one of those boats with a patched sail? Or will he curse his own limited vision, his lack of initiative, his caution, curse even his affection for his family and his homeland, the sum of which kept him here when he had a chance?

My God! I'm staggered by this line of thought. *What* chance? Damian has no such chance! Because you, Kay, are against it, remember? Dead set against adoption. *Dead* set.

CHAPTER

11

The wall surrounding the school grounds is splashed with flowers on either side—phlox and spiderwort and shrub roses in pink, coral, and magenta. The playground, pounded bare except near the edge, is shaded by clumps of bamboo and alder, and the school, a one-story building of lemon-yellow stucco with a terra-cotta roof, has doors and window frames painted robin's-egg blue. None of it looks as grim as Damian's sighs would imply. I pluck up my courage and go in at the central door.

I find myself alone in a long corridor. Facing me is a row of hooks, at the moment empty, above which a series of posters depicts what to do in case of air raid; the menacing planes above the fleeing children are emblazoned with the sickle moon and star. From behind the doors along the inner wall comes the faint hum of voices.

I move on down the hall. There, eye-catching with its bronze and blue logo, one of Mike's letters is posted.

Dear Damian:

I was delighted to get your letter telling me everyone is well, including Erasmios. I don't understand what you mean by "two kinds of Greek"—do you mean ancient and modern? I didn't know the ancient tongue is used any more, yet you say "the older one" is employed by writers of books and teachers in school, and "the other one" by everyone else. I should think this would be very confusing . . .

Victorian fatherly, I think, reassured. Concerned, yet aloof. Nothing at all like that other: *". . . and when you wake . . . it's as if God changed his mind and started over . . ."*

A bell clangs, the doors to the classrooms fly open, and the children spill forth, pouring themselves exuberantly onto the playground. As I flatten myself against the wall I see a woman beckoning from the end of the corridor. She ushers me into her office.

Our sole mutual language is French, it turns out, in which neither of us is fluent. As I contrive an explanation of who I am—*"la femme d'un homme américain qui s'intéresse au biens du petit Damian"*—I am interested to observe some of the more obvious differences between the genus Retired British Schoolma'am and Greek Assistant Principal: where Mrs. Meade is brittle, blunt, and opinionated, this woman is graceful, feminine, quiet-spoken.

The school has one hundred and four pupils, she tells me, ranging in age from six to twelve, this being the *dimotikón*. I nod to show interest and comprehension. Damian, she goes on, is a good boy with no criminal habits.

"*Mais naturellement!*" I exclaim. We regard each other in silence. I rally my remaining vocabulary. Does Damian have any difficulty with his studies? ("*Damian, a-t-il des difficultés avec ses études?*")

No, no, he does what is expected of him. Though he could do better, you understand, *Madame la Mère Américaine*. He is inclined to hurry through his lessons . . . It would be inadvisable to visit his classes. A stranger who does not speak Greek—pointless and distracting. Dismissed early? Perhaps an exception . . . The ability to make exceptions is a mark of wisdom, is it not?

"*Oui, bien sûr, Madame la Directrice!*"

Damian and I emerge into the dazzling heat. Peeling off his long-sleeved shirt, he stuffs it into his briefcase. At the schoolyard gate he leaps like a goat over the four steps below, sends his briefcase spinning in the air, races to catch it. "We are free! We are free!" Then, abruptly sobering, he falls into step, walking sedately with serious face.

"You have met Mrs. Meade? You like?"

"Oh, yes." (True of first question, anyway.)

"And *kyría* Samoglou? She gives good report of me?"

"The headmistress? I am pleased to report she says you do not have the habits of a criminal."

My attempt at humor falls flat. "What means this?" Damian cries, outraged. "I not burn down the school? Not steal? Not kill? What you think of me, American mother—I not do bad, but also not do good! She say *nothing* good about me?"

"I got the impression you're doing quite well, Damian." Soothingly.

He kicks at a pebble. "But she not *say?*"

"Well . . . she did say you often hurry through your work."

Damian sighs. "She speaks truth. But what would you? The *lethrini* swim many together, and the waves dance and the wind sings—I feel like prisoner indoors, American mother!"

"It's not really cold out, Mom—it's never really cold when it's snowing! That's a super sled Dad gave me—was it really his when he was little? I bet he never went as fast as I do! Will you time me, Mom? Come out and time me!"

"Later, David . . . Later . . ."

Damian is free. I am in prison. Mine is a life sentence, with no hope of parole or pardon.

From Petrá to Molibos the coast makes a great slow curve like a hand cupped. Damian and I are the only ones traveling afoot. We can be seen from fully half a mile away, and the noise of the infrequent vehicles carries that far, yet each as it passes blasts us with its horn.

"They play games," Damian says tolerantly. "Is long empty road. Boring."

"As long as they don't think they're playing football and we're the ball," I remark, and am rewarded by his laugh. It wasn't all that funny: doesn't anyone joke with him? No. No woman, anyway. Not Mrs. Meade. Certainly not Verek. Well, maybe Zoë.

The bare land rises (dry-brush watercolor) in great rocky sweeps to meet the sky. I look back at Petrá, at the dome of the church high above the town, and then eastward to Molibos, where the ruins of the fortress crown the hill against whose steep sides the serried houses cling. "Like survivors after a flood," I remark.

"Yes, the Turks," Damian nods. "Again and again they come. No hills high enough—they sweep over everything like angry river." He stops to inspect a squashed tortoise about four inches long; meditatively, he pokes it with the toe of his sandal. "For my father, too, no place to hide. Or for my uncle Yeoryio." Picking up the flattened carcass, he turns it over and looks at the underside. "From their own people," he says bitterly. "Bad as Turks. Greeks bad as Turks to Greeks." I say nothing. "You know what they do to my uncle Yeoryio? You understand?"

"Yes . . . I think so."

He drops the battered disk in the dust and we walk on. "Is why my uncle wears his hair long, to— how you say?—to put thumb to nose towards Colonels. Colonels make law nobody can wear hair long or have beard. No short dresses—law say that, too. Mrs. Meade very bossy, she make me study very hard, she never say I do well, she never praise me, but she old woman wears short skirt to say go-to-hell to Colonels. So I like."

The sky swings slowly past as we walk; it's as if we're standing still while the strange and desolate landscape paces by us in stately dance. We take solemn note of the marble-sized droppings of sheep, of rocks where lichen is a splash of vivid orange. In the intervals when no car can be heard, I am doubly aware of the silence: of our footfalls on the asphalt, of the sleepy twitter of birds within a gape-eyed chapel, of the constant hiss and drag of waves foaming among the stones at the edge of the ribbon of beach. From time to time a burst of plaintive music drifts down from a distant hut where a soldier lounges on duty; now and again that strand of barbed wire is strung like an afterthought along the narrow strip between the road and the shore, and every fifty yards or so there dangles the triangular sign: ΚΑΡΠΟΙ.

"My aunt Verek say when God made the world, he made many rocks he not use. These he threw into the sea. That was Greece, she say—rocks with smile of God on them. You like?"

"I like. Very, very much I like." Then, pleased I can decipher the letters, I ask what *karpoí* means. "Do I have it right? That's the way you say it?"

"Kar-*pee*," Damian corrects me, "Means 'fruit.' " He regards the sign dubiously. "But not here. I not know English word." He clenches a fist, then explodes his fingers. "Is warning. Do not swim here, American mother. *Boom*. Finish."

"Oh . . . mines." I regard the rusting signs with new respect. "Have they been here ever since the war?"

"War against Germans? No, no! Put there last week, American mother. Greeks always at war. Maybe we not shooting, but we at war. For many hundred years we at war with Turks. Sometimes very much blood and many dying. Other times they come and live quietly here and everything look friendly. But always we *quietly* at war because we want them go home."

"Are you telling me you Greeks expect the Turks to invade? That's why the mines—the *karpoí?*"

"Why not? Sneak in enough Turks, my uncle Niko say, and U. S. of A. will say, oho, more Turks than Greeks on Lesvos, give Lesvos to Turks. We say *ókhi*—

— 124 —

no! So sometimes we put mines here"—he gestures—"other times move mines someplace new. Turks not know where they are, Turks stay home."

"But if you very plainly label where they are"—how "very Greek" can one get?—"won't the Turks know, too?"

"Who will tell them? I not." He glances up at me impishly. "You not."

We are nearly to Molibos. Rounding the turn before the hotel, a figure in uniform comes strolling toward us, walkie-talkie to his ear. *"Yeiá sas,"* Damian says politely, and, *"Yeiá sas,"* the soldier replies, flicking me an all-inclusive glance from beneath his helmet. Very Greek: his walkie-talkie leaks bouzouki music.

"Soldier not tell them," Damian grins.

ΜΟΛΙΒΟΣ, reads the sign as we enter town, and immediately beneath: ΜΙΘΗΜΝΑ.

"Mithímna is ancient name. Means 'drunken song.' " Damian seems to have appointed himself his uncle's deputy as guide and instructor in all things insular. *"Molivos* is modern name, means 'town of lead.' Not nice name, not pretty. Is because Turks hit with many, many lead balls, from—how you say 'very big guns'?"

"Cannons?"

"Cannons, yes. You want see the castle?"

I peer up at the jumble of rocks above the red-tiled roofs. It looks a long way off. "Another day, perhaps."

"Tower in Pyrgotafos much older, also no soldiers there. We go tomorrow, hokay? We make the peek-neek—you like?"

"I like." I smile, and my God! I think, stunned. I *would* like.

East of Molibos we climb down to walk along the beach.

"Here no *karpoí*—no mines," Damian says. "Soldiers watch Turks from castle. Like eagles they keep watch on sea." And he mimes sweeping the horizon with binoculars.

Well, of course it wouldn't be anything like picnicking with David. We'd always had to act the heavy parent: "No diving into strange waters . . . No climbing above stone walls . . . No sledding into the road . . ." But I never said that, did I?

Damian and I pick our way over the litter of plastic sandals, plastic wrap, plastic bottles—all the non-biodegradable junk of a people not obsessed by neatness. I find the going rough, for the beach is thickly strewn with stones, some as small as hens' eggs, some as large as footballs, all tumbled smooth and rolling treacherously underfoot. They come in apricot and slate blue, buff and violet, muted where dry, intensified where the waves lap them. I'm tempted to collect one or two, for a remembrance.

A remembrance? Of what?

"We go back by road now," Damian says. "From here more *karpoí*."

"How do you know? I don't see any signs."

"Signs not down by water, American mother." Patiently. "*Karpoí* by water, for Turks. Signs by road, for Greeks."

I gaze at him as if, for the first time, my American eyes have him clearly in focus. "Damian," I say abruptly, "do your aunt and uncle worry about you, do you think? Warn you not to do this, not do that? Or are you pretty much on your own?"

We scramble onto the road. "My aunt Verek all the time telling me what to do, American mother, what to say, how to be. But where to walk or not walk, no. I have eyes. I look for myself."

Closer to Pyrgotafos (if one can trust the lack of signs) the beach is again free of mines, but we keep to the road anyway. The village doesn't seem to be getting any nearer, though that could be the heat, of course. We pass two more of those ubiquitous chapels, each no larger than a one-car garage, and then stop for a good look at the tower, which Damian tells me is the *pýrgos* of Pyrgotafos. However, we don't go over to explore it. The Germans' minibus is parked by the base, and we can see sun-helmeted heads darting about the top like waterbugs.

"My uncle Yeoryios say tourists act like they own all Greece," Damian scowls. "March through olives like summer storm, take pictures of *táfos* from near, from far—ask hundred, ask thousand questions. Almost as bad as government men from Athens!"

I cast about for a safe topic. "All these little churches, Damian—are they ever used now?" For we are passing yet another deserted chapel, its door fast, its windows shuttered.

"How you mean 'used'?"

"You know—on Sundays, with the priest and the people and all."

"No, they just for one family, for the dead."

"As a memorial, you mean? Put up in memory of the dead?"

"*For* the dead," he says patiently. "Each family

like to keep their own bones. More friendlier than in *ostothíki*—in bone house. Better each family have little church, put bones in there. This one"—he tips his head—"is for family of Voufounos the cheesemaker. Nice and friendly, close to his cheese factory—I show you."

We round a bend and there on the outskirts of the village (at last!) is a whitewashed building. In its open doorway a man is leaning; catching sight of us, he lifts his hand in languid greeting. I remark that cheesemaking must be hard work.

Damian shrugs. "If old and tired, like *kýrio* Voufounos, yes. If young and strong, not so hard as hoeing olives, I make guess." He glances at me. "Not far now to house of my *koumbáros*. I think you tired, American mother. Tired from long walk."

"A bit." I reflect that American years may be easier on a woman than Greek years, but Greek miles are surely longer than American. And then, on impulse: "What was your mother's name, Damian, do you know?"

"*Málista*. Of a certainty I know." His tone is the same as that first time he spoke to me: "*How do I do? I do well . . .*" "Her name same as yours: Katerini." Then, when I am silent: "She from Eressos. Her father, my grandfather, very brave man. Try to get rid of Colonels, but he too old. Not too old for fight, you understand, but too old for caught, arrested. When they question him, he die."

"That's why they took your father?"

"Yes, for sure. And my uncle Yeoryio. My grandfather say nothing, he very brave, very, very brave. Die without talking. But *they* know fox does

— 128 —

not nest by himself. Kostas lucky, he very young, too young to cause trouble, they think. Not true! Fifteen-year-old Greek can cause much, much trouble! But they not catch him. Kostas very brave, too, likes danger, is very quick. So he is safe. But I wish . . ."

We turn onto the staircase lane. Our sandals sliding on the gritty stone with a soft abrasive *shiuh, shiuh* sound very loud, almost as loud as the cuckoos calling from the rooftops.

"What do you wish, Damian?"

"I wish he not call you *kyría* Katerina. That my *real* mother's name." His eyes black as midnight slant up at me. "What you call yourself in U. S. of A., American mother? You tell my uncle Kath-er-in—like so?"

"No one but my mother and father ever called me that. To my husband I'm Kay. To my friends, too. So I'd rather you called me Kay than American Mother. I'm . . . I'm not your mother, Damian. I'm not anybody's mother."

He nods. "I know. Your son dead. My mother dead. Is better not pretend, yes? But is not correct to speak as if I have as many years as you. My aunt Verek say is not correct."

"In the United States children often call adults by their given name—what you call their saint's name. Sometimes they say Miss—Miss Kay—or Aunt Kay. It's what we call a courtesy title."

"But you not my aunt. You my friend, like Kyriakos." He smiles suddenly. "So. Go and rest, *friend* Kay. Tomorrow we catch big fish! Show my American father—" Again, he hesitates. Then: "My father dead, too, friend Kay. How I should call your husband?"

"Whatever he . . . whatever he thinks is right."

"Yes. He will know what is correct. But I hope he not say to call him American father—you understand?"

CHAPTER

12

Long before the stars pale, a cat comes lamenting down the lane, stopping outside the gate to deliver himself of several verses and then wandering on, his cries of loneliness and passion echoing between the houses. Lucky beast, I think: all he risks is a boot hurled from a window, whereas you, Kay—

Friday. Mike will be coming today, and how will it be between us? More of the same? Which is to say, a hell of a lot of nothing? A shared silence, Mike called it. "That's what this marriage has shrunk to, Kay: a list of things not to be mentioned, not to be said. A damn long list that grows longer and longer . . ."

Quarter to five on the ghostly face of my watch. I pull on my jeans and a clean shirt, run a comb through my hair, and slip out into the gray light of the courtyard. Easing the gate closed, I hurry the short way up and the long way down, and find the square by the harbor deserted and silent.

On the glassy water a single boat, squat and untippable as a turtle, dozes near the wharf. Its burnt-orange sail is neatly furled against the lemon-yellow mast; a low cabin amidships nestles among piles of yellow-ochre nets; its trim is a fresh, intense peacock blue, and its name is painted on the prow in cadmium red: ΠΟΥΛΑΚΙ ΜΟΥ.

As I admire this carnival craft, Kyriakos emerges from below deck. Pulling the boat close through liquid-gold water (the sun is just spilling over the horizon), he leaps ashore.

"*Khristós anesti!*" Shoving back his black cap by way of salute, he gives me his broken-toothed grin.

"*Kaliméra*," I reply uncertainly.

"*Kyría*, you are a believer, surely? In our blessed Lord?"

Am I? "I . . . hope so."

"So—I give you the greeting for this time of Easter. 'Christ is risen'—is what we use these forty days our blessed Lord walks here with us. You have not this custom?"

I shake my head. More's the pity, I think. It would add a certain yeastiness to an exchange with an IRS auditor, say . . .

"So, I teach you—"

But Damian has come plunging down the lane. "If I am late I am sorry! I make long way 'round past the house of my *koumbáros*—I think maybe friend Kay still sleeps."

"Of a certainty you are late!" Kyriakos says severely. "What good the I-am-sorry? Never make a lady to wait, not at any time for any thing. Remember that and you have happy life." He winks at me. "But Katerina forgives you—look, she is smiling." He digs into his pocket and brings out a paper sack. "For you, *krýsi mou*. Now you can greet your friends. Eleven long years you have lived, aieee! From me, no sympathy!"

Damian fishes out a lump wrapped in gold foil and offers it to me. "It's my birthday, friend Kay," he says solemnly.

"Yes, I know—thank you—"

"So make me a wish." His eyes dance. "Wish for me what you wish on a birthday in the U. S. of A."

Happy birthday, David. Happy birthday, my darling. . .

I manage, but just barely: "Happy birthday, Damian."

"*Kroniá pollá,*" Kyriakos says. "Means 'many years.' Much better wish than 'be happy just today.' "

"*Kroniá pollá,*" I repeat obediently, and whatever has me by the throat lets go; perhaps in another language one is safe.

Kyriakos extends a callused hand. "You owe me one, Damiane. I give you already my good wishes." And he pockets the candy. "But now we stop these ceremonies, the day grows old. You tame *Pouláki Mou,* Damiane, I help the lady Katerina aboard."

"Wait one little minute, please. Kostas comes."

"*O Kostas?*" Sharply. "Who invites Kostá?"

"Kostas invites Kosta." Damian does not look at me.

Kyriakos scowls. "It's your birthday—you want Kostas, we wait."

I stroll to the edge of the wharf. Schools of miniature fish dart past; in the crystalline shadow of my reflection a starfish sprawls . . . So Kostas wants to crash the party: so what?

"He comes," Damian says with relief.

The cab skids to a halt beyond the plane tree and Kostas, festive in butter-yellow shirt and white pants, strolls toward us waving and smiling.

"It's my birthday," Damian says, again with that touching solemnity. He offers Kostas a gold-foiled lump.

"*Kroniá pollá!* From who you got the candy? *Kyría* Katerina?"

"From friend Kyriako," says Kyriakos pointedly, "who invites him and his American mother to go fishing on his birthday. Now comes his uncle, who is so late I ask myself who is lucky woman—"

"You talk English, you talk nice," Kostas says, grinning. He cinches his belt tighter across his flat belly.

Kyriakos, too, gives a hitch to his belt. "Hokay, we vote. This is Greek custom, *kyría*. Before ship sails, captain must ask crew: is it hokay where they go? Crew of *Pouláki Mou* numbers two: *kyría* Cunningham, Katerina to her friends, and Damianós Mikhaïl Demetríou. I ask crew: does this *ponirós*—this sly and jealous fox—come with us? Katerina, you speak first. Is for you, the voyage. For Damian the sea is always here."

"Why not? Surely there's room?"

"I, too, say yes," Damian says stoutly, hauling on the rope to bring the boat snug against the wharf.

Kostas gives him a friendly cuff on the shoulder. "Always plenty of room on *Pouláki Mou*," he laughs. "Kyriakos makes big haul sometimes, sometimes very small"—he pinches his fingers as if he were plucking a flea—"so small can be tucked in pocket!" And leaping lightly aboard, he turns to extend me a hand.

When his crew (and the self-invited fox) is settled on the piles of netting (dry, this crew member is pleased to find), Kyriakos casts off, gives the starting rope a single powerful tug, and nods approvingly as the motor settles into a smooth cadence. Mounting the raised portion of the deck at the stern where he can see over the cabin, he expertly mans the tiller with his foot. If Kostas is a bandit, Kyriakos is a pirate . . . a pirate chief, I think idly, admiring his arrogant stance. I should have brought my sketchpad . . .

"What kind of boat is *Pouláki Mou*, Kyriakos? It's very steady, though of course the sea is calm." Indeed, as we slide across the gently heaving water one would imagine the sea is breathing in its sleep.

"*Kaïki*. It is made first by Turks—*gayiq*, they call it. But we Greeks made many improvements." He grins. "Of course."

"Do you ever use the sail?"

"If motor dies. Also we have oars. Do not worry, Katerina, we get back to Pyrgotafos hokay."

"Sail very good when motor would scare fish," Kostas says lazily. "Some fishes have big ears."

"*Pouláki Mou* is very safe boat, friend Kay," Damian assures me. "Even when seas are angry. Wide and flat, like hand on waves." He makes patting motions, as if the sea were a contentious dog.

Yawning, Kostas lies back on the nets, his hands locked behind his head. "Not fast, of course, Katerina. More like duck than gull. But of course nothing can be everything," he adds courteously, and smiles at his host.

"Very true—a taxicab does not win the Grand Prix." Acidly. "Driver of taxicab must be very special man, I think. Oh, yes: not drunk, not crazy, not blind, but better sometimes deaf—I am right?"

Kostas looks at him, his eyes sleepy. "I could sail this boat alone—one man—*stó Tourkía* and back. Like gentle donkey, this boat, easy to ride on smooth, smooth sea."

Damian scowls at him. "My friend Kyriakos go fishing when no one else dare to go!"

Kostas laughs. "Oho, Kyriakó! What you catch from stormy waters? One big fish? Many little fishes? What you catch?"

"Why expert sailor like you does not buy Greek boat?" Kyriakos twists his finger against the side of his nose. "Why he buy German taxi? I ask *myself*!"

"More easier get rich, *fíli mou*. On Mytilene is many boats, here in Molivos only one taxi. Besides, old boat is like jealous lady—always you must spend, spend, spend!"

"So how did you, expert sailor, have money to buy taxi?"

"I not spend it on women," Kostas says, and shows his teeth.

Kyriakos says something in Greek, and Kostas laughs.

"Now they talking like sailors," Damian says tolerantly.

At least they've stopped needling each other . . . "Just as well I don't speak Greek, then," I smile.

"When my father was a young man," Kyriakos tells me, "it took four, five men to run a boat no bigger than *Pouláki Mou*. There were no motors, everything was done by men. Even the nets were pulled in by men. Life was hard and fish cheap. Now, even with motors costing much money and petrol many *drachmés* a liter, fishing is a good life. Work not so hard and price of fish high. But one problem: a man can never be sure the fish will be there."

"Fisherman like you always in luck, I think,"

Kostas says with a smile. "Somebody always glad for what you catch. Always happy to pay you good money. But with taxis is different. Maybe nobody wants go for ride. Maybe strike spreads like winter storm and no tourists come. What happens then? Greeks not ride in taxis, much too poor. But Greeks always hungry. If not hungry himself, can buy from you, sell to man who is."

Kyriakos is giving Kostas that look again: *shut your mouth or I'll shut it for you.*

I grope for something pacific to say. "How clear the air is! Look how far away we can still see the tower!"

"From top you can see very, very far," Damian assures me. "Can see Turkish coast from Baba Burnu to Assos—I show you!"

"You go up on tower? Aieee—I think your aunt Verek will *zzkk!*" Kostas makes a gesture of cutting his throat.

"We were going to picnic there today." I glance at Damian doubtfully. "I didn't know Verek had forbidden it."

"Not Verek. The law says no, Katerina. Very dangerous—two, three children die there already."

"The law forbids child by himself, not with father or teacher," Kyriakos points out. "Child alone has one-half brain, two children together, no brain at all."

Damian is indignant. "You think I make friend Kay to climb down inside? I am not crazy fool! We go up outside, where is easy. We go down same way, very slow, very careful—not going to fall!"

I'll have to make some excuse . . . get out of it somehow . . . I shade my eyes: there's a small fleet of *kaïkia* coming toward us out of the dazzle of light. *Be-*

cause of course I can't go picnicking where a child has died . . .

"The *maríthes* are many at Skála Sikamínias," Damian remarks regretfully. "But we not go fish there, friend Kay. That is east. We go north by west. You want know who those boats are? I tell you. I know all boats that fish off Akra Kórakas. First is Lefteris Koukas from Petrá, then Mathias and Kristos Attakos from Molivos, then Petros Manesis, and—yes, there he comes, always last—Stefanos Stathakos—"

"Enough!" Kostas snaps. "Katerina does not want know these fishermans, does not want hear list like teacher counting noses!"

I could say I've changed my mind, I'd like to go to Mytilene to meet Mike after all . . . No, Damian will think I'm backing off, that I'm scared. Which I'm not. Not of the climb, anyway. And Kostas—Kostas is bound to misinterpret my last-minute switch. He'll put it down to his fatal charm (joke in Greek, hahaha, more joke in Greek). I'm trapped. I said I'd climb the tower. Now I've got to.

We're rounding the point. There is the castle, as Damian calls it; there are the tile roofs spilling like faded petals. Kyriakos cuts the motor and gets out the lines.

"You're not going to use the nets?" Fishing with a line! Why, we could do that from shore. But with nets—that's practically biblical!

"Not for *barboúni*, friend Kay," Damian says kindly.

"Net must be only at night, Katerina," Kyriakos explains, "so fish not see it. He is not going to swim to his death to please us—we must be one little bit smarter than he is."

We gaze as if hypnotized where the colorful little gourds ride on the water, languid partners of the peaceful waves. Not one of them gives that encouraging bob that signals some fish has taken the hook; wherever the *barboúni* are, they are not here. The light off the water, the quiet, voices in the village so faint as to be dreamlike, the repetitive motion of the waves induce in us all a kind of trance. A shared silence . . .

Well, I would break ours! *Khristós anesti,* Mike, I'll say. Welcome to Greece. Let me introduce Damian, who chooses to call me "friend Kay" because—

Kostas jerks his line. Empty. He mutters under his breath.

"Did my husband reach Athens all right?"

It has occurred to me I should have gone myself, last evening, to the hotel, perhaps even dined there, instead of at the café on the square in Pyrgotafos. I should have gone to the hotel and phoned Athens: made some gesture of interest, for God's sake, in Mike's whereabouts. But I'd been so tired, blood-and-bone tired.

Kostas shrugs. "No way to know for sure. Hotel say all phones now strike." He frowns, attaching more bait. "Voula not even know how many come today. But I meet plane, of course. I bring husband, do not worry, Katerina."

At least the planes are moving: that's a comfort.

"Where did you learn English, Kostas? In Germany?"

"I learn German in Germany. I learn English in school, but I not have special teacher like Damian. So I learn more better in Canada. I work two years there, in Greek restaurant." He glances at Kyriakos, and laughs. *"I cook the fish—me, Kostas Demetriou, best fish cook in Toronto!"*

"They hide *you* in the kitchen?" Kyriakos winks at Damian.

"Canada not like Greece. They have only young girls waiting tables—beautiful young girls."

"All young girls are very beautiful, everywhere," Kyriakos sighs. "What a shame a man has only one life."

Kostas shrugs. "No good those girls in Canada. Free for the asking, you understand? No dowry. A man must be very rich to take a wife with no dowry."

"After Canada you went to Germany?"

"No, Katerina, by then the Colonels gone. Is safe to come home. I work here three years; then I go to Germany. Too late, best times already over. The money is sick, the money is dying. Soon no work for Greeks. So once more I come home." Again, that expressive shrug. "Here things not good but not bad either. With luck and if he is clever a man can live."

Kyriakos tips his pole. A silvery fish about eight inches long dangles at the end of the line.

Kostas laughs. "Six of those and you have enough for one meal if you not hungry."

"Much more than some will have." Pointedly.

The boat stirs, the water begins to dance, and a light wind stirs my hair. I marvel at how blue the sky is.

Kyriakos nods. "We go back now, weather is changing."

"You can tell from the color of the sky?"

"*Kyría,* it is my job." Dryly.

"I am good sailor, too," Kostas says. "I show you. Captain entertains ladies, crew works. I am crew."

Damian mutters under his breath.

"Do not worry, he will not sink us, I do not permit it," Kyriakos grins. "So, famous sailor, start the motor. Is not hard, if you have back of mule—"

Kostas makes a gesture that very clearly indicates less talk would be welcome, then seizes the rope. Half a dozen violent tugs later, he stops to catch his breath.

Kyriakos laughs. "Not so easy to start as taxi, maybe?"

Kostas glares. He yanks the rope again, and then again.

"Open the throttle," Damian moans.

The motor coughs, sputters, then settles into a roar.

"*Close* the throttle!" Damian puts his head on his knees.

"So I was not born under a seashell," Kostas shrugs. He engages the gears and we lurch forward. Kyriakos roars in Greek. " 'Gently! Sweetly!' " Kostas mocks, and laughs.

Damian says in an urgent voice, "Keep wide of the harbor, uncle. There are rocks you do not see, just under water—"

"You have good crew." Kostas nods to Kyriakos. "Wide awake, like frightened bird." He has assumed Kyriako's stance of one foot on the tiller, one hand on his hip. I think: my God, he *is* beautiful. I wonder if he'd pose for me . . . No, risky to ask.

I can still see the fortress. From this distance it looks more picturesque than useful.

"Do you really expect the Turks to invade?"

Kyriakos shrugs. "Who knows what Turks will do?"

"So if they come, is not first time for Lesvos," Kostas says. "I give you my tourist lecture, Katerina, no charge. First is Aeolians, they come from Thessaly. Next come Persians, Athenians, Macedonians—once even Egyptians come. Everybody comes to Lesvos!"

"Wasn't that a Roman aqueduct the Germans wanted to see?"

"Romans, yes—you have heard of this Julius Caesar? He made big name for himself when he take fortress at Mytilene. Before that he was nobody."

"After the Romans came lots of tourists, mostly making trouble," Kyriakos says with a grin. "Seljuks, Byzantines, Venetians, Nicaeans—"

"Spaniards from Catalonia—they are bad, very, very bad, I not tell ladies and children what they do." Kostas moves the tiller, and we curve toward the northeast.

"Worst is when Greek does to Greek," Damian says. "Like to uncle Yeoryio. That is the most worst of all. Greeks to Greeks," he repeats incredulously. "That is great, great sin."

He is obsessed by this, I think with concern. And of course he is right. Treachery and torture, bad enough when it's the enemy, become utterly unspeakable, utterly vile, when it is one's own countrymen . . .

"No, worst is the Turks," Kostas declares. "I tell you, Damiane, than Turks is nobody worse. They come next after Spaniards."

"And stay five hundred years," Damian says gloomily.

"No, after Spaniards come Genoese," Kyriakos says. "In 1354, it was. Emperor of Byzantium gave

— 142 —

Lesvos to a Sir from Genoa who marries his daughter. That is castle they live in, there in Molivos. That was the best time—everybody happy, some getting rich, and for one hundred years nobody fighting, nobody killing. *Then* came the Turks, in 1462. My own grandfather remember when they leave, just before the first Great War, and you are right, Damiané, after five hundred years we Greeks were Greek again."

"If we all those other things for many hundreds of years, why we not forget how?"

"Greeks forget how to be *Greek?*" Kyriakos stares at Damian in incredulity. "Impossible! We are not Turks because Turks come, we are not Germans because Germans come."

"We not Americans because Americans come," Kostas says with cool impudence. "Too bad—we be rich, then, too!"

Language gap again . . . "And you, Kyriakos, where did you learn English?"

"In prison camp. Much better than university for speed, *kyría*. Learn or die!"

"My brother Mikhaïl, father of Damian, never learn English," Kostas remarks. "Too busy always, must work from daylight to dark in the olives." He moves the tiller slightly, and it seems to me we're now running due north. "First they are my father's, he die. Then they are my brother Mikhaïl's, gone ten years, I think he die. When you are a man, Damiane, they yours. Remember what I tell you. Your uncle Yeoryios use the olives, but they not his. Borrowed only."

So much for Mrs. Meade's speculations. But if the trees are Damian's by right, you'd think his uncle would want him adopted—adopted and safely out of the country. Maybe Yeoryios *does* want that. I have only Mrs. Meade's opinion to the contrary.

Kyriakos takes the tiller. "You want we should pay little visit to Turkey, maybe inspect Turkish prison?" And we turn southeast, into the sun.

"I not want olive trees," Damian says sulkily. "I rather go to sea."

"Yes, sure, why not?" Kyriakos squints up at the mast, at the May wreath swaying. "Greek sailors lucky—can always drown in sight of land!"

CHAPTER

13

The harbor at Pyrgotafos is vibrant with *kaïkia* even more colorful—lime sail, scarlet trim; apricot sail, aquamarine trim—than *Pouláki Mou.* Black-clad women are making their selections from the baskets of fish on the wharf; old men are already at their card games under the plane tree; and somebody's *mikhaníki*—a sturdy three-wheeled vehicle like a mechanized mule ("by motorcycle out of tractor")—has tipped its load of lumber across the entrance to the church, much to the diversion of onlookers.

Kostas goes off in his taxi, having promised to bring Mike directly to Zoë's; I'm concerned about the shortness of time before the birthday party, I explain, arrangements for which I feel must be made by my husband himself. Kyriakos chooses a table by the water, and there the three of us eat oranges, and thick bread with honey and unsalted butter, and drink strong American-style coffee, Damian's laced with hot milk. Out of sight beyond the turn to Molibos children are whooping and shouting in the schoolyard; the sound is a cloud over the sun. As I watch Damian thread honey across the surface of his coffee, I become aware Kyriakos is studying my face as if it were a portent-filled sky.

"*Kyría,* Kostas says you have a great grief—this is true?"

I can only look at him, and nod.

"This is a curse, you think? It is punishment you do not earn?"

Carefully, Damian returns the dipper to the honey bowl and looks away, at the water dancing and glittering like hammered silver. I say nothing.

Kyriakos puts his hand on my arm. "A curse no matter how strong cannot cross water. I tell you, Katerina, I am Greek, I know about curses. So smile sometimes, *kyría mou,* with your eyes as well as your lips. Here you are safe."

Damian bursts out laughing. "So *that* is why, yes? Is why Greeks cross so many seas! To escape a curse?"

Kyriakos laughs, too, tousles Damian's hair, and deftly intercepts the check. "This is my country, you are guest here. I come to America, you pay." Glancing past me, he gives a quick fierce scowl, as quickly erased. "Here comes my cargo for Assos," he mutters. "Pray for quiet trip and no Germans sick. Or maybe I forget to bring them back? I joke, of course." And he sighs.

"*Kaló taxíthi,*" Damian says with a grin.

At least I can buy the bread for the picnic, I console myself as Damian and I seek out the bakery, a dark cavelike shop tucked behind the post office. We pass a quartet of women seated on the steps where the lanes join, the baskets at their feet piled with mending. Farther along, a trio of women sit winding wool. Each time: a sudden silence, frank stares, smiles, then "*Kaliméra!*"

"It's very friendly, living in the village, isn't it?"

"Yes, is very nice, the all-together," Damian agrees. "When my uncle Yeoryios put water pipes to our house, my aunt Verek say she miss the *óli mazí* when she wash clothes at the fountain. You want swim, friend Kay? I know where is smooth rocks, no mines."

"I'll have to get my swimsuit. What about you?"

"I swim in my shorts. They dry fast."

I put my tank suit on under my jeans and shirt, add a towel to my satchel, and so we set out up the coast road, stopping for cheese at Voufounos'. He's not in his shop; Mrs. Voufounos says he's taken the bus with their daughter Eleni to see the doctor in Mytilene. "*Kýrios* Voufounos has tired heart," Damian explains.

All along the edge of the road toward the sea there's a narrow strip a yard or so wide where yarrow and sea lavender, broom and mullein fight for roothold, then the land drops away to the water. Abreast of the tower we pick our way through this ribbon of stubborn green and go down to the shore. The "smooth rocks, no mines" Damian promised me are at the mouth of a shallow stream mumbling its way to the sea between banks of wild lupine.

"Water good for drinking," Damian tells me. "I think is why tower is here, built over source—is correct word?"

"It's correct, but we'd probably say 'spring.' " I turn on my back and float idly; the water is as placid as a mill pond. Against the bright sky the tower looks like an oddly symmetrical mountain. A bit wider at the base than at the top, its sides are patched with greenery, the cracks in its massive stones having been invaded by whatever could take root. "Who built it, does anyone know?"

"Some say Romans—they leave mark on wall by the spring, I show you. Others think not so old as that." He flips onto his back and wriggles his toes. "Many sailors not know how to swim. My uncle Kostas say that is stupid, man who goes to sea should make friend of the water. He does not go to sea, that Kostas, but he is half fish already, my uncle Yeoryios say."

I float like a piece of driftwood, letting the limp little waves lap me slowly eastward. "Look, I'm a sailboat. How long until I bump into Turkey?"

"Maybe a day, maybe a week. When you reach channel you go faster, friend Kay. Sea like river there." He rolls, dives, and comes up on the other side of me. "Sailors fall off *kaïki*, drown, maybe fish eat, maybe buried in Turkey—Turks not bother to say. Happens many times, my uncle Kostas tell me." He laughs, as at a private joke. "I ask my uncle Niko one time what he want me to be when I am a man. What you think he say?"

"Priest?"

A gust of laughter. "No, no! Not uncle Nikos! Never!"

"Politician? Poet?"

"No, no! 'What I want you to be?' uncle Nikos say. 'I want you to be—alive!' " Damian flips backward, resurfaces, and shakes the water from his eyes. "My uncle Yeoryios say it is enough that when I am a man I am Greek. My uncle Kostas say why not rich Greek? My uncle Nikos say rich man is not free, he does not own money, money owns him, he is servant of money. What you think, friend Kay? Is not funny way for to talk? No one of my uncles has money, but they talk about it hour by hour. Like me: I not have boat, but I think boat, I talk about boat, very, very much. What you not have that you think about all the time, friend Kay?"

A husband . . . a son.

"I'm tired . . . I think I'll go lie in the sun." I can scarcely get the words out. "You needn't come with me if you don't want to."

"No, I come, too."

We wade ashore. Leaving the buoyant water, I struggle against the familiar illusion of a giant hand pushing me down, trying to push me under; I feel as if I've had a foretaste of old age.

"I ask stupid question, you are angry, friend Kay?"

"No . . . no, of course not." I manage a smile. "I'm just tired, as I said."

Damian is silent; I wish I hadn't been so curt. But I *am* tired, though I can't think why. It's good just to lie here, lie here in the warmth, the flood of sunlight . . . it's restorative . . .

"You will cook soon, friend Kay," says Damian from far away.

I wake with a gasp. "Was I asleep long?"

"Not many minutes. But sun is strong. Come, I show you the spring. Is cooler there."

I pull on my jeans and shirt over my almost-dry swimsuit, and follow him along the stream to the tower.

No wonder ancient peoples told tales of giants! Here at the base the stones are a good five feet high and easily ten feet long; each must weigh tons. Even the smaller stones, higher up, are massive—how did anyone get them up there? As for its size overall, I would guess the tower to be about fifty feet high and some thirty feet along each side of its squarish top, and broader by perhaps twenty feet or so at the base. Whatever was it built for? Surely nobody would go to such lengths simply to be able to keep watch well out to sea, not with those respectable hills of Molibos and Pyrgotafos handy. But if the structure was intended primarily for defense, was it large enough? To be of any use against an invasion in force, I mean.

I say as much to Damian.

"But spring is very good, friend Kay. Gives good water, and never stops. Water very important for soldiers, important for everybody. We have not much water in Pyrgotafos until Turks dig wells. So for many hundreds of years before Turks come, tower is important to keep enemy from spoiling it."

My wits must have withered. " 'Spoiling'?"

"Yes. So if you drink, you die."

The narrow stream slithers out like a little snake through the thicket of bamboo rustling against the tower. I gaze down into its limpid water, the stones on its bed like opalescent scales. "Poison it, you mean, Damian . . ." Man against man . . . You'd think it would be enough, in this barren land, to contend with stony soil and untimely frost and drying winds. Water, life-giving water, should be sacred: inviolate absolutely! No wonder the ancients assigned gods to springs, to the rivers, to the sea . . .

"Two ways in, friend Kay. Can splash like fish up the little river, but easier to use steps Romans build."

Damian leads the way around the bamboo to a

barely discernible trail that threads between the thicket and the great lichen-stained stones. A few feet along and we come to rough steps leading steeply down to a narrow slit beneath one of the immense blocks. This opening, scarcely more than a yard wide, is further constricted by the gutterlike channel for the over-flow from the spring. The top of the opening being just below ground level, no way could an invader coming from the sea have known it's here, I think, even without that concealing patch of bamboo . . . or not until he came close beneath the walls, where he'd likely be met by rocks hurled from above, or hot oil, or a hailstorm of arrows.

Passing from brilliant sun to filtered shadow, we descend the uneven steps. Damian scrunches over to slip through the narrow opening; stooping still lower, I follow. Intense darkness confounds me. I can see nothing.

"Slowly, friend Kay. More steps go down—two, three, I not remember how many—but always they are slippery. Everything smooth like floor of church. If we have lamp I show you where it tells who does this work. Which soldiers, which legion—story is there in stone, forever. Very much work to have nice drink of water, you think so?"

The blackness is thinning out, is taking form. I catch the glimmer of water. Light seeps thinly from above as well as from the passage behind us. Now I can make out the walls on either side, a hollowed chamber perhaps ten feet across, and—I stand erect cautiously—the crude stone vault that spans the cis-tern and the ledge on which we stand. Overhead is an opening that leads (as if we were in a well) to daylight, but on a slant, for I can't see the sky.

I state the obvious: "The defenders of the spring didn't have to go down the outside after water, did they?"

"No, very simple come for drink down long safe hole. Very easy for to climb, good safe steps cut in rock. Not break if soldier wear bronze. You have word in English for straight-up-and-down stairs? In Greek is word for everything."

"Ladder," I smile. "And 'long hole' is a tunnel."

Squatting, Damian cups his hands. "Drink from spring, friend Kay. Who drinks from spring in Pyrgotafos never knows fear."

I crouch beside him, dip, and drink. Though the water is remarkably clear and good, I can't see that it changes me in any way. Perhaps it takes time.

"Actually the tunnel might be a danger," I remark. "Somebody could always sneak close on a dark night and then climb up. If those steps are cut into the stone, the defenders wouldn't even have a rope ladder they could haul up."

"Not sleeping like babies, friend Kay, everybody dreaming happy dreams. Always one man stands watching. Feel here—"

His hand guides mine along the top of the opening. There's a kind of shelf, I find, a projection wide enough for a man to stand on and from which he could no doubt pick off any attackers coming, of necessity, one by one and hunched over, through that narrow, low entrance.

"Rock very useful," Damian says with satisfaction. "Is where to stand for to guide pail into water, is also from where to kill Turks, or Persians, or whoever is enemy." Then, more soberly: "Is also what kill boys who fall when climbing. They not fall in water like off *Pouláki Mou,* splash to side and climb out. They hit head, maybe break back on this sticking-out rock, slide into water and drown."

My God! The children—the children who died! "I'm not crazy, I don't make friend Kay to climb down *inside,*" Damian had told Kostas scornfully. Those children—two? three? God knows how many!—had died *here*—here where my hand has touched—right *here,* in this cave like a serpent's mouth, fangs ready, waiting . . .

I turn and plunge through the passage, stumbling up the steps, scraping my knee, not knowing, not caring I've broken the skin. The sunlight, the blessed hot sun and the sea glittering . . . red earth, blue sky, blue water—out in the channel a ship with a deep blue sail . . .

"I am sorry, friend Kay," Damian says humbly. "I not forget your son die. I not know talk of Greek boys dying make you so sad. Boys fall many years ago, I not know names. Always for many thousand years boys dying. *Everybody* die, friend Kay!"

"Yes . . . I know." *I know it but I can't accept it. It isn't right. It isn't the way it's supposed to be. Everybody else's, maybe, but not mine: that's the way it's supposed to be . . .* "Let's decide where to have our picnic. You choose, Damian." *Anywhere but here.*

Damian is not easy to deflect. "Nobody die up there, up on top, not for many hundred years. How we know where no boys die? Is not for sure *any* place where *no*body die, not ever—"

"All right, all right!" I manage a smile. "The top of the tower it is."

— 153 —

"The easiest way up is on the side away from the sea," he tells me eagerly, and flinging his string bag over his shoulder, he leads the way.

The coastline here is roughly an inverted V, and the three sides of the tower that face the sea have, paradoxically, stood firm against the onslaught of time and the weather; it's the landward side that looks as if it's been dynamited: some violent disturbance has loosened a number of the huge stones and sent them tumbling. We clamber past and strike a trail that zigzags steeply up the slope. Damian scampers up with the stamina of a mountain goat, and I after him as best I can. We reach the top, and I sink onto a hummock of dry grass, and look about me . . . and catch my breath.

From horizon to horizon sweeps the resplendent sky, flawlessly blue. I feel a sudden lifting of my spirits, as if a clean wind has caught me unaware. I am—and this is unexpected, too—glad I've come (to Pyrgotafos? to the tower?), and thankful I've conquered, or at least won a skirmish against, whatever sent me fleeing from the grief-polluted spring below.

On every side facing the sea there is a waist-high bulwark of crenellations, now crumbling, which must once have afforded considerable protection against invaders' spears. Clearly the defenders had an excellent view out across the strait and along the coast from Pyrgotafos (if, indeed, the village existed then) almost to Molibos. A donkey goes slowly along the road toward the village, laden with bales of straw or grain of such a size I'm reminded of an ant lugging a huge crumb of bread. The inevitable army trucks rumble past. And in the channel a line of low-slung vessels is immobilized.

Damian is perched in a crenel where wild leek and cornflowers bloom. The wind, faintly aromatic, blows steadily from the north. He sniffs deeply. "I smell the fires of Troy! Keep watch, friend Kay! Watch for signal who is victor!"

"What are those strange-looking ships sitting out there?"

"Turks, looking for oil."

"Right there? Not a mile away?"

"Turks looking for oil all along our coast. Makes government very mad, my uncle Nikos say. Of course we look, too, all along their coast. Better if we find it, I think. Lesvos very poor. Did my uncle Kostas tell you about catastrophe with oak trees?"

He hands me the string bag, and I take out bread and cheese. "No, I don't think he did." The bread has an unfamiliar smell, almost earthy, and inside its golden crust it is a strange color, a very pale gray. However, it is delicious, with a fresh, nutlike flavor. Even the cheese is good, though it has a fearsome smell.

"Very bad what happened." He chews hungrily, swallows. "Very bad for Kosta, too. When he come back from Canada after Colonels gone, he and my uncle Yeóryios wait for my father to come. I am very small but I remember the waiting. Others come—Pétros Mánesis, we see his boat this morning, and Manólis Siphnéos of Skoularis—and others, all with eyes very strange. I remember the eyes, friend Kay. Like they long time staring at black night. Staring at deep cave. Staring where is nothing, nothing, only black. Staring for so long a time the black is around their eyes." He breaks off another piece of bread, but does not eat. "We wait and wait, but my father does not come. Others come, many others, but not my father."

"Mrs. Meade told me," I say gently.

"Yes." He puts the bread in his mouth and chews slowly, as if it has a strange taste. "At last my uncle Yeoryios say is no use to wait more, *o patéras* is not coming, he is dead. I am sad because I never see my father, I not know his face. Is very strange not know face of my father, friend Kay. My aunt Verek say pray for soul of my father, pray he rest and be happy, but I cannot think for *who* I pray—I see nobody in my mind. When you pray for your son, there is his face before you, is it not so?"

". . . Yes." Very carefully, I begin to peel an orange.

"I make long road to oak trees," he says apologetically. "So now with my father dead my uncles must choose. My grandfather gave to his sons this way: olives to my father, house to Kosta, and oaks to Yeoryio. But Yeoryios has wife, needs house. Kostas needs way to make living, and bark of oak trees is very useful for turn skin of goat or sheep into leather—English word?"

"Tanning."

"Bark very good for tanning. Yes. So they change—"

"Exchange."

"They exchange. Kostas has oaks, Yeoryios has house, and at same time he can work in olives, keep for me until I am a man." Damian sighs deeply. "I think he hopes then we work together. My uncle Yeoryios loves olives how I love ships. He say if you sleep under fig tree, when you wake your head like stone, but sleep under olive tree, you wake as if in high mountains, air like wine on tongue." He kicks at a rock and sends it rolling. "So—comes bastard leather. *Plastós.* End of tanning business. Young men leave, go to foreign lands, wherever they can get work. My uncle Kostas go to Germany, and there for three years he works. I miss him very much. Always he is laughing, is brave, is full of plans. I am very glad when he comes bringing money to buy taxi. Now he will stay."

"Three years! I didn't realize he was there that long. What did he do—work in leather?"

"No, with the vines. Germans lost war but are very rich, can pay other people do their hard work. My uncle Kostas say in Germany hardest work for lowest pay done by Yugoslavs and Greeks." His tone is bitter, no doubt in unconscious echo of Kostas.

From the willows along the watercourse drifts the call of a dove. I hear a sadness in it, a longing.

"Friend Kay, are you sick for home?"

"I am, a bit," I confess. "I wasn't until a moment ago."

"It is the birds." He breaks off a piece of cheese.

"Birds?"

"Yes, their song. They like enemy that creeps through tunnel and leap at you when you not looking—*flut!* you are finished." He munches thoughtfully. "My uncle Kostas when he work in Germany say he think he cannot live without *tón koúko*—here they are everywhere. In Germany some stupid bird is all the time making sound like sick sheep. Kostas say he is not woman, he does not weep for home, but it make him want to curse." Delicately, like a cat, Damian licks a finger. "What kind birds you have in your village?"

"Thrushes . . ." Treacherously, the memory of the warm green melodious evenings (*"Mom, let's eat outside, okay?"*) seizes me by the throat. I say with difficulty, "Their song is like liquid silver. It would seem strange to you there, I think, Damian—we haven't any cuckoos either."

Mountains to the southwest wear towering crowns of thunderhead. A flock of untidy-looking sheep boils along the track that skirts the tower; an old man, shouting and whacking with his crook, manages with the indifferent help of his dog to keep them from spilling through an opening into the green-striate field beyond.

"*O Sokratis,*" Damian says, gazing after him with affection. "Is as deaf as stone. Lives on edge of village, near to uncle Kostas's oaks." He points toward a thrust of land running like a buttress down the hill to which Pyrgotafos clings. "See there the roof of my uncle's house? Looks like red sail against green water, you think so?"

It is the comment of a boy whose heart is with ships and far horizons, I think, watching the silver-green of the olives foam and swirl beneath the wind like a tide against the shore.

"When I am a man I think I have a problem, friend Kay," Damian goes on moodily. "Easy to say no to uncle Yeoryio when it something he not want either." He scuffs at a stone, not looking at me. "But when is what he want very much—hard, very hard to say no."

"Perhaps it will all work out." Gently. "We have a saying, 'Don't borrow trouble.' "

"I know, not necessary. Trouble come find you, don't worry." He kicks at the stone again, sending it skidding under a tangle of vine. A moment later, so faint it could be a thought, not an actuality, I hear a single stroke of sound. It seems to come from somewhere beneath our feet—somewhere within the tower.

"*What was that?*" I don't know why I'm so startled.

"Stone fall down secret way, friend Kay." Damian lifts the mat of vine. An opening as narrow and rectangular as the top of a flue gapes at us blankly. I stare down into blackness.

"I can't see anything. But it goes on a slant, doesn't it? What did it hit, do you suppose? It sounded much too near to be—you know—by the spring."

Where the children were smashed and broken . . . Where they died they died they died . . .

"Not straight like mast of ship, friend Kay. More like leg of dog." He gestures. "First this way, little bit. Then down to spring."

Of course he has explored it, I think helplessly. It may be forbidden that children be up here at all, certainly forbidden that they climb down inside, but what are such prohibitions to a boy like Damian? "*I had to see if I could do it, Mom! I had to try, didn't I?*" Damian, like David, has to *go*, has to *do*, has to *be*. Always will have to, as long as life lasts.

"My uncle Kostas think when the tower built, is no Pyrgotafos. Not born yet." Damian gazes toward the village spilling down the hill to the harbor; there is an almost adult affection in his glance. "I think my uncle Kostas makes mistake—I cannot think world ever had no Pyrgotafos." He grins. "Is always here, always. Like sun and moon."

The children must have been running about, shouting and laughing. One of them must have stumbled, must have fallen through the vines. No: Damian said it was all a hundred years ago; there may have been no vines then. Probably they were climbing down—"I dare you!" "You go first!"—and they'd not been as skillful (or as lucky) as Damian. They'd groped for a foothold and not found it . . . had found it, but the rock crumbled, or they'd been in a hurry and had slipped . . . had plunged helplessly, fingers clutching frantically at the walls but catching no handhold anywhere . . . plunging like a stone forty, fifty feet to strike that granite ledge . . .

Someone had to run to tell the mother. The mother had to send word to the father . . . send someone to tell the father toiling in the sun among the olives . . . send someone to the wharf, to wait until the weary sailor put in from the sea. No one had had to run for me. I'd heard the screech of tires, the car against the tree, the woman's screams. No one had had to send for Mike, call him out of conference, leave a message at his desk. He'd swung off the train at his usual time, had come striding across the green toward the cluster of cars, of people, had come running to where I crouched by David . . . to where I was pleading, "David? David—it's Mother! David—"

Wait for me, wait for me. . . . Don't leave me yet come back come back oh wait for me . . .

Kyriakos is wrong. Some curses are strong enough to cross all the seas that wash all the shores of all this anguished world.

CHAPTER

14

Now that Damian's birthday is over—over but not done with: you *wait,* Michael Cunningham, you just *wait!*—I am thankful to be horizontal, at least, though God knows I can't sleep. I seem to be in the clutches of more acute than usual post-party blues. I ask myself: why didn't I say the hell with it when Mike didn't show up, and cancel the whole affair? Because, if I had, Damian's birthday would be ruined, and I, not Mike, would be ruining it, and I couldn't do that. And because Mike would never forgive me. "Some flimsy excuse, Kay! What a pity you can't be depended upon to take over when I'm not there."

Well, maybe he wouldn't go that far, but he'd be thinking it.

Everything should have been so smooth and easy. Kostas was to bring Mike directly to Zoë's, I would formally present Damian, whereupon Kostas would convey us—that is, Mike and me—to wherever Mike decided to have the birthday party. To the *tavérna* in Pyrgotafos. To the *tavérna* in Molibos. Wherever: arrangements would be made. And then Kostas would transport us to the Hotel Silver Bird. (And high time,

— 161 —

too.) So when two o'clock came and went, and two-thirty ditto, with no sign of Kosta's taxi, my sole reaction was to feel a bit uneasy.

"That Kostas—he makes detour, goes see Roman ruins," Damian assures me. "Tourists pay more drachmas, friend Kay. He not think you worry."

At three o'clock, Kostas returned. Alone.

"Katerina, I not know what to think. Your husband is not on plane. I am ten minutes late though I drive like maniac—I like to kill these tourists, to them clock is like *tó vivlío* to donkey—but everyone say no American come. I think somehow he send message, airline has wireless working. No message." He smiled consolingly. "He comes on next plane, Katerina, you will see, but I cannot wait, I have tourists for Silver Bird. Next plane comes in time for bus at four o'clock. Four o'clock from Mytilene, six o'clock to Molivos. He will be on that bus, Katerina—you will see."

"I hope so. He'll be awfully disappointed if he doesn't make it—he's been counting the days until Damian's birthday. Which reminds me, I'd better go and make arrangements, don't you think? After all, somebody has to."

I'd have no difficulty, Kostas agreed, especially with Damian to act as interpreter. Meanwhile he'd go to Molibos, collect Mike from the bus, and bring him on to Pyrgotafos. "Then begins *tó paniyíri*—the celebration." Smiling hearteningly.

Damian and I found his air of cheery optimism (real or fake) far from infectious. We trudged morosely down to the café on the far side of the square and gloomily reserved the longest table available. And then we trudged back to Zoë's, where we fretted until half past six, at which time Kostas returned. Alone.

"No one on bus, Katerina," he said soberly. It seemed to me there was more than sympathy in his eyes, there was pity, as well. "Only old Voufounos and his daughter."

Zoë nodded, smiled, and shrugged, as if a husband who doesn't turn up when he is supposed to were the most normal thing in the world—what else can a woman expect? And I must stay with her until tomorrow, Saturday; my room won't be needed until Nikos comes. "She say maybe Nikos bring news," Kostas added. "She say if you here in this house, you will know news at once."

I accepted gratefully. I dreaded being alone in the hotel, not knowing why Mike was delayed, not knowing where he could be—much better to be with friends, however new. Besides, with the phones on strike, Mike couldn't reach me there in any case.

So here I am, in Zoë's bed, wishing it were already morning, wishing I could sleep, telling myself it's no use to fret, but fretting anyway. Why *wasn't* Mike on either of those planes? Could he be sick? But he's never sick. Hurt, then? Struck down in that crazy I'm-more-macho-than-you-are Athenian traffic? Well, Alex and I managed to jaywalk unscathed. *What*, then? Mugged? No, not in Athens, not a tourist. Tourists (Mike said so himself) are sacred. So stop worrying, Kay, you dimwit; it doesn't help. You just have to wait until Nikolas Paradellis comes tomorrow. (Today?) Perhaps he and Mike will come together. Yes, of course they will.

But still I can't sleep.

As soon as I agreed to stay on here, Kostas took himself off, I suppose to get ready for the evening's festivities. Around seven o'clock a brief shower treated us to breathtaking flares of lightning followed by prolonged rumbles that rolled about the heavens in the most satisfying way, and for a short while I forgot my frustration and worry and, dressing, found myself confident that Mike would put in a belated appearance. And so I did more to my eyes and lips than I usually bother to do, and I sleeked my hair behind my ears, switching to that pair of dangly earrings that has a multitude of tiny silver bells cascading down—Mike had tucked them into my Christmas stocking two years ago. Daubing on a touch of scent, I was thankful I had, after all, brought along the smoke gray pleated chiffon. It was only later, as Damian and I set out for the waterfront—we were eating early (early for Greece)—that I suddenly reflected I had had to get ready alone, I was setting out for this child's birthday party alone—*alone!*—and I was seized by a sense of betrayal so acute I could have wept.

How *could* he, how *could* Mike fail to be here?

Though the cobblestones were still islanded by rainwater, the plastic-corded chairs and the oilcloth cover of our table were already dry, so we could sit out in the open under the dappled sky. I'd hoped for a spectacular sunset to lift my spirits, but in this I was disappointed, too; the rain having rinsed the color from the sky, the sun slipped unnoticed behind the horizon as my guests dutifully assembled.

Oh, Lord, that party! To begin with, the mix was wrong. Wednesday night the ingredients were highly compatible; tonight we just didn't fizz. I missed Zoë's cheerful leaven. She had smilingly refused to join us— she and her daughters as well. The celebration was for family, she said; they would be out of place.

"I tell her she *is* family!" Damian said in exasperation. "She is mother of my *koumbáros!* Kyriakos comes, I tell her, and he is not family! But she say no."

So in Zoë's merry stead we had Verek frugally rationing her smiles. Also we had Yeoryios, whom Kostas—and where on earth *was* Kostas?—evidently had not warned about Mike's absence, for his first reaction was plainly one of annoyance, as if he'd been trapped into a compromising situation a prudent man would prefer to avoid. Kyriakos, too, frowned and glanced about as if, under the circumstances, he wasn't sure he cared to stay.

"Your husband is not here? Kostas does not meet plane?"

"My husband wasn't on it. Obviously he's been delayed, but with the phone strike, there's no way he could let me know." I glanced at Damian, then away; his whole body drooped. Did he share my suspicion that this no-show of Mike's was no accident, was stage-managed by him to force me into the forefront, so to speak, of their relationship? Or was it just that the boy had done a bit of boasting? *"On my birthday my American father is going to . . ."* It would be only natural.

"When Boréas blows, nothing goes right," Kyriakos said somberly.

Verek muttered something nobody troubled to translate.

Greece being the most male-chauvinist of male-chauvinist countries, perhaps the whole problem was simply that I, in the absence of my husband, I, a foreigner and a woman, had presumed to act as host. Not that I had much success in the role! The waiter continually ignored my signals and leaped to place bottles of wine before Yeoryios and Kyriakos. And why hadn't I thought to invite Mrs. Meade? *She* wouldn't object to a mere female heading the table.

Following Verek's remark, the silence had grown so heavy I'd been afraid it would sink us altogether. "You can see the lights on the Turkish coast," I'd offered nervously, toying with my wine. "It looks so near, you'd think you could swim across."

Yeoryios frowned. "Do not try, *kyría.* You would drown."

"Nobody make proper *paniyíri*," Damian said mischievously.

"Is not subject for joke."

"Look!" Kyriakos mimed applause. "He makes entrance like film star, *o Kostas!*"

"I am late, I am sorry." Lighting up the table with his smile, Kostas slid into the one place remaining, which happened to be diagonally across from me. He was wearing very lean American jeans and a pale blue silk shirt that clung to his ribs; more than ever he looked like a beautiful, slightly decadent god. "I try to get call through to Athens. No luck. Very bad, this strike. Stupid." Filling his glass: "Your health, Katerina! My brother! My sister—"

Solemnly, we drank. Then at Yeoryio's suggestion we all trooped into the kitchen to choose what to eat. When we returned we could see the Germans' minibus parked beyond the plane tree and toward us—toward the tables next to us, that is—that spirited group wending its jolly way. As they took their seats, they sent us a veritable barrage of greetings.

"Guten Abend! Guten Abend, unsere Amerikanische Reisegefährte! Ach, der tapfer Seemann! Guten Abend, Herr Kapitän Karandonellis!"

I smiled, bowed, and replied (I hoped) suitably. Kyriakos mumbled a response. Yeoryios and Kostas affected to be unaware of their presence.

"Rain tomorrow." Yeoryios refilled glasses. "Good. The olives are still thirsty. Storm today was only a taste."

I said, "At home we say red at night, sailor's delight."

"In Mytilene storms come always from the sea. They come from north, south, west—every way but from Turkey."

"No, from Turkey comes other kinds of bad weather." Kostas aimed a smile at Kyriakos. "We lucky, we can always ask 'our brave sailorman' what cooks in Assos."

"So I take Germans to Turkish ruins," Kyriakos snapped. "Is it worse to escort tourists by ship than by taxi? From the one *drachmés* are dishonorable, from the other not?"

Yeoryios was watching me. "You don't drink your wine, *kyría*. You don't like?"

"Oh, yes, very much." I took a generous swallow. It certainly was strange.

"Retsina. After one glass you are used to it, Katerina," Kostas smiled. "After two, you like. After three, you prefer. After four—"

"After four, better no more," said Damian, and for the first time this evening (and, I think, looking back, the only time) everybody laughed.

Yeoryios helped himself to a garlicky yogurt, and

passed it to me. "This business of your husband's, what Nikos Paradellis calls Beta Beta Beta—how it works?"

"Advertising, you mean?"

"Yes. I want sell my olives—I go to this Beta Beta Beta and I pay them. What they then do for me? They choose what to say in the newspapers?"

"More or less, yes. And in magazines and on the TV—"

"It is one very big company? Has offices in London, where your husband goes?"

"Yes, and in Zurich and Rome."

"Not in Athens?"

"I don't think so."

"Greece is poor country," Kostas said, smiling. "Cannot buy from Americans, my brother. Can only sell to them."

Yeoryios nodded. "Very true. Can only sell, whatever we have. Olives, wine—"

"Whatever of value we have and they do not." Solicitously, Kostas offered me a dish of what looked like pale pink pudding. *"Taramasalata.* Made from eggs of fish, Katerina. Very good."

Something about his smile made me feel like an outsider. Something was wrong . . . but what? My husband had not come when expected: was that my fault? Perhaps not, but at the very least they must be embarrassed for me; it is always awkward when the husband isn't where he's said he'd be. And of course in their experience there is always the possibility he never would be, and no one would ever know why.

Sea birds were circling a fishing boat whose sail gleamed coral against a sea of beaten pewter. I moistened my dry mouth with wine and said, "I wish I could roll up that view and take it home with me."

"Can only sell, we Greeks, whatever we have that is very old and worth much money," Kostas persisted, as if I hadn't spoken. He lifted his glass to his brother. *"Yeiá sou."*

For a moment Yeoryios did not respond. Then: *"Yeiá sou,"* he said heavily, and emptied his glass.

I said, "Isn't it forbidden to sell antiquities?"

Yeoryios shrugged. "A man plowing turns over gold coins. Law says he must report what he finds. If he obeys, he can do nothing until authorities come. They are busy men, also not in a hurry. He must wait: he cannot plow, cannot plant. At last authorities come. They dig up whole field. Everything is ruined." He reached for the wine. "If a man has sense, he pockets the coins and says nothing. When he can, he sells them."

"Is stupid law," Kostas nodded. "Stupid laws make only trouble for honest men."

"Do not worry, Katerina," Kyriakos said. "You are not among thieves. Greeks are very honest people."

Kostas laughed. "Any man is honest who is afraid of beatings."

"Ókhi, we are honest because we are poor," Yeoryios said roughly. "A poor man must trust his neighbors, or he lives like in a cage with wild beasts."

Damian turned to me. "How is it in the U.S. of A., friend Kay? People are honest?"

I said reluctantly, "At home it really is a terrible problem, especially for the old. People put many locks on their doors, and still they aren't safe. I don't know what has happened to us—it didn't used to be like this, or so my parents said."

Yeoryios said harshly, "To steal from his own people a man must be willing to crawl like a snake."

In the fading light Kostas' teeth gleamed. "But from his enemies is hokay—it is natural to steal from enemies."

Yeoryios nodded solemnly. "Yes, that is honorable. But a true Greek will not steal from his brothers."

I said, "I think in my country the poor look on those who have more than they do as not really *being* their own people."

"Here in Greece, Katerina," Kyriakos remarked in a peace-keeping voice, "our ancestors were very good at this advertising." He swirled the wine in his glass. "You have been to Olympia? But you and your husband must go. There you will see the *zanès*—the statues to Zeūs—set along the road where the athletes march into the stadium. These statues—never say we Greeks are not a practical people!—are paid for by money taken from any athlete who in any way cheats. On the statue is put his name, and the name of his city, and what he did that was dishonest. There it stands for all to see forever. Shame to his name, to his line, to his city—forever! Now that, *kyría mou*, is advertising!"

"And you, my friend, blow like Boréas!" Yeoryios scowled. "How many such *zanès* are there? Fifteen? Twenty? After century upon century of games! But where are today's monuments to the police who arrest the innocent? To the informers who drink with friends and report what they say in their wine? To the jailers and torturers, paid by their own government, all of them deaf, deaf to the screams of their victims, who beg for mercy in their own tongue— Greek begging for mercy from Greek!" He banged his glass on the table. "Set up the *zanès* before the Parliament, I say! Line the walks of Platéia Syntàgmatos—line Athena's Way up to the door of her temple! Advertise—advertise our shame! And let us not forget"—he glared fiercely around the table—"a suitable memorial to the *friends* of Greece who sold us these weapons Greeks turned on Greeks!"

"There wouldn't be room, my friend," Kyriakos said quietly. He laid his hand on Yeoryio's arm. "Have more wine, *fíleh mou.*" Then, with a smile for Damian: "Come, you are very silent. It's your party, after all—make us a speech!"

"I am thinking," Damian said shyly. He glanced at me. "I am thinking one country not so different from another. U.S. of A. not so much different. Only here we have *koûkous* and there not."

"You talk nonsense!" Yeoryios glowered. "Greece is poor, U.S.A. rich, very rich. Very proud also—like rich man, very proud! Never is so proud a country as this U.S.A.!" Abruptly, he turned the full tide of his bitterness against me. "I am only one man, one poor man, *kyría,* but I know this: rich man always think he know what poor man need. And always he is wrong. I also know this: I want your rich country leave my poor country alone. It may be our fate to lose an island or two. Let *us* lose them—please don't do us a rich man's favor and *give* them away!"

Damian was gazing at his uncle with shining eyes.

"For what it's worth, Yeoryios," I said, my heart pounding painfully, "I voted *against*—"

"You Americans think you can sit like rich man

behind big desk and tell poor man what he should do. Did you not say, 'Here, Russia, take this piece of Poland'? 'Ho, Turkey—you want little bite of Cyprus? Come, help yourself!' " Again, he drained his glass. "You forget it is not playing cards you are giving—it is the *land* where people are born, the *land* where they plant their food, where they hope to be buried when they die! I do not want you do this to *my* land, to *my* village, U.S.A.! I do not want my dead brother's son go to your America, become one more rich American who think he can play with other peoples like toys!"

I said hotly, "Yeoryios Demetriou, I tell you there is *no* possibility of Damian coming to America, *that* I can promise you!"

And felt sickeningly disloyal to Mike as I said it. And feel so now, remembering. But I would say it again. *Will* say it, if I have to!

"Hush, Katerina," Kostas said. "Forgive my brother, I beg you. He has hard life and many griefs. For one little minute he forgets you are guest here, you are our guest—" and he signaled to the waiter to bring more wine.

"Now wait just one minute!" I managed a laugh. "Tonight you are *my* guests—my husband's and mine—no, I insist! It's embarrassing always to be accepting, never to be allowed to make the smallest gesture in return. I am *embarrassed*—"

"So you should be, to talk of such things," Kyriakos said with mock severity. "No, Katerina, you are our guest—you cannot help yourself!"

So say a pretty thank-you, Kay, and be grateful . . . At least the Germans had left, I was relieved to see. Since they'd skipped their usual formal farewells, I could only assume their departure coincided with Yeoryios's anti-America diatribe.

"And I ask pardon if I offend," Yeoryios was saying in a low voice. "I who am Greek should know how great is the distance between peoples and their government! It is unjust to blame a man for what his leaders do—how can he, one man, stop them? They do what they please—"

"No more!" Kostas cried. "You ask pardon, and you repeat sin at same time! Is celebration, to dig up old ghosts and fight again old wars? *Kroniá pollá*, Damian!" He clinked his glass against the bottle. "Come, Katerina, tell us how you make celebration of birthdays in your rich country!"

"We . . . have a cake, with candles." *Hang on, Kay. Don't think of that festive supper, uneaten . . . of the pile of presents, untouched . . .* "One candle for each year . . . and of course gifts."

"Is for children or for everybody?"

"For . . . everybody. Of course, for someone very old, perhaps just a few candles, as—as symbols, you know—"

"More safe," Kyriakos said gravely. "Not to burn down the house. I tell you a story, Katerina *mou*, about my grandmother. My mother's mother." He looked around the table. "Fill your glass, Yeoryio. Is long story, my grandmother had long, very long life. She had one hundred and six years when she died, and never was she sick, never in her whole life. She had eighteen children by her first husband, who was my grandfather. After he died, she married once again—she was then forty-six years of age—and she had three more children. You do not believe me? I tell you it is truth. Sometimes she did not even have the midwife—she sent for her older daughter, my mother's oldest sister, to help her. They spread a blanket in the field and she lay down and gave birth. This was in Attica, you understand, where women work in the fields."

He glanced at Yeoryios, who was shaking his head and scowling.

"When she was very old," Kyriakos went on doggedly, "my grandmother decides she wants to die. I say to her—I love her, Katerina; you know how it is possible to love someone who is far ahead of you on the road?—I say, 'Maybe for you, *yiayiá*, the rules will not hold. Maybe you will live a thousand years.' 'No, I have lived long enough,' she says, and she lay down on her bed and will not get up. They send for the doctor. In her whole life it is the first time—now, when she has her birthday for one hundred and six years of age. The doctor came and he said, 'I can do nothing for her, she is not sick.' My grandmother refused to eat, just drank a little water only. Three days later she die. Always she have the strong mind, you see. She decide to die—she die."

Kyriakos looked around the table and cleared his throat.

"This is what I want tell you, Katerina. When my father died, my grandmother send word to my mother, 'Tell my daughter now is the time for her to be strong. Tell my daughter also she will recover from this.' "

Lying here sleepless in the dark, I think of how, at Kyriakos' words, Damian turned to look at me, his eyes black pools in the lamplight. I think of his voice as he said, "You understand, friend Kay? You understand what Kyriakos wish to say?"

"Yes, I know," I told him in a low voice. "I wish I could be strong like that, Damian. I don't seem to be able to. I'm not brave, you see. So I don't think I shall recover."

I think of how I stopped, then, how I sorted my words over. "Perhaps because I had only the one son," I said.

Kyriakos nodded. "Not enough iron for an anchor," he said.

CHAPTER

15

Where is Mike?

The question sabotaged the birthday celebration. It plagued my dreams. And now it gnaws at me every moment like a fox at my vitals.

How *could* he allow himself to be delayed? Because that was nonsense, what I was thinking yesterday—Mike would never deliberately absent himself on Damian's birthday! So when he saw he wasn't going to make it, how could he let the time slip by with no explanation, no excuse? Forget the strike: the planes are still flying, aren't they? Surely he could have sent a message somehow, if he'd wanted to! It's all so unlike him!

Maybe he couldn't. Not only couldn't make it: couldn't send word, either. Maybe . . . I could ask Voula if she's heard anything. If there's been a plane crash anywhere. But if the phones are closed to Athens, how would she have any news? Radio . . . But then Kostas would have heard, wouldn't he? Not necessarily. I don't even know if Mike got to Athens. His plane could have gone down between London and Rome . . . between Rome and Glyfada . . .

Kostas couldn't have heard anything. He's off to Eressos with a carload of tourists from Petrá; I gather a substantial fee is at stake. "Always Nikos comes today," he assured me. "He will tell your husband about the bus, Katerina. No need for taxi from Mytilene." No, obviously Kostas has heard nothing . . .

Damian has gone to school even though it's Saturday, although because it's Saturday, only until one o'clock. And so I prowl the walkways and unexpected open spaces of the village, looking for something, anything, to sketch. Nothing seems worth the trouble: not the swallows cutting secret codes above the squat belfry of a church; not the donkey women (as Damian calls them) making their melodious way down the narrow lanes, their little beasts top-heavy with baskets of beets and lettuce, oranges and eggs; not even the boat propped on oil drums on a rocky beach east of the village—could that be Kyriakos busy with caulking pot and brush? Too far away to tell.

As I make my way back to Zoë's through the first spattering of rain, I find myself thinking (as if such thoughts were part of the very stones beneath my feet) of all the women who have waited for their men hour after endless hour, day after anguished day. Damian's mother, bearing her child alone. Verek, when they were "interrogating" Yeoryios. The wives and daughters of those who were returned at last from the islands . . . or who weren't. It's a wonder we women aren't all demented. A time for us to be strong . . . Perhaps. But *God* it's hard!

Mike, where the living hell are you?

Sometime before three Damian stops on his way home to see if there is any word. I'm explaining (falsely cheerful) that no, not yet there isn't, when

Nikolas Paradellis comes quickly up the outside staircase. He is astonished to find me here.

My disappointment and dismay that he is alone are so acute for a moment I feel sick. "Didn't anyone tell you?" I say brightly. "The hotel was over-booked, so your mother very kindly took me in."

"But your husband?" Nikolas looks about him, pride and embarrassment in his glance. "My mother's house is not modern, *kyría*. What does he say to this?"

"Mike's not here. I don't know what's delayed him. I was hoping"—I still manage to speak lightly, to smile—"you'd have some word, Niko."

"He's not here in Pyrgotafos?"

What's the *matter* with Nikos? Is he slow-witted? "Kostas went to Mytilene after him yesterday, but he didn't come!"

Nikos's homely face is comical in its bewilder-ment. "Please, *kyría mou*, I am sorry if I am stupid. Still I do not understand. Your husband stays in My-tilene? You have had quarrel?"

"Of course not! He's not *here*, I keep telling you—he's not here in Lesvos. He wasn't on the plane!"

"But he must be here, *kyría*! I myself drove him from hotel to airport. I waited—we were early, al-ways I think it best to be early—I have pleasant time. He is very nice man, your husband. Very friendly. We talked, then he goes out to the plane—"

"You *saw* him? You saw him get on?"

"No, naturally not. But they announce plane for Mytilene, we say good-bye, he goes out the correct gate. Where would he go but to the plane? And there is only the one, after all—he could not make mis-take!"

And there aren't any stops . . . What was that awful story I read once, years ago? It was in all the papers: something about a door blowing off, or something, just as a man was passing, and he'd been sucked into space, into nothingness. And the man's bride (he'd just been married) saying over and over, "I can't believe it, I can't believe it—" Over and over, like a—a lifeline.

If something like that had happened, Nikos would have heard.

Mike took the plane to Mytilene. Fact. Accept it, Kay. And don't break down in front of these Greeks. They've had it much worse than you for much longer. So don't break down, you hear?

Damian leaps to his feet. "Maybe my uncle Kostas back from Eressos. I go ask him. I not know *what* I ask, but I ask!"

In less than an hour (it seems longer) Damian returns. He and Yeoryios are flanking Kostas as if he's under arrest.

"Listen to my idiot of a brother!" Yeoryios roars, splashing across the courtyard with angry strides. "Listen to his story, *kyría mou,* and forgive him if you can! He is idiot! *Idiot!*"

"I, too, ask you to forgive me, Katerina," Kostas says in a troubled voice. His eyes meet mine pleadingly. "I try to do only what is best. Now I tell you everything. It is true I meet plane. So much of what I tell you is true. I say your husband is not there. Not true, Katerina. He is there—"

"You met him?"

"Yes, Katerina, yesterday, in Mytilene. But I not know what is best to do. Your husband drunk—he very very drunk. I put him in taxi, I drive to Hotel

Silver Bird. He very difficult, Katerina *mou*. I get him
to room, I lay him on bed. I think maybe he will—
how you say?—get more himself—"

"But he never drinks! Not like that, anyway!"

"—be more himself in time for birthday," Kostas
goes on doggedly. "I think we can tell some story—
he takes wrong taxi from Mytilene, blah-blah-blah so
you not know—"

"Idiot!" Yeoryios roars again. "What is five drops
too much wine? Is this a sin, a crime, that you must
lie to *kyría* Cunningham, who is his *wife*—you think
wife believes husband is a saint? Wife is fool? So you
cut her into small pieces with worry—you make her
to be broken into small bits"—Yeoryios makes crumbling motions in the air—"and eaten up with fear!"

"But where is he *now?*"

"At hotel, of course, *kyría*," Kostas says with
dignity.

" 'Of course'?" Nikos echoes. "So why does he
not come to birthday feast?"

"He sleeps. I cannot wake him. I go for to get him
and I find he sleeps and sleeps. Not pretty to see—I
not want you to see him like that, Katerina. I not want
Damian to see."

My God, I think, my heart sinking, what can Mike
be thinking of *me* now? Because of course he must
be fully himself. Hung over, maybe, but certainly lu-
cid, and wondering where on earth *I* am. At least I
hope he's wondering. I hope he wants to know. And
that dear Voula will be too tactful ("—not my business—") to say I've gone off with Lady Killer Kostas
. . .

"You do *kyría* Cunningham one more favor," Nikos says sharply. "You drive her to Silver Bird. I

come, too. I want make sure you make no more plots to keep in repair her marriage!"

"Believe me, Katerina," Kostas says in a low, intense voice, "I am sorry if I make you to worry. I want only what is best for you. I not want your husband, American father of Damian, to make big fool of himself before whole village!"

"I'm sure you did what you thought best, Kostas," I say coldly. Need he use a sledgehammer to drive home his point? "Now I really must go and—and welcome my husband."

"I go, too," Damian says.

Oh, no! Mike would hate it if Damian were to see him now! I say hastily, "No, I think it would be much better if you go home with your uncle Yeoryios."

His eyes are smoky. "I go with you." Firmly. *"Friend* Kay."

We set out. Nikos keeps turning his head to stare at Kostas, puzzled. In the back seat with Damian, I gaze out stoically at the slanting rain. *Drunk . . . hung over . . .* I still can't believe it. Did the conferences go badly, and alone and despondent in a strange city, he thought what the hell, let's forget it . . . and then somehow miscalculated? But that's so unlike him! All right, then: had our quarrel—the coolness between us, our estrangement (call it what you like)—tipped the balance? And then there he was, in that unpressurized plane. High altitudes multiply the effects of alcohol, everybody knows that. He could have had a beer or two, and then got on the plane . . .

A beer or two wouldn't make him dead drunk, no matter what. It had to be hard liquor, and plenty of it.

At ten o'clock in the morning?

Besides, Nikos saw him to the plane. Did they have anything to drink while they waited? I'll be *damned* if I'll ask. Checking up on my own husband! God, it's so *demeaning* . . .

"When you saw my husband in Athens, had he, in your opinion, been drinking?"

Nikos turns to face me, his light gray eyes somber in his gaunt face. "Not a drop, *kyría mou.*" Formally. "I swear it."

Damian stares out the window.

Kostas well in the lead, we stalk across the lobby of the Silver Bird without bothering to check at the desk; like a posse, I think. As we troop down the hall, I wish I'd asked which room, and gone on ahead. This is no time for an audience.

Kostas knocks at 1B. After a moment, he knocks again, frowning. "Maybe he still sleeps, Katerina."

Nikos says, "You are certain this is the room?"

Kostas glares at him.

"Try the door," I say in a low voice.

It appears to be locked. Kostas shakes the door handle. I lean close to the plastic paneling and say, medium volume: "Hey, Mike, it's Kay . . ."

Nothing. Not a sound.

We straggle back to the lobby, where Kostas plants himself in front of the desk. "*Kýrios* Cunningham is not in his room? Not in hotel? Goes for walk? Goes for swim?"

Voula shrugs. "I do not know." Indifferently. "I do not think I see him today." She glances at me curiously.

My God! I think in panic, perhaps he is really ill! Isn't there some dreadful disease—something very dangerous, even fatal at times—whose symptoms can be mistaken for drunkenness? Diabetic coma—that's it! Except that Mike isn't diabetic. What about concussion? A blow on the head can cause slurred speech and an unsteady gait. Drowsiness, too. Maybe somebody tried to mug him, and he, all unaware of the extent of his injury, not remembering anything, simply went out to take the plane. But Nikos would have noticed . . . if I can believe what he says.

"In any case, I'm moving in with my husband," I tell Voula. "May I have the key, please?"

She glances at the row of cubicles behind her. Several contain chunks of metal the size of a tennis ball, each with key attached. 1B is empty. "If he is not in his room then he must be out, madam, for he has taken the key with him."

I point out that it's raining—it's been raining all afternoon. "Perhaps he is not out," I say coldly. "Perhaps he is ill. Surely you have another key?"

Nikos says impatiently, "Voula, stop making difficulties and send for the housekeeper!"

The elderly housekeeper, entirely in black even to her apron, speaks no English and possibly not even Greek, for she addresses not a word to anyone. She produces a formidable ring of keys, selects one, and unlocks the door. Smiling apologetically, she steps back, and Kostas flings open the door.

The room is empty, the bed ominously smooth.

What is it about hotel rooms that makes them instantly depressing? Their very inoffensiveness, I suppose; their overwhelming neutrality. Pictures you can't recall later, curtains you don't notice even when you're looking at them, chairs that fit no one . . .

Mike has never been here. No one real has ever been here.

I open the wardrobe door. There is Mike's suitcase on the floor. I stoop and touch it: it's real, at any rate. And still locked.

"Well," I say, "at least you got him this far, Kostas."

I'm not sure what, if anything, I mean by this. I'm taken aback when Kostas bursts out passionately, "You think I still lie to you? Because I want protect you, Katerina, now I have not your trust? I swear, I *swear* from this moment I tell you only the truth! Here to this room I bring your husband—"

"The key! I find the key!" Damian shouts from the bathroom. "On the shelf! He leave it on the shelf!" Emerging, he gives the outlandish chunk of metal an exultant twirl about his head.

Confiscating this potential missile, Nikos puts a question to the housekeeper, who answers at some length.

Kostas interrupts brusquely. "You, Niko, translate for Katerina, yes? Then she will see if I tell truth or no!"

"The woman says the American gentleman was intoxicated when he arrived yesterday afternoon," Nikos relays impassively. "She does not see him except that one time, when he first arrive." The housekeeper is backing out the door, still smiling apologetically. "She goes for chambermaid. Perhaps chambermaid saw *tón kýrio* Cunningham this morning. She may know how he feels."

But the chambermaid, a painfully thin child who can't be over fourteen, is no help at all.

"She say she not see no one this morning."
Damian clearly relishes his turn as translator. "She
say she come to this room at nine o'clock, to make
neat the bed. Nothing to do, bed nice and neat." Here
the chambermaid sends an uneasy glance at the
housekeeper, who frowns. "Maid say she not notice
anything strange about the room. Any sign someone
has been sick? uncle Nikos asks. What sort of sign,
please, sir? A smell of—I not know word—"

"Vomit," says Nikos impassively.

"Is no need translate every breath!" Kostas roars.
"Stupid girl say she see nothing, no sign *o kýrios* is
sick—"

"No one falling down drunk," Damian says with
gusto. "No, she say, nothing like that, sir. Room is
very *íremo*—"

"Serene," Nikos says. "Bed not slept in."

Again Kostas bursts out angrily, this time in
Greek.

"My uncle Kostas say that not true, that is dirty
sinful lie." Damian is as unflappable as a U.N. interpreter. "He say he put your husband on that bed with
his own hands."

"Did you open the bed?" Nikos sticks to English,
to speed matters up, perhaps, or perhaps out of
courtesy to me.

"No, naturally not—I am very busy! *Kýrios* Cunningham wants go out, wants salute the sea. 'The sea
the sea the beautiful sea,' he says, like priest in
church."

Nikos puts a question to the now thoroughly
frightened chambermaid, who answers in a breath-
less rush.

"She says the bed was very little disturbed, *kyría mou*. She did not change the sheets, but smoothed the covers only. That is good: your husband cannot be seriously ill."

The maid and the housekeeper, suitably tipped, withdraw.

"But where *is* he?" I open the French doors and step out on the balcony, as if, insanely, I think Mike might be lurking there. The rain has stopped, and the wooden deck is beginning to dry. There is a low table and two chaise longues on which under yesterday's sunny sky Mike and I should have been lounging. By ourselves. Without Damian. *Especially* without Damian, who is now poised on the slippery railing like a gymnast. (Does he think this all a game?)

Kostas, Nikos, and I consider the railing. No more than twenty inches high, it could scarcely confine a toddler, let alone a man with little sense of balance. Some ten feet below, a flower bed has disciplined rows of some spiky blooms, not one of which appears so much as bruised. No one could have fallen here, leaving no mark, to rise and stagger off toward the water that glimmers so seductively beyond that fringe of trees . . .

We hear a door open, a woman in a scarlet bikini comes into view, and as we watch her make her sinuous way down the neatly raked path to the sea, I find myself wondering if one can get to the beach from 1B without going through the lobby.

Damian hops off the railing. "There are stairs, friend Kay. I see where they go."

I wander back inside. God, how I hate waiting! And I can't do *anything*—I can't scream, or sob, or beat my head against the wall. I have to wait, wait, *wait*. Act controlled, in full command of myself. A credit to my country. "The American never got hysterical." And all the while I don't feel in the least composed, or cool-headed. Certainly not courageous. *Damn it, Mike, where are you?* Oh, God, I'm scared . . . I'm so scared . . .

I'm standing there gaping at Mike's suitcase, at his address tag: *Michael Cunningham, Hotel Silver Bird, Molibos, Lesbos.* Readdressed in Athens, obviously. Nikos must have told him where I'd be. No, wait: I left my forwarding address with the Hotel Caledonia; they'd have told him . . . They *did* tell him, for heaven's sake! I must be losing my so-called mind. Mike phoned to the Silver Bird on Wednesday. Kostas told me Voula said he'd called . . .

"I wonder what happened to Mike's carry-on bag?" Fretfully.

Kostas smites his forehead. "Aieee! I think he leaves it on the plane, Katerina! He gets off, your husband, waving tickets, ticket for return to Athens, you understand, and also for luggages. Husband want get on plane and go back to Athens. No, I say, no, here is where you want come, mister sir, here to Molivos—"

Damian bursts into the room, his eyes shining. "Very easy to go out, friend Kay, and the lady Voula not see! Stairs down to hall below, where is rooms all along side toward sea, and at far end is one more door going into garden."

"Do not worry, Katerina," Kostas says quickly. "Your husband last night sleeps like baby. He cannot by himself get up, go down these stairs, and no one see nothing, no one hear nothing. No, do not worry!"

"So, Mr. Expert Detective, what you think did happen?" Nikos asks acidly.

"I think husband sleeps and sleeps, wakes with very sick head. Fresh clean air off the sea will clear away fog, he thinks. He goes for walk—why not?"

"It is now five o'clock of a rainy afternoon," Nikos says pointedly. "This makes one very long walk." He turns to me. "I think, *kyría mou*, we must notify the authorities."

"Yes . . . I'm afraid—I mean, I can't think of any logical explanation—" *Oh, yes, I can.* My insides knot with fear.

"No, too soon," Kostas says firmly. "First we look. Much better we, his friends, find him, Katerina. Much less talk. Give me key, *kyría mou*, I leave with this Voula. Then we look."

Mike doesn't have to be drowned. He doesn't have to have gone swimming where there are mines. He could have fallen . . . He could be anywhere along the shore. He could be resting somewhere, couldn't he?

Oh, sure.

As Voula speaks to Kostas, little puffs of smoke escape her mouth; she looks as if she's on fire. Damian edges closer to watch.

"What friend, uncle Kosta? What she means, the lady Voula—'Your friend the wine merchant must have been too generous'?"

"*Wine* merchant!" I echo, startled and incredulous.

Kostas scowls at Damian. "He is not my friend, Katerina. He is tourist who comes on plane, American tourist who wants ride to hotel. He helps me get husband into taxi. I give him ride for free, I say, if he help me get husband, quiet, no fuss, into room."

Nikos narrows his eyes. "You do not mention this tourist."

"Why I should make big story? How much trouble husband make in Mytilene, how many people watch, how much noise—"

"What did he look like, this maybe–wine merchant?" Nikos asks Voula. "It is possible I see him in Glyfada."

"Not fat, not thin. Not old, not young. How to describe a nobody?"

"I'd like to speak to him, Niko," I say. And to Voula: "Which is his room, please?"

"Mr. Sanzio is not here, madam. This morning he took the bus to Mytilene."

Sanzio! Well, of course—I expected it, didn't I? Then why this burst of adrenaline . . . this feeling of being followed? Sanzio had a perfect right to prowl around Athens, to come to Mytilene, to Molibos, whenever he pleased. It's just that that isn't the way his schedule read. Or is it?

"He does not stay long, this wine merchant." Nikos scowls.

Voula shrugs. "He has not much business here. This is only hotel for tourists in Molivos. Small cafés have Greek wine, for Greeks. No business for this Sanzio."

"This kidnapping is getting to be a growth industry . . ." No, that had been Ben What's-his-name, the nice husband from the Bronx. *"Lucky to get him back . . . usually they don't, not if they've gone to the police"*—that had been Sanzio.

"Well!" I give an explosive little laugh. "All this

fuss and no doubt my husband has just gone out to—
to explore your charming village!" I stretch my lips
in a smile. "If he comes in, please tell him I've gone
for a drive. I wouldn't want him wondering where *I*
am!" I turn the smile on Kostas; it feels glued on. "I'm
so sorry. I forgot to bring in my luggage."

Voula says politely, "If madam would sign the
register?"

I am riveted by the sloppy, almost illegible *M.
Cunningham* near the top of the page, just above a
rather ornate *Raphael Sanzio*. Surely there couldn't be
any connection between that garrulous little guy
whose bald pate had popped so unexpectedly into
view on the Parthenon—if it *had* been Sanzio—and
Mike's disappearance, could there? Because he
wouldn't be so open about who he is, would he? If
he really *is* somebody named Sanzio, that is. *Raphael
Sanzio:* it certainly sounds fake. But so does anybody's name, actually. "I'm Katharine Cunningham
. . ." Oh, yeah?

"Come, *kyría* Cunningham, we have much to
show you," Nikos says quietly. As we cross the now
nearly dry courtyard, he adds in a low voice, "We
cannot wait, *kyría*. I think we must go to the mayor.
He will know whom to call, how to get the army to
watch along the beach—"

"No, not yet," I say in a tight voice. It's as if I've
been playing Scrabble blindfolded, and somehow the
presence of Sanzio here in Molibos has made a number of the tiles fall into place, forming words whose
meaning, though I can't really see them, yet I do see
. . . "Listen, Niko, I sat with that wine merchant on
the plane to Rome. I—I think"—I draw a deep
breath—"I think my husband is kidnapped, and

somehow this wine merchant is involved. First he manages to get a seat next to me, or just happens to—either way, he finds out all about Mike and me, because there are these letters, you see. Letters from Damian, plus copies of Mike's. And I lost them. I mean I thought I lost them, but now I'm sure he took them. This fellow Sanzio stole them. Then he followed me to Athens, and he trailed you to the airport, and—and wangled a seat next to Mike, and got him drunk, and then, somehow, last night, he—he took him somewhere—"

"Please, *kyría mou*, no more of this," Niko says firmly. "You are upset, it is natural, but this is a story for the films. Only very rich men are kidnapped. Very, very rich, or very powerful. Your husband— forgive me, *kyría* Cunningham, but I have seen his letters to Damian—he is fine, good man, but he writes like simple man of simple tastes—I am right? Not rich. So we must not waste time—we must have many peoples to search the beaches, perhaps he has broken bone—"

"Nikos, *you* be sensible, please!" I think of our walk back from Petrá, of soldiers everywhere. "No one can lie on any beach on Lesvos for a whole day and not be seen! The soldiers watch everywhere all the time—maybe they're looking for Turks, but they'd never overlook Mike! No, *listen*, both of you"—for Kostas is back from his stint as bellhop—"that man, that wine merchant, knew all about Beta Beta Beta— you know, my husband's firm—and he—Sanzio, I mean—was very knowledgeable about kidnapping. He brought the subject up, and then he went out of his way to plant the idea that the f-families had damn well better not go to the police. I tell you, my husband has been kidnapped!" I am seized by another fit of shivering. "If he's drowned, there's nothing we can do to help him. But if he's k-kidnapped, there's no hurry—"

Nikos exchanges a glance with Kostas, muttering in Greek. Kostas barely nods, then turns to me, touching my arm briefly.

"Speak very soft, Katerina. Nobody must know what you fear, especially that Voula."

"I think there is law one must report a man missing," Nikos explains. "Kostas is right, *kyría mou*. Voula would go to the police fast as the wind. She would not want trouble for hotel."

Damian's back is toward us, his hands balled fists in the pockets of his shorts. He appears to have shrunk slightly, to have withdrawn into himself. It occurs to me that fear—gut-wrenching fear—is contagious. If you're on the same wavelength, that is.

"If we go to the police now," I say in an anguished whisper, "don't you see he'll—it'll be like with Damian's father—they'll panic, the kidnappers will panic, and no one will ever see or hear of Mike again!"

In my mind's eye I see the sapphire waters sparkling about *Pouláki Mou* as we round the point at Molibos—three miles of sun-dappled, treacherous currents, and bodies washing up on the Turkish shore . . .

"Yes," Kostas nods, "that is true. If your husband dead, is no hurry. If he kidnapped, we must each time put foot down very, very careful—"

"I think, *kyría* Katerina," Nikos says slowly, scowling at Kostas, "you must have this chance. You would not forgive us otherwise."

CHAPTER

16

For one brief, bewildered moment I can't think where I am. Acoustical-tiled ceiling . . . angled chair upholstered in orange linen . . . fishnet curtains filtering the early morning light . . . Still half asleep, I turn to see if Mike's awake—and there's no one there, of course. But here he *has* been, not thirty-six hours ago, his head on that very pillow.

Where is he now?

For the dozenth time I sort over the possibilities. He went for a walk to clear his head, and somehow slipped, and fell, and now lies out of sight of passers-by, so badly hurt he can't even call for help. He did go down for a swim, after all. Late Friday night or early yesterday morning he went swimming on one of those stretches where the mines are—he wouldn't know about the mines; how could he?—and he set one off, and now he's lying there as broken as David . . .

Surely the army would hear any detonation, and surely they would go to check, and the news would sweep through the villages. Would I have heard? Yes, of course: Melita works for the mayor; the mayor would be told; Melita would tell me. For once no news really is good news, Kay: Mike has not—repeat *not*—blown himself up on a mine.

But if he did go swimming, by himself and in the dark, he could have lost his footing, couldn't he? He could have struck his head, and the tide—even Damian's little, little tide—would be enough, if a man was unconscious . . . Or perhaps he swam too far out, and was caught in those currents Damian keeps warning me about. This very moment Mike may be no more than driftwood in the channel, his hair flaxen seaweed, his flesh nibbled by *barboúni*, the crabs picking his eyes . . .

I slide my hand over the empty sheet and I think: *this is how it feels to be widowed.* No one else in the room, in the bed. Just you, Kay. And silence: now, and tonight, and tomorrow, and forever, right to your life's end. *Oh, God! Oh God oh God . . .*

Perhaps I'm not widowed. Perhaps what Nikos dismisses as "a tale for the films" has really happened, and right this moment Mike is at the mercy of some brutal gang of kidnappers. He's confined: manacled: bound in chains: locked in a closet too small to stand up in, too small to lie down in. He's shut up in a chest of some sort . . . like that cedarwood chest at Zoë's. They'd have to gag him, of course. Tie him up so he can't move.

And if I go to the police, the police will turn out the army, with their bouzouki walkie-talkies and their trucks with hallooing, waving soldiers, and the gang will kill him. Strangle him, drop him in the sea, and everybody will say he drowned while swimming. No, they'd drown him first, so the autopsy would be okay. You can be drowned in a basin of water; you wouldn't even struggle, if you were drunk enough, or drugged—

Drugged! Of course! Of *course* Mike hadn't been drunk! That wine salesman drugged Mike, and Kostas couldn't tell the difference!

I'm out of bed like a shot. If Mike is—was—drugged, it changes the focus, all right, though just how, I'm not sure. At least he isn't lying injured anywhere nearby: I know that much. We—Nikos, Kostas, Damian, and I—spent the remaining light last evening combing the area around the hotel: the gardens, the beach, the road toward Petrá, the road toward Molibos. To keep from arousing curiosity in any onlooker, we'd hiked about as if we were exercise freaks, I chattering like the most dim-brained tourist: "Is that an olive orchard? Oh, *do* let's explore it!" Sickening . . . And now that it's daylight, Kyriakos will be searching along the coast; Kostas promised to alert him. So I can forget the likely places and concentrate on spotting the unlikely ones, and looking there.

Five past six: no one at the desk. A thickset man in a shabby seaman's jacket is hosing down the steps to the drive; otherwise I see no sign of life about the hotel.

I take the road that turns inland, towards Vafios. The farmers are already at work. *"Kaliméra,"* says one with guarded courtesy as he opens the flaps of his plastic greenhouse. I cast about for a way to get a look inside. Of course—my camera! With the apologetic smile of the dedicated shutterbug, I take two shots of the clusters of tomatoes still as green as the leaves shading them. A swift glance down the rows reveals no sign of Mike. Naturally not: did I think the farmer would fail to notice a six-foot stranger bound and gagged beneath the potting bench? And that heap of soil in the bin isn't capacious enough to conceal a body.

Make up your mind, Kay: are you looking to find Mike alive or dead? If you're convinced he's dead you might as well cut the comedy and head straight for the mayor or the police or whoever's in charge here. Only if Mike's alive does this playacting make the slightest sense . . .

I spot a watering trough in a field, with a pump propped against it. The trough looks large enough for two, maybe three bodies. Clambering across the ditch, I scramble up the slope to take an "artistic" shot (in case anybody's looking). Then, elaborately casual, I tip up the wooden cover and peer in.

Nothing. Bone-dry, and except for a drift of dead leaves, absolutely empty.

The road dips to cross a dry streambed, and from here on there are only rocks and yellow sand, in which nothing grows but scattered clumps of thistle and now and then a cactus. If Mike came this far (and it's absurd to suppose he did) he'd be conspicuously *here* somewhere. He'd be plainly visible, for in all this barren waste there's no place for a man to hide—or be hidden.

A faint clamor of church bells sifts across the vacant air. I decide it's a signal to turn back. In the silence and the solitude of retracing my steps, I can't help but ponder my behavior. Am I more than slightly demented, that I should concoct this scenario of violence and crime to explain Mike's disappearance, and then, despite the fact that there's no one in sight, obsessively keep up my pose of casual tourist on an innocent stroll? No, I'm not demented. *I'm just not going to fail Mike as I failed David.* I'm not going to assume that because he's *my* husband, nothing can happen to him. Nor am I going to panic, so that everyone from Petrá to Pyrgotafos knows I think Mike may be kidnapped.

As I round the last turn before the sign for the Silver Bird, it occurs to me suddenly that I don't even know where Sanzio was Friday night; that is, I don't know where his room was in relation to Mike's. (Ours . . . mine.) Voula would know. How to get it out of her without fanning her curiosity?

A tour bus mutters impatiently at the end of the drive, and the lobby is aswarm with elderly women, sun-visored and camera-slung. Voula is calling the roll. "One-B—certainly, madam." Scarcely lifting her eyes from the roster before her, she scoops out the contents of my box. I collect my key—and an envelope, an ordinary white envelope neither particularly clean nor, for that matter, particularly dirty; it has the look of a letter that has spent some time in a jacket pocket, and it is addressed to Mrs. Michael Cunningham in Mike's handwriting.

I balance it in my hand: it seems curiously weightless. There's no stamp, no postmark on either side: it must have been hand-delivered. By whom? Mike himself? He wouldn't—my God!—play with me like this, would he?

Of course not, Kay. Don't be daft.

Then where is he? What's happened to him?

I cut through the flock of twittering gray-heads and as soon as I'm out of sight around the corner I rip open the envelope, my fingers like ice.

Dear Kay:

As no doubt you've noticed, I've been kidnapped. Show this to no one. Tell no one. They want $100,000—in drachmas, not dollars. When you have it they'll tell you where to leave it.

It isn't even signed. Didn't they give him time? Maybe he couldn't think how . . . maybe nothing seemed right. My eyes burn with sudden, unshed tears. Damn it, did *Love, Mike* strike him as too personal, too much of a commitment?

Voices on the stairway. *Pull yourself together, Kay, you hear?* Two latecomers, giggling like schoolgirls, hurry past. *No one, but no one, must suspect there's anything wrong.* I force myself to walk, not run, for the safety of my room.

The little chambermaid is making up the bed. Flustered, she tries to gather up her equipment and vanish.

"Wait, *parakalō*—uh, *kaliméra*"—I thumb through my traveler's phrase book for something—anything—that will convey what I want to know: which room did the "friend" of my husband have on Friday night? I find the phrase for *where is,* I find *husband*—thank God the Greek is given phonetically—but there's nothing for *friend* or (strange oversight) *room*. The intensity of my anxiety for Mike's safety must have sharpened my mental faculties, for suddenly I recall the rate notice posted behind the door, and there it is: *room—domátio.* And how about *philosophy* and *Philadelphia*—I know the "filly" part means *love,* but couldn't it stretch to mean *friend,* too?

I toss these Greek words together like a salad, and

my dear little chambermaid watches me with eager sympathy, and never laughs, bless her. And then her face lights up, and repeating *neh! neh! neh!*, she points at the floor. Unless I mistake her meaning entirely, Raphael Sanzio had the room below. But are we talking about the same man? Swiftly I sketch a round face, a few strands of hair carefully placed. She laughs, nods, and combing across her hair with her fingers, goes into her *neh!* routine again.

I thank the child and tip her, and she slips from the room, leaving me to brood over how little I've really learned. So Sanzio spent Friday night in the room below: so what? All that signifies is that no one else—no stranger, I mean—may have had as good a chance to overhear whatever was happening in this room. If Sanzio himself wasn't up here lending a hand, that is. Or bossing the job . . . Because of course he's in this right up to his bald pate—he *must* be! How far can you stretch coincidence?

I read and reread Mike's note. I don't for a moment doubt it's from him, though the handwriting, cramped and shaky, is nothing like his usual fluent scrawl. *"And why were you so sure, kyría, it was from your husband, if, as you say, the handwriting differed from normal?"* *"Well, because of the wording."* "As no doubt you've noticed . . ." Who else but Mike would use such a phrase in such a message? Tongue-in-cheek humor, a pinch of bravado, more than a little bitterness: it could only be Mike.

My God, I'm so scared! Because it's up to me. To me alone. Even if Mike didn't warn me, I'd never go to the police. That would be signing his death warrant. "They want $100,000—" We don't *have* a hundred thousand dollars—he knows that! Lying around handy, that is. If I were home, I suppose I could raise it somehow, given time. Borrow on his life insurance, or something. No, I guess only Mike can do that. But I'm *not* home. And there *isn't* time. Every day, every hour, God *knows* what's happening to him! Do they feed him? Bring him water? Oh, God . . . *Mike* . . .

Hold it! Don't push the panic button, Kay. Hang on, hang on. Time enough to self-destruct when he's safe.

I go over the note once more. Damn it, it says so much, yet so little! Why didn't he give me a clue how to raise the money? Or doesn't he have any idea either? Maybe they didn't give him a chance, just snatched the note before he had time to sign it and rushed it to the hotel—

Who did?

That, Kay, is the jackpot question.

It had to be somebody who knows where I am, obviously. And they wouldn't just hand it to Voula; they'd have to know which room (i.e., which box) is mine. Or have savvy enough to look in the register. (Except that I don't remember seeing that out when Voula's not on duty.) No, wait—all they had to do was leave it at the desk; she would put it in my box later. Which means it could be anybody. Anybody at all.

The elderly tourists have been shepherded outside and Voula is enjoying a peaceful cigarette. Casually, I display the envelope. What time did my husband leave this, does she know?

Voula is sorry, she has not seen *kýrion* Cunningham this morning. When she came on duty at seven, the envelope was already in the box. Then: "Your husband is not staying, madam? You would prefer, perhaps, a single room?"

"The one I have is quite satisfactory." Dismissively.

Confound it, for all she knows Mike could have been with me last night, couldn't he?

In the deserted dining room, I order toast and coffee. It seems heartless to eat, but starving won't help Mike, wherever he is . . . In another room in this hotel? Highly unlikely. In any one of the various houses in Pyrgotafos? Possible, I suppose. In the hold of one of those fishing boats? In a farmer's shed? In a back room of one of the shops in Molibos or Petrá? Behind the altar screen in that church on the hill? (Oh, come *off* it, Kay!) How about in one of those many, many little memorial chapels?

The multiplicity of places where it's conceivable Mike might be overwhelms me. I'm trailing honey over my last piece of toast and trying to pull my forces together when *of course!* I think—of course he couldn't tell me where to get the ransom money! Anything he said would have tipped them off we're not rich, and they'd deep-six the whole project, and him with it, as not worth the risk . . .

Kostas is crossing the lobby. "Katerina!" He takes my hands in his. "Cold, cold! No good to freeze in fancy hotel! I bring you message from Zoë. She wants you should spend the day with her. Also Verek wants you should make visit. Come, I take you now for ride in taxi. They both in church until ten o'clock, you have time for to choose."

"And Damian?"

"He in church, too, Katerina. Nikos take him every Sunday. Is duty of *koumbáros* when father dead."

As I leave my key, I catch the expression of lively interest on Voula's face. Perhaps I'd be well advised to play the role of Deserted Wife. (Voluntarily deserted, that is.) Embarrassment, grief, anger—whatever a woman treated as a piece of left luggage is likely to feel. I give Voula a so-he-left-me-see-if-I-care smile and tell her sweetly, "Should my husband come in again, just say 'no message.' "

Kostas slides behind the wheel. "What you mean, Katerina, 'comes in again'? You have seen your husband?"

"There was a note in my box, and—uh—and"— *tell no one, show this to no one*—"and I'm letting Voula think it's from Mike," I stammer. "You know, to keep her from suspecting anything."

"It is not from your husband?"

Trust no one—is that what Mike meant? I feel as if I'm walking over a bog, the ground quaking beneath my feet, and no way to know which step will send me plunging in over my head.

"The Germans are inviting me to go to Eressos with them tomorrow." Smooth as a polished pebble, the lie rolls out.

Kostas glances at me in surprise. "To Eressos? Not Argala?"

"Yes—yes, you're right. Argala—that's what they said."

I hope I'm better at acting than I am at lying.

The coast road toward Pyrgotafos winds east and south, into the sun. I'm fumbling for my dark glasses when Kostas sends a troubled glance at my face and says tenderly, "You are very sad, Katerina *mou?* You need woman to talk to? Not just Greek woman who can only smile, but maybe English, who can share your heart? You want we go to Petrá and see this Mrs. Meade?"

In spite of her incisive tongue, her abrasive manner, perhaps I would find her company a comfort. No, on second thought, *not* Clementine Meade. She'd take one schoolma'am look at my face and demand, "*Now* what's the matter?"

"I don't dare, Kostas. It'd be just like me to blurt out all about it, and the English are very law-abiding, you know. If Mrs. Meade knew I think Mike's been kidnapped, she might feel obliged to report it. I don't say she would, but I don't know she wouldn't, no matter how I tried to dissuade her."

"You are right—she go always her own road." He indicates the binoculars on the dashboard. "Kyriakos lend for us. He fix boat, cannot look along shores today."

And here I'd thought . . . I should have looked myself, earlier. "What's wrong with *Pouláki Mou?*"

"Lets in water. Is old, old boat with many holes."

I pick up the binoculars and καρποι leaps into view, and then the rocks, and the water beyond. "From the top of the tower we could see almost all the coast from Pyrgotafos to Molivos, couldn't we?"

"You want I go up and look, Katerina? Too steep for ladies, the tower. Good only for goats. You wait below, hokay?"

"Nonsense, Kostas! Damian took me up on Friday, remember. And if you think I can sit and do nothing—well, I can't!"

Kostas sighs. "Is very hard, the waiting. Almost

more hard than the knowing." He looks at me appraisingly, then nods. "Yes, you are right. Very good you should climb the tower, know for sure everything is hokay from there. Only be careful, Katerina *mou*, and not to fall. If you fall and are hurt, I kill myself." And he laughs, I suppose to show he's joking.

We start up. The climb proves easier than it did with Damian; although Kostas goes first, he lets me set a slower pace, and where the trail is steepest, he turns to offer me a hand.

"You are true mountain climber, Katerina!" he says warmly. "Also as brave as you are beautiful! Your husband is lucky, lucky man, I hope I get chance to tell him."

I save my breath for the scramble up the last few feet.

Once at the top, I bring the glasses into careful focus on the shore toward Molibos. Slowly, slowly I trace the edge of the sea down past the stretch with the ΚΑΡΠΟΙ signs, past where Damian and I floated in the buoyant water at the mouth of the stream from the tower's spring, past Voufounos' cheese factory and the patches of land devoted to cabbages and cauliflower, until finally all I can see is a scattering of masts behind the roofs of Pyrgotafos, the gulls sunning themselves on the tiles. In all that distance there is nothing whatsoever that warrants a closer look. God knows I don't want to see Mike sprawled somewhere, badly hurt or worse, yet not to see anything is singularly disquieting.

"The water is like glass . . ." My voice breaks.

"Katerina *mou*," Kostas says gently, "you want

to weep, I have good shoulder for catching ladies' tears."

"Oh . . . no, thank you. Once started, I might not stop." I manage a smile. "I'd soak that handsome shirt of yours. Here—you look, Kosta. Just to check." And I move back against the crenel where Damian perched—was it only two days ago? *"We wait and wait, but my father does not come."* Were his words an omen?

In the quiet I can hear the stream muttering past the rocks, the waves whispering along the shore, and from the barren fields to the north, the occasional comment of a sheep's bell. And then once again I hear from somewhere below us—from somewhere *in* the tower, I swear it!—a sound so faint it is more as if I've sensed it than heard it.

"What's that?"

But I know what it is: it's another pebble falling, as that one fell when Damian sent it skidding under the vine.

"Is what, Katerina?"

"I thought I heard something—a little noise in that passage—you know, the one the children fell down . . ."

"A rat, without doubt." He strolls over and lifts the vine to peer down. "Do not worry, Katerina. He will not come into the sunlight." He tosses a fragment of rock down the shaft. I hear it strike the side; then, after a scant second or so, there is a faint *tunk!*, followed almost at once by a barely audible splash.

"That's it! That's what I heard! Something fell into the spring—it must have struck that stone shelf where the sentry stood . . ." *And where the children died.* That projection is a demon, a malevolent stone demon crouched in wait, fangs bared, hungry for prey . . . "Did anyone look in there?"

"Last night, Katerina, I look. I find nothing. You want I should look again? Maybe I go down inside, like defender of Pyrgotafos, make very sure husband is not caught?"

I get a quick picture of Mike's body stoppering the passage like a dropped cork. Is Kostas kidding? "Of course Mike isn't in the tunnel!" I say almost crossly. "Your stone would never have fallen straight through, so don't go risking your neck!"

Showing off . . . "Uncle Kostas likes danger, likes to take risks." Though maybe the climb down isn't all that tricky, if you take your time. Still, that may be why I haven't been frank with him about Mike's note. Perhaps I don't trust him not to try to play the hero. It would be just like Kostas to pull some damnfool stunt that would blast whatever chance Mike may have . . . a conclusion Kostas promptly reinforces.

"For you, Katerina, I risk everything! For you I gamble my life!" His voice is ardent, his eyes laughing; I'm not sure if he intends this as a declaration of undying devotion or as gallant if ill-timed banter. I opt for the latter.

"Thanks, but no thanks. Look, there's Melita!" I point to the coast road. "She's running—is she late? I didn't know she works Sundays, too."

Kostas shrugs. "Mayor must eat every day. Most times I take her in taxi. Today more important I help my poor Katerina."

I'm really vexed. "For heaven's sake, we could have given her a lift! What must Zoë think—and after all her hospitality, too! Besides, Melita likes you, you know. I saw her watching you Wednesday night. You mustn't be unkind."

"More kind not be too kind, Katerina," he says soberly. "She has no dowry. A woman has no dowry, she must be very, very beautiful." Then, deliberately: "Any man would marry you, even if you have nothing."

This I choose to ignore. As we start down the zigzag trail, Kostas in the lead, I remark impersonally, "I thought what the wife brings to the marriage remains hers, that it's a kind of social security—if he abuses her, she's not trapped."

"That is true. But the man can use the dowry, Katerina. She brings land, he can plant it. She brings house, they can live in it. She brings furniture, he can maybe rent house." We negotiate the steepest turn. "Maybe he even let her have the money." He turns to laugh at me over his shoulder, and, *my God, he is beautiful,* I think. (The artist in me thinks.) "Dowry is big help for young people—no waiting for father to die. Also helps get not-so-pretty girl a husband." Easier now: we're nearly down. "My friend Nikos is poor man, he must work and save for to find husband for each sister before he can think to look for wife. Now I hear there is new law, no man can demand dowry before marriage. For Niko this is no help. He has his honor, and honor, Katerina *mou,* is worse tyrant than any law."

We clamber over the fallen rocks, circle the bamboo thicket, and then at my insistence, Kostas goes down to check the spring.

"All hokay." He takes my hands in his, as if to

warm them. "Water very still, not deep—I see for sure no husband in there. This is truth, Katerina. All I say to you since yesterday, since I make vow no more lying, everything is truth. *Everything*, Katerina. Every word."

CHAPTER

17

"Why should my mother build a fire in her oven for one dish only when the baker has space in his?" Nikos lights yet another cigarette. "Many women in the village leave food to be cooked as they go to church, and bring it home afterwards ready for the table." He smiles, shrugs. "Americans not the only ones efficient."

Kostas had let me out at the Paradellis gate just as Despina came up the lane bringing the *moussaka* wrapped in a cloth to keep it hot.

"That's more than efficient, Niko. It's—it's civilized." I'm shaken to find myself close to tears. Over what—Niko's words, the sane and decent communal life they describe? Or am I moved by envy, a yearning for the *óli mazí*—the all-together—in which my life, God knows, has been conspicuously lacking?

Nikos gives me a searching look. "Come, we sit on the terrace, we do nothing, like birds in the noonday heat. It is very good to sit and talk while others work—makes a man feel rich and powerful, like a king." He puts glasses and a bottle of wine on the small wooden table, offers me one of the rush-bottomed chairs as if it were carved and gilded, and pours the wine. "So we have our own private *kafeneîon.*" He seats himself across from me, then leans forward to add softly, "I have no news, *kyría.* The phones still strike. Melita says there is no talk at the mayor's of accidents. My mother and my sisters know you are very worried over your husband's absence, that it is not a matter of a quarrel, as you pretend. But do not fear, they say nothing."

"Verek must know, too. Kostas tells me she wanted me—or at any rate she invited me—to s-spend the day with her." Why the *hell* must my voice shake so? Because I'm terrified, that's why. I'm scared to death. *Well, ain't that a shame? Pull yourself together, dammit! Quit thinking of yourself. Think about Mike.*

If I think about Mike I will fragment, right here and now.

"She will not talk either, that Verek," Nikos remarks.

"I know . . . Oh, and we went up in the tower to search the beaches—Kostas had Kyriako's binoculars."

"Very good. All those working in the fields see you. That is excellent." He stubs out his cigarette. "Whole village will think you do not know if husband drowned or run away." He smiles without humor. "Greeks think no one but Greeks capable of deception . . . Greeks or Turks."

How sad his eyes are . . . I wonder if I can trust him, if I ought to tell him about the ransom note. Why Nikos and not Kostas? Didn't someone say he's a Communist? In which case he'd be all for kidnapping a rich man, wouldn't he? No: Kostas said Nikos is "maybe atheist." Then how come he's Damian's godfather?

"Tell me, *kyría mou*, this ring you wear on your left hand—it is your wedding ring?"

"Yes, of course." I regard the plain circlet in surprise. What else could it be?

"When you became betrothed you wore it on your right hand?"

What is all this, verbal therapy? Evasive action? Throw up a bulwark of words, and hide behind them . . . "No, that's not our custom," I say cooperatively. "We have what we call an engagement ring. It's worn on the same finger"—I study the wide gold band Mike gave me—"until the wedding day. I didn't have this other ring because once Mike decided we'd get married, we just went ahead and got married. He's very good at putting across an idea . . ."

Mike is: *Mike is.* Hang on to that, Kay. He *is*, he still *is*.

"We Greeks are a frugal people. We use same ring as for betrothal. First, about-to-be-bride wears this on left hand; then, when she marries, it goes on right hand." Nikos lights another cigarette. "Very strange about customs. Very different from one country to another."

"Yes, I've noticed that." I toy with my glass; the wine is the color of the tile roofs below, a soft, pale russet. "I am alone here—a stranger in your country—but oddly enough I don't feel alone in my trouble. Mike's disappearance somehow seems to be the concern of the whole village."

"But of course! You are not stranger here, *kyría*

mou, you are guest! In Greek we use same word for both: *ksénos*. In your country you feel no duty to help those from far away?"

"No more than we do our neighbors, anyway." I think this over. "Maybe not quite as much, as a matter of fact. After all, visitors go, but neighbors stay. One has to face them."

"When your son died and all came to comfort you—you think they did this only because they would have felt shame not to come?"

On the sunlit water a motorboat slides silently toward Molibos, its sound drowned by the radio next door. "I . . . I let it be known that I—that I wanted to be left alone. No one came."

". . . *Keep them away, Mike! I won't see anybody! I can't do it! They don't want to come, anyway—they dread it—do them a favor and tell them to stay away* . . ."

"Here we would know better," Nikos says gently. "In Greece, *kyría mou*, only the dead are alone with their sorrows. Perhaps it is because we are a sunken country—"

"Sunken?" I say dully.

"Submerged." He draws at his cigarette. "That is better word? We are a submerged country. We live on the tops of the mountains that are above the water, and are separated and divided by the water and the mountains, and this makes each person important, you understand? Here your grief would be of great concern. You could not hide in your house and let your loss consume you."

"Pyrgotafos is a very small village where everyone knows everyone else," I say defensively. "I imagine it would be different in Athens."

"Athens is not Greece, *kyría*. Athens is an infection, a boil! There the sun is poisoned. Pollution! No one does it as well as we Greeks—in this as in everything we excel! Where once Athena stood guard in the violet air, now she cannot see her city. I live there only because I must, because here there is no way to provide for my mother and my sisters. I am not fisherman like Kyriako, one taxi is enough for Molivos— what can I do?" His voice is bitter. "*Kseniteiá*—it is a common fate for us Greeks. Means loss of a man's native soil. We are ever journeying, looking for our chance." He studies the tip of his cigarette. "I tell you, *kyría*, if I could not come home at the end of each week out of that thickened smear to this clear bright light—we Greeks live by our light—I should give way to madness."

We are both surprised when I put my hand on his arm. "You smoke too much," I say impulsively. "It can't be good for you."

He looks at me with burning eyes. They are an unexpected light gray—which wave of invaders from the north is responsible? "You do not have the right, *kyría* Cunningham, to worry about my health," he says coldly. But he does not move his arm, and after a moment I withdraw my hand.

"If it is true that civilization consists of man withdrawing from nature"—I attempt a smile—"you can console yourself that Athens is fast becoming the most civilized city in the world!"

For a long moment his anger smolders. Then, abruptly, he drops his cigarette on the concrete floor and rubs it out with his shoe. "You are right, I smoke too much. Also I cannot afford it. Tell me, *kyría*, is it true, as Kostas says, that you do not want Damian to go to America?"

— 213 —

"Not quite. What I don't want"—I choose my words with care—"is for Damian to come and live with my husband and me. When my son was . . . killed . . . last year, it was while I was working. For me the house is full of him still. I could not bear to see anyone else—another child—in his place at the table . . ."

It sounds so ungenerous, so twisted in on myself. Only another woman could understand—another woman whose child is dead through her own fault. How many such women can there be? Surely not many, the whole globe around. I am set apart: a monstrosity, an aberration of the species.

"Tell me, then, why you came."

"To Greece?"

"To Mytilene. To see Damian."

"Because my husband insisted. I knew he was—*is*—seriously considering adoption." Carefully, I sip the wine. "I cannot have more children, you see, and my husband . . . misses our son very much. He needs a son—son or daughter—" *I will not weep. I will not.*

"You love him." Not a question: a statement of fact.

"Yes . . ."

Nikos is making notches with his thumbnail along the edge of the table. He does not look at me. "Tell me about your work."

"It's not really work, Niko. I mean, I don't have any set hours—I can do it whenever I like. I have a room at the back of the house where there's a good north light. I make drawings—paintings, sometimes—to illustrate children's books. You know, the pictures—"

"I know this word," he says with dignity. "You

were there, as you say 'making illustrations,' when this accident occurs?"

"Yes, I was there, in the house." I speak as if he were a police officer, or a judge. As if he has a right to ask, and I no choice but to answer. "My son was killed right there—right in front of the house—while I was d-daubing away—"

"While you were at work to interest and amuse the children—possibly to teach them, these other children: that is your grief also? You feel at fault because you were doing for other children when your own son was in danger?"

"You're too generous. I was doing it mostly for me. We don't need the money—not really—and it doesn't bring in all that much, anyway. I was doing it because I wanted to paint, and it was one way I could do both—be both painter and wife, I mean. Painter, wife, and mother. And now I've failed at each. But the worst—believe me, Niko—the very worst to fail at is the last, is mother."

"And all my life I want to be a poet," Nikos says with quiet intensity. "But like you I ask myself: have I enough gift? Would it be wiser to risk nothing, do only what everyone tells me is my duty, and in this way make no one angry and no one to laugh? And I, too, say *ókhi!*—no!—and I link arms with myself. Like you, I must do what it is in me to do—no one owns my life! So days I work in the Sarris Travel, and all other times I write." He smiles wryly. "Even now: even now I write. I look at you, I listen to you, I think about you and your husband and your son and your work and your grief and I write a poem—what else? I shall call it *Vásana*—I think in English is 'Tribulations'—"

"Niko," I say, "I heard from my husband today. It is true—he is kidnapped! He really is!"

Nikos stares at me. Glancing about the empty terrace as if we might be overheard, "How did you hear?" he mutters. His expression is as guarded as if we were conspirators.

"There was a note from him in my box at the hotel. Voula says it was there before she came on duty at seven."

"You are certain it is from your husband?"

"Positive." I reach for my bag and take out Mike's note. "I'll read it to you—it's hard to make out, his writing is messier than usual."

"That would be natural, if he has been bound."

"Yes, I thought of that." My mouth is dry. " 'Dear Kay: As you may have noticed, I've been kidnapped—' "

Nikos smothers an exclamation. Then: "Forgive me, *kyría mou,* he says that? 'As you may have noticed—'?" Incredulously.

"That's one reason I know it's from Mike. He's trying to be funny, you see, so I won't worry so much. That's—that's the way he is." Was. Used to be, before David. "He goes on: 'Show this to no one, tell no one.' Then . . . then he says how much they want, and he'll let me know later where to put it . . ."

"But you tell me."

"I have to, Niko. I have to trust you, because"— *of course!*—"I have a favor to ask. You're the only one who can do it."

"Ask," Nikos says simply.

"You go back to Athens tomorrow, don't you? Will you please, *please* somehow get in touch with Mr.

Bingham—that's my husband's employer—I've got his address, his cable address as well—it's s-silly, really—*Bilcun, New York*—" Mike made jokes about that, too, I remember, my eyes stinging; rather impudent jokes. "Tell him what a—a mess we're in, and ask him to lend me the money. He needn't worry, I'll pay him back."

"This Bingham, you say he is boss? Your husband does not own the Beta Beta Beta?"

"Good heavens, no! Mike just works there—he's far from being the top man! Tell Mr. Bingham I need the money right away—please will he cable it at once—"

"You do not tell me how much you need, *kyría mou*," Nikos says softly. "Believe me, though you do not care to show me the note, I do not already know."

I feel my face grow hot. "Niko, my God, I don't suspect *you!* It's—it's one hundred thousand dollars! Maybe that doesn't sound like much, but it's more than I've got at the moment. Just the same, tell Mr. Bingham not to worry, I'll pay him back. And whatever you spend on phones, or cables, or whatever, I'll pay you back, too."

To Nikos the sum obviously is a staggering one. His eyes widen and he says something like "Eh-kah-toe hee-lee-*ah*-theess!" in a tone almost of reverence. Then he reaches for his cigarettes.

"When you talk like this I must smoke, I am sorry. 'Pay back pay back'—you are not fallen among wolves, *kyría mou*. So do not speak so: please, no more! Phone strike may end at noon tomorrow, but lines will be very busy, very tangled. I go to my cousin who works in Bank of Greece—surely they have ways to speak to America. Never fear, I reach this Bingham

— 217 —

boss." He inhales with satisfaction. "So now we know two things about your husband's captor. One: he, or they—I think there must be more than one; your husband is not old woman, easy to toss in sack and carry off—one of these captors can read English, otherwise they would not have him to write his own note, too dangerous. Two: he is smarter than they, so it is our hope that—*kyría*, what have I said?"

"Sorry." I wipe my cheeks. "It's just that—well, you're so *nice*, Niko"—I manage a shaky laugh. "Like a brother—a very clever, very comforting brother."

He gives me an enigmatic look; then he, too, laughs. "I am very glad I am not your brother, Katerina—you permit I call you this? Three sisters for dowries are enough for one man!"

He doesn't pay me any stupid compliments, I think gratefully; he really *is* nice. "Why do you think—I mean, know—Mike is smarter than they are?" Even though they did manage to nab him. What of it? That doesn't prove Mike's stupid. I was perfectly willing to share a bottle of wine on the plane, wasn't I? It didn't occur to me the wine might be doped. Trust, unfortunately, isn't a matter of I.Q., it's simply a sign of where you're coming from . . .

"Because he makes a message to you with his 'As you may have noticed'—a message they could not have told him to write. This way he can hope that when there is another note, you will look for something to make you sure he wrote it. He will not want you to pay the money for nothing."

"You mean, if they . . . get careless with him, he wants me to save my hundred thousand?"

"I think he thinks more of how to keep his captors from being what you call 'careless.' I think you can be sure he has made clear to them that he must write the notes, that he has for you a secret code, otherwise you will think him dead and not pay. So I think he is safe until after he writes where to put the money."

"Yes . . ." Bleakly.

"Katerina," he says, looking at me as if he were memorizing my face, "in my country it is the men who handle the money. Even when the money belongs to the woman, the man takes care of it. So when I ask you questions, say to yourself he is not being impudent, this Nikos, but you are guest here, you are under his protection, he has duty to look into this matter. So, I ask you: how will you pay back this money to Mr. Bingham? Suppose he is bloodsucking capitalist and wants to know. What shall I say?"

"Tell him I will sell the house. Mike never liked it anyway," I add with a tremulous laugh.

"You can do this? It is possible in America for wife to sell the house without the husband's signature?"

"Well, it's my house, actually."

"It is your dowry?"

"We don't have dowries, Niko, you know that. But yes, it's mine. My parents left it to me. When they died, I mean."

Nikos looks very tired. "And this house does not please your husband?"

"Well, it's—it's awfully big for just two people."

And for one? It doesn't bear thinking about.

"And you are happy there? You wish to stay, though house is very, very big and possibly costly?"

"It's not beyond our means," I say stiffly, "if that's in any way relevant."

Nikos stares at the glowing tip of his cigarette.

— 219 —

"Do not be angry, Katerina, but we must think of everything possible. I ask myself who could have captured your husband, and I answer: it is possible, nobody. No—listen, Katerina—suppose a man would like to have the use of his wife's money, but he cannot ask her for it, she is grieving. Much of her money is in form of a house, a costly house. Perhaps he has debts—"

"My *God!*" I leap to my feet. "You mean you think Mike is *faking?* My *God*, Niko—and you talk about being friends!"

He has stubbed out his cigarette and risen wearily to his feet. His light gray eyes are on a level with mine.

"I am trying to find your husband for you, Katerina. Where we look depends on *why* he is missing, as much as *how*. You think what I say is not possible? He has no reason to make such a plot? If he asks you to sell your house, you would sell it? You would not make excuses—it was your parents' house, here you brought your son—you would not use these polite ways to say no?"

"*I have to have these three weeks when I don't have to get myself past that damn tree—is that asking so much?*"

I stare at Niko, stricken.

"How does he sign this letter?" he goes on relentlessly. " 'Do not worry,' 'your loving husband'— it would be natural, *kyría*, to end with some such reassurance."

"He didn't sign it at all," I say, adding—I can't stop myself—"as perhaps you've known all along, Niko."

CHAPTER

18

As soon as I can without being blatantly discourteous, I make my escape and set out on the walk back to Molivos. I refuse Niko's offer to escort me, on the excuse that I need to be alone, to think things out. What I do *not* need (though naturally I don't say so) is any more heart-to-heart chats with Niko. For if that's what he thinks of Mike—that he's capable of faking a kidnapping, and for such a reason!—if that's what Nikos thinks of me—that I'm the kind of wife who could goad a man to such deception!—then surely any effort he puts out to find Mike must be the shabbiest pretense. I doubt he can even be trusted to try to get my message through to Bingham!

I feel I'm on a treadmill through time as well as space. Three steps: two seconds. Ninety steps: one minute. One minute farther along the road toward the inevitable time when I shall know whether Mike is alive or dead. One minute over and done with between where I am now, tormented by worry and doubt, and where I shall be then, when I know. Perhaps my road will end in an hour, when I reach the hotel. Perhaps it will end tomorrow, perhaps not until next week. Maybe not even then! How long did they hold that fellow Sanzio was reading about? *Fifty-four days* . . . an unimaginable eternity.

I pass Voufounos' cheese factory. Must be plenty of room in its cool depths to hide a man . . . or a man's body. But Voufounos would know he (or it) is there, and Voufounos, surely is not a kidnapper—not the Voufounos who was almost too weary to lift a hand in greeting. As a profession, kidnapping must be rated as fairly demanding physically, I should think.

Mike could be anywhere, anywhere at all. And what good would it do to know where he is? How could I rescue him? How could anybody? Of course if I were *sure* where he is I could go to the mayor, or to the police, and urge them to make a surprise swoop. But you'd need highly trained commando-type soldiers, and invisibility, and immense, incredible luck. Because how could they help knowing we're trying? And it would only take a moment—one stroke of a knife across his throat—to silence him. My only real hope—Mike's only hope—is that they honor the ransom, and release him when it's paid.

Which might be dangerous for them: that's the trouble. Mike could identify the kidnappers, couldn't he? Even if they kept him blindfolded? Because voices have patterns, as maybe they know. And Mike is an excellent mimic, though they wouldn't know that; he'd have no reason to mention it in the letters. Still . . . . THE VICTIM WAS RELEASED UNHARMED—how often does that happen? It's much more likely that, once they have the money, they'll dispose of the only possible witness against them . . .

Of course there is no word for me at the hotel.

"No, madam, nothing. Phones still on strike in Athens." Voula gives me a look of veiled amusement. No doubt there is something amusing about a woman whose husband, having sent her on ahead so as to be free of her for a few days, then drinks to avoid her, then simply decamps. "One moment, madam—your passport. Also that of your husband. The police have finished with them." And Voula, checking each as if to make sure of the name, hands me first mine, then Mike's. He can't get far without it, as I am sure she knows.

I take a glass of sherry onto the balcony overlooking the sea, and there I wait out the rest of the endless afternoon. I can't seem to get my thermostat set correctly: if I sit in the sun I feel feverish; when I retreat to the shade I get to shivering. If only I were home, I could at least appeal to the police—or could I? No: no more than here. But I'd hear my own language . . . familiar, friendly, *known* sounds. I wouldn't have this sense of displacement. What did Nikos call it? *Kseniteiá* . . . something like that. Oh, come off it, Kay! What you're feeling is nothing peculiar to you; it's the usual anguish every victim's family has felt. Commonplace. Ordinary. Welcome to the twentieth century.

But at least they have each other, these families. They can shore each other up, they can comfort one another. I have no one, no one. I can only wait, and do nothing: nothing! This is hardest of all, this pretending that I'm not really worried, that I'm sure Mike will come to his senses and just turn up, embarrassed and contrite and pledging not to be naughty again. So I sit here and fiddle with my drink; or I take out my pencils and make a show of capturing the view; or (Kostas coming to check on how many will be going on Monday's plane, reports that Verek wants to know why I go to Zoë and not to her) I smilingly refuse an invitation from Herr Professor Furchtwanger to accompany his group tomorrow to Mytilene and beyond—two early Christian basilicas are there, at Argala and at Loutra; a pleasant distraction they would prove, dear American *Freundin*. No, thank you, I reply; I am expected at the home of—I almost say "my Greek son," but recover in time: *"zu dem Haus von meiner Freundes greckishes . . ."*

And so the interminable afternoon crawls past, and it is evening, and I dine, or mime the gestures of one dining, and it is night, and I go to bed and pretend to sleep, and give up, and try to read, and can't do that either. And now it's Monday, and I'm exactly where I was: adrift, alone, no end in sight. In truth it's worse than after David, I reflect as I set out for Verek's after a bleak and obligatory breakfast. Food, sleep, domestic chores: these I had attended to without conscious thought, but somehow, on a submerged level, they had helped. Now I've no house to clean, no meals to cook. I have absolutely nothing to divert my mind. My thoughts are free to sandblast my spirit raw.

Mike . . . Mike . . . Are you, too, afraid every waking moment, and when you escape into sleep, do you, too, dream of empty rooms, and blood on snow, and sirens wailing nearer? Do you dread they won't release you when the money comes—if it comes? Have they, with careless cruelty, let you see their faces, so you already know they have no intention of releasing you? Nikos thinks you're very clever to fix it so they can't kill you, at least not until you tell me where to leave the money. But they could kill you then, couldn't they? Perhaps they already have. Perhaps you've already written that next note, and now—but I would know, wouldn't I? I'd know if you weren't there anymore, weren't anywhere anymore—wouldn't I?

Verek must have been watching for me. As I enter the courtyard, she comes out on the porch, and for a moment it is like that first time, but only for a moment. Now she hurries to the stairs, she comes swiftly down. Approaching me closely, she stares at me, her lips pressed tightly together. Then—and I don't expect this—she takes both my hands in hers, clasping them strongly, and of course it's all I can do not to cry. (Why *must* I threaten to go to pieces whenever anyone shows me the slightest sympathy?) And now she ushers me ahead of her through the door under the porch.

The center of the room is filled by a huge wooden-framed loom strung with threads of ruby, crimson, indigo, and wine. A long table against the wall holds the finished cloth; the orderly piles make a vivid abstract. Overhead hanks of wool hang like the leaves of a fantastic forest. Here, obviously, is where Verek lives, not in those sterile, nearly empty, overly neat rooms above.

She gestures for me to sit. I consider thanking her, but know I'd feel absurd speaking words that are not understood. Yet simply to smile and nod my head seems so stupid. Silence between women is unnatural, unnerving.

Verek seems to find it so, too. Having brought me a cup of coffee and some sweet biscuits, she goes over to a row of photographs on a shelf above the fireplace in the corner, and leaning forward, she kisses the first picture. *"Patéras mou."* Awkwardly balancing my cup, I rise and come nearer. They are all wedding pictures, I see: assorted young couples gazing self-consciously at the camera. *"Mitéra mou."* She kisses the first picture again. *"O patéras kaí i mitéra Yeóryiou tou."* One kiss only. *"Mikhaïl kaí Katerína."* Kisses, sighs, shakes of the head. *"Yeóryios kaí Verek."* A deprecatory smile, but no kiss.

Does Damian look like his parents? I have time for only a quick glance at the two incongruously solemn faces before I must, in all courtesy, turn to look at Verek's own wedding picture. The youthful Yeoryios could be taken for Kostas, I note with uneasy surprise; though his hair is cropped short, city-fashion, he has a dashing pirate's mustache; his face is handsome, self-confident, unlined. And Verek—Verek is beautiful: her face is smooth with youth, serene, strong, classic. A goddess on a Greek coin. *How cruel* . . . I can't look at her, for fear she'll read my thoughts.

She seats herself at her loom. Sipping my coffee, nibbling at the nuggets of sugared almonds, I feel conspicuously useless. Verek's movements are rhythmical, unhurried, apparently tireless; her expression is stoic, withdrawn. Where does she get her—not serenity: that's akin to sainthood, and there is little, I suspect, of the saint about Verek. Fortitude? Yes, that defines her: fortitude, endurance, constancy—qualities I conspicuously lack.

By eleven o'clock I am thoroughly sick of my thoughts and of the silence in the room—silence between women, I mean; the shuffle and click of the loom make a kind of pulse, a rhythm of life that keeps the stillness from being too oppressive. When at last Verek rises, smoothing her apron and collecting a basket and knife, I get thankfully to my feet and follow her out.

The sun is strong, the soil hot. As we go down the row of tomatoes, reaching cautiously under the scratchy leaves for those ripening early, I'm aware of a dusty, yeasty, greening smell that is oddly comforting, as if some things in this life are proceeding according to plan. I'm so sheltered, it seems to me, so pampered—lights at a touch, heat at the turn of a dial, food obtained without physical effort—has all this ease of existence allowed me to cosset my grief? Would I have "got over" David's death by now if I, too, had to heat water in a kettle, or plant and weed and water and harvest my salad greens myself instead of buying them prewashed in cellophane packages? Would such tedious, repetitive tasks have dulled the sharp edge of my anguish? I don't think so. I think I have some innate weakness of spirit, some flaw in my soul. Mike, after all, lives in the same unnaturally sheltered environment I do; he spends his working days in even more synthetic, more exotic surroundings than I, yet he knew David's death was his "time to be strong"—and he *was* strong. And I saw this as a fault, a lack of love, not as the strength of love that it was, the love that chooses life.

Oh, Mike—if they give you any choice, choose it again! Choose life, my beloved! Choose life!

And so as we start down another row and I hold the basket for Verek while she picks, I fall into an argument with Mike, an amicable argument in which I find myself taking both sides. Not, of course, that Verek's grief could ever have been as anguished as mine, I point out—you don't really miss what you've never had, right? *No,* by God! False, totally false, like all those other scraps of folk "wisdom" with which we flog the grief-stricken. *Time heals* . . . Bullshit, Mike. *It's all for the best.* More of same. *God never gives you a burden greater than you can bear.* Now there, Mike, we have the ultimate blasphemy. The hell he doesn't!

Up in the kitchen, Verek and I sort and trim and wash and dry, snap tips off, peel and slice. And so we go on living, she and I, our grief ever inside us, hidden, hidden within, our hands making the motions expected of them, obedient, dutiful. I watch her out of the corner of my eye and I marvel. Who would suspect the passions, the hungers unfed? Does she see me in similar light? Do I appear unnaturally serene, eerily calm in the face of my husband's inexplicable absence?

Yeoryios comes in promptly at noon, and we take our places at the oilcloth-covered table in the kitchen. Man and wife make the sign of the cross. Raising his glass, Yeoryios says something that might be a toast. A hint of laughter in her voice, Verek replies. Then he lifts his glass to me.

"I say also to you what I say to my wife: 'Health to your hands!' Means the hands that cooked this meal, they deserve thanks." Investing the gesture with a simple dignity, he breaks the loaf of bread, giving some to me, then to Verek.

And you, Mike? Do you have food, too? Did your captors pray over it, not in gratitude but mockingly, ridiculing the devout? Do they treat you decently, or do they feed you not out of compassion but for their own amusement, leaving your hands bound, tossing the food on the ground, making you grovel like a dog? Or don't they feed you at all? Laughing, they cram food in their mouths greedily, while you watch, hunger cramping your cheeks . . .

My hands shake, and my bread drops to the table.

"No harm, *kyría*. Be thankful you do not let the bread fall to the floor. That is stepping on the foot of God."

After that, naturally for the next few minutes no one says anything. My hosts eat as if the task is too serious for conversation, I as if it were a duty. When we've finished, Yeoryios brings out a bottle of wine, remarking that we'll take *tón moskáto* below, it's cooler there. And so we go down to the weaving room and sit at one end of the long table.

"Now I ask question everyone asks." Yeoryios fills the assorted glasses. "Is my country very different from your country?"

I look around the room—at the lamp burning before the Madonna and Child in the corner, at the bright-hued hanks of wool above the loom, at the dazzle of light through the unscreened doorway, at the firewood stacked outside. As I consider my reply, a cuckoo calls from the topmost branch of the dead tree in the courtyard; the falling notes seem as alien as . . . as the candles and the icons in the gold-shadowed church.

"Here nothing is the same but the stars, the sun, and the grass," I reply. "No, that's not entirely true. We, too, have many sparrows, and in our gardens we have roses. But they are not as lovely as yours."

"*Eliés*—olives—these grow where you live?"

"Oh, no, it's too cold. I never saw an olive tree until I came to Greece."

"No olives," Yeoryios says slowly. "You think a Greek can be happy where it is too cold for olives? Where the sun is too weak?"

"Many Greeks come to America and do well."

"I do not ask can a Greek survive. Kostas survive the Canada, Kostas survive also Germany. I ask can a Greek be happy? Is very different question."

We aren't talking about Kostas, and we both know it.

"I think Damian has resilience," I remark. "He is not a—a tender flower that wilts when it's transplanted."

"Much depends, *kyría,* on moving a plant at the right season, and with familiar soil about the roots. Kostas was grown, a man. Damian still speaks with child's voice. Is very bad time for uprootings." He drains his glass, frowning. "If you and your husband wish for Damian to go to America"—reluctantly—"Damian must choose. I would be satisfied to have him who is my dead brother's son for my own. But what can I do? I am a man fighting with copper coins against gold."

"Damian cannot be bought!" I say hotly, and then, because this exchange seems to be veering wildly off course, I pull myself up short. Anyone would think I *want* Damian to come to America! That's not it. What I want, I realize, is for my refusal to have some significance, some weight. If Mike wants Damian for his adopted son, and Damian is willing, yet I say no, if Mike then agrees not to push it, wouldn't that show he still loves me? In spite of everything?

I say earnestly, "Yeoryios, believe me, I *don't* want Damian for my son! No, truly"—for he gives an exclamation of disbelief—"for me that part of my life is over. I . . . I can't go through it again. That's why to any proposal of adoption, Yeoryios, I vote no. *Ókhi.* But my husband does not feel the same. It's—it's entirely possible that having Damian for a son is more important to him than my disapproval. So he—he and Damian—may vote yes. I most profoundly hope they don't." I try to smile. "I hope Damian sticks to his plan to be a sailor."

"Means nothing. He is very young, too young to know what is best for him. When I was his age I wanted to be soldier killing many Turks. Sometimes, *kyría mou*"—Yeoryios leans forward to fill my glass— "sometimes I still do."

You better think this through, Kay! Do you want Mike and Damian both made miserable by your intransigence, just so Mike can prove his love for you isn't as dead as your son? What faster way to kill love than having to prove it, prove it, prove it? Each new proof piling another stone on the cairn . . .

Yeoryios must have been giving Verek the gist of what I said, for she flashes me a look of woman-to-woman sympathy . . . sisterhood. I cast about for some way to ease us all back onto safe ground.

"Tell me, Yeoryios—that mark above the door: does it have some special meaning? I noticed one at Zoë's, too."

He glances up at the sooty cross. "You have not this custom? During that service which ends on Easter morning, at the moment when all the candles are put out and everything is darkness, the priest lights first his new candle, and then each one—men, women, children, everyone—receive new light from his. Then—it is now three, perhaps four in the morning—all the village walk home carrying this new light. As we enter the house we trace the cross there above the door. Then we, too, make new the light in our house. We light the candle before the holy picture and we light the fire on the hearth. For us this is truly the first day of the year, *kyría*—life and light begin for us on this day of Easter."

I feel again that vague jealousy, that yearning . . . But there's no way Mike and I can rekindle anything, I know that. Certainly not through some primitive though charming folk ritual.

"And you, Yeoryios—do you take part in these Easter customs?"

"Of course—am I not Greek?"

"At home it is mostly the women who attend church, or so it seems to me."

"Here, too, *kyría*, the women are often the more faithful." Yeoryios looks at his wife with that expression which is not so much more gentle as less harsh. "The lives of women are much subject to change, to forces not seen, not truly known. It is only natural they turn to God for comfort. If I were a woman, hour after hour I would be on my knees."

"I would have thought the same is true of men."

"Yes, you are right—a man's life is a leaf blown in the wind. He must work and he must fight, and who can say if his trees will bear fruit, or he and his comrades be victors? Still, we leave to the women much of the praying. No doubt we feel that is one more way in which God intended them to serve us." Though he speaks seriously, I could swear there is a twinkle in his eye. "And the fasting—this, too, is woman's duty," he adds dryly, "for God knows they are better at enduring suffering than men."

Does he?

Deliberately, I echo the question Kyriakos put to me: "You are a believer, surely?"

Say yes, oh, say yes.

"I believe I believe," Yeoryios replies slowly. His eyes beneath his heavy brows betray his resentment. (What would Nikos have said? "You do not have the right to inquire after my spiritual health . . ."?) "Like all men, I wish I was more sure of what I truly believe." Then, pointedly: "What do you believe, *kyría* Katerina?"

That there is nothing outside the plane window, and in a moment we shall all be sucked into nothingness and forgotten.

I say in a low voice, "I wish I could be sure I believe in anything at all."

He gets to his feet. "I must go back to my trees." But it is not a dismissal, for after a moment he goes on quietly, "It is a gift, to believe, *kyría mou.* It is also a reward." His face is all at once very hard. "Every man's life gives him reason to deny God. You must not look for the reasons *no*. You must hold only to the reasons *yes*."

CHAPTER

19

The long, long, long afternoon crawls by. I am parched, dried up by the silence, worn down by my thoughts.

Ought I, after all, have gone to the police? *No, Kay: not again!* You believed—you still believe—that would only ensure Mike's speedy death. Don't make your tough decisions twice.

Tell no one. If only there were someone I could trust, whom I could talk it over with—someone who's been through it and survived, like Verek. *Damn* the language gap—we might as well be on separate planets! Why didn't I tell Yeoryios about the ransom note? What if I need his help later, yet it's obvious I haven't trusted him? *Tell no one*—that's why I didn't. But I told Nikos, and *he* doesn't even trust Mike! (Or says he doesn't.) At least I didn't tell Kostas. Or Damian—yet.

But Damian is only a child. And not even mine.

"That part of my life is over . . ." For anyone who can have only the one child, being a parent is as great a gamble as marriage used to be. So what in God's name possessed me to agree to it? How could I have

been so foolish as to lay all my bets (so to speak) on this first, last, and only? How could I have assumed that this child, because he's blood of my blood, bone of my bone, is inviolate? Evil can't touch him, danger and death will pass him by, at least for my lifetime . . . My God, how could I have been so selfish? As if my own safety or even my survival mattered at all! But of course I didn't know. You don't know anything about anything until it happens to you. You can be told, and you think you know, but until you've been there, you know nothing. Not with your blood, your bones. Until I held David in my arms, no way could I have known I would gladly lay down my life for him. Gladly. For him, or for his brother or sister . . .

"*. . . the first day of spring and it's snowing . . .*" I remember your train was late, Mike, and you came in looking more than usually drained. It was a tough day for you, too, I see that now, though I don't think I did then, not really. (Happy birthday, David. Happy birthday, my dearest son . . . my dead son.) "When I was a boy I used to catch the flakes on my tongue," you said, Mike—remember? You fixed yourself a drink then, and staring out at that damnable snow pasting over the window like disks of wet gauze, you went on: "Now the air is so filthy it isn't safe. Cockeyed, isn't it?" A long, deep swallow. "Whole damn world is cockeyed, Kay. Stick out your tongues, kids, and you'll catch the plague. Swim in the river and if the cops don't get you the sewage will. Open your windows and let the bright early morning acid scour out your lungs. God, what a hell of a world, Kay. What a hell of a fucked-up world for . . . anybody . . ."

For children. You almost said it, Mike. A hell of a fucked-up world for children—true, oh, very true! A world where the fathers—some of them, but not you, Mike!—devise weapons that will kill the children but leave the sleds intact. A world where some of the mothers—me, for one, though you didn't say it, Mike, thank God for that!—let the children go out and get themselves killed, and that without the benefit of any advanced technology: plain old-fashioned neglect is enough . . .

When at last Kostas' cab rolls up and he and Damian emerge, I feel like a convict who catches a glimpse of parole.

"Kosta, may I hitch a ride to the hotel? I'm hoping Nikos will call from Athens. Besides, Verek must be thinking she'll never be rid of me."

"Uncle *Nikos?*" Damian says in bewilderment. "He is in Athens?"

"Of course. Doesn't he always go back on Mondays?"

To my distress, his eyes grow bright with tears. "Why does he not look for my American father? All this day I think he is looking, that Niko! What, then— is money so important to my *koumbáros?*"

I say soothingly, "He only pretends to go because he always goes. But Nikos will phone America for me—I can't from the hotel, you see; everybody would know my husband is not angry, he is truly missing, and they would call the police." Kostas is looking at me narrowly. How can I tell Niko and not the others? It just isn't going to work . . . "I'll just say good-bye . . ."

Verek must think me already a widow. She presses my hands, and after a moment's hesitation, kisses me on both cheeks. I can only pray she hasn't the gift of second sight. Or does she know something I don't—that I haven't been told?

We stop by the olive trees. Beyond a curious hump shaped something like a haystack, Yeoryios is hacking at the ridges of stony soil. At our approach he leans his heavy-bladed hoe against one of the great gnarled trees and comes striding across to meet us, each step scattering shards of baked earth before him.

"Thank you for your hospitality," I say formally. "I must go now and wait for word from Niko. He phones America for me, to try to arrange for money for my husband's ransom. I've heard from him—he is kidnapped, just as I—I suspected."

Imagined. Hallucinated.

Kostas swings around to stare at me, incredulous. Yeoryios flicks him an impassive glance. "You are certain, *kyría?* In these days almost everywhere a man is safe in Greece."

Avoiding Kosta's eyes, I explain about the note.

"Is it much money you need, *kyría?*" One would think, so matter-of-factly Yeoryios puts the question, that it is an everyday occurrence: the ground is dry, we need rain; my guest needs much money for ransom . . .

"They want one hundred thousand dollars."

Yeoryios's eyes harden. "You have such money?"

"I—I can get it, I think."

"One hundred *thousand* dollars!" Damian exclaims. "This is very much money!" He calculates swiftly. "Is nearly four million *drachmés!*"

Kostas flips his hand at him to be quiet. "Katerina, you think someone can send you this money?"

"God, I hope so! I don't know for sure. But I don't

know why he wouldn't—my friend—I told Niko to call my friend—"

"*Téssera ekatomíria!* This is very, *very* much money!" Damian is clearly dazzled. "Enough to do everything!"

"Everything?" Kostas snaps. "What everything?"

Damian gestures widely. "Enough for doctors for uncle, pay for taxi, fix *Pouláki Mou,* marriage gifts for sisters of my *koumbáros,* television for his mother—everything! Enough for *everything!*" he repeats, in case any of us has failed to grasp his point. "Maybe even money extra!"

"My taxi already paid for, I thank you! In Germany I make good pay. Is not like Greece, where a man works for nothing."

Yeoryios throws him a hard look. "To owe money is no sin. Honest man always in debt. What they pay grape pickers, those so generous Germans? Or maybe with your face you find easier work?"

For a moment I think the two will come to blows. Then Kostas shrugs, turning away.

"So I owe money," he says sullenly. "A little. Is not your business, hokay? So stop the blah-blah-blah." He glances at me. "Come, *kyría mou,* time we go." And turning on his heel he stalks off toward his taxi.

"His *filótomo* is injured," Yeoryios says dryly. "He wants to be the big shot always. You, Damiane, no, you do not go with them. Make yourself of use here. Good night, *kyría* Katerina."

"Good night, and thanks again, Yeoryio." I extend my hand, and am surprised, and a bit moved, when instead of clasping it he bows over it, though he does not touch it with his lips.

"Do not thank me, *kyría mou*—we are friends."

Kostas is clearly angry, and with me. "You do not tell me about your husband's letter!" We hurtle out onto the main road.

I say pacifically, "He said to tell no one, show it to no one."

"But you tell Niko! Why you tell Nikólas Para-déllis and not tell Kostás Demetriou? Because I try to help you, I try to keep you happy, I lie to you about drunken husband? So now you lie to me! Letter is from the Germans, you said! The *Germans!*"

"I'm telling you now—you and Yeoryio—because I've had time to think," I explain. "Sitting there with Verek, I've had hours and *hours* in which to do nothing *but* think! Besides, Kosta"—for I truly want to placate him: I need his help, but more than that, I'm troubled by that scene in the orchard; what earthly difference does it make if his taxi is paid for or not?— "besides, Yeoryios didn't hear about my husband a single second before you did, so calm down and don't be mad. I *hate* it when anybody's mad!" And that's the truth, I think bleakly. "As for Niko, I had to tell him before he went back to Athens, don't you see? He has much more chance of getting a call through than I ever could. Besides, how could I phone? Even if there weren't any strike, how many phones in Molivos are there?"

"The mayor, the doctor, the hotel, and the police," Kostas says gravely, then flashes me his beautiful smile. "Hokay, Katerina, I forgive you. I make big scene over nothing. We forget it. Only no more lies, *agápi mou*. You don't like for me to be mad, don't act like enemies. You agree?"

"I agree."

I am pleased to be promoted once again from *kyría mou* to Katerina.

"A message for madam," says Voula as we come in. "A phone call from Athens—your husband says to tell you he returns tomorrow."

Utterly confounded, I can only stare at her.

Kostas says incredulously, "He says he is *kýrios* Cunningham? In *Athens?* Please—no jokes!"

"He gives no name. I ask, but he says you will know, madam. But it is from Athens, this call, I am indeed certain. The line is clear, he speaks good Greek, I do not make any mistake. He says he has word about your husband who returns tomorrow."

Sick with disappointment, I turn away. Obviously, the one who comes tomorrow is Nikolas Paradellis—who else would be calling from Athens? And he's coming—I'm sure of it—because he feels obligated to tell me in person, he can't just give me such a blow over the phone, that he can't reach Bingham. Or *has* reached Bingham, and he won't send the money. Or—

"I see you to your room, Katerina. You very tired, after a long, long day." Kostas puts his hand under my elbow. When we reach the little hallway he slips it to my shoulder. "Give me key, poor Katerina, many hours of Verek, *aieee!*" He follows me in and closes the door. "Tomorrow we go to Mytilene, learn what Nikos has to say. Don't look so sad, Katerina. If Nikos cannot get the money, we try another way. Try Mr. Sarris, try Mrs. Meade—always there is another path for brave man or woman. Do not lose heart, Katerina! Is not the end of everything for you, I swear it!"

His voice is warm, his eyes full of pity—and for

a stranger! How could I have hesitated to tell him about Mike's note? "Thank you for everything, Kosta—you've been marvelous!" I extend my hand. "You think Nikos expects me to meet him tomorrow—that's why he phoned?"

"He wants we should come, that is clear." Kostas does not release my hand. "I meet you here at ten o'clock, *mátia mou*. Perhaps there will be paying passengers—"

"Of course *I* will pay—good heavens!" I attempt, gently, to withdraw my hand. His clasp tightens; he lifts my fingers to his lips, never taking his eyes from my face, as if the very intensity of his gaze will keep me captive. Good grief, when did this happen? I know Kostas is mercurial, but ye gods! *"Póso kostízi?"* I attempt a laugh.

"For you, special price," he declares fervently, his eyes glowing, whether with ardor or laughter I can't tell. I have the feeling I've been out of the game so long the rules have changed. "For you, Katerina, anything—" and he pulls me toward him.

"Kostas, no! Look, I'm sorry—I didn't mean—you *must* not!" For his arms are around me, I'm caught hard against his chest, and he is kissing me on the forehead, the eyelids. His mustache brushes my cheek as I turn my face away; the sensation is so alien to anything I've ever experienced I have the absurd notion that none of this is happening.

"Why must I not?" He kisses my ear. *"S'agapó,* Katerina, *koúkla mou! S'agapó polí polí!"*

I will not struggle, it's so undignified! Tomorrow Kostas will be ashamed, will hope I've forgotten. "No—Kostas, you must *not* do this! *I* must not!"

His skin so close to my lips is like bronze satin.

"Katerina," he says fervently, his breath warm and (God help me!) sweet on my face, "listen to me, Katerina, Katerina—*s'agapó eilikriná*. There are many kinds of love, many kinds to give, to share—love is good, Katerina, it is very very good. Let me show you, Katerina—for you are hungry, I see it in your face, I see it in your eyes—it is no disgrace, Katerina, to want love—"

"No—*please*, Kostas!" I haven't breath for more.

"Yes," he says huskily. "Yes yes *yes*, Katerina!"

He is kissing me again and again on the throat. His lips are smooth, firm, warm against my pulse. I feel my body—my God, what is the *matter* with me?—becoming receptive, and its treachery enrages me.

"No! I *mean* it, Kostas—absolutely *not!*"

He holds me away from him an inch or two, and his eyes, black fire, gaze into mine. At once I work my hands between his chest and my breast, my palms flat against the silk, against the smooth bronze skin. I push as hard as I can, and his arms tighten. I can feel his heart racing. Damn it, he's so alive, alive!

"*Why* no?" Fiercely.

I have no idea where the words come from, but there they are when I need them. "Because you are a good man, Kostas, and I—I am a good wife."

I'd hate to have to prove either . . . Giddy with relief, I realize he's released me. For a long moment we stand motionless, facing each other, his eyes searching my face. I pray mine expresses something of what I'm thinking: *I'm sorry, I'm sorry, Kostas, if somehow, something I said or did . . . Oh, God, I'm sorry . . . There's no other man for me but Mike, you see. I'm sorry . . .*

Without another word he is gone.

I go to the mirror and stare at my face. What did he see there? He saw something. I am, I realize, in a turmoil of conflicting emotions. "You fool, you," I tell my face, spacing the words for emphasis, "you have got to smarten *up!*" To be in trouble, to be in need of rescue, to turn to a man for friendship—well, what did I expect? For a male—and God knows few men are more male than Kostas—it may be the ultimate aphrodisiac. It's not his fault. Somehow, something I said or did made him think I'm . . . available. *Now* I've got a fine line to walk! I do need his help—his and Niko's, his and Yeoryio's—I may not be able to manage without them. How the *hell* am I going to handle this from now on?

When the phone rings, for one wild moment I'm afraid it's Kostas, wanting to apologize.

"One moment, madam." Voula's voice: cool, impersonal, borderline unfriendly. "It is the United States calling."

My nerves are in such a state I have to choke down laughter.

"Mrs. Cunningham?" The silky voice could be in the next room. "Mr. Bingham is calling. Hold on, please."

And then there is the homely, warm, down-to-earth blessedly *American* voice of Joshua Bingham. "Kay, my dear—I am wondering if all is well. I had an astonishing conversation with a friend of yours today. He says you and Mike are separated—can that be true?"

"After—after a fashion."

"This friend has suggested a course of action which I might take. It seems a bit drastic—would this really be of help?"

"It might be"—I search for a safe word; is Voula listening?—"it may be vital. Please, could you do it today? Would that be possible?"

"I'll attend to it at once." Briskly. "Plenty of time, it's only one P.M. here, you know. Just thought I'd check with you first. I don't want to do anything— ah—interfering. And Kay, my dear child—if you like, I could come and perhaps help effect an—ah—a reconciliation?"

For a moment I'm tempted. A man I can rely on, a *safe* man, who speaks my brand of English, who thinks in English. But is it conceivable that a man's employer would drop everything and fly across oceans and continents, simply because of a marital spat? Never. It would be obvious I'd told him the true state of affairs. If to him, the kidnappers would reason, why not to the police? And they'd jettison Mike with all possible speed.

I reply firmly, "Thanks anyway, but I'm afraid this is something we have to work out alone if it's going to work out at all."

"Very well, dear child, you know best, being— ah—right there on the ground. Good luck, Kay, my dear. If there's anything further, your friend can let me know."

When I hang up, I'm amazed to realize I'm hungry. As I cross the lobby to the dining terrace, I glance out the open front door; Kosta's taxi is gone, I see with mingled relief and—not disappointment, surely—rather an uneasy feeling of something not finished. . . . At least it is gone.

The mockingbird in the locusts chooses to give a nocturne, and the *barboúni* is fresh and perfectly grilled. I reflect on my conversation with Bingham.

Not a word out of place, I think smugly. Bingy and I could qualify for the Diplomatic Corps. Even if Voula was listening—and of course she *was* listening: a phone call from the U.S.A.!—we said nothing to tip her off. If he sends the money today, it might be here by tomorrow. Maybe Nikos will be bringing it. It's almost funny, to think of a reputed Communist phoning the head of one of the best (though certainly not the biggest) advertising firms in New York, and helping, if all goes well, to rescue a dyed-in-the-wool capitalist. I feel buoyed by optimism and hope. *Some* things are going right, after all! Nikos did reach Bingham—how could I have distrusted him?—and Bingham is sending the money. I have resources: I'm not totally dependent on the possibly volatile goodwill and certainly purely voluntary help of strangers.

I smile at the Germans as they come out for a belated meal. They've been to Neapolis and Loutra—the basilica at Argala was a disappointment, but at Loutra there was a most interesting mosaic. Perhaps if the Frau Cunningham is not otherwise occupied, a stroll about the charming town of Molibos would be a pleasant way to pass the evening? One has heard rumors of polygonal walls of an archaic temple dating from the eighth century B.C., but here in Molibos their precise location no one seems to know . . .

Professor Furchtwanger's knees and nose are, if anything, an even more ardent pink than before; the lady archaeologist crackles with enthusiasm; the elderly gnome of a scholar crinkles his eyes at me and beams. Though it's true I'm tired after my "long, long day," it's not the kind of tiredness that makes one sleep. A stroll about the town in the cool of the evening may be just what I need; furthermore, I'll be well chaperoned, in case Kostas takes it into his head to give it one more try.

Down to the harbor we trudge, and up to the castle, which proves to be nothing but a great un-even-surfaced space open to the sky and surrounded on all sides by the crumbling remains of twelve-foot-thick walls. The going is easy, however, for the moon, slightly past the full, pours its cold light with such liberality we could have dispensed with flashlights. Its effect on the professor is to make him even more garrulous; he keeps up a continual babble about his explorations of Molibos and environs, how he has recorded them with the "artist's eye" of his camera: Roman remains . . . Venetian . . . the tomb, Aeolian, perhaps? . . . the tower—incomparable! such beauty of age! imbued with *soul*, do I not agree? calling to mind Tyrene . . . Mycenae . . . secret postern and concealed spring . . . *"Ach, die Geist der Vergangenheit in den Steinen wohnt!"*

When he draws breath, I feel obliged, as guest, to murmur my own appreciation of the joys of setting foot where Ancient Man has trod, et cetera, adding that I wish my own Latin were not so vestigial, for I would like to have translated with a bit more facility the dedication (or whatever it was) to those who built the access to the spring. I am surprised when it appears that for all his ubiquitous perambulations, the professor is unaware of the existence of this Roman thank-you note, and am pleased I've been able to add something to his travelogue.

It's close to eleven when we reach the Silver Bird, and we part with many cordial wishes for a good night's sleep (for which, I am grateful to realize, I am now more than ready). "No," I say, still smiling, "thank you very much but tomorrow to Ayiassos I cannot accompany you. Not even by the icons in the monastery am I tempted." I am too tired to think of a reason, so I don't give one.

Voula is not on duty. A swarthy fellow in an ill-fitting jacket—could it be the gardener, moonlighting at the desk?—after some pantomime on my part (for he speaks no English) hands me my key and—my heart skips a full beat—another envelope. This time it is addressed to Mrs. Katharine Cunningham.

Like a sleepwalker I go through and past the *Guten-Nacht*ing Germans. I do not open the envelope until I am safely in my room, the door shut and locked behind me.

The writing is, if anything, even more spiky and shaky than before, the lines wandering up and down the dirty paper. *Blindfolded.* He wrote it blindfolded.

This is no joke, Kay. I really have been snatched. They want a hundred thousand bucks in unmarked drachma notes. Tell no one—repeat, no one. Put it in the tomb—they say you know where. Love to Jimmy. He would hate it here.

As before, it's unsigned, but it's from Mike, all right. If I had any doubts, which I don't, that mention of Jimmy would convince me. It was our private family code for *I'm losing patience, so pay attention, you hear?*

I hear you, Mike. Mike darling, my darling, my love, oh, my love, I hear you.

CHAPTER

20

"Sit by me, Katerina." Kostas holds open the door on the passenger side; in the midmorning sun the taxi is almost blinding with fresh polish. "Rear seat for mister king and queen."

Smiling, friendly, open, and no more than arm's-length affectionate, Kostas seems the same as ever; one might think yesterday's feverish scene never took place. Or that he tried his luck, and having lost, pocketed his dice with a commonsensical shrug. As if, after all, no one could fault him for trying.

A man and woman emerge from the hotel, the gardener/night clerk following with their exceedingly elegant luggage, six russet leather suitcases zippered into matching blue and russet tweed slipcovers, each bag large enough to hold my entire traveling wardrobe tripled. Kostas has some difficulty stowing it all in, and says one of the "lady bags" will have to ride up front.

"Quite all right," I say graciously.

"On the seat, Katerina. No room on floor. And next to window, please, or I cannot work the gears. So please to move closer."

Cautiously, I hitch myself six inches over.

We're halfway to Petrá when the man speaks.

"Ask Johnny what time we get to this Meatburg."

Evidently he is addressing his wife, who replies, "You ask him." Indifferently.

"You tired of talkin' to the natives?"

"You're the one who wants to know."

On our right the sea flashes silver; two little islands dance in the sun.

"Say, Johnny—what time *do* we get to Meatburg?"

I glance at Kostas. Apparently he is deaf.

"He doesn't want to talk to you, either," the wife says, and laughs.

The man leans forward. "Listen, Johnny, I asked you a question. What's the matter—you no speaka da English?"

Kostas turns his head slightly, his eyes still firmly on the road. "I not know you speaking to me," he says agreeably. "My name Kostás—Kostás Demetríou."

"Now, Johnny, who the hell else in this shitty cab you think I'm speakin' to? So when I ask you, Johnny, how far it is to Meatburg, you just gimme a rough guess, okay, Johnny boy? Boy oh boy oh boy?"

I turn and survey the speaker. His face hangs in folds like a Great Dane's; in spite of the breeze from the open window it is gleaming with sweat. Sloshed, and at ten in the morning. Why the *hell* does he have to be an American?

"Now we all know why everybody loves you so," the wife says.

"And you just love the natives, don't you? You

just love to watch them go dancey-prancey every night. So *you* ask him. Ask pretty Johnny boy!" The wife is silent. "Go on, *ask* him!" In silence thick enough to smother us we drive through Petrá and turn south on the road to Kalloni. "You don't want to embarrass Johnny, is that it? You think Johnny's upset because although he drives this shitty cab there every damn day, he doesn't know how far it is to Lean Meatburg?"

"You make me sick," says his wife.

The man sways forward, taps Kostas on the shoulder. "Damn it, Johnny, you gotta have *some* idea behind that pretty face—"

Kostas slams on the brakes so abruptly we all lurch forward. Cutting the motor, he leaps out and yanks open the rear door.

"You want walk to Mytilene, mister? Is not far— maybe one week!"

"Cut the comedy, I've got a plane to catch, Johnny boy—"

"*Demetríou!*" Kostas jabs at the card taped to the back of the driver's seat. "*Mister* Kostás Demetríou. Printed in English, for barbarians who can't read Greek." He turns, hawks, and spits. "Is ancient word meaning ignorant foreigners who don't speak *elli-niká*—who go *baa-baa-baa* like stupid sheep!"

I stare at my hands, clenched in my lap. My heart is pounding, my mouth dry. The naked fury in Kos-tas' face appalls me. How he detests the "barbari-ans" who invade his country! Does that include me? Mike and me?

The wife is saying placatingly, "He's sorry he was rude, though he's too stupid to say so. Now let's get moving, okay?"

"*Not* hokay! Mister must not hide in mouth of woman, mister must speak with own tongue!"

"Say you're sorry, damn you," the wife says in a low voice. "I've got a plane to catch, too."

"What the hell—all *right*. I'm sorry I hurt your tender feelings—*mister*." The man speaks in a singsong, like a child mocking a playmate. Kostas slams the rear door and, simmering, slides behind the wheel again. The burning sky, the baked and scalded slopes, the air flickering in the heat all seem cooler than the temper he is struggling to control.

"So now I answer your question, if you ask polite. The question: 'Mr. Kostás Demetríou, how far to Mytilene?' "

"Yeah, that's the question. Cor-*rect*, Meester Tahxi Mahn!" And he laughs.

"*Say* it," says Kostas in a deadly tone. His hands tighten on the wheel until under the bronze the knuckles are white.

"Go on, go *on*," says the wife. "We'll sit here and cook until you do—is that what you want?"

The man nearly chokes on the words, but he gets them out.

Kostas grins. "And I answer, also very polite: for you, Mytilene is fifty dollars from here." He starts the motor.

"Why, you—you goddam *pirate!* It was twenty *to* the hotel, and that's all you're gonna get for the return! I bet you threw this temper tantrum on purpose, *Mis*ter Kostas Duhmee*tree*-oo. Kostas—hey, that's rich! How much it gonna *Kos*tas?"

"Jesus," breathes the wife.

"Each," Kostas says. He turns off the engine. "Also pay now."

*They'll report him. I can't stop him. There's nothing I
can do to make him behave. They'll report him and the police will ask questions, and somebody will say, oh, that's
the woman whose husband left her, and the police will start
checking—oh, God! Stop it, Kostas! Mike—Mike will be
killed if you—if the police—*

The man is paying. His face a mottled purple and
his hands shaking, he fetches two fifties from an inner compartment of his wallet. These Kostas pockets
without changing expression.

"You just did a job called extortion, you know
that?" the man says thickly. "Which happens to be
a crime, pal. God damn you, I'm gonna get your li-
cense for this!"

"I tell you one more thing," Kostas says, and
laughs; I realize with a sense of shock he's enjoying
himself. "From here to Mytilene you not speak. Not
so much as one little word! In Greece is law against
bad language in public. You go to police about me, I
go to police about you, and *I* speaka da Greek!"

There is silence for the next forty kilometers.

The plane is coming in as we turn through the
gate. Kostas makes short work of emptying the cab.
"Kaló taxíthi'!" and he leaves them standing helpless
by the untidy heap of their luggage.

Nikos is clearly delighted to see us.

"I didn't know if you wanted me to meet you,"
I tell him. "Then I thought maybe you hoped to bring
the money. But it's too soon, isn't it?" Nikos glances
across at Kostas, a quick, covert look. "He knows,"
I say. "Also Yeoryios and Damian—I had to tell them,
Niko. It didn't seem to make sense not to." If the
money hasn't come yet, why is Nikos here? "Whatever did you tell Mr. Sarris?"

— 252 —

"That I have family trouble, my godson's family is in trouble and I must go. I have good news for you. Your Mr. Bingham makes no difficulties. He is cabling the money."

"Yes, he phoned. Don't worry, he was very discreet—you must have coached him very well."

"He is a man with brains—"

"How soon comes the money?" Kostas cuts in impatiently. "Katerina is much worried—is not important, how smart is this Mr. Bingham."

"My cousin says telex takes usually two to three days to Athens, then perhaps another three or four days to Mytilene. Because of the strike, of course, it may be longer."

"But that could mean next *week!*" I fight back tears of disappointment and dismay.

"Courage, *kyría mou*. I told my cousin they are not to play usual games with your money. I said this is very, very big deal I hope to pull off with your help, and if he gets money through quickly, before the deal collapses, I will see he is not forgotten."

Kostas says abruptly, "Maybe is Greek miracle—maybe money is already here."

"Not possible. Besides, Katerina needs her passport to prove who she is."

"I have it with me—Voula returned it yesterday, Niko. Why don't we give it a try?"

Kostas executes a snappy U-turn and we head back toward the city.

The Bank of Greece is in a narrow building near the bus stop, on the south quay. Nikos says it is better if I go in by myself, since his cover story for this whole caper is that I am a rich American woman about to build myself a house; it would not be likely that any Greek having hopes or expectations of profit from such a project would show up at the bank, and what other reason could be given for their escort? So: "Courage, Katerina. Alone is safer."

It appears that I have arrived at an inconvenient time. The desks behind the partition on the right are vacant, and the man behind the grille at the end (oddly dressed for a banker in a blue denim work shirt, and tieless) declares himself unable to help me. He asks me to wait. "There are complications, you understand." He does not elaborate.

Is he intending to check up on me? But I haven't so much as told him my name . . . I subside onto a bench against the wall, where I try to calm myself by studying the decor. Window draperies fall from ceiling to floor in folds of deep red, contrasting nicely with the white walls and the black slate floor: strong basic colors, each of them, fostering the notion of fiscal strength . . . I become aware that the "complications" impeding attention to my problem seem to be a cup of coffee and a cigarette, and that others, later arrivals than myself, are not only presenting their demands—in Greek, true—but, between puffs and sips, are being attended to. I take my place at the end of the line.

At last it's my turn. No sooner do I explain that I'm asking about funds from New York than I'm shuttled to one of the unoccupied desks. "He returns shortly, *kyría.*" Sip. Puff.

And so he does: another young man in blue denim, tieless, this one with a two-day beard. He shakes his head. "Nothing yet, *kyría.* Come back tomorrow before one-thirty, when we close. Or you could telephone; it will save you time."

Through Voula's switchboard?

"Unfortunately that's not convenient. I have a friend who often comes in to the airport—could he inquire for me?"

"Certainly, but I could not give him the money, you understand. You must come in yourself. There are papers to be signed."

"Of course." I hope my panic doesn't show in my voice, in my eyes. Will they want to know what I'm doing with that much money? Ask me to show proof I'm really building a house? "It's a considerable sum I'm expecting," I say offhandedly. "There will be no difficulties?"

"If everything is in order, *kyría*, what difficulties could there be?"

"It—uh—it would be awkward for me if you don't have enough." I can only hope it's good protective coloration to appear to be an idiot.

"It would be more awkward for me, I assure you. Have no fear, *kyría*. This is not a bank in a small village, after all." He gives a little smile.

"Thanks for trying, anyway, Kostas," I say dejectedly, and am about to get into the front seat again when Nikos takes my elbow and steers me toward the back.

"Come, Katerina, we have things to talk about."

"Cannot talk in front seat?" Kostas demands, turning.

"About some things, no. For some things there must be space. It is not so crowded here." He climbs in beside me. "Also I wish to smoke, and have no wish to set Katerina on fire." And he lights a cigarette, and smokes it in silence, and lights another, and smokes that one, and lights a third, and still he does not tell me what it is we have to talk about. We are nearing Petrá when Kostas says that as Damian's uncle, perhaps he can get him excused early, a remark that appears to goad Niko into saying what he has to say.

"I have come on purpose to tell you something, Katerina, which I now dread to tell you for fear it will end our friendship." When I stare at him, bewildered and frightened: "I have bad news," he goes on quietly, "and if I had not asked questions, you would not hear these answers yet. But I must tell you, and you must know. It is this: you cannot adopt Damian, even if you, your husband, and Damian himself want it very much. So do not put your heart on it. Greek law forbids. I am sorry."

My insides have given a sickening lurch . . . a reaction I am taken aback to realize is clearly not one of relief.

"Are you sure?"

"Very sure. It is true neither you nor your husband has Greek blood?"

"No. I mean, yes, that's—that's true. We don't."

"Or are members of the Greek Orthodox Church?" I shake my head. "Means no?"

"Yes, we are not." I can barely whisper. Oh God oh God . . . I *know* Mike has let himself hope . . . he has daydreamed . . . How can I tell him? He'll think I'm glad. I'm not glad, not really. Though in a way I am, because it's settled, it's not up to me—but at the same time I'm not glad at all. Not at all.

"I am very sorry, Katerina," Nikos says gently. "After the war—the Big War—many hundreds of children whose parents are dead are flown to the U.S.A. and adopted, no doubt by good people, but not Greek, and children now are not Greek either. So this is to protect the children, so they do not lose the language and the faith of their people. I am very sorry, Katerina, it is the law."

"Why you ask questions?" Kostas says sharply.

"Because I think I remember something about this, it is in the newspapers one time. Because I also think Katerina must not make plans, Damian must not make plans that cannot come true."

After a moment, I manage awkwardly: "It's not your fault, Niko, after all."

"I am glad you are not angry with me. It is human to be angry with the one who brings bad news."

We're stopping before the school. The gate, the wall, the trees are out of focus. *Mike came for nothing. He came and risked his life—perhaps has lost it—all for nothing.*

"I'll tell Damian, Niko," I say huskily, "but in my own good time, okay?"

Damian piles exuberantly into the front seat, tossing a ritual "What's new?" over his shoulder.

"All quiet," Nikos says, and Damian turns to give him a sharp stare. Then he sinks back in his seat to gaze in silence at the sun-washed slopes. We're skirting Molibos when Nikos adds, "Things not so bad as you think, Damian. This man I phone, the boss of your American father, he is sending the money."

"Good." Damian doesn't turn his head.

He knows there's something more. The sooner I tell him the better, I suppose; he has a right to know he's off the hook. But I'm reluctant. Worse: I'm dreading it. The words will put an end to Mike's dream. After I tell Damian, the dream won't exist anymore . . .

We have passed the cultivated fields that lie outside Pyrgotafos and are abreast of the tower when, finally, I ask Kostas to let us out. "Damian and I will walk the rest of the way."

We get out, and Kostas drives on.

"Why is my *koumbáros* come from Athens?"

"He has news he wanted to tell me himself, because he is very kind. Shall we walk along?"

"Where you want to go?"

"To your house."

"Past the tower is shorter." We turn off the road and are making our way beside the noisy stream when Damian goes on, still in that aloof, withdrawn voice: "It is something you can tell me, too, friend Kay?"

"It's something I must . . ." And so I tell him, bluntly and simply, using (they are burned in my memory) Niko's own words. "So you see it is a law your people intended for your protection, Damian, and to keep you Greek." *I must sketch him . . . Can I bear to? But I must have something of him to take back . . .*

We've reached the bamboo thicket. Absently, Damian plucks a blade and begins to shred it. "I never think I be sorry to feel safe from going, but I am," he says slowly. "I am very sorry. I think I wish I have two lives, one to live here a Greek, one to be your American son. He very lucky to be your son, your David. He had a good life, I am thinking, *fíli mou,* but too short." He gives me that sidewise look. "You are also sorry about this law?"

"Yes . . . and surprised to be sorry, like you." We both laugh a little, tentatively, as if testing a language in which we once were fluent but now have almost forgotten. As we leave the shade and set out once again in the brilliant light, I am astonished to hear myself add: "I have something else to tell you, Damian—something I've told no one else."

When did I choose? When did I decide Damian is the one I can trust, and not Nikos, or Kostas, or Yeoryios, or even Kyriakos? Maybe I've been making up my mind all along, just beneath the surface, so to speak. But Damian is only a child . . . Surely one of the adults would be a better choice? Well, I'd better be sure I'm right: once I confide the location of the drop there'll be no turning back . . .

As we make our way past a shepherd and his dozen or so sheep—Damian: *"Kaliméra, Babá Katsánis! Tí néa?"* *"Kaliméra, Damiané! Isihía!"*—I mull over my reasons, dredging them up as best I can and hauling them into the daylight for a closer look.

Niko first. Could he possibly have any connection with the kidnappers? Well, consider this: didn't he put forth, and in the strongest possible terms, his suspicions that Mike is faking, that he isn't really kidnapped at all, and then bingo! in the second note: *"This is no joke, Kay."* You'd almost think Mike overheard what Nikos said. When did he go back to Athens? "I am here only the one day—" Okay, say he left last Sunday afternoon: did he have time to go and have a chat with those guarding Mike? Maybe . . . And don't forget he did book us into the Silver Bird. He did see Mike to the plane . . . that plane on which Sanzio, it just so happens, was also a passenger.

Too many unanswered questions about Niko. Not the ideal confidant, not with Mike's life at stake.

So take Kostas. Or, rather, *don't* take Kostas! Clearly he is a man with a hot temper, a man with little or no regard for law who may think foreigners

— 259 —

fair game for any kind of extortion . . . In connection with which I shall dwell only briefly on that scene in the Silver Bird Sunday afternoon. What was he after—some quick (and free) sex, some genuinely reciprocal lovemaking (I doubt that!), or—most likely, but least flattering to either of us—a solid basis for blackmail? I wish I could dismiss this last notion out of hand, but I can't.

Yeoryios: another question mark. He detests Americans—"Don't your rich country tell my poor country," et cetera—but does this make him a kidnapper, an extortionist? Somehow I can't believe it. He was genuinely shamed by his wife's refusal to offer me hospitality. Still . . . given the chance to get in ahead of the kidnappers and empty the cache of $100,000—in drachmas, presumably untraceable—would he resist the temptation? As Damian said, such a sum would certainly pay for doctors. And Yeoryios does blame Americans as accessories before and after the fact, supporting the Colonels who are responsible for his injuries.

All right, how about Kyriakos? When he was needed to search up and down the coast, did he go? No, his boat was (conveniently?) unusable. Other than that he hates the Germans, is not rich, and has an on-occasion leaky boat, I don't know anything about Kyriakos. He's simply one big question mark.

Which leaves me with Damian. Granted, he's only a child, but couldn't that be a plus? He hasn't been corrupted, at least not yet. Nor humiliated, like Kostas. Nor crushed, like Yeoryios. Nor embittered, like Nikos. Never in this world would he nip in ahead and filch the ransom—I would bet my (Mike's) life on it! And, since he *is* only a child, he wouldn't devise some macho ploy to find and free Mike single-handed. Besides . . . besides, there is no one else.

"This is something only the kidnapper knows, Damian." I pitch my voice low, though no one's within earshot in the fields or on the lane. "I've heard from Mike again—from my husband. He tells me where to put the money." I reach into my bag and hand him Mike's note. "I don't know for sure where he means. I've got to ask you—to trust you, you see. There's no one else I dare ask."

His eyes are dark pools in his solemn face. "You do not trust me before?"

"No, I—well, perhaps I didn't *not* trust you—it's because it's not about myself, don't you see?"

He nods. "Better not until earned. What I do to earn this? I cannot think." The words, the voice, are not quite a child's.

Nothing: you've done nothing, Damian, just been. And what you've been—what you are—I love. I trust you because I love you. And I can't say it, I can't ever tell you in so many words, it would be such a betrayal . . .

He stares at me for a long moment, then lets his eyes drop to the paper. He tips it one way, then another, as if the sun's reflection bothers him. "I am sorry," he says at last, shamefacedly. "I cannot read this. Always my American father prints his letters on that machine."

"It says to leave the money in the tomb—that's the important part. That's what I'm trusting you not to tell a single soul, Damian. Not *anybody*. I don't know how they'll know when it's there—they have ways, I suppose—friends who will tell them. But what tomb can they be talking about?"

"There is empty burial room on my uncle Yeoryio's land." Damian says reluctantly. "Only other tombs would be in the—how you say 'burial place for everybody'?"

"Cemetery."

"In the cemetery in Molivos. If they mean one of those, how they will know which we choose? Unless they watching cemetery every minute, which is foolish. Easy to catch criminal who sits and watches, like cat at hole of mouse." He frowns.

"This tomb on your uncle's land—could my husband be there, do you think?"

"Not possible, friend Kay. My uncle works almost every day in olives—he would hear something, he would see."

"The tomb is near where he works?"

"But we walk past it yesterday. That small, small hill"—he gestures—"in olives."

"Sort of sandy and grass-covered?" I remember it vaguely. "Who knows about it besides your family?"

"It is not secret, friend Kay," Damian replies, flushing. "Is why town is named Pyrgotafos: means tower-tomb. Tourists come, poke noses in, take many pictures. You want go see?"

Once you know it's there, the tomb is obvious enough. It's in that haystack-shaped mound I barely noticed yesterday, the one just within the olive grove; the land is so undulating one more mild swelling hardly calls attention to itself, especially with the concentric circles ("rain-catchers," Damian calls them) of Yeoryio's hoeing as camouflage.

We've kept to the road past where his uncle is working, and now we slip silently from tree to tree, dodging behind the great hollow trunks of the patriarchal olives (these ancient veterans are somewhat scattered, with younger, smaller trees interspersed). Obviously Damian has been here many times before without his uncle's knowledge; it has been his game, I suspect.

The entrance to the tomb is a narrow gap between two rocks, in plain view, as I point out, of any observant passer-by.

"Is nothing to hide." Damian, too, speaks just above a whisper. "Tomb is empty for maybe two hundred years—ever since Turks, who knows?"

The gap is scarcely wide enough for me to squeeze through. Damian follows somewhat more easily.

In a few steps we've gone from brilliant day to late dusk. There is a strange smell of soil, dried up, worn out, reduced to dust. Once my eyes adjust I can see quite well. We're standing some two feet below ground level, in a space barely high enough to straighten up in and just about as wide as we can cover if we both stretch out our arms. Carefully, for the floor is exceedingly uneven, I move over to examine the walls. They're of smooth stone fitted without visible mortar; I can't tell if they're weight-bearing or merely some kind of facing.

Why *this* location for the money? To implicate one or both of the Demetriou brothers? No—too obvious. No one would believe they'd use a drop on their own land. On the other hand, either Yeoryios or Kostas very well might, and for precisely that reason: that no one would think they would. Or are the kidnappers being exceedingly crafty, counting on folks to assume the Demetriou brothers must be involved because it's so obvious they ought not to be? Probably none of the above. Probably the drop—where did

I pick up the term?—has been chosen simply because it's convenient: relatively isolated yet of easy
access to a public road, where anyone has a right to
be, and not be questioned.

"I show you something more, friend Kay." Damian keeps his voice low. "I show you passage to other
room."

"*Another*—" My heart constricts. Perhaps . . .
perhaps the whole kidnapping was conducted with
ruthless efficiency, consolidated, modern fashion, and
in there, in this second room, will be . . . Damian is
removing a stone from the wall opposite, and I am
eager to help. "Two, three more," he says. The stones
slide out easily, and we lower them cautiously to the
floor; a thud might bring Yeoryios running.

"How did you know these stones come out?" I,
too, am whispering.

"I come here often for to play. One time when I
am escaping from Turks—did not your son play such
pretend games?—I see there is this hole, this little
tunnel through—look there—"

Beyond the opening it is not entirely dark. Peer-
ing in—the passageway is roughly twenty inches
square and two feet deep; the stones we removed
merely blocked the opening, no more—I can make
out a space that may be as large, or even larger, than
the room in which we stand. What faint light there
is appears to be filtering from above.

"Mike?" Softly. And again: "Mike?"

Silence. Only the muffled stroke of Yeoryio's
hoe . . .

"What's in there, Damian, do you know?"

"Burial room, friend Kay. This where we are is
prothálamos. We learn about such things in school.

Lesvos a history book, my teacher says, with many, many pages. I say nothing—I not go boasting about what my uncle finds."

"You mean your uncle Yeoryios?"

"Yes, he find this passageway, I am sure of it. Two, three years ago, when Kostas is in Germany. I say nothing to Uncle Yeoryio that I play here—he has forbidden it."

"But you play here anyway?"

"I want to know what is here," Damian says simply. "Why I am not to go here. Is something to be afraid of? No. No bones of dead, nothing. I dig about. I find . . . almost nothing."

"Damian"—what more ideal, more quiet, more safe place than this in which to be entombed?— "Damian, when were you in there last?"

"Not since I know for sure you coming, friend Kay. But do not fear your husband is in there—how he is in there and we not hear him?"

Mouth slightly open as if to breathe in the slightest sound, I hold absolutely still. All I can hear is my own heart . . . I think . . .

"Maybe we wouldn't hear him if he's in there . . . if he's bound and—and gagged . . . if he's unconscious, I mean, or—or hurt . . ."

Damian puts his foot on the wall and hoists himself up. Before I can stop him, he has thrust himself forward and is wriggling through. I hear him drop to the ground amid a rattling of loose objects.

"Damian! Are you all right?"

"Yes—hokay—nobody here but me, friend Kay." His voice comes through eerily. "I have here for my American father a gift—I find it that other time." I hear some scuffling, the sound of things being moved about, and then Damian reaches through to hand me something . . . a metal disk of some sort, cold to the touch: a coin, perhaps. I hold it up to the meager light from the entrance and I catch the gleam of gold.

The light grows stronger, moves in swoops and plunges, now all at once fills the *prothálamos* with dazzling brightness. A lantern . . . Someone is in the entrance holding a lantern!

Its light falls impartially on the golden coin in my hand and on Verek's face, cold and accusing.

CHAPTER

21

Behind me I can hear Damian scrabbling like a cat at a window.

Her eyes blazing, Verek spits out a comment.

"Friend Kay, please to give me your hand."

"Damiané?" Verek's voice softens with relief.

I reach through, Damian heaves himself up, and a moment later he has wriggled through and tumbled lightly to the floor. Verek addresses him in a tone that is such an accurate echo out of my past my heart constricts. *"What are you up to now?" "Did it ever occur to you to ask?"* Women the world around scold in the same cadence: fear laced with relief and anger.

Damian is explaining, tipping his head winningly, turning on the charm. A smaller, younger Kostas . . . Will it work with Verek? It must have, many times, or he wouldn't try it now . . . It works. Verek lets out her breath in a smothered exclamation of vexation, gives me an enigmatic look, and eases herself back out. We follow meekly.

Verek has gone to speak to Yeoryio, who sets aside his hoe and comes striding toward us. "Please— to the house!"

When the amenities have been observed—I am offered a glass of lemonade, a fig in syrup; obviously I have not committed any cardinal sin—Yeoryios says heavily, "You go to this tomb, *kyría*—why?"

"To—to see if my husband is there—"

"No, *kyría*, you do not think that. You know I look. At once when you say he is missing, he is being held by enemies, I look. You do not believe me?" His eyes bore through me.

Does he think I have been lying? "When *you say* he is missing—" Does Yeoryios, like Niko, think Mike is faking? Or does he—do they—does everyone think I'm making this all up? That I've fantasized the whole thing? Or that Mike and I together, for some mad reason, between us have concocted this insane deception? Crazy Americans—who knows what they'll do?

"Of course I believe you! But Mike could have been put there later—he could have been put there last night—"

" 'Put there'—if he is dead? Is that your meaning?" I nod. "If he is dead, Katerina," he says more gently, "he is there"—he gestures—"in the sea. Too much risk to keep a dead body on land. Somebody sure to find, to ask questions." He gazes at me piercingly. "So—you and my nephew go to the tomb. You find there is no husband there, not alive, not dead. But still you search! My wife says you find something—"

Quickly, I offer Yeoryio the coin. A head in profile, the gold but slightly worn.

"*I* find it, uncle! *I* give it to friend Kay for my American father! It is not right he makes for me many gifts and I not give him nothing!"

— 268 —

"Where you find this—in burial chamber? Where I forbid you to go?"

"I play I am Trojan soldier hiding from Akhilleús, my uncle. I am Akhilleús waiting for to leap on Éktor, bravest of the Trojans. I not know is another room until one month ago." Damian crosses himself. "I not think is anyone buried there."

"No one is," Yeoryios says slowly. "Now." The word hangs in the silence while I, sick with fear, try to sort out its meaning. Then: "You play games too, kyría—you and my nephew? I tell you this is no game." He taps the coin in his callused hand. "Is no prize for most skilled digger. What is found on my land is mine. *Mine.* It is not your business, not your husband's business. It is nothing to do with you!"

"I'm not playing games!" I say hotly. "I am trying to find my husband! I couldn't care less what you find on your land or what you do with it—all I want is my husband safe! I'm not lying to you, Yeoryio—my husband is in danger! He really *is* kidnapped—they will *kill* him if I don't hurry and—and pay the money—"

Tell no one. Show no one. My God, whom *haven't* I told?

"I believe you, kyría Katerina. You speak from the heart." Yeoryios pauses again, studying my face. Then, deliberately, like a man taking a calculated risk: "It is three years now since I make more orchard. I must put in new trees among old; old cannot yield forever. So I dig, and I find rock, not far under the soil but not solid—you understand? I dig farther to see if this is stubborn rock I cannot move, or maybe far from its fellows so when I dig it out there is still much soil for the tree—a Greek cannot be defeated by a rock, *kyría*, or where would we live? When I have him uncovered, I see he is not hard to move. But when I have him out, there beneath are more rocks— it is no good place for tree, after all—but what I find is strange is there is small mouth between these rocks—small hole not round and smooth like for snake but in form of triangle. I am now very curious. This hole that I dig is near, but naturally not over, the *táfos*—the tomb, empty for hundreds of years, robbed long ago by Venetians, or maybe by Turks. I bring an electric torch and I look. What I see, Damian!"

Yeoryios turns to his nephew, who is listening wide-eyed. "Like a school of golden fish—not many, a few scattered—but gold, shining like little lamps. I put the rock back. I plant my tree though I know it will not thrive. Then I go to *thálamos*, which I now know is *prothálamos*—the true burial chamber is beyond, deeper. I search and search, for I know there must be a passage in, a passage which is closed after the tomb has received its dead. I search many days, *kyría*, and at last I find it. And I open it, and I crawl in. *Thávma!* What I find! One casket of bronze, with bones. Golden cups, not many—"

Verek interrupts with a sharp comment. Yeoryios shrugs.

"My wife worries you will report this coin to the authorities. I think you do not love them any more than we do. Also you do not wish to make them to notice you. So I do not worry you will make list for authorities of what I find." He clears his throat. "Six plates. Four goblets. Five cups. One armband. One breast plate. Twenty-two coins. And this"—he taps the coin in question—"makes twenty-three. I am surprised it is there for Damian to find; I think I search everywhere, everywhere. You are thinking maybe it is not so much treasure, after all? Is tomb of perhaps not very important leader, or maybe somebody else find it, many years ago—somebody who help himself quietly, like me. Because all these things I sell. I have the money safe, *kyría*, so you see"—Yeoryios coughs, as if the words stick in his throat—"I have money for my dead brother's son, for his lessons with this Englishwoman—he has no need for your husband's money. But I cannot say this. I dare not tell even those Help people. Where would I, poor man with small orchard, find such money? So I let them to send it, this Beta Beta Beta, and I let your husband."

Yeoryios is right: the last thing I want is for the police (or anyone else) to go mucking about the tomb. I wish I could go off by myself, away from Damian's shining eyes, away from Yeoryio's proud but shame-filled gaze, away from Verek's smoldering glance . . . go off and somehow reason this through. *Tell no one—repeat—no one.* And already I've told Damian, and as for Yeoryios, if he's in any way mixed up with the kidnappers, he already knows where the money is to be put . . .

"It may be several days before I have the ransom money," I say reluctantly, "and meanwhile please everyone act so that no one—no outsider—takes any interest whatsoever in the tomb, because"—*if I don't trust you, you won't trust me, and you'll watch to make sure Damian and I don't go digging farther, and they—the kidnappers—will see you watching and they'll think I did tell you, and they'll kill him—they'll kill Mike—*"because that is where they've told me to leave the money," I go on without a pause.

I'm watching Yeoryio as I speak, and there's no mistaking the incredulity that leaps to his eyes.

"*This* tomb? *This?* On Demetriou land?"

"Letter to friend Kay say to leave it 'in the tomb,' " Damian tells him. "No other is *the* tomb, I think!"

Troubled, Yeoryios turns to talk to Verek, I assume to tell her what I've said.

"My uncle says if you must put money in tomb," Damian mutters rapidly, his eyes on his uncle's face, "then it is true your husband is captured. He says that if this tomb on our land is the place for the money, then it is clear someone in Pyrgotafos or perhaps in Molivos is one of these pirates—who else would know of it?"

"My nephew is good interpreter," Yeoryios says dryly. "I say also that doctor of archaeology in Athens is not in business of kidnapping American tourists, and among no other Greeks is our unimportant little tomb much known. Only here, only in my village."

"I am grateful"—I can't keep the bitterness from my voice—"that you believe my husband really is in danger. Nikolas Paradellis does not think so—he told me he thinks my husband himself is trying to get money from me!"

"He says this, *O Nikos?* He says your husband *does* do this, or he says merely that it is possible?"

"Nikos says it is something I ought to consider as possible. I could see he believes it himself."

"You may tell him, *kyría*, that I, Yeoryios Demetríou, believe your husband has fallen among pirates. You may tell him also I say that in this life not to believe in danger unlooked for, in disaster not deserved, in death too soon, is to see with eyes of innocent child. In grown man is stupid." He smiles bleakly. "My friend Kyriakos say the gods punish the stupid, *kyría mou.* I think we must try very hard to be clever, you and I."

Verek leans forward and addresses her husband urgently.

"My wife wants you to know whatever is put on our land is put there by God and for use of family. The law says otherwise—we talk of this before. What is the law? Government, nothing more. Government can change. Family is forever."

Damian, who has been growing more and more restless, now bursts out: "The bones, *theîe mou!* These bones you find—where are the bones?"

"In cemetery, of course. In bones room."

"In Molivos?"

"Naturally."

"But, uncle—how you know bones are Christian?"

Yeoryios smiles. "I make sure. I baptize them."

"Are they still in the box of bronze?"

"I told you—I sold the box." Scowling. "Why you ask so many questions?"

"Because I am afraid for you," Damian says shyly. As if he finds his present mantle, that of guide and interpreter for and protector of adults, somewhat too large for him, dragging slightly on the ground. "If law says do not sell these things, perhaps one who buys is no true friend, and will go to the police and say, 'Look, look what I buy—' "

"Do not fear for your elders, we are not babies! It is against the law to buy, too, little one! You buy a treasure, too bad, you have to give it back to authorities, who tell you you are lucky you lose only your money, not your freedom!"

"Is it then a Greek who buys?"

"I do not know who, but it is not a Greek."

"Then when he leaves the country, and all his luggages are looked at and he is caught, he will say he buys from you."

Yeoryios glances at me. *He's hiding something . . . he's protecting someone . . .*

"Uncle Kostas!" Damian says joyfully. "He goes to Germany many times! Always he comes home for Easter, for my saint's day, for Christmas—it was uncle Kostas, wasn't it? He sold this box, these golden cups and coins you find—he sold them in Germany! He is so clever, very good actor, that Kostas—he can make everyone to think he has nothing! Who would suspect simple worker going back to German vineyards?" And Damian throws back his head and laughs with glee. "Then did you give him some of the money, uncle? Is that how he buys his taxi?"

"I do not give him the money." Yeoryios tousles Damian's hair. "He gives me my share—that is only right, for all the risk is his. But, yes, you are correct—with his share he buy his taxi."

Only the cab isn't paid for . . . or is it? I recall with some uneasiness Kostas boasting his cab is free of debt, and Yeoryios pointedly reminding him it better not be, not on his earnings . . . Was Yeoryios questioning the division of the profits? Or did he mean Kostas would be well advised to keep up a pretense of not having much money? Evidently Yeoryios himself hadn't gone for medical help (if my sources are reliable), but was that because his share wasn't adequate to meet the costs, or because the entire village would wonder where he got the money? And there would be whispers, and jokes, and guesses . . . and the authorities, no doubt, have many ears . . .

"Yeoryio," I say, much troubled, "what would happen if you were caught? You or Kostas?"

"Prison." The word drops like a stone. "Our freedom is in your hands, *kyría mou*. I tell you what I tell you not because I trust the tongue of a woman to be still"—he smiles without humor—"but because I must. I cannot have you report the coin Damian finds. I cannot have you hope to take it with you to your country. What Damian says is true: they would find it in your luggage and you would tell them where you got it—oh, yes, *kyría*, you would tell—'in Pyrgotafos,' you would say, because why not? They know you have been here, you merely tell them what they already know. And men from museum in Mytilene would come, they would see someone has been digging—"

He is almost begging me . . . He *is* begging me, this proud, heroic Greek. I cut him off. "Don't worry, Yeoryio, I know the coin is not mine to keep. I agree with Verek: what's found on your land is yours. I'll not say anything to anybody, I swear it. And now I must go—there may be news for me at the hotel."

Yeoryios, too, gets to his feet. "You do not talk now, not while husband is in danger. But what of later? When husband is free, and all is well? You may be thinking if both uncles are in prison, authorities will give nephew to American parents!"

I shake my head. "You knew I would say nothing or you would have told me nothing. If you or Kostas were to wind up in prison—which God forbid!—because of anything I might do or say, you know very well Damian would simply wash his hands of me. And he'd be right!"

"Wash my hands?" Damian regards his hands with some bewilderment. They are indeed very grubby.

"Have nothing to do with me." I manage a smile.

Yeoryios walks me to the courtyard gate. "I was once in prison, *kyría mou*," he says softly. "Though that was not dishonor, you understand. Those who truly loved Greece were then all in prison. But never again, I tell you. I cannot breathe behind bars. My heart will burst."

"I will say nothing, now or ever, I promise you. You have my—my word of honor. Besides, I'm not Greek—it's not *my* country's treasures you have taken. As for what's right or what's wrong," I go on hastily, "who am I to judge? I'm only too willing to bend the rules myself, I notice, when it's a question of my husband's safety!"

Damian touches my arm. "I go feed Erasmio. You want come say hello?"

I can hear a car, still some distance off.

"Kostas will drive you, *kyría* Katerina. I think you have enough walking for one day."

"All right." Though being alone with Kostas is nothing I particularly look forward to. "In just a moment, Damian." I watch him make his way down the path to the vegetable patch, shoulders slightly hunched, hands thrust into the pockets of his shorts. Clearly there's something he wants to say to me in private. Well, it will have to wait.

Turning back to Yeoryios, I find myself speaking in a low, hurried voice but with the utmost—and, I would have thought, totally uncharacteristic—frankness. "If anybody asks me anything—I mean if—if you're in any trouble about selling those cups and coins and things you found—you know what I'll say? What about Yeoryios Demetriou's *own* wealth, I'll say—wasn't that a—a Greek national treasure? And wasn't it Greeks who robbed him of it? So leave him alone, I'll tell them, he's just trying to swap one for the other!"

Yeoryios gazes at me, not smiling, but not (I think) shocked, either, but rather with (it seems to me) warmth. Kinship, perhaps. He says something under his breath, but in Greek, and Damian is not there to translate.

Then, in a voice he hasn't used with me before: "I see, Katerina, you are able to understand my grief. I think in your woman's way you share it. You understand what I would do to repair my loss: I would do almost—though not quite—anything. *Anything.* And that is why I fear so much what *you* might do, to have a son."

I shake my head. "Damian is quite safe from me, Yeoryio, don't worry." I hear Kosta's taxi turning into the lane, and add hurriedly, "I can't possibly have him legally—ask Kosta, he knows all about it—and as for stealing him"—I manage a smile—"I wouldn't dare! *Some* Greek treasures, I feel sure, are protected by Zeūs!"

I find Damian leaning against Erasmios, his arms around the beast's neck. He straightens when he sees me and makes a pretense of playing with the blue-bead necklace.

"I tell Erasmio I am very glad my uncles don't need money—is nice, nice feeling!" He smiles at me, uncertainty in his voice. "Is it not lucky, friend Kay, that my uncle Kostas has time to sell the treasures in Germany before he has no work there and must return home?"

What if . . . what if, after all, Kostas didn't manage to sell all the treasure? Or sold hastily, without getting full value? If those treasures had to be smuggled out of Greece in great secrecy, surely they had to be sold—and sold by experts—without stirring the slightest ripple, certainly without alerting anyone in Greece. How could Kostas have realized anything like their true value? And how did he—an immigrant worker—know to whom, and where, and even (relatively uneducated as he was) for how much?

"Very, *very* lucky, Damian!" I say with the heartiest reassurance I can muster. "And let's not worry Kostas, okay? He has enough on his mind trying to help me get my husband back. So I won't say anything about that coin you found, and don't you, either. We'll leave that to Uncle Yeoryio—okay?"

And for the life of me I can't figure out why I said that . . . what my subconscious is trying to say. (If anything.)

Though we are alone on the drive back to Molibos, Kostas is reassuringly proper, yet friendly. (". . . a fine actor, my uncle Kostas . . .") He chats the whole way about the Germans, "who go everywhere in Lesvos, everywhere, but never in taxi, always in the little bus. Though sometimes, it is true, they walk, like foot soldiers, first here, then there, like tireless bees looking for sweetest flowers . . ." It's a safe topic, impersonal, unprovocative. I don't have to say a word, just listen . . . or not, if I don't care to. If I have other things to think about.

At the hotel Nikolas Paradellis is pacing the lobby, his cigarette trailing blue smoke.

"Nikos! Is the—has anything happened?"

"Nothing. Here all is quiet." He gazes at me with something very close to exasperation. "I worry very much when you do not return. Why so long to walk and talk to Damian? Why Kostas does not bring you to hotel? Maybe you walk back—maybe you must be alone, to think your thoughts which cannot be happy ones—and walking back, you have met with an accident!"

"You are like silly hen squawking after chickens," Kostas says scornfully. "How Katerina gets hurt? She is too large for eagle to carry off, and here we have no wolves." He claps Niko on the shoulder. "Now is your turn to keep her safe. I go ask if I have tourists for tomorrow. You want ride to Mytilene, Katerina?"

I am acutely aware of Voula, smoking peacefully behind the desk. "Couldn't you do that errand for me, Kosta? You know, the one I spoke of—"

"Yes, hokay, no problem!" He gives me his warm smile, a smile that cools abruptly as Herr Professor Furchtwanger comes herding his flock toward the terrace. "Everywhere—I tell you they are everywhere! Is not three years of Germans enough for one man's life?" And he stalks across to speak to Voula.

Nikos asks me if I'd like a beer, and we take a table by the railing. "Katerina, I ask you a favor, as your friend I ask it. As godfather of Damian I ask. Please, tell me where you go. Always. Please."

I am truly astonished. "Whatever for? And how can I?"

"What will you do tomorrow?" Doggedly. "If you know, tell me, please."

I am about to confess I have no particular plans when, as if on cue, a voice at my elbow, speaking German, invites me and my husband to join him on his return visit to Ayiassos tomorrow. It is Herr Furchtwanger, beaming, hung about with cameras like a Christmas tree. "I have in my little bus much room, for many of our number grow fatigued and here at the hotel will stay—oh, disgraceful! Not to see site of ancient city of Brisa!"

"No, thank you very much indeed," I reply unhesitatingly, my German flowing like cream. *"Kýrios* Paradellis here has very kindly invited us to join him on—on a picnic!"

"My misfortune. I cannot, then, persuade you"— he glances about, as if under some vague prompting to locate my elusive husband—"to admire the historic town of Mithimna in the beautiful light of evening? I wish to memorialize on film the sunset bathing the walls of the castle, the stones of the tower. You who are a true artist, Frau Cunningham—you at me will laugh, but these remembrances I store up, and then in the winter, in the tedium of the cold weather, my little pictures I paint!"

"Thank you, I have had a long day and am somewhat tired."

As Furchtwanger bows, turns, and strides purposefully off, Nikos mutters that he begins to agree with Kosta, these Germans are an infestation. The barman sets glasses and two opened bottles of beer on our table; behind him is Voula, a slip of paper in her hand.

"A message for Mrs. Cunningham."

It's from Bingham, I see in one swift anxious glance—an extravagant message that spurns cablese.

No quarrel worth this suspense. I pray for
your speedy reconciliation. Please let me know
when you welcome him back. Remember Mike
is devoted to you, as are we all, so forgive.

My eyes brimming, I hand the cable to Niko.
"Very competent, our man in New York," he says solemnly, and fills my glass.

CHAPTER

22

"—settled by colonists from the Tródia," Nikos is saying, "nearly three thousand years before Christ." I force myself to pay attention: *what* was settled? "There were stone houses inside strong stone walls with many defenders—some think the tower is one such." He nods toward the structure where it looms a hundred yards or so off the road. "I think it is not so old—maybe dates from the Trojan war, fifteen hundred years later."

Nikos, perhaps to justify his continued absence from his job, perhaps to ensure he's kept posted on my whereabouts, has appointed himself my escort, along with Damian, who also is AWOL, having flatly refused to go to school. Right after breakfast this morning—my God, it's Wednesday already! *Six days—* counting today, Mike has been missing *six whole days!*—right after breakfast the two of them walked me from Molibos to Pyrgotafos, where they made me drink a lemonade in the *tavérna,* and now they walk me back again, more slowly. No doubt it's good therapy, but the way seems very long, the sunlight blinding, and as the day moves on toward noon, the heat savage. Damian behaves like a half-grown hound, making numerous side trips to check out any possible place of concealment: a rude shelter for sheep, a shed for a farmer's *mikhaníki*, an isolated chapel. Nor does Nikos choose topics I can safely tune out: the philosophy of educating an elite for leadership, the difficulty of publishing poetry, the integrity of the writer and how to protect it—"Freedom of the press means only freedom to choose which lies to read," he remarks—every now and then an intelligent comment on my part is called for, and so I must not allow myself to dwell only on Mike—Mike's danger, Mike's distress of body and mind, the first likely date of the arrival of his ransom, the tricky business of effecting the exchange . . . *if* they have any intention whatsoever of effecting an exchange . . .

"I think it not so old," Nikos repeats, for I am eyeing him blankly. "You want to go up, Katerina? There is much to see from the top."

"Kostas and I climbed it Sunday morning. He had Kyriako's glasses, and we searched all along the coast." I can't keep the weariness and discouragement from my voice.

"Kyriakos looks today. His boat is all repaired. There will be nothing, Katerina. Your husband is not in the sea."

"How can you be so sure?"

"If he is kidnapped they will need him to convince you to leave the money. If he is author of all this, then do not worry—he is alive, well, comfortable—"

"Niko! Please! I *know* Mike is not faking anything!" If I can't convince Niko Mike is really kidnapped, I think irrationally, then it's hopeless, I'll never get him back. "I'd *rather* he were faking, damn it! At least he'd be snug somewhere, as you suggest—he'd not be afraid, sick, perhaps in pain! Do you realize he's been shut up somewhere *six days*— if he's been t-tied all this time, his legs must be h-horribly cramped!" *They'd have to gag him. They'd have to chain him . . . gag him . . . drug him, maybe. Oh, God, if they were to miscalculate . . . give him an overdose . . .* As for being safe, they don't need him anymore, Niko. I got a second message, and it tells where to put the money. I mean, Mike tells me. So now all they need to do is to collect it—"

"It tells where to put it?" Incredulously.

"Yes—why not?" Oh, why not tell him? Hanged for a sheep, et cetera. Though I won't show him the note, of course. I'm not going to tell anybody about the Jimmy code. That's family . . . private to Mike and me. "I'm to put it in the tomb."

"That is what it says? 'In *the* tomb'? It speaks of only one?"

"Yes. I assume they mean the tomb among the Demetriou olives."

"I do not like this, Katerina," Nikos says slowly. "It is clear your husband could not have thought of this himself—unless of course Damian writes him about this tomb."

- "Why don't you ask Damian?" I say coldly.

"You are angry—"

"Of course I'm angry! How can you *think* Mike would plot to—to terrify me this way! To get money from me! You said you thought he was nice—'very nice man,' you said—"

"Katerina," Nikos says quietly, "I have choice, and

for me I choose what is less bad, as you do for you. Tomb on Demetriou land is very, very old. Sometimes old things are forgotten, but not when they are in the name of the town—when one is reminded every time one says the name. Kostas takes tourists on trips all over Lesvos, but by request of Yeoryio *not* to the tomb which is in his olives; tourists are a plague, they radiate destruction. Besides, there is nothing there for tourists to see. So who would think of this tomb as place for the money but someone who lives in Pyrgotafos? Or in Molivos, but I think not. In Molivos are many good hiding places. So naturally I prefer it to be your husband. It is very great dishonor to come from a village where someone is terrorist like this, a pirate who captures the American father of my godson!"

Only a failed poet, I think wearily, would contemplate his own loss of honor at such a time.

"This second note—when did it come?"

"Monday evening sometime, after dinner but before—oh, ten or so."

"Again it is in your box, Katerina? And again no one sees who put it there?"

"I didn't ask—Voula is eaten up with curiosity as it is. But she wasn't on duty. At least she wasn't when I came back from a walk and—and there it was."

"If only we could go to the police!" Nikos says crossly. "For us everything would be easier." He scowls up the slope at Damian, who is bounding down like a mountain goat from one of the ubiquitous sentry huts. "Police would find out where everyone is when these notes appear. Maybe they do not find out who puts them, but they find out who cannot, and that would be of comfort. Now we do

not know. It could be me, Nikos. It could be Kyriakos, Kostas, Yeoryios—could be Voufounos, Taour-
ouflis, Stathakos the mayor—"

"Ye *gods*, Niko! Your own friends! Damian's own
people!"

"Are they not human beings, swayed by human
need?"

"But the *mayor!*" I say, half laughing, close to
tears. Nikos is right: there's no way to know whom
I can trust. "At least I know it isn't you, Niko—you
were in Athens when the second note came."

"Ah, but my fellow conspirator put it there. My
good friend the mayor put it there—he sends word
to me through my sister Melita—he needs money for
Molivos' harbor which is no good for tourists' ship,
they must anchor far out and trembling old women
must climb down into little, little boats—"

"All right, all right! It could be anybody!" I feel
an irrational anger. I know he's trying to help, but
can't he see I need to trust *some*one?

As we near Molibos, Damian rejoins us, walking
solemnly by my side. The soft swish of the waves,
the sighing of the wind, the bells punctuating the
slopes where the flocks graze now give way to the
staccato cough of *mikhaníki* motors, the rasp of a
handsaw, the chatter of a radio. I look at Niko spec-
ulatively. Suspicion, I find, is highly contagious . . .
and chronic. One might argue that even his insistence on accompanying me everywhere is hardly innocent. True, this way he knows I'm "safe," but also
he knows at all times precisely how far I've come in
unraveling my problem . . . Why not put him to a
test? See what he says?

"You know, Niko," I say confidingly, "yesterday

when I awoke I had a kind of—of waking night-
mare. I was thinking of all the places Mike might be,
either alive or dead, and I've looked—or one of us
has looked—in almost all of them, I think, except—
well, except in that cedarwood chest in your mother's house. And then I thought of some kind of coffin—quite large, and—and of stone, I think—there
may have been more than one. That was the most
vivid . . ."

Nikos is gazing at me with blazing eyes. Then:
"There are such chests in every house in Pyrgotafos,
Katerina. The bride brings this chest filled with bed
linens when she comes to her husband. If your husband is dead—if he has been dead since Friday
night—he is not in one of these chests, *kyría mou*.
Impossible! Here we must bury our dead within fifteen hours of the soul's passing—it is the law, the
rule of the church. We do no indignities to the body,
we return the body to the soil, but quickly, quickly.
Because of the climate, you understand. I truly believe that unless your husband has been thrown into
the sea, he lives, Katerina. We would know it otherwise."

I stare blindly into the dazzle of light to the east.
Trust a poet to put it plainly . . . There is a change
in the sea, it seems to me. Instead of the docile,
tamed, rhythmic splashing, now it grabs impatiently
for the shore, snatching greedily at the rocks. An
omen, I think: it doesn't have Mike yet, but it will
. . . it will.

"To dream of your husband in a coffin: that is only
natural," Nikos says. "It means nothing. Such a
dream would anyone have who, like you, is torn with
worry. Damian is right—I must take you to the cem-

etery. If you dream of *sarkofágoi*, we must go and look. Dreams must be respected. Kyriakos would say it is how the gods nudge us along the way they would have us go."

We mount the broad steps that lead in a sweeping curve to the little plaza before the cemetery gate; this stands half open. We go in. The cemetery, I find, is not large, covering little more than an acre. It is a crowded, cluttered place of stone tombs like great shipping crates, of flat slabs in sandy stretches patched with weedy clumps of grass, of narrow cobbled walks and flights of leaf-strewn steps, of willows and a fig tree and a huge cedar. Along the far side a low, windowless, cement-block structure looks completely out of place.

Nothing is like anything in my dream.

Nikos leads the way to the building and opens the door, which has neither lock nor latch. He gestures for me to enter.

As my eyes adjust to the gloom (the only light is from the open doorway), I see there are heavy shelves set around three walls, and on these shelves are stout wooden boxes, similar in design to but somewhat smaller than packing boxes for books. Each is marked with the Greek cross and some lettering, which I do not try to decipher. The air is very dry, with a strange, faintly animal smell, not pleasant, not unpleasant.

There is nowhere here that Mike could possibly be concealed, alive or dead.

"When I was about fifteen," Nikos says in a dreamy voice, "I would come here to the ossuary and look at these bones. I would try to see if I could tell who is rich man, who is poor, who is good, who is bad." He shakes his head. "Impossible to tell. My friends say I make them melancholy—I fear this conversation makes you the same, Katerina."

Damian is looking about, a curious alertness in his manner. "I wonder which—" He breaks off.

"Which is your mother's?" Nikos says gently. "In the corner, with the Demetriou. I bring you again, Damiane. For now I think *kyría* Katerina has had enough."

We come out into the light and the heat of life once again.

"Some of these tombs are true *sarkofágoi*—word comes from the ancients' Greek, it means 'to eat flesh,' " Nikos remarks conversationally as we make our way toward the entrance. "We use the word for the kind of stone—it has much lime in it—from which the tombs are made. In three years there are only bones, you see, and these we move to the ossuary. Same for those in the wooden coffins"—he gestures toward a section where there are only simple stones flush with the ground. "Bottoms have only slats, to make easy the work of the worms."

When I can find my voice: *"Moved?* You mean you *dig up* the dead?"

"Why not? It is only bones, Katerina—it is not a person any longer. Cemetery is small—all cemeteries in Greece are small, we have not much land, after all. Each must take his turn."

Damian looks interested. "How they know who is ready to come up? Hokay if wait too long, but if dig too soon—aieee!"

"Family remembers," Nikos says shortly. "Also is duty of keeper of cemetery to keep records, who goes to ossuary, where next to dig for newest coffin, and so on. Not to worry, Damiane."

I clear my throat. "What about the Pyrgotafos ossuary—did anybody look there?"

"Ours is only a very small village, Katerina. We
bring our dead here to Molivos."

"More friendly, the *óli mazí*," Damian says cheerfully. He leaps onto a slab, then, at a word from Niko,
leaps lightly off.

We descend a lane so narrow and steep it is more
like a rain gutter, past Spyros Armenis the ropemaker, and on to the square by the harbor. There sits
Kyriakos the searcher-for-Mike, at a table with two
other men, playing cards. *Pouláki Mou* is moored near
the wharf, for all the world like a faithful hound
sprawled patiently outside a saloon.

Kyriakos tosses down his hand, rises, and strides
to greet us.

"I tell Katerina you search along the shore today," Nikos frowns. "Why you are here, lazing in
the shade, drinking coffee, playing *khartiá?*"

"Waiting for you, my friend." Kyriakos claps him
on the shoulder. *"Pouláki Mou* and I go up and down,
up and down from Akra Korakkas to Skoularis.
Nothing, Katerina, give thanks always to Poseidón.
No husband drowned anywhere. So now come, forget the heat, come for a sail. *Pouláki Mou* wants show
off how fresh, how clean, how everything fixed like
new."

"Maybe friend Kay is hungry," Damian says. *"I
am hungry!"*

"I take you to Pyrgotafos, we eat some good *mez-
éthes* in *tavérna*. I bring you back to Molivos, maybe
you like swim ashore to hotel like mermaid, Katerina!"

I begin to suspect Kyriakos may have been

— 290 —

drinking oúzo with his coffee. But so what? I certainly don't feel like going on to the hotel, putting up a front before Voula, asking for messages, avoiding that room from which I am convinced Mike was abducted; I don't want to sit alone on that balcony, pretending to eat . . .

"Thanks very much, Kyriakos, I'd love to sail to Pyrgotafos."

"Damian and I come, too," Nikos remarks dryly, "so all is proper."

"Not to worry, *mátia mou*. Katerina is safe wherever she goes." Kyriakos flashes his pirate's smile. "Kostas say she wear virtue like a crown."

Nikos says levelly, "I am not surprised he knows."

As *Pouláki Mou* rounds the point and purrs toward Pyrgotafos, I can see a dozen little fishing boats about half a mile offshore, heading toward Molibos.

"They are late," Damian observes.

"Winds are fickle as young girl's heart," Kyriakos says. "Makes for slow voyage."

Nikos is inspecting the shoreline with Kyriako's glasses. "You have much trouble with your boat?"

"A gash along the side. Two planks sprung. Takes me three days to caulk and mend. I do not know how it happens, who does this or when." Kyriakos scowls. "I think first some idiot swing against her when she is at anchor—but this would not push in from beneath."

"Why you not use sail today? You invite Katerina to come for a sail." Pointedly.

"Wind is off the land. Hard to run in close by sail."

"Sail is stored below? Katerina would like to see how it is stored."

Kyriakos stares at him. "What is this? You make questions like policeman!" His voice roughens with anger. *"Kyría* thinks maybe I have her husband stored like cask of fish waiting for market? So then I, a madman, invite her aboard?"

"She would like to look," Nikos says stonily. "She must look everywhere."

"No—" My instinctive protest is as much against the shock on Damian's face as against the implication in Niko's words, but Kyriakos has jerked up the hatch, and, bowing in mock deference, he beckons me forward.

Folded sail, coiled ropes, assorted buckets . . .

"Go down and look *under* the sail, *kyría,"* Kyriakos says, his eyes stormy.

"*I* look," Nikos says. "Katerina does not wish to examine your boat, she is too trusting. I trust nobody—nobody! I look God himself in the eye and say *prove it."* He slides below, lifts a corner of the sail, looks under the bow and toward the stern, two areas I cannot see in their entirety from where I stand. Climbing out again: "Nothing," he says.

"I am sorry for you, Katerina." Kyriakos resurrects his broken-toothed grin. "You have madman for friend."

"I do not know from which direction danger may come," Nikos says evenly. "If the notes she received from her husband are genuine and he is indeed abducted for ransom, who knows what such men will do?"

Kyriakos turns to me in astonishment. " *'If'* he is abducted—you have doubt of this?"

I say wearily, "Nikos thinks Mike himself may be trying to get money out of me."

Kyriakos turns and gazes wordlessly at Nikos. Then: "Yes, I speak truth, you have madmen for friends, *kyría mou*. Yeoryios is crazy for olives, Kostas for women; I am crazy for fast ships and freedom, but Nikos—Nikos is crazy for crazy ideas. Crazy!" He waggles his fingers by his head. "Not much left up here. Too bad!"

"If her husband makes a drama of all this," Nikos says calmly, "then he cannot love her or he would not put her through such torment. If he does not love her he could be a danger to her."

Waves slapping the bow punctuate the silence following this remark.

"I see, my friend," Kyriakos says gently, "it is not your brains you have lost. I am sorry."

Oh, God, whatever next? I take up the glasses and turn to inspect the shore. What is the matter with these Greeks? Must they be so . . . emotional? If Nikos fancies he's in love with me, will he really, *really* try to find Mike? And perhaps not a single one of them—not Kostas, or Kyriakos, or Yeoryios, *or* Nikos—not one shares my conviction that Mike most certainly *is* kidnapped. Perhaps each, for reasons of his own, prefers to think there's been a quarrel, that Mike and I are on the verge of divorce, that this is Mike's way of getting "alimony." Perhaps the only one who truly believes Mike is in danger is Damian . . . Damian who cannot be a son to him . . .

My face must be more expressive of my thoughts than I realize, for Kyriakos touches my arm and says, "Be glad you cannot have him, Katerina. Nikos tells me about this law. Do not grieve. Damian will be happy here. You think because some Greeks want be rich not tomorrow but now, this minute, all Greeks think only to be rich. Not always true, *kyría mou*. A man works hard all his life so when he is old and rich he can sail his own boat. Damian will sail his boat when he is poor, which is while he is still young. Is this not better?"

"See the troubles my American father has because he is rich, friend Kay." Damian is perched like a gull on a pile of rope. "Better to be poor and live quietly. The hawk sees the bird with the brightest feathers."

"You talk like wise old man," Nikos says, smiling.

"Too bad you are not so wise as your godson," Kyriakos remarks.

"I am what I am," Nikos says shortly. "If I am a fool, too bad."

We drift all along the shore where the current might have taken him, searching with naked eye, searching with binoculars.

"Friend Kay and I go swimming here." Damian tosses the comment into the unhappy silence as if to stir it up, to disperse it. "I am surprised when she not find the water cold. Comes from Vosporos."

"No, cold current is farther out. It comes from north, and goes to east and south. But here it is turned, going more west. Look!" And Kyriakos tosses a fragment of cork overboard. "See how it goes slowly toward Molivos. Here by the tower water is not so warm. Nearer the point the current from south comes in close, swimming much better there, Katerina— warm, warm like in Persefoní's pool."

"Swimming not good there at all," Damian laughs. "*Karpoí* there, Kyriako."

"Now, yes—that is true. I speak of when they will be moved, *Damiané*."

Through the glasses I can see the little triangular signs, the litter among the stones, the shimmer of bamboo against the base of the tower, the green marking the course of the little rills that now and again find their way across to the sea . . . but nowhere do I see—does anyone on *Pouláki Mou* see—any sign of Mike. Nothing. Mile after mile of nothing.

I am giddy with fatigue and hunger when, at about quarter past two, we put in to the dock at Pyrgotafos. Kostas is waiting by his cab.

"Good news! All flows smoothly, no road blocks! We make happy trip to Mytilene, Katerina and I!"

"First all must eat," Kyriakos says firmly. "Katerina is hungry, I am hungry, and Damian could eat a wolf."

"But won't the bank close at three?" I say anxiously.

Nikos guides me to a table. "It is closed now, Katerina. It is Wednesday, after all."

"Today bank has hours from eight to half after one, also from five to eight in the evening," Kostas intones in his tourist-guide voice. Then, flashing his searchlight smile: "In Greece is nothing boring, Katerina, day after day the same—even the banks play games. I take you special. Do not worry—for you, special price!"

"For Katerina, special trip, my friend." Kyriakos signals the waiter. "Katerina goes first class, she goes free, and better she not go alone."

And so I am well escorted when, at four o'clock,

we—Kostas, Nikos, Damian, and I—set out for My-tilene. I spend from five-thirty to six in the bank; shortly after seven-thirty we are back in Pyrgotafos, mission accomplished. I am intoxicated by hope, and in a state bordering on euphoria: at last something has gone right!

I have been afraid, of course the bank might make difficulties over the size of the transaction. Nothing of the sort! Mr. Two-Days' Beard assures me he has already verified the code number by phoning telex, that everything is in order if I would let him see my passport . . . if I would sign these papers. "Thank you, madam, always the formalities, is it not so?" He then asks me how I would like the money. When I say in thousand-drachma notes, he looks at me with such ill-concealed curiosity I'm framing an explana-tion (coached by Nikos) of what I'm going to use it for—"My fondest dream, a little haven by the wine-dark sea"—when he asks me how I'm planning to carry it. "You will need a shopping bag, at least, madam!" Kostas, laughing, goes to buy one. And in this canvas sack the bank official stashes thirty-eight packets of thousand-drachma notes (one hundred notes per packet) as casually as if they were grocer-ies. Damian insists on carrying the sack to the taxi; it's too heavy for ladies, he says. Kostas hefts it, and agrees, it must weigh all of six kilos, he says gravely.

As we hit the road for Molibos, I remark that as long as one has one's papers in order, the Bank of Greece appears not to care one whit whether you're getting one hundred dollars or one hundred thou-sand.

"Sending it *out* of the country, Katerina," Nikos says dryly, "would be another bucket of fish."

He waves aside my thanks as we let him out at his gate.

"Katerina, you cannot spend this night alone in a hotel. Do not argue. I tell my mother you come here tonight."

I fight back sudden tears. Damn . . . Damn! "I'm not arguing. But I—maybe I ought to stay where Mike would expect me to be, Niko. Where he would come looking for me. Or—or *they* would expect to be able to reach me, to tell me where he is, I mean. Where they've—they've left him—set him free."

"You will put the money in the tomb tonight?"

"Of course—as soon as possible."

"Better after dark," Kostas says. "So nobody see."

But they'll know it's there . . . whoever "they" are. Somehow they'll know—won't they?

"Katerina, they would not telephone you through hotel switchboard—much too dangerous," Nikos says firmly. "If they pick up money tonight, perhaps by morning will be a note at the hotel saying where is your husband. Perhaps not—perhaps is too soon, also there may be hindrances, someone always in lobby, tourists photographing the dawn—much can happen. We can only hope hotel all asleep, same as before. Perhaps they release him and not even bother with note—then no problem. But if money is gone and husband does not come and no word either, nothing—I rather you be with my mother, Katerina."

I stare at him for a long moment. Then, to Kostas, quietly: "Please drive me around to the hotel so that I can see if there's any message . . . any further instructions. If not, we'll go back to your brother's and I'll do what I have to do, and then I'll walk back to Zoë's."

"My pleasure, Katerina *mou*." Kostas is looking at me with—I can't mistake it—pity and concern. Like Verek, he thinks I'm a widow, I'm sure of it. Already, or soon will be.

As we swing into the hotel drive, there drawn up before the door is a jeep, not khaki, like the army's, but dark blue. Lounging against it, smoking and chatting, are two white-helmeted young men in dark blue uniforms. *Police. My God, they're police* . . .

They straighten, discarding their cigarettes as we pull to a stop (what else can we do?), and stroll over.

"Kostás Demetríou?"

"*Naí* . . ." Unhurriedly, Kostas gets out. Damian and I slip out the other side. I can't say about Damian, but I am sick with fear. If they search the cab . . . If they see the sack . . . *"What house by the sea, kyría? Where?"* And then they'll question Voula, of course. And then me: *"Your husband, kyría—where is he?"*

Kostas is slouching against the cab in an attitude of utter nonchalance, but stationed where he will best block their view of the interior, rear. There is an exchange of Greek, low key, not, it seems to me, accusatory . . . I catch the word *Sanzio.* More Greek . . . Damian is examining the jeep with every evidence of pleased curiosity, so I can't ask him what's up . . . and wouldn't, in any case. As for me, I'm not being precisely ignored, but any interest the police pay me appears to be extracurricular, so to speak. I decide to act the American Tourist.

"Excuse me." I address Kostas, my tone halfway between arrogance and impatience. "Will you be long, do you think?"

"No, *kyría*." Deferentially. "There is no problem,

kyría. They wish merely my help in a matter concerning a tourist, but it can be postponed. Please to attend to your concerns, *kyría*. I shall be at your service."

In a state of high nerves I stride briskly into the lobby, collect my key (the box is otherwise empty), and go to change into something that'll be less visible than white duck pants on my way to leave the ransom . . . if, that is, the police haven't already spotted it in the back seat of the taxi and confiscated it. I choose wine silk trousers and long-sleeved shirt—dark shades of red all look black at night, I reflect, and then, too, the outfit has a certain formality that may get me past the police without it shrieking "radical" or "conspirator." I put flashlight and a few toiletries in my bag, on second thought toss in that navy silk knit, just in case, and am recrossing the lobby when the lady archaeologist waylays me apologetically. Did my husband and I accompany the Herr Professor Furchtwanger to Ayiassos? At dinner she has missed him. He does not return also? I'm afraid I'm a bit short with her, explaining that no, we did not go to Ayiassos, but that no doubt the professor has stayed over—ruins at sunset and moonrise hold for him a fascination—and I hurry on out onto the entrance steps, where I find Damian and Kostas waiting by the cab, and the police gone.

"I must go to Petrá later, Katerina," Kostas says as we head back through Molibos. "Body washes up there this morning early—no, Katerina, it is not your husband!" For my face (I am sure) reflects the anguish that explodes within me. "Is short, fat fellow, this dead, with not much black hair. No papers, which makes problem. His clothes not Greek, so police ask at hotel in Petrá, at Silver Bird. Voula say maybe is this wine salesman who left for Mytilene on Saturday. Maybe he does not go to Mytilene, who knows? Will she go and look? they say. She is not happy to go, that Voula. Is much better that I go, Kostás Demetríou, I see this man for longer time than she, I see him for whole drive from Mytilene. I come every day at six o'clock, she say. They wait. They wonder why I am late. Not late, busy, I say—American lady wants go to bank in Mytilene not in morning, when everybody else go, but in afternoon, special trip, private. Hokay with me, I tell them, she pays extra. Is very rich, I tell them. Beautiful lady but spoiled, very spoiled." And (incredibly) he laughs.

"They didn't look in the cab?"

"No, to them taxi is like innocent donkey: deaf, dumb, harmless. Besides, Damian makes them nervous for their jeep. They tell him not to touch anything, but he cannot help himself. He strokes it like he thinking maybe to buy it."

Very competent, my men in Molibos . . .

And then, inevitably, the reaction: Why Sanzio? Why is he dead? Are the kidnappers fighting among themselves? If so, over what—the division of the money? Or are they quarreling over Mike's release—when, where, how . . . or if?

Mike . . . oh, Mike, Mike . . . It is a prayer, a placation, a chant, an incantation. As long as I say his name, he is alive. It is a bargaining, a propitiation, but with whom and in what currency I do not know . . .

Yeoryios offers to go with me to the tomb. I shake my head. "This is something Damian and I must do by ourselves. I think somehow we must—" I'm about to say "placate the gods" when, under Verek's steady gaze (though I know she cannot understand my English), I feel compelled to change it to a stammered, "s-say a proper prayer."

Verek disappears into an inner room, returning with a large two-handled willow basket, a candleholder like a spiked saucer, and a short honey-colored candle, which she first warms with her hands, then gently impales on the spike.

"My wife say to leave the candle burning," Yeoryios tells me. "This candle was blessed in the church on Easter morning. She say it will keep the evil spirits away from the money, and, if God wills it, it will let the money buy your husband's safety."

Covering all bases . . . The thought prompts an unwelcome shiver of laughter, which I choke down.

Verek transfers the packets of notes into the basket with reverent care, counting them as she does so. (For whom?) Then she covers them with a cloth, tucking it in on all sides.

"Looks like bread for *paniyíri*," Kostas says cheerfully. His successful evasion of search-and-arrest has buoyed his spirits indecently.

Awkwardly, I take the candle. "Yeoryio, Verek, Kosta," I say, embarrassed at asking the same pledge twice yet superstitiously compelled to do so, "I ask you once again to tell no one—"

"Already we promise," Yeoryios says with offended dignity. "If one promise is no good, two such are double no good."

"Yes, I—I know. I'm just making a ceremony. But you see, you three—and Nikos, of course—are the only ones who know where the money is to go. Except the kidnappers, naturally. They must feel absolutely safe, that it's truly safe to come and collect it. So I ask you, and I will ask Niko, not to watch to see who comes."

"You have my word, Katerina, and my hand on it." Yeoryios takes my hand in his; it is like clasping a rough piece of wood. He turns to his wife and (I assume) repeats our exchange, for she crosses herself. *"Neh neh neh!"*

"And I give you my word of honor, Katerina *mou,* that I will not go to the police and I will not watch to see who comes," Kostas says, serious for once. "As I hope for heaven"—he, too, crosses himself—"this I say to you is truth."

With no more ceremony Damian and I pick up the basket between us and set out down the shadowy lane. A mockingbird is filling the soft evening with music . . . Does Mike hear one such, wherever he is now, at this moment, the sun not long down, the moon not yet risen, the air cooling, sweet, sweet with flowers on the tangled hillside? The world is so beautiful, no one should be feeling such loneliness as washes over me, such loss, and grief, and guilt, and dread. And how Mike may be feeling I cannot bear to think. The agonizing pain of cramped limbs bound too long . . . thirst . . . hunger . . . terror and rage. Fear is my constant companion, as it must be his; it is my bedmate, my other self. *What if, what if* . . . I don't dare think ten minutes ahead or I lose my courage—what's left of it. *Tomorrow at this time I may see his face . . . Oh please, God . . . please . . .*

Damian has lit the candle, and thrusting it ahead of him through the narrow opening, he slips through. I follow, holding the basket as carefully as if it indeed contains the ceremonial bread. Someone—Yeo-ryios, no doubt—has replaced the stones of the passage into the burial chamber; by candlelight it is impossible to tell just where they are.

Damian sets the candle on the floor, and I put the basket beside it. It does look like a picnic lunch, I think absurdly. Or as David and I used to do . . . we'd leave a candle burning, and a snack out for Santa Claus . . . I look up and meet Damian's eyes.

"I, too, pray, *fíli mou*," he says softly. "I pray for the safety of David's father."

I reach out my hands, and he takes them, and so here we stand, our hands clasped, the money and the candle between us.

"I ask my mother to help," Damian says in a whisper, his eyes wide, the candle making dancing lights in the expanded pupils. "I ask her and I ask my father, too . . . to help, to pray. Do you believe, friend Kay, that this can be?"

"Yes," I say. "Oh, yes!"

And I do believe it, at least here, at least now.

The candlelight is dazzling, blinding. "We'd better not leave it burning," I say in a whisper. "It might be seen from the road."

"Not needed any longer, prayers already gone to heaven," Damian says confidently, and blows it out.

We return to the house hand in hand. As we approach the courtyard gate, I say, "I feel . . . not so alone. I feel comforted. Do you, too, Damian?"

He doesn't answer at once. Then: "Nobody tell me what color my mother's eyes are, but I think black, like mine. But just now, she look at me from yours, friend Kay, though yours blue like *thálassa*. This is very strange, and I do not understand, but I like."

He looks up at me. In the light from the open doorway I can see him smile.

"I . . . am very glad . . ." is all I can manage.

I wish I could say I saw David looking at me from yours, Damian, but I didn't. I don't. I see his eyes only in Mike's . . . only in Mike's.

CHAPTER

23

I am awakened by a cry—a woman screaming something—some phrase—over and over. The sound spills out from somewhere down the lane . . . No, it's in the street below: the cry flung against the house walls, rebounding. And then there is the sound of someone running, stumbling in panic, the footsteps sharp on the stones, and again the cry: *"Panaghía mou!"*

I sense Zoë sitting up, staring, as I am, into the pitch dark. There's desperation in the cry, and anguish. Perhaps I ought to go and help. Is anyone—

The cry comes again, much farther away, and then the faint, distant sputter of a motorcycle.

"What *was* it she said?" I ask urgently, knowing full well Zoë doesn't understand my English. *Damn* not knowing the language! And again: "What *was* it?" Anything this night could bode disaster.

Zoë pats my hand. *"Panaghía mou,"* she says soothingly, and on her tongue the words convey no tinge of panic. She curls again into a plump ball, and promptly goes back to sleep.

I have no idea of the time. Though it has been a long and exhausting day, I found it hard enough to get to sleep the first time. Now, my thoughts spiraling, I find it impossible.

The money . . . is it still in the tomb? Or have they already come after it, crawling in through that narrow opening, sending a pencil of light here and there . . . Now they've seen it, they've snatched it, they've gone back to their lair . . . They're counting it, gloating over it, dividing it . . . Is Mike watching? Oh, God, I pray not! They'll never free him if he is! Perhaps he can hear, though; he can hear them counting, quarreling . . . Maybe he's already freed! Maybe right now—this very minute—he's stumbling along some unmarked lane, his legs scarcely obeying him. Doggedly, he keeps going, not knowing where he is, where the lane leads him, his one thought to put distance between himself and his captors before they change their mind . . .

Or maybe he's still prisoner, he's still bound, gagged, blindfolded, forced to listen as one of them argues it's too soon to free him, first they must make their own getaway. Then how is he to be freed once they've gone? And another says, openly, bluntly, in some language Mike understands, that he can't be freed—he can identify them—he's heard their voices, which they haven't bothered to disguise. Perhaps, with cruel carelessness, they've even addressed each other by name, never intending for a moment to free him . . . as he's known, he's known all along . . .

Or perhaps they haven't collected the money yet, it's still in the tomb because the kidnappers think it may be watched. Or perhaps they don't even know it's there. It's the wrong tomb entirely. No, it's the right tomb, they do know it's there, but they heard that woman scream and think the police may be about. And it will still be in the tomb in the morning, for any amateur archaeologist/tourist/camera freak to happen on, and report to the police. And they will confiscate it, and ask questions, and prowl about, and Mike—Mike will die . . .

Stop it, Kay! Think about something safe, and calming, and sleep-making . . . Nikos, who promised so calmly, and sensibly, and—and consolingly, not to watch the tomb. And why not? He has no intention of watching—why should he? He'll pick up the money in his own sweet time, and meanwhile, he wants me here so he can watch where I am . . . Probably he told Zoë to keep me "safe" here . . . What! Do I now suspect Nikos again? But Kyriakos thinks Nikos is in love with me—isn't that a motive? Nikos thinks I have money, that all Americans are rich . . . He knows I own a house, a big, an absurdly big house . . .

It's no use. I tell myself I must sleep, that I'll need all my strength, all my courage, all my self-possession. For Mike's sake I must, I *must* sleep . . . The window is taking shape as the sky pales toward dawn before at last I escape into that blessed oblivion.

This time it's a tolling bell that awakens me. The strokes fall across the village like a hammer on stone.

Bong . . . Bong . . . Bong . . .

Zoë is braiding her hair by the window, the sky her halo, pearly white, dazzling.

"Someone has died, Katerina," says Nikos from the doorway. "I go to ask who."

Gone . . . Gone . . . Gone . . .

Not Mike! Please, God—not Mike!

Almost at once Nikos returns. So sure am I that someone has come across Mike's body—that the kidnappers, the money safely theirs, have dumped his mute and helpless body in a ditch, in an empty chapel, on the beach—anywhere—and the woman who ran screaming in the night had stumbled across it . . . I am so sure of this, the picture is so clear, the details so sharp, it is a moment or two before I grasp what Nikos is saying.

"Old Voufounos died in the night, Katerina. His daughter ran for the doctor, but he died before the doctor came."

Zoë: "O Evánghelos Voufounos? Khardiá?"

"Naí." He regards me soberly. "Please to accompany my mother when she calls on the widow, Katerina. It will comfort the family if the American mother of Damian does them this courtesy. No, do not be alarmed"—for the bell is tolling once more—"it is again for old Voufounos, to make sure everyone has heard." Then, at a question from Zoë: "Thío." And to me: "Funeral is at two o'clock."

"Today?"

"Certainly today. Have I not told you it is the law? Also there is no need to wait. He has brothers in Molivos; his wife and daughter are here in the village. No problem."

And what of Mike? The money—is it still there? I can't ask. Perhaps Damian will think to look. As for any word at the hotel, surely Kostas will check? Or, in the face of a death that everyone knows has really happened, does Mike's predicament diminish in urgency? For everyone but me, that is . . .

Zoë, Nikos, and I set out. His sisters are not expected to pay condolence calls, Nikos explains, being very young and as yet unmarried. They will of course attend the funeral; everyone in the village will be there.

I begin to suspect my inclusion in this expedition again is intended as therapy: engage the American in a real tragedy, perhaps we can be spared her hysterics over her pretend one . . .

"Niko, you must tell me what is correct. Is there something I should say—something that is the custom?"

"Leave to my mother to speak good of the dead—after all, you did not know him. For you is enough, 'sillipitíria mou'—it means, 'my condolences.' "

I practice the phrase as we go down the lane.

"Do you think I ought to wear a hat, or a black scarf, like your mother?"

"You are not yet a widow, Katerina," Nikos replies evenly. "My mother wears the scarf in mourning for my father, not for old Voufounos."

"I'm sorry. I didn't realize your loss was recent, Niko."

"My father died with Damian's—they were arrested together. My mother will wear black the rest of her life, unless she remarries."

"I see. I've noticed many Greek women wear black, but I thought it was—you know—a practical color."

"In this climate?" Dryly.

"But Verek wears black, and yet Yeoryios lives."

"That is for her father. My sisters do not wear the black because they are young and of another generation. It is not the law, you understand, but the custom. Sometimes it is to avoid gossip, but with my mother it is the true grief. I remember my father very well. He and my mother made a good marriage."

"They married for love, you mean?"

"That I do not think. They did not meet until the

wedding—she is from Athens and my father was the schoolmaster in Molivos. But if we do not marry the women we love, we Greeks"—his smile is melancholy—"we try very hard to love the women we marry, and in this my father succeeded." He glances down at his mother. "He said it was not hard."

Voufounos' house abuts onto a small square, stone-paved except where one severely pruned sycamore emerges to give anchorage for the clotheslines stretching like the ribs of a maypole to the surrounding houses. Today these lines are bare, no doubt out of deference to the dead. Chairs have been set out along one house wall, and already floral wreaths are hung by the Voufounos steps; propped next to these, a six-foot-high elongated flat object covered with purple cloth unmistakably marks the house of the dead. Men with black armbands stand by the door, cigarettes trailing smoke. They step back to let us pass.

Inside, four black-clad women sit in a row on straight-backed chairs. As Zoë tearfully embraces each, Nikos presses the first woman's hands and bends to kiss her cheek. To her mumbled question, *"mitéra Amerikána Damianoú tou,"* he murmurs in reply, and she gives me a toothless smile. I stammer my phrase of condolence, and allow myself to be urged into the next room.

It is small, crowded, windowless. In the center is the coffin—a bier, actually, I suppose—with a row of folding chairs on either side. To the dead man's right, Mrs. Voufounos and her daughter, both in starkest black; as Zoë slips into the empty chair beside them, they neither move nor speak. On Voufounos' left, two men with black armbands are graven images: the brothers from Molibos, no doubt. Nikos seats himself next to them, and someone brings a chair for me, placing it slightly to one side as if not to play favorites.

In silence we all contemplate the dead.

The bier is covered with a purple cloth trimmed with gold braid. A single tall candle at Voufounos' head and three at his feet flicker in the draft from the door. His body is tucked all about with flowers: lilies, carnations, roses. He is dressed in what must be his best (possibly his only) suit, freshly pressed, somewhat shiny, thin, cottony-looking . . . saved for Sundays and feast days, perhaps . . . From where I sit, at his feet, I have an excellent view of the pattern of his socks, for he wears no shoes; it seems strange that feet so informally clad should be so still. His head rests on a pillow with an elaborately embroidered snowy white pillowcase (from his widow's bridal chest?), and his hands are tied together with a purple scarf. A gold-paper something—perhaps a prayer—is tucked into his unresisting fingers.

My mind, which until this moment has been curiously blank, has just entertained the notion that there is nothing here to be afraid of—certainly not poor old dead Voufounos—when his daughter bursts into sobs, rocking back and forth and wailing, *"Patéra mou! Patéra mou!"* I stare at my clenched hands, my eyes burning. *Better you should weep for him than he for you, Eleni . . .* Her mother sits like a stone.

Nikos rises and touches my arm. I yield my place to a newcomer.

In the entrance, one of the old women offers Niko a gilt-framed picture of a vigorous-looking young man; Nikos kisses it and passes it to his mother. I am handed a small glass half full of some dark amber liquid. Fire courses down my throat and warms my chest.

Nikos carries his glass onto the steps, where he pauses to light a cigarette. When Zoë and I emerge, he is down in the square, talking with Yeoryio.

"*Kaliméra, kyría* Cunningham," Yeoryios says formally.

"*Kaliméra, kýrio* Demetriou."

It seems an occasion for Greek only.

Yeoryios tips his head, and I move away from the cluster of people. When we are more or less alone (the square is still nearly empty), Yeoryios says quietly, "The money is gone. This morning early I go to see. I think if we do not get your husband back today, *kyría mou*, we do not get him back at all."

I know just saying this can't make it happen; nevertheless, at the sound of the words my heart constricts painfully.

"Where is Kostas? Did he check my box at the hotel?"

"Nothing, *kyría*. Empty. Now he takes tourists to plane—what a capitalist! No time for paying visit to new widow! But he returns for funeral, of course."

"And Damian?"

"In school. I tell him it is best he do as usual— makes less talk."

I try to picture Damian trapped in a classroom on this of all mornings, attempting to appear interested, attentive. "Yes," I say faintly. "I suppose you're right . . . There's nothing I can do?"

"No, *kyría*, I am sorry. Nothing for you but wait. Wait, and pray."

The classic role for women, I think bitterly.

Now people are gathering, two or three drifting

in together, to talk in quiet voices and stare at the house. "You see we do not leave those who grieve to grieve alone," Nikos says as we start back. "To stay away is a disgrace. The farmer toils in the fields on Sundays and on saints' days, but when someone in the village dies, he puts down his tools and comes: death is after all the most important thing in life."

"Ought I to send flowers, do you think?"

"No, you are guest here—a stranger. It is not expected. My mother will bake a *kolivozoúmi*—a funeral cake—and I will bring a bottle of *koniác*."

I feel cut off, isolated. That's all I am here: no more than a stranger. I stare bleakly after Zoë as she sets out for the marketplace, and something of what I'm feeling must show in my face, for Nikos says quietly, "If you wish it very much, Katerina, flowers from Damian's American mother would be of much comfort. No one wishes to impose, you understand. I have noticed it is not the custom among foreigners to make gifts, except perhaps in what we call a 'play for power.' When we Greeks give—and we give often—we do so simply for friendship."

" 'Play for power'? What on earth do you mean?"

Nikos shrugs. "A parent gives a child a gift. It is to show his love, he thinks, but also he hopes to bind the child's gratitude. A young man makes a gift to a young woman to win her heart—more than her heart. Your husband sends gifts to Damian, to help him, true, but also to prove—perhaps only to himself—that he is a good man, generous."

"Is that so wrong?"

"Not wrong, but not so right, either. Best way is not to know the giver, Katerina. Give, but put no name on the gift."

"All right, I'll not say the flowers are from me. That's what you want? No one to know whom they're from?"

"They will know, just the same." Nikos smiles. "And you will be all the more praised because of it. If you follow the road to Sikminia for two kilometers, you'll find the woman who makes the wreaths."

I'm grateful for the walk. It's something to *do*, something to be *doing*, to fill the void, the rift, the vast crevasse in time between *now* and *then*, when Mike is back . . . or is not—is not ever coming . . . A steady breeze off the sea tempers the sun. Small birds skim across the road like cards flung, to be caught in a row of fig trees. The oil rigs are busy again in the channel, though whose they are I cannot tell. *If they dump his body out there, and it's . . . retrieved . . . will anybody bother to report it? Or will they just throw it back . . . a nuisance catch . . . trash fish?*

I make my way across the square (now nearly full) to leave my modest wreath with one of the old women in the outer room. Returning to Nikos's, I find Zoë has put out a plate of food and a bottle of retsina; this consumed, we set out, Zoë on Nikos' arm, his sisters and I more or less escorting one another.

Three black-robed priests have joined the people in the square. More stools are brought, are soon filled. Latecomers stand about, quietly talking, watching the door of Voufounos' house, gazing thoughtfully at the wreaths that now cover the house wall.

"That's the mayor," Nikos says in my ear, indicating a short, thickset man with hair almost as long as Yeoryios'. "Over there—the man speaking to Papá Andrónikos—is the notary; we call him the matchmaker because he signs the banns. And there is Ioanna the weaver; the baker you know—"

It seems to me everyone I have ever met or heard spoken of in Pyrgotafos is here, with the glaring exception of Kostas Demetriou. Surely he should be back from Mytilene by now?

Propped against the cropped tree in the center of the square are three religious banners. Several boys about Damian's age squat nearby, squabbling over a game of pebbles; in their bright shorts and striped shirts they look like tropical birds let loose in a flock of ravens. Beyond the tree Kyriakos is talking with a thin, bent old man Nikos says is the ropemaker from Molibos. On the far edge of the square I see Yeoryios and Verek, silent, unmoving.

"Who's that behind the mayor?" For my attention has been caught by a fellow as conspicuous as a rooster and almost as raucous. Conversing loudly with himself, he has dispensed with jacket and tie; beneath his unbuttoned vest his shirt blazes forth like a sunset.

"Mayor's brother, Stefanos Stathakos. For him he is almost sober."

Exactly on the hour of two a bell tolls thrice. After a few seconds' silence, it sets up a continuous clamor lasting a full minute. A man emerges from the house, retrieves the coffin lid, and returns within. The crowd begins to stir.

Again the door opens. Eleni Voufounos hurtles out and plunges down the steps. With a cry like the shriek of a wild bird—shrill, unmusical, defiant—she flings herself across the square, the crowd parting before her like the Red Sea, and begins to beat her head against the stones of a house wall. The assembled crowd, now silent, shifts slightly for a better view. I am horrified: someone should *stop* her, she'll injure herself! But now an old woman moves to her side, stroking her shoulder and murmuring to her. Eleni, trembling and wailing, allows herself to be led back inside.

Ceremoniously, the three priests don their chasubles; these are of fine white linen elaborately embroidered in gold and silver, with bejeweled icons of the Christ on the back. As the priests pace slowly toward the house, three of the little boys resignedly pick up the banners, while the others drape themselves with three wreaths each, one around the neck, one on each shoulder. Like victorious ponies, I think. (And am immediately ashamed.)

Now men are maneuvering the coffin out of the house and down the steps; they appear to have difficulty keeping it horizontal. One of the priests clears the way through the crowd, chanting in a strong, melodious voice and swinging a censer in a wide arc; layers of pungent incense mark his passage.

Zoë and I fall in with the silent throng that follows along the narrow streets behind the priests, behind the boys with their banners, behind the four bearers and their burden, behind the widow and now silent daughter, behind the brothers and the neighbors and the friends and fellow townsmen. It all seems so theatrical as to be unreal: the chanting, the incense, the extravagance of flowers piled about the body—a body clearly visible in the gap between the lid and the bier; one can only hope the blossoms keep the weight of the lid off old Voufounos's face. It's a scene from an opera, I tell myself; it's a stage performance, nothing to touch me, thank God, nothing to remind me . . .

At the church door the lid is lifted off and set to one side, and as the mourners follow him in, old Voufounos is borne high, a fallen warrior on his flower-covered shield. Again the chanting and the incense and the solemn circling around the body by relatives and friends, again the dazzle of the candles and the shimmer of gold and silver icons, again even the anguished daughter kissing and caressing her father's hands: all, all helps insulate me, helps protect me from being tricked into reliving the unbearably familiar, unbearably beautiful rite I endured after David. *"He cometh up, and is cut down like a flower . . . He shall gather the lambs with his arms, and carry them in his bosom . . . We commit the body of this child to the ground . . ."* Here—and for once I thank God for it—I am sheltered behind my blessed ignorance of the language, I can keep it at arm's length, a piece of theater . . .

Suppose Mike is dead—is this how I will have to bury him? With rites that are nothing to either of us, with pomp he would scorn, with prayers whose meaning neither of us knows? Shall I have to say good-bye in an unknown tongue . . . bury him among strangers . . . leave him to the speedy attention of the busy worms?

They carry old Voufounos down to the harbor, where the kind services of Erasmios are available: there he stands, drooping in the shade of a fig tree, and nearby is a simple two-wheeled cart with a high seat and a space behind just large enough for the coffin. As Yeoryios untethers the burro and backs him into the traces, the pallbearers set down their burden, one of them removes the coffin lid, and everyone gazes once again on the sunlight playing on the face of the dead man; some touch his cheek or kiss his hands. Then again the lid is balanced on top, and the coffin is lifted into the cart.

The little boys with their banners set out steadfastedly for Molibos, followed by Papa Andronikos, chanting (what happened to the other two priests?), followed by Erasmios and the cart, followed by all the rest of us. Yeoryios is the only one (besides Voufounos) who rides; aside from holding the reins, his main task is to keep the coffin steady over the frequent breaks in the pavement. Everyone else, even the widow and grieving daughter, must walk in the blazing sun, past the *karpoí* signs just beyond the tower, past the sentry hut (for once with no music playing) where two soldiers stand at rigid attention, must walk in the blazing sun the two miles or more to the wide steps that mount the slope to Molibos cemetery.

The cart can go no farther. The coffin is eased out, eased down; once more the lid is removed and the indifferent dead is bathed in sunlight; once more his stillness is assailed by inarticulate cries of grief and parting. The lid again in place, the four bearers lift the coffin and begin the long climb.

Halfway up there is a wide landing, and here everybody is glad to rest. The bearers step back and yield place to four fresh; there is another repetition of farewell kisses, caresses, tears, and cries of grief. Shamefully, I feel impatient: they're overdoing it . . . why prolong it? The mayor's brother may feel the same, for every stop he refreshes himself from a flask he carries in the inner pocket of his vest.

We reach the cemetery gate. The lid is removed,

and this time Eleni flings herself on her father's body. "*Patéra mou! Kýtaxeh patéra mou! Apístefto!*"

"What is she saying?" I whisper to Niko, shaken.

"She begs us to behold her father's body—that she cannot believe what she sees."

So we sat, Mike and I, two carved figures, not touching, not weeping. And I, too, told myself *I can't believe it, it hasn't happened, I don't believe it happened, in a minute we'll be back to before, and none of this will have happened* . . . But I did believe it. Just as Voufounos' daughter believes it, however she may scream and cry. Are her extravagant demonstrations of grief any help at all—a healthy catharsis—or do they only intensify the pain she's feeling?

Now the procession enters the cemetery and winds along the shady, leaf-strewn paths to the grave, which is, of course, already dug, though not, it seems to me, very deeply. The coffin is set down and the lid removed (for the last time, I hope fervently). Again the daughter flings herself to her knees, wailing, "*Patéra mou! Patéra mou!*" As someone draws her gently back from her father's body, my eyes sting with sympathetic tears. What! Do I weep over a stranger's grief, I who stared dry-eyed at the coffin of my own son?

How can I bury him, Mike, when I still can hear him call? "Come and see!" And very clearly I answer, "Coming—coming right away!" And I go. Oh, yes, I go. And I say, "David, ye gods, use your head! Not into the road, David—it isn't safe!" And he doesn't go down, Mike. He laughs at my fears, but he doesn't go down. "Just a minute, I'm coming!" I say. And he waits for me. He does, Mike. He listens to me, his mother. Who loves him. Who always made time for him. Who always put him first . . .

— 319 —

The priest is chanting again, melodiously, this time with a layman (at any rate he wears no vestments) responding. And now the mayor's brother commences to imitate the antiphon, not joining in but coming like an echo, a beat or two behind, mockingly. He emits short bursts of crowing and yammering in a pseudo-devout intonation that convulses some of the children on the edge of the crowd. The mayor turns on his brother a glare of such ferocity that Stefanos backs away, loses his balance, and stumbles into the open grave.

As Kyriakos strides forward with the clear intention of hurling him out over the heads of the crowd, Stefanos seizes a shovel from the nearer grave digger and begins to parody his activity, tossing a whirlwind of sand onto the pile on the far side, stopping, jerking upright at exaggerated speed. Abruptly he stops, tilts forward, and (I can't quite see) apparently makes brushing motions with his hand. Kyriakos, too, has been brought up short on the edge of the grave, staring in. Then Stefanos strikes an attitude like an operatic tenor, caterwauling in Greek at the top of his lungs. A ripple of appalled laughter washes over the crowd.

"He says, 'This bed is taken, gentlemen!' " Nikos tells me, not taking his eyes from the drama before him. "He says, 'Try next door!' "

Stefanos has stooped, is grasping something—what? a root?—no! oh, God! a hand!—he's shaking a hand and shouting, *"Kaliméra, kýrie!"*

With a gasp of horror the crowd surges forward, cutting off my view, but not before I have caught a glimpse of what it is that Stefanos Stathakos is hauling out of the grave, hauling it toward him as if it were a brazen intruder, a trespasser, pulling an arm, a jacketed shoulder, a head of blond hair—

"*Mike! Mike!*"

My cry wilder, more shrill than Eleni's, I am running, stumbling down the shallow steps, thrusting, pushing through the crowd, pleading in English (all Greek forgotten): "Oh, *please!* Please let me through! My husband—it's my husband! Mike! *Mike!*"

The priest turns and makes a regal gesture to stop me. I duck under his arm, hurtle myself to the edge of the grave—and gaze, in an exultation of relief, into the sand-encrusted death mask of Hermann Furchtwanger.

CHAPTER

24

Embroidered robes flowing, Papa Andronikos strides forward. He puts a brief question to me, and when Kyriakos answers for me in the negative, with a flick of his hand he indicates I am to be removed from the graveside; another flick of his hand instructs the grave diggers to place Furchtwanger's body to one side; and when the two workmen have scooped the body up and slung it behind the excavation in a gesture singularly devoid of deference for the dead, Papa Andronikos proceeds unhurriedly to complete the prayers for the legitimate claimant of the site. The chief mourners leave. And now one of the grave diggers jerks the embroidered pillow from under old Voufounos' head and tosses it out of harm's way; then, stooping, they both drop the coffin into the grave as casually as a man would heave a chunk of rock into a foundation trench.

Nikos touches my arm. "The rest is not our concern, Katerina. Come, we speak once more with the family."

Kyriakos says something to him in low, urgent Greek. Nikos nods, and taking my arm, steers me through the stagnant crowd and out the gate. Here it is like running the gantlet: on one side, the widow, the daughter, the female relatives; on the other, the men. I am still numb with shock, and I cannot think of the phrase Nikos taught me; I press the women's hands and say, "I am so sorry, so very sorry," over and over. As I reach the end and am about to accept the wine being offered all the women, Nikos puts a paper cup in my hand. "Better the brandy. Drink, Katerina."

He is right: before its warming fire the deadly chill spreading from the ashes of my terror slowly dissolves.

Nikos says softly, "The mayor goes for the police. Kyriakos says we must hoist sail and be gone before they arrive."

We go down the long flight of steps at a pace just this side of headlong. Yeoryios and Nikos swing onto the seat at the front of the cart; Verek and I tuck ourselves on the wooden bench along one side, Zoë and her two younger daughters opposite. "And Melita?" I ask, looking round.

"Gone to the mayor's," Nikos says. "And Kyriakos will stay behind, perhaps take a drink or two in the *tavérna*, and listen to what is said. Is often useful, what one hears in the *tavérna*."

"I didn't see Kostas anywhere, did you?"

"You do not see Kosta because he is not here." Yeoryios flicks the reins and Erasmios moves forward with maddening slowness.

"Perhaps he has trouble with his taxi."

"Yes, I hope so," Yeoryios says grimly.

We're all talking around and around the one subject in the forefront of our minds: *Hermann*

Furchtwanger—how did he die? Where? And who put him in the grave? Someone is bound to tell the police about my behavior. They'll surely wonder why I screamed out my husband's name. And what did Kyriakos say to Papa Andronikos about me? If only we could get together on a story . . . because of course the police will come asking questions. They'll be poking around and poking around, and the kidnappers will panic, and—I hear the sound of a car. Is that Kostas, at last? No: it's a jeep, a dark blue jeep pulling up by the cemetery steps. Two police get out and start briskly up.

Despite the jolting (the cart has no springs) and despite the silence—no one is in the mood to talk—the journey back seems shorter than the going. Halfway along, Erasmios of his own accord quickens his pace, his necklace of blue beads swinging jauntily, and as we come near the tower, attempts to turn off on that side road that skirts it at a distance. Yeoryios addresses the beast sternly in Greek, pulling its head back toward the shore road.

"He wants go short way home," Nikos says. "If you are in some hurry we can walk from here."

"I do not like for donkey to tell me which way I can go!" Yeoryios gives Erasmios a smart whack with the reins.

We pull up before Nikos' gate. Everyone except Yeoryio climbs down. Verek kisses me on the cheek. "Katerina," she says warmly, *"tí thráma, o Voufoūnos, naí? Ándras sou—ókhi, ókhi!"* And she climbs into the seat by her husband.

As I enter the house I have an irrational sense of sanctuary. Though the police can find me here as easily as on the road, I don't feel so vulnerable. Still

. . . I wish Kostas were back. I want to ask him about Sanzio: did he drown, or was he—like poor Hermann Furchtwanger—murdered? Because of course *he* must have been—he certainly hadn't tucked himself away in Voufounos' grave. Would Kostas think the two deaths are connected? Would he—do any of my friends—think either death might be linked to Mike's kidnapping?

"Niko, don't you think it's odd it's taking Kostas so long? And isn't he supposed to bring Damian? God, I *hate* it when people don't turn up when they should!"

"He goes to Eressos, Katerina. He tells his brother it is to Mytilene, because when tourists must go to the plane, they must go, it is understood. But to Eressos—this is pleasure trip that can take place another day. Kostas is very"—he rubs his thumb and fingers together—"he likes money. Do not worry, he will soon come with Damian. Please, Katerina, go to sit on the roof in the cool air. I bring ouzo."

"Nikos," I say, accepting the tiny glass, "what does '*tí thráma*' mean?"

"Means 'what a tragedy.' "

I stare at him, at his young/old face, his tired, ugly, kind, too-intelligent face, his surprising light gray eyes; and at what I read there—pity, compassion, acceptance of irrevocable loss—I turn away. From somewhere deep within, as air seeks the surface of water as it heats, grief rises. I try my usual tactics: take a slow breath, deep, deep; think of something else . . . anything else. This time it doesn't work.

David . . . David, it's Mother! . . . Look at my son, look at my David! . . . I can't believe it . . . Mike, Mike,

— 325 —

I can't believe it . . . He's dead, do you see? Dead . . . he's dead he's dead and it's my fault! Because I didn't go . . .

I become aware of Niko beside me on the bench. He sits quietly, his elbows propped on his knees, waiting. Now he rises and goes into the house, returning after a moment with a towel wrung out in cold water. I press it to my face.

"You weep for your son."

"Yes . . ." *And for Mike, for Mike!*

"It is time."

I dry my face. "What a good friend you are."

"No friend." When I look up at him, startled, "I love you, Katerina," he says quietly, "and not as a friend, not as a brother."

"I am . . . very sorry."

"Do not be. I am not sorry. Though for me it is a source of pain that when I tell you I love you, I must do so in a language in which I am clumsy, and perhaps you are offended. I offer my love as a tribute, Katerina. Believe me, it does you no dishonor."

"I know that, Niko," I answer in a low voice. "Although not everyone would think so. Most people would think that I must have done something—I must have tried to win your regard. I can't help but feel at fault—"

"That is nonsense. It is not your fault. Is the flower at fault whose beauty pleases us, the bird at fault whose song enchants us? You cannot help what you are, and what you are, I love."

"Oh, Niko—" I struggle for composure—"how *can* you? I've—all along I've presented myself in the worst possible light! I've told you I caused my son's death, that my husband—he blames me, I know he does—

— 326 —

how you can imagine you are in love with me *I* cannot imagine!"

"I love you, I do not worship you, Katerina," Nikos says calmly. "There is much difference. A man worships perfection, he loves faults. Surely you do not imagine that your husband no longer loves you because you were—you told me this yourself—because you were busy at your work when your son was killed? Was he not also busy at his work? Yet you still love him, Katerina—you have told me this also."

Yes, but Mike is no poet . . . Resolutely, I use the present tense. Being no poet, *he* doesn't love me for my faults; ergo, he doesn't love me. How could he love me *because* I neglected David? No one could! What kind of reasoning is that? Lunatic. And it *was* my fault. Not Mike's—not to any degree whatsoever. At home the fathers don't raise the sons, however they divide the duty here in Greece. At home the mothers raise the sons . . . whoever's at home, that is. Or they fail to, like me. David's death is my fault. Mine. So how can Mike still love me?

Yes, but Nikos does. I have to believe it. I can't see why this should be so—I haven't tried to be seductive, or charming, or even particularly friendly; I've just been myself, however I happened to feel at the moment. So if he does love me . . . if he can . . . perhaps I still have something in me worthy of being loved . . . No, *worth* doesn't enter into it. Mike said that, once. Or something like that . . .

"I don't love you because of you but because of me," he'd said. "You don't love me because of me but because of you. Nobody gets loved because they deserve it, but because they're lucky, I swear. They just happened to be handy when the one who loves them was looking for someone to love. How the hell else do you explain those decent guys whose women are bitches?" And then he'd laughed . . . That was a long time before David, of course.

I say shakily, "What are you trying to do, Niko—patch up my marriage?"

"I try to make you a gift," he smiles, "American style. I try to make you think kindly toward me."

"Never think I don't! Just the same, I *am* sorry, because I wouldn't do anything to hurt you, believe me—"

"Katerina, I do not suffer. What I feel for you is my joy—I think perhaps my only joy. Do not begrudge me." He does not move to touch me, but his eyes travel over my face, as a sculptor's fingers feel the marble.

I catch the sound of a car approaching. "I hope that's not the police," I say fervently. "I hope it's Kostas, with Damian."

"Your Greek son." Nikos's eyes, those light gray eyes that are his sole good feature, glow with a strange fire. "You may find others in other countries—this is possible, I think, because you have a mother's heart, Katerina—but always Damian will be your son in Greece. And I am Damian's godfather, which makes a link between us nothing can break." He reaches toward me and I put my hands in his. He lifts my right hand to his lips and kisses it. Releasing this hand, he stands for a moment looking at the fingers still caught in his. Then, slowly, he bends and kisses my wedding ring.

"I was wrong," he says in a low voice. "No man who is married to you could willingly do anything to cause you hurt. Your husband must be, as you say, held captive for money. I believe it truly now. Forgive me, Katerina. I am . . . too quick to see evil. Too quick, and, I fear, too slow."

Kostas' taxi coughs to a stop by the courtyard gate. I follow Niko through the house and down the outside stairs. Nikos gives Damian a friendly cuff on the shoulder, puts a question to Kostas, and gets the answer, "Ókhi."

Damian has given me one quick glance, then away. He says nothing: no greeting, no question, nothing. His face is as I first saw it: adult, closed, as expressionless as he can make it, yet not cold, for behind that shuttered façade burns—hostility? No, not this time, at least not toward me. It's more as if he's . . . given up. As if, for now, he's robbed of hope. I want to put my arms around him. No child's face should wear such an expression, of grief tightly reined in . . .

My heart constricts. *He knows. Damian knows.*

He swore no oath—he made no promise not to watch. He watched, and he knows: the one who took the money is someone known to him, someone he loves.

I can read him as if he were my own.

It could not have been much after three-thirty when the body of poor Furchtwanger was unearthed in the cemetery. By four-thirty I was back at Zoë's; ten minutes short of an hour later Kostas brought Damian, and at five-thirty exactly the police come looking for me.

There are, it seems, a few questions they'd like to ask me. With the assistance of *kýrion* Paradéllis, because they do not speak English. If the *Amerikaní* will be frank with them, and answer honestly, much unpleasantness will be avoided . . . And they give me an our-mothers-warned-us-about-women-like-you look: wary, cold, stern—and curious.

"They want to know what are these words you shout when the body is found, and why did you shout them? I tell them whole village knows what is the trouble, you quarrel with your husband and he leaves and you do not know where he is. They say they know what whole village knows; now they want hear what *you* say."

I put on what is truly an Oscar-winning performance as the Deserted Wife. I explain who I am and that I have come to Greece at my husband's insistence. That he wants to adopt a Greek child and I do not. We quarrel. He leaves—I do not know where he is, but I think not far away; after all, I have his passport. (Cardinal Rule Number One when lying: stay as close to the truth as possible. Besides, Voula will have told them I have it.) Naturally I worry, and when I am there in the cemetery and everything makes me very melancholy—it reminds me of the death of my son, I am again in my mind burying my son, I am sure they understand—and all of a sudden there is this very dead man—my husband, too, is blond—I cry out my husband's name, what could be more natural?

Nikos translates. The corporal consults his notebook. He mouths: "My-ick! My-ick!"

"That's right," I say, "I called out, 'Mike, Mike!' " And with these words I start again to weep, and it doesn't take any acting ability at all. Repeating Mike's name conjures up again the terror that gripped me at the sight of that blond head, lolling at such an un-natural angle . . . *Mike, Mike! Where are you? Are you still alive, still warm, still breathing, or are you, too, cold, clay-cold, gone far away, staring blankly, uncaringly, into the faces of those who find you?*

The private would be only too happy to leave me to my emotions. The corporal is made of sterner stuff. He puts a sharp question to Niko.

"He wants to know when you last saw your husband."

"Two weeks ago, at the airport in New York." I explain yet again our separate travel plans.

"And when did you expect to meet him here?"

"On Friday. He came—he came on Friday, and then he—he left! That same night!" My face is contorted with grief, and I give it full play.

"You have not seen or heard from him since that time?"

Careful, Kay. "I haven't seen him, but he has—twice he's written me. *Surely* they don't want to know what he said, do they, Nikos? What a husband s-says to his wife?"

The corporal is a gentleman, or else he is a man with an active imagination. He does not demand to see my letters from my husband.

"But what about money, he wants to know," Nikos says, and my heart gives a lurch. How did they get onto that already? And however will I justify the need for one hundred thousand dollars—and in drachmas! "To buy my heart's desire, a little house by the sea—" A likely story! Not if I'm really Ye Deserted Wife . . . deserted because I hate Greece and all things Greek!

I can manage just one word: "M-money?"

— 331 —

"Yes, Katerina. If you have not seen your husband for a week or more, and you do not know when he will return to you, what do you do for money, the corporal wants to know. Greek officials always anxious not to have problems with tourists who have no money, you understand. We are hospitable people but practical, too."

Behind the two policemen, Kostas winks at me. "Tell him hotel bill is hotel's problem," he says cheerfully. "For food you have friends. For travel you have private taxi, no problem."

"Oh—that!" I'm so relieved I nearly laugh aloud. "Good heavens, I have credit cards! If I need money—well, normal amounts, you know—no problem, as you say, Kosta."

"And the German?" Nikos says. "He asks when did *i kyría* last see him." Impassively.

I try to think. "Alive, you mean? At supper, Tuesday evening. You remember, you were with me, Niko."

As Nikos turns to address the police in rapid and confident Greek (I mean he is neither humble nor timid), I suddenly conjure up the figure of Hermann Furchtwanger, bedecked with cameras like a booth at a fair, his face healthy, pink-cheeked with warm blood coursing, his smile cheerful, eager, his eyes kindly, trusting, like a large, friendly dog's. *"I wish to memorialize . . . the sunset . . . At me you will laugh, but my little pictures I paint . . ."* No, Herr Furchtwanger, at you I will never laugh.

"How did he die, this German?" Kostas puts the question so abruptly even the police are startled.

Nikos glances at Damian, then away. "Neck broken," he says shortly. "Like a man hanged."

"You mean"—I quickly fight down a wave of nausea—"he was—was climbing, and became entangled?"

"No, Katerina, there were no marks of rope on his skin, nothing of that. Police say his neck was broken from one sharp blow against the spine."

Like the children falling in the tower . . . Was Furchtwanger insane enough to try that passageway, in the dusk, and alone? Obviously he hadn't been alone, if that's where he fell. There, or from the fortress wall, which would have been closer, more convenient to the cemetery . . . more than a mile closer, and downhill . . . more or less downhill. Either somebody was with him, or following him, or was there already . . . somebody who knew where he was going, as Nikos knew . . .

As I stand there smiling apologetically at the two policemen, wiping my eyes, giving them a watery smile, I see one thing clearly: *they could all be in it.* Nikos, who watches my every move. Yeoryios, who works right by the ransom drop, so convenient, that tomb. Kyriakos, whose boat—how else had it been damaged?—undoubtedly was what transported Mike from the hotel to . . . wherever. Kostas, who sold those artifacts in Germany, where he worked in the vineyards, and where Sanzio was buying and selling wine . . . It was all falling into place, making a pattern like a spider's web, first one strand, then another. And there's no one I can trust, not for sure: I see that now. No one but Damian. If I make one stupid move, I'll be caught, entangled, and Mike—oh, God, one false step on my part, one wrong turn, can cost him his life!

If it hasn't already.

Nikos talks earnestly to the police; they bow briefly to me, and take themselves off.

"They want to know where they can find you if more questions needed. I tell them you stay here with my mother and me, the godfather of your husband's Greek son."

Zoë's house might be safer for me than the hotel, at that. Because tonight is *it*, I'm convinced of it. Either Mike will be released—which is highly unlikely; the discovery of Furchtwanger's body must have changed everything—or he won't. Not ever. And I just don't see how the kidnappers can hope Mike could reappear and remain silent. Even if he's promised not to talk, they know he's bound to be questioned, and not politely. No: even if they're sure he can't identify them, they can't let him go. Which means if he's not already dead, he will be by morning. And once I believe him dead, I'll talk, and they know it. So they have to shut me up, too. They have to make me disappear. From the hotel it would be easy. With Mike dead, and me, too, they'd be safe: there'd be no one left who's not involved to some degree, however slight. *Except Damian.* Damian would still be left, and Damian knows who took the money. Maybe he wouldn't talk, but they can't be sure. To be safe, they'll have to silence him, too.

All this goes through my mind in no more time than it's taken Kostas to tell me there's no need for him to go to the hotel, because "in the morning and again now I look in your box, Katerina. Nothing."

I hear myself, with no perceptible hesitation, thanking Niko, accepting "for one more night" his mother's hospitality, and then, to Kostas, the question that's been nagging at me for hours: "What about Sanzio?"

For a moment Kostas looks honestly bewildered, and I'm struck by the notion he has forgotten him.

"You remember Sanzio," Nikos says grimly. "Drowned. You go to identify."

"It is Sanzio, as I think." A shrug. "He is very dead. It is true he has drowned, but police worry because back of head looks as if he hit it on rock, not easy to do while swimming in quiet sea, they say. Or maybe he hit head as he fell off of boat. If it is as they hope, a nice, simple drowning, everything quick and easy. If somebody hit him on head"—Kostas sighs, apparently out of sympathy for the overworked police—"many questions, Katerina."

"Sanzio never went to Mytilene on Saturday after all?"

"For certain not, Katerina." Patiently. "He gets on bus, he gets off bus—if police are smart, they ask driver where. I say nothing. Is obvious Sanzio is kidnapper of your husband. Me, I like it—if Sanzio gets push into next world, not so many kidnappers to worry about! Is easier for husband to escape."

Nikos, it is clear, does not share Kosta's optimism. He launches into rapid Greek, and the two exchange remarks earnestly. Damian, withdrawn and apparently deaf, holds himself aloof from any attempt at translation.

"Katerina," Nikos says, turning to me with a frown, "if it is true, as Kostas thinks, that kidnappers quarrel among themselves, I ask myself, what do they quarrel about? How to divide the money? Perhaps. What to do with husband? Very likely. We can only pray that those who say, 'Free him,' are the winners. That they can convince their fellows it is much smarter always not to be murderer—for all other crimes one can find excuse, but never for murder: that neither the gods nor men can forgive. I tell Kosta this dead German in Voufounos' grave must make for the kidnappers many complications. We must give them this one more night to free your husband. If by morning they do not give him back to you, I say we must go to the police."

So now here I lie, listening to Zoë's breathing, and I wait. Overhead footsteps go back and forth, back and forth. Nikos, too, must be awake, his thoughts as disturbing as mine. Why doesn't he go to bed, damn it, and give me a chance? The night won't last forever. Already the window grows gray, then silver, as the waning moon, late rising, washes the courtyard with light. And I lie here and I tell myself Mike has no one but me. David died because I wasn't there. If I go, if I'm *there*, Mike won't die: it's as simple as that . . . *Except I don't know where.*

Pyrgotafos: tower and tomb. If the money was to be in the tomb, why not the victim in the tower? Not very imaginative, perhaps, but neat . . . and unlikely: where could they put him? Okay, so what did Furchtwanger come across, then, that they had to kill him? Of course he tried that passageway down—any zealous archaeologist would. Was one of the kidnappers stashing the money somewhere? Not if Furchtwanger was killed on Tuesday night, when he was on his photo binge. The money wasn't even in the tomb Tuesday night—I didn't bring it from Mytilene until late Wednesday afternoon, and by then Furchtwanger must have been dead and . . . and already stored in the first available gravesite, the next one scheduled for use, where digging would cause no comment. The murderers wouldn't plan to leave him there, of course, to be found later and many questions asked. Of course they expected to remove him as soon as it could be done safely, and then dump him in the channel . . . perhaps he and Mike together . . . and they would both wash up days or weeks later, evidence of just what happened long since eaten away. Bad luck, Voufounos claiming the site so soon.

Why didn't they leave Furchtwanger's body where it fell? Or was pushed . . . was thrown. "Must bury within the day, *kyría* . . . the climate, you understand . . ." So Furchtwanger, dead, would be a danger. The shepherds pass that tower every day. They might be old and deaf, but surely they would not be unaware of a dead body . . . and consequently of Mike, if Mike were somewhere near . . . But where? Tied, slung in a netting, perhaps, gagged and bound, hanging like a . . . a ripening cheese in that passage? Why not? I hadn't gone down it, had I? So how do I know—wait! Kostas dropped a stone down it. The passage was clear then, Kay, for God's sake. Clear on Sunday morning. *But not necessarily clear when poor Furchtwanger went clambering around, cameras unleashed and flashbulbs at the ready, on Tuesday evening . . .*

Okay, then if Mike was there, why didn't the kidnappers play it safe and finish him off then, too—dump him in the same grave with Furchtwanger? Because Tuesday night the money hadn't come. Because I might demand further evidence that Mike was alive before I left it, docilely, unprotestingly, cooperative as all hell, in the tomb. Until I left the money, Mike had to live.

As he doesn't, not any longer, does he, Kay? Here—here's my husband's life. Help yourself. I hand it all over to you—no questions asked.

CHAPTER

25

Someone is blowing gently on my eyelids. *"Mike?"* But it is only Damian.

"Come, *fíli mou*," he whispers. "I have news." Against the pale outline of the moonlit doorway I see him slip outside.

Zoë's breathing keeps slow, keeps even. Sliding cautiously out of bed, I pull on my silk trousers and shirt, grope noiselessly for my flashlight, glide barefoot across the room and ease the door shut behind me.

The house is dark; Nikos, it seems, finally sleeps, but I have no doubt the least noise would wake him. As silent as smoke we cross the courtyard and slip out the gate, where I stop to put on my sandals.

"What is it? What's happened?"

Damian puts cautioning fingers to my mouth. They are trembling; this shocks and scares me more than his stealthy coming, more than his silence now. Without another word I stumble after him up the staircase lane to the turn leading down to the harbor.

I try again. "Where are we going? Why did you come for me?"

He pulls my face close to his, his voice so low I can barely make out the words. "I not know who to ask for help, friend Kay. You the only one I know for sure is safe. I not know if they all in it, too." He shivers. "If my *koumbáros* Nikos . . . if my uncle Yeoryios . . . if my friend Kyriakos. I not *know*—"

"Who took the money, Damian?" Urgently. "You saw, didn't you?"

"Yes—no—I saw, but I not see face—"

He knows. He wouldn't have to see the face. He doesn't trust me, either.

"I think maybe they going to free him," Damian goes on in that same anguished whisper. "Free him, or—or maybe not. If planning not, you and I, friend Kay, must s-stop them—"

With that he turns and plunges down the steep-stepped lane, and I, slipping and sliding on the cobblestones, curse the fitful moon that dodges in and out between close-packed clouds. The lane is blotched with shifting shadows like patches of camouflage, and I pray I don't turn an ankle or stumble over some obstacle, to send it clattering and banging against a house wall, and wake the village.

We reach the square. Here Damian hesitates, looking about him as furtively as any thief. Not a light shows. Under the plane tree chairs are tipped together like drunks, and cats prowl stealthily from one to the next, silently scavenging.

The one he saw couldn't be Nikos, or Yeoryios, or Kyriakos—he wouldn't "not know" about them, then.

"It was Kostas, wasn't it?"

The words are ashes in my mouth. Kostas, beautiful as any statue. Kostas the merry, the graceful, the proud . . . and the daring, and the ruthless, and the amoral . . . And if he did this, Kostas the cruel, as well. God, yes! Kostas the cruel, cruel, cruel!

Damian seems to be having trouble breathing. Then: "I see him take the money, friend Kay. I hide in the great olive and I watch, and I see him come. This morning he say nothing to nobody. He pick up tourists as if world same as always. He drive me to school. He come back in afternoon same as always. Say nothing—he say nothing to me—" A trickle of silver slides down his cheek. "I am thinking maybe he takes the money to put in more safe place. Then I know that is stupid, that is thinking like baby. He takes money because he wants money. So then I think, maybe if we stop him, friend Kay—if we save my American father and make my uncle to return the money—everything be the same, the same like yesterday . . . like last week . . ."

No, Damian. We can't ever do it. Nobody can. Worlds can't be put back, pasted together, no cracks. Besides, Sanzio is still dead. Furchtwanger is dead. And the one didn't drown, or the other fall, all on his own, no help from any man. And you know it.

"We'll worry about your uncle Kostas when we have Mike safe," I say curtly. "Why did you come for me *now*, Damian? Have you anything more to tell me besides that Kostas took the money?"

Damian brushes his cheek angrily. "I acting like baby. Forgive, please, friend Kay. Yes—I cannot sleep, so when uncle get up and go to taxi, go gliding out in taxi with no lights, no motor until he reach the lane, I run to follow. I am too slow. He turn past the tomb, not stopping. He takes I think maybe short way to Molivos. I think one boy not enough. I think also you have right to fight for your husband, friend Kay. So I come for you."

"You don't know where he went, then?" Disappointment roughens my voice.

"I am thinking maybe *Pouláki Mou* still here. Then to move husband he will need taxi. But *Pouláki Mou* is gone, friend Kay." He points to where five or six *kaïkia* are frozen in the silver light; they all look more or less alike to me, but Damian seems sure. "Maybe Kyriakos go early for to fish . . . but maybe not. I think we must look along the sea. We must find *Pouláki Mou*, friend Kay, before—before they dump biggest catch back."

His voice is bitter, and despairing. As we hurry onto the shore road for Molibos, I too feel a most anguished powerlessness; I am torn between the urge to give him a comforting hug and the far more impelling impulse to run and run, to search and search anywhere, everywhere . . . I resist both.

"Listen, Damian," I say briskly, "we can't run up and down all over Lesvos looking for Kostas and his taxi, or search all the shores for one small fishing boat. There simply isn't time. We have to find *Mike*. So *think*—think hard!" The admonition is as much for myself as for him. "So far everything has gone according to plan for the kidnappers—at least, as far as we can tell from here—except for one thing: the almost immediate discovery of both deaths. Sanzio washed up in Petrá almost at once—"

"How you know?"

"Well, the police were going to get Voula to identify him. I don't suppose his appearance was much . . . much altered yet."

"Fishes leave him alone," Damian nods. "You are right, friend Kay—cannot be long in the sea."

"And the police say Furchtwanger's neck was broken"—I have a sudden vivid recollection of that lolling head—"so he c-could have fallen. Okay, that's what we *know*. Now let's do some inspired guessing."

We are approaching the dark and silent building where Voufounos worked himself to an early death. Beyond is the turn where one can see the tower . . . and can clearly be seen from the slopes above as well as from the sea. Instinctively, we slow our steps and, reaching the turn, shrink back into the shadow of a tangle of wild grape.

"Now he said—this was Tuesday night—Herr Furchtwanger said he was going to take pictures of the fortress and the tower. Don't you think it likely he came upon the kidnappers? And they killed him. Of course we've been all over both places, but still . . . Is there any place in either where somebody might be held captive?"

"In castle is always soldiers, watching for Turks," Damian says reluctantly. "How your husband could be there, and they not know? Or this German come with camera, and fall, and they not see? Soldiers there all day and all night, friend Kay."

"Okay, scratch the fortress. Furchtwanger could have fallen off the tower. Or fallen where the children fell, down that passageway to the spring." My voice is rock steady. "He could have been trying to climb down in, maybe to take a shot of the sky—he was always talking about his camera having an 'artist's eye'—maybe he wanted the evening sky framed by the opening. And he slipped."

Or was pushed. Or thrown.

Cautiously, we move out into the moonlit road. The gibbous moon behind its flocked veil has turned the sky luminous from horizon to horizon. In the blurred light everything seems out of focus: the clump of bushes, the fragment of wall . . . Something streaks across the road, and I freeze.

"*Ghátos,*" Damian mutters. "Only a cat, *fíli mou.*"

"We know so little!" Try as I may, I can't keep the desperation out of my voice. "My God, all I really know is that Mike was alive to write that note I got Monday night—*five days* ago!"

"You say it is hard to read, but still you know for sure it is my American father who writes it." I can't tell if he intends the statement as a question or a consolation.

"We have a—a kind of code, Damian. Mike says, 'Jimmy would hate it here.' That's how I know."

And I wasn't going to tell anybody about Jimmy . . . Strange—now that I know Damian can't be ours, I want to share—I want him to know all about us.

"Jimmy?"

"My son had this friend, Damian. An imaginary friend whom he called Jimmy. I mean, Jimmy wasn't really there—and yet he was. And my husband or I would say, 'Listen, David, you and Jimmy had better do thus and so'—you know, meaning, 'Pay attention, you two!' "

"I not know other boys play this game," Damian says shyly.

"Oh . . . Did you, too?"

"*Naí.* I once have friend nobody see but me. I call him Leftéris." He laughs softly. "I am glad my

American brother make friends in his mind. What kind of boy was this Jimmy?"

"... *Jimmy would hate it here ... Pay attention ...*"

"Damian! Oh, my *God!* I've been thinking all along Mike's been blindfolded! You know—because his writing wandered all over. But what if it's because it's pitch dark?"

"Pitch?"

"Very, very dark. Is there any place in the tower where there isn't any light at all? David was afraid of the dark—he said it was Jimmy—"

"I think is not much light in the passage, but it is not pitch, not at first. When we climb down, we have no candle, no torch—"

" 'We'? Who do you mean—who was with you?"

"Nobody." Damian's teeth gleam palely in a smile. "Only Leftéris, friend Kay. So we—I— go very, very slow, feel very careful for where to put feet. And after passage bend is very pitch dark. But where passage bend, is nothing," he adds thoughtfully. "No wall on one side—for three, four feet I feel nothing. I cannot see how *much* of nothing is there, but I know the nothing part is not high enough for soldier to stand. Maybe is just a little shelf, for weapons—I not know. I not go for to see," he adds, embarrassed. "Leftéris say maybe better not explore—maybe other boys climb in there and . . . and find something to make them to fall . . ."

We stare at each other, and then, in wildest hope, we both gaze at the tower looming on our left like some monstrous stone sentry slouching on endless duty through the interminable centuries.

"They'd have to have some place for their food, wouldn't they? The defenders—they'd need a good-sized storeroom for their food!" Somehow I manage to keep my voice low. "That's where Mike is, Damian—he's *got* to be!"

Damian puts his hand on my arm, to calm me; one would think him the adult and me the child. "Best to go up the stream, very, very quiet," he whispers. "Nobody hear our feet because of water talking to itself. Maybe nobody there but my American father—maybe they off somewhere, thinking what next. But maybe everybody there—"

And maybe there's nobody there at all. Maybe we've guessed entirely wrong, and Mike is somewhere else, somewhere I've never even thought of, miles from here . . . Eressos or Petrá or—or somewhere, one of those places Kostas is always taking tourists—says he is taking tourists—

I've taken perhaps a dozen panicky, impetuous steps forward when Damian, hissing, pulls me into the shadowy opening of a lane—nothing more than a sheep path, actually—that gapes on the landward side. *"Pouláki Mou!"*

And there she is: squatting silently about a hundred yards offshore, no lights showing, immobile: a vessel in a frame from an old-time movie, colorless, her burnt orange sail black in the moonlight, her lemon-yellow mast a ghostly white.

"They see us if we use the stream," Damian whispers. "Safer other way. Also from top we can see if anyone swims to shore, we can hear if anyone busy in tower . . ."

The path is nothing much more than a ditch,

wandering like a straggling sheep first this way, then that, but always keeping roughly the same distance from the tower, as if it were skirting it, looking for a chance to attack. There is a rude fence on either side, waist-high, formed of stones heaped together casually, which gives me the illusion that as long as I sneak along, crouching behind its shield, I can't be seen from above—though I don't look up, to check. If there's anyone up there, watching, I hope we're no more than a . . . a drifting shadow, a cloud shadow blowing in eerie silence along the periphery of their vision. For the first time, I see Damian is barefoot.

A sudden sharp rattle sets my pulses pounding. Stumbling to their feet, several sheep, their hoofs like drumbeats on the rocky ground, come prancing over to gawk at us across the stone barrier. By some miracle they don't set up any mindless *baa-aa*-ing, but the clatter of their hoofs as they move along with us is as loud as applause, their bells like castanets, hollowly echoing. We might as well have had a motorcycle escort, I think bitterly, as at last they lose interest and sink back out of sight, I suppose to sleep.

We reach the tumbled stones, and now, before we start the ascent, on a single impulse we both risk a glance upward. Nothing: no head showing above the crenellations, only the jagged outline of the worn stone teeth against the sky. I take obscure comfort from the fact that Damian and I assume the same stance: mouth slightly parted as if to drink in the faintest sound . . . I can hear nothing but the sighing of the wind through the dry grass, the soft complaint of the sea against the beach, the impatient mutter of the little stream, out of sight beyond the clump of bamboo, and, somewhere far off, a dog barking.

"Damian," I say, very low, "if there's anybody at the top, you get down as fast as you can and get help. Never mind me, understand? I'll go first—this'll give you a chance to run like hell for that sentry hut over there and get help."

"Hokay, friend Kay. But if nobody at top, I go down the passage—"

"No, Damian. *I* go down—don't argue, we haven't time. I have to be with my husband or he will die—I *have* to. And it's better this way, much better. You can run faster than I, and you can get help much faster because you speak Greek. So I'll go down, and if there's nobody there I'll come back up and we'll look somewhere else. But if Mike is there, you go for the soldiers. If he's there, he'll have been tied up all this time—he must have been—and he'll never be able to climb out on his own. I'll stay and comfort him and you go for help—"

"*Ókhi.* No, friend Kay—not soldiers. Soldiers ask too many questions. Then no way for to save Kosta, too." Stubbornly.

Oh, God, he still thinks the impossible is possible! And there's no time, no time, no time to dissuade him!

"All right, you run for—for Nikos, or Yeoryios—whichever is quicker from here—"

"Uncle Yeoryios stronger," Damian says, a sudden joyous confidence in his voice.

"Okay, get Yeoryios—but only if Mike is there by himself, you hear? If Mike is alone, I'll call out, 'Oh, Mike—Mike!'—just his name, get it? And you run for Yeoryios. But Damian, if there's anybody else, there wouldn't be *time*, don't you see? If any of the kid-nappers are there, I'll scream out their names, too, so that no matter what, *you* will know who they are, and can—can take care." My helplessness to keep him safe is a leaden weight. "If I call out any other name than Mike's, you run for the soldiers—*promise* me, Damian!"

"Maybe too dark to see. Maybe you not know names," he says doggedly. "Maybe strangers—is possible. What you shout then?"

Oh, God, he's so hopelessly loyal! "I have a flashlight," I tell him. "Okay, if there's anybody else there, I'll just scream—as if I've come by myself, get it?—but I'll add their names if I know them. *Now* will you promise to do as I ask? You *will* go for the soldiers?"

Because if you don't, we'll never make it. Mike and I will die. We may die anyway . . . Maybe I ought to go for the soldiers now . . . But if Mike's there, and they hear us coming, he'll be dead by the time we reach him. His only hope is for me to get down there quietly . . . and then what? I don't know! I don't know! My God, I wasn't cut out for this kind of thing . . .

"Hokay, friend Kay," Damian says slowly. "I promise."

Without another word he starts to climb, moving as swiftly and as silently as mist rising. I pause long enough to slip off my sandals: better not the scrape of leather on rock, and besides, I'll be more sure-footed, climbing not only up but down as well . . . All my senses seem keyed to an extra dimension: the wind is purer, sweeter, more scented, the rocks be-neath my feet and hands seem warmer than the night air, holding in their warmth the promise of the coming day. And from the top (which is, as I expect but still am relieved to find, empty of other human life— and a good thing, too, considering Damian's insubordination in preceding me) there's no sign of Kosta's taxi anywhere . . . Well, he would hardly park it by the tower. The road to Molibos stretches empty, a scratch across the empty land. *Pouláki Mou* is in shadow, a small blurred islet immobile on the great breathing shadow that is the sea, the sea that stirs and shifts like some vast living presence, waiting . . . On the horizon a pinpoint of light blinks rhythmically.

"Mikrá Assía," Damian whispers. "Tourkía."

"*Naí*," I whisper in return, and his hand touches mine.

The clouds break beneath the wind, and beyond Molibos the sea grows brighter as a finger of silver sweeps down the coast to bathe *Pouláki Mou* in such clear light I can see the figure of a man crouched over the nets . . . He's hauling a net across the deck . . .

"Kyriakos!" Damian is disbelieving. "Does he fish, then? Here? Or maybe just pretending?"

I feel no surprise, only a dull acceptance. Kyriakos, too: of course. And of course he'd have to pretend to fish, so the soldiers watching the sea won't think him of any importance. I suppose he's waiting to take Mike well out into the channel. They can't risk another body washing ashore almost at once— Sanzio was more than enough. Forget Sanzio, for God's sake, Kay—keep your mind on the problem before you. Which is—perhaps we're already too late, perhaps Mike is already aboard—no: there goes the net over the side! If Mike were already aboard, they'd hoist anchor and get under way, wouldn't they?

Damian touches my arm. "Give me your torch."

Hunching over, he holds the glass against his belly and presses the switch. For a split second there is a faint glow of light, as quickly doused. Without a word he hands the flashlight back, I clip it securely onto my hip pocket, and we move across to the corner where the mouth of the passageway is concealed beneath the vine. Lifting the tangled mass carefully aside, I peer down into utter blackness, utter silence.

"Damian—" My impulse is to hug him, perhaps even kiss him on the cheek, but something in his face holds me off. "Wish me luck," I say painfully. "And pray I find him."

"I pray, friend Kay." I can barely hear the words. "And God guide your feet."

"And God speed yours."

The words come easily to my tongue, as if I've been saying such things all my life.

CHAPTER

26

The descent proves easier than I expect. The niches, at good and safe intervals, are deep enough to give me a secure foothold; when I look up I can see the night sky, unnaturally bright, and against it the outline of Damian's head. The passageway, too, is narrow enough so I can rest by leaning back against the wall, and this I do, briefly, once or twice, until I feel something—a piece of rock, perhaps—move slightly behind my shoulders; not much, just a little, but I'm so terrified I'll dislodge a chunk and send it splashing into the spring, to alert . . . whomever . . . that I don't give in again to any temptation to rest. Time enough for that when Mike is safe.

Beneath my fingers the niches feel dry, bone-dry, the stone not solid, exactly . . . more like a kind of petrified sponge. The air, too, is so dry I imagine I can almost smell the water in the spring. I have the sensation of being utterly alone, that no other living thing whatsoever is in this tunnel, nothing, no insect, not even a fragment of moss, not even a frill of lichen—certainly nothing so . . . warm, so wetly alive as that rat Kostas conjured up.

My legs are tiring. Did I think this easy? Not easy
. . . A ripple of fatigue runs across my instep, a
shadow of cramp follows . . . tightens . . . and I
cling with both hands, weight on the other foot, and
I *will* it to go away . . . and it does.

Down again. Damian is farther away. How far to
the dog-leg angle? I can't have passed it; I wouldn't
be able to see the sky. *My God, I can't find the next
niche!* Oh—farther over, is it? Then I must have
reached the elbow. So far so good.

And so I grope, and set my foot, and test my
weight, and grope with the other foot . . . and again
. . . and again. And now I can't see Damian, I can't
see the sky, I'm truly alone in this eye-stretching dark.
Once more, a foothold . . . and on my left *there's no
wall.*

Gingerly, I stretch forth my hand. No wall at
shoulder height: at waist height: but down here, down
by my knee, stone once again. So there *is* an opening, just as Damian reported, an opening as wide as
the passage and three feet or so high. How much
space there is beyond this gap I can't tell, for I can
see nothing. It's totally dark, a velvet blackness
against which fanciful lights prick and dance across
my eyeballs.

Shifting my weight to free my left hand, clinging
to the niche with my right, I ease out my flashlight
and turn it cautiously—*don't drop it, Kay, for God's
sake!*—until my thumb is over the switch. I aim into
the opening and slide the switch on.

The beam of light slices across the little cave . . .
rebounds from the back wall . . . loops to show the
roof some three feet above the opening . . . slides
down one side (glint of metal—a hook? a ring?) . . .

skitters across the floor to flick here and there, prob-
ing the corners. So panicky am I that this ideal, this
perfect hiding place is empty that it is a heart-stop-
ping second or two before I take in the truth of it:
that *there he is*—that bundle dumped in the corner like
a discarded sack is Mike—*is Mike!*

Doesn't he know I'm here? Is he asleep? Why
doesn't my flashlight wake him, then? Maybe he's
drugged . . . maybe he's hurt . . . *maybe he's dead—*

He's not dead! He can't know I'm here, that's all.
There's something wound around his head . . . a
cloth, a tape . . . something . . . wound around and
across his eyes, his mouth . . .

I tip my head back to look up where I know
Damian is waiting, and I call—not loud enough to
carry to *Pouláki Mou*, just loud enough for him to
hear—I call out, joy and anguish intermixed: *"Mike!
Thank God I've found you!"*

And now as I clamber onto the floor of the cave,
Mike gives a convulsive shudder, strains toward my
voice, tries to sit upright. And I am crouched by him,
I'm lifting him in my arms, embracing him, my lips
on his bearded cheek, on the layers of tape that
blindfold him, on the cruel gag of tape across his
mouth, inches wide, many-layered. And I am saying
over and over again, "Oh, Mike! Oh, Mike—Mike!"
Which is scarcely brilliant or poetic or even original,
but, by God, makes my point. *Here he is—here Mike
is, and alive! Alive!*

He's straining to say something . . . a muffled,
anguished sound . . . I can't make it out. His hands
are behind his back, the wrists bound—wrapped—
with that same shiny plastic tape. I see he's tried to
remove it, and from his face as well, by rubbing his

arms and his head on the rocky floor of his prison; his cheeks, his chin, his hands are all abraded, are scraped raw, are caked with blood. Rage seizes me, and I say in a choked voice, "Oh, my darling, I'll get this damn stuff off you as fast as I can!"

And because what I want most of all is to hear him say he loves me (if he does), I look first for the end of the stuff that's over his mouth . . . I find it, just back of his jaw. I try to prop the flashlight so I can see what I'm doing . . . see if I've got it started . . . Damn it, it clings as if it's glued.

Damian should be going for the soldiers and the hell with saving Kostas! How long to run for Yeoryios? Five minutes—six at the most. And to wake him, and Yeoryios to dress and come? Another ten, maybe. Say fifteen minutes total. Please God, don't let them come ashore after Mike for just fifteen minutes—

"Let me give you more light, Katerina," says Kostas' voice cheerfully.

I snatch up my flashlight and whirl about, catching him in its beam. I see him rasp his nail across a match and reach to light the lantern hanging behind an outcropping of rock. And I leap at him, my flashlight a club, to strike, to stun him—I really think as I leap I want to *kill* him.

Laughing, he catches my wrist. "Why you are angry? Is not husband alive and safe, ready now for freedom?" And Kostas plucks my "weapon" from my grasp. "Two-cell torch too small for cracking heads, Katerina, you need three-cell at least," he says gravely, his eyes dancing. Then: "How did you find him?" Idly curious, friendly, for all the world as if we're on top of the tower admiring the view of the sea, as if we're relaxing on the terrace of the Silver

tiful woman? Why I should kill your Mike? Have I
not ransom safe? Before you come my plan is very
simple: I drive taxi to Mytilene, I take early plane to
Athens, I take boat for—do not ask where, Katerina.
Change clothes, change name, change passport,
change luck, change whole life. Plenty of time. I leave
tape on husband's eyes—he cannot pull it off, eyelids will tear; be very, very careful, Katerina, use much
olive oil, remember what I say—and with eyes blinded
and hands behind his back, he is not going to climb
down. Maybe I free his mouth—yes, that would be
honorable. Still I have plenty of time—tonight he
cannot shout very loud, and old Sokrátis with his baa-
baa-ing sheep is too deaf to hear—"

"What a swine you are, Kostas!" I say in cold fury.
"It might be *days* before anybody came this way! Mike
could *die*, damn you—die of hunger or thirst!"

"No, no," Kostas says soothingly. "When I reach
Athens I phone Voula—I tell her to tell Niko the answer to his puzzle is in name of our village." All the
time he's talking to me he's working at getting the
tape off Mike's mouth—there seem to be at least three
layers, wound around the nape of the neck and across
the jaw in what strikes me as an excess of silencing.
"By the time Voula bother to see Niko, and Nikos to
find answer and look in *pýrgon*—in this tower—I am
gone on little, little boat. Or on plane. Or maybe in
car—who knows? I am gone like the lark in winter
and I am safe, and so is husband. Everybody happy.
But now, Katerina—now I must change my plan."
He sighs. The tape has broken off on a diagonal, and
once again he has to locate the end, and restart it. "I
cannot leave you here, to run for help. I cannot bind
you, like your husband, because when in the morn-

ing Nikos finds you vanished from his house, he will call the police, the army, the mayor—he will turn Lesvos heels over head to find you, and you will say, Oh, that wicked Kostas has done all this, and telephones will hum, and police be waiting in Athens for my plane. And I cannot kill you," he says tenderly, "because you are too beautiful, and you would trouble my dreams—what good a man be rich and with whole new life, where he has handsome car and fine clothes and respect and even servants, if he not have pleasant dreams? So now I must think of another way."

He has the tape down to the last layer. Causually, as if he were opening a package, he pulls it off on either side as far as the corners of Mike's mouth, where he slashes it off and then taps the loose ends down onto the red and angry skin, leaving Mike's mouth still taped firmly shut. God! it must be painful! Because of course somebody has been stripping off that gag every day, hasn't he? More than once every day. Mike's had to have water, at least. I ache to comfort him—he seems only semiconscious; didn't they feed him?—but I don't dare move for fear of distracting Kostas. *Ten minutes. Please, God, give me ten minutes . . .* If I can just keep him chattering on and on, glorying in his "accomplishments," boasting and explaining . . .

"Tell me, Kostas, did you do all this by yourself, or was Nikos in it, too? I mean, how did you get my husband onto the same plane with Sanzio, so he could drug him?"

"Katerina, never did I choose to capture *your* husband!" Kostas says, hurt. "Would I do such a thing? American father of my dead brother's son?

— 359 —

Never! It is true that in Germany we entertain ourselves with plans for kidnappings on our own—this
Sanzio is what you call 'fingerman' for big, big business—very convenient his wine-selling, good curtain
over, I am right? So when he lands in Mytilene with
husband already drunk from drug, and tells me hokay, now we do this by-moonlight job—is American
slang for extra work regular boss know nothing
about—at first I think no, I cannot do this; and then
I think, do not fight your fortune, Kostas Demetriou,
the gods have chosen for you, do not be ungrateful.
Besides, always I plan for husband to live, Katerina.
That Sanzio, he has different idea."

"You mean you killed him because he wanted to
kill Mike?"

"Very greedy man, that Sanzio. He thinks I have
more treasures for him to sell, or maybe I plan to sell
them myself. I am thinking he has not been honest
with me, that when he sells he gives me not all my
share. 'Ask for not too much ransom,' he tells me.
'Ask only what wife can get without eyebrows going
up from Mytilene to Athens.' But four million drachmas is modest sum for one man to start new life, Katerina. For two men, too small. So I make sure that
now Sanzio pays me what he owes me." Kostas sits
back on his heels and gives me his most dazzling
smile. "Aha! Strategy! I have all solved. I take you
both to *Pouláki Mou*—nobody bother Greek fishing
boat. You spend rest of night and maybe half of day
with Kyriakó while I go off to Athens and vanish into
blue sky—"

"Kyriakos!" I wail, horrified. Another of Damian's friends proved worthless, treacherous!

"Yes, he is waiting now for me to bring Mr. Mike.

He helps me for to sail today. He was angry I scrape bottom of his boat on Friday night, but it is not I, it is that fool Sanzio, I say. Husband is angry he is drugged and fights shadows, I must calm him, he is strong but I am stronger—remember that, Katerina *mou,* you choose the lesser man, poor Katerina!—and while I hold him, Sanzio steers *scrawch scrawch* over rocks. We are lucky we get to tower, I tell Kyriakó, more lucky we get back to harbor. So Kyriakos say he must share the catch, since it is his boat that has hauled it ashore. I agree—why not? Can always refuse to pay later." He shrugs. "Come, Mr. Mike, on your feet and we go down. And Katerina"—he has slid that wicked knife into its sheath, I'm relieved to see—"you be sweet wife, good wife, and not do stupid plotting to save husband, because I not have one little bad dream if I kill him. I am sorry to make you sad, but it make me very sad to think of you in husband's arms—I be happy to have excuse to make you widow. So—no screams, no runnings, no hitting with flashlights—" And he laughs, his beautiful teeth gleaming, his face—God help me!—as beautiful as ever. *Because he intends to kill us, no matter what he says. If Kyriakos is expecting him to bring Mike, then Kostas never intended to leave him in the tower; he's planned all along to take him out into the channel, and then—*

"Ladies first, Katerina. That is polite, yes? Then I lower husband with rope, and we all three stroll like tourists across the shore and make midnight swim to *Pouláki Mou.* Tourists always slightly crazy; nobody pay any attention what they do." He is uncoiling the rope from the hook—one end appears to be tied to the ring adjacent, and the other end already has a loop; this he works over Mike's head, pulling his arms through so the loop is about his chest. Now he hauls Mike to his feet; Mike's whole body sags and his legs buckle; his head wobbles as if his spine is rubber. "Remember, Katerina, a good wife obeys, for sake of husband."

"I trust I may use the flashlight," I say coldly, and I clip it to my pocket, and start down.

The storeroom, it turns out, is little more than fifteen feet above the spring, and the descent (for me, at least) is relatively easy, though the flashlight is no help at all; I'm certainly not going to look down, not down toward that ledge. As I grope for each foothold, the shadows cast by my arms, my upper body, swoop in macabre dance across the rocks by my face. I *will not* think of the children who fell, but only of Mike . . . Mike swaying above me as limp as a puppet on strings . . . as an effigy on a gibbet. When at last I find myself balanced on that shelf I am quick to slide farther, to swing down onto the rim of rock by the little rill and the entrance. I try to guide Mike's feet, but he is either unconscious once again or nearly so, for his legs buckle helplessly, and he spills over, slow motion, to plunge into the water and sink.

I've made a grab for the rope. It scorches my hands. I scream, "Kostas! Stop—he'll drown! For God's sake pull up on the rope!"

It tightens, and Mike resurfaces, arching and twisting like a fish on a hook, head thrown back desperately as he fights for air.

Kostas swings down to land lightly beside me. "Come, Katerina, help me to pull in our so-big fish." It takes the two of us to haul him up, for Mike seems exceedingly heavy, a dead weight sagging on the end of the rope. At last we have him safe, sprawled face down on the edge of the spring.

"Mike could have *drowned* in there, you know that? With that God damned gag over his mouth!" And I reach down and jerk it off, and with one swift motion roll it in a wad and throw it in the spring. Mike gives no sign he's aware his mouth is free; his silence, and his indifference to my touch, scare me.

"Do not be rough, Katerina," Kostas says reprovingly. He has stripped off his shirt and now is peeling off his jeans. Under these he wears skimpy swim trunks, of the kind that has a woven belt. "What you wear under those so-charming *pantelóni*, Katerina? Something which in moonlight look to soldiers like American swimming clothes?" He is transferring his knife in its sheath. "Hold torch on Mr. Mike—I must make him ready for to swim to *Pouláki Mou*." And Kostas jerks off Mike's soaked jacket, and loosening his belt, grabs his trousers by the bottoms and yanks them off, too.

I unbutton his shirt and gently ease it off. Yes, I suppose at a distance Mike's briefs could be taken for swim trunks and my bra and panties for a bikini. Maybe Kostas really means to get us out to *Pouláki Mou*. Maybe we'll actually swim out there. I can do it easily, and so, I suppose, can Kostas—but Mike? Weak as he is? Say we do make it: we won't just drift about, killing time for twelve hours or so until Kostas is well away. Mike and I will be killed, both of us, and promptly. And Kyriakos, too, I bet, just as soon as it occurs to Kostas that Kyriakos' cooperation lacks commitment. We'll all three be killed, and dumped in the channel, and then Kostas will sail back to Pyrgotafos and find that Damian has gone for Yeoryios . . . He'll have to kill them, too. *My God, I haven't thought of Damian in—what? Five, six minutes? Damian—*

"Come, Katerina, no more delays. Make yourself to look like crazy American tourist who goes swimming in midnight sea. Do not worry—I am in a hurry and have many problems, and so no heart for making love. Also of course with husband right here is not proper, *agápi mou.*" Regretfully and courteously.

"I'm fine as I am," I say curtly. "This silk is so thin it will soon dry once we get there." Besides, I don't want poor blinded Mike wondering if I'm doing a strip act.

"Hokay, whatever you like," Kostas says agreeably. He is rolling his clothes into a small bundle and tying it to his belt. "Leave husband's clothes here, Katerina, you can get them later. Mine I need for to travel to Mytilene. A Greek cannot walk about the town nearly naked. Causes talk."

Four minutes . . . three minutes . . .

"What about your shoes?"

"I leave them in taxi. I think far ahead, Katerina. Better the naked feet for swimming, for climbing up and down. Now we go before Kyriakos think we have forgotten him." He slides Mike's left arm over his shoulder and hauls him to his feet. Mike is a rag doll, a sack of potatoes. "Put other arm around shoulders, Katerina. I go first, then husband, then you— not polite, maybe to make ladies go last, but here I think safer." A flash of teeth.

Edging our way through that narrow passage, Mike more or less suspended between us, is so difficult that at last Kostas is silent, which is a relief.

And as we struggle, *He didn't ever intend to return to Poulâki Mou*, I think, *or he'd have come in his swimming trunks, not dressed ready to—to decamp. He really did intend to leave Mike in the tower, helpless, wrists bound, blindfolded . . . Helpless, or dead, more likely . . . Of course, dead! Only I was there—I was there!*

We're out in the open, and past the bamboo. The sky is almost cloudless, and the moon bejewels the placid sea. *Poulâki Mou* has drifted somewhat farther toward Molibos, it seems to me . . . or dragged anchor. "How do you ever expect Mike to swim that far?" I say despairingly.

And where is Damian? Where is Yeoryios?

"Do not worry, Katerina, I swim with one hand and hold husband up with other—no problem! Come, act like all friendly, maybe planning a little song and a little dance in moonlight, but walk, walk along—"

I stop, panting as if I'm out of breath. "What about Furchtwanger?"

"A pest, *kounoúpi*, also a German, which is to say has the blood in his veins of invaders of my country. Come, walk along, Katerina, we talk as we go. Possibly he is a danger, this German. He comes looking and looking, and I ask myself, has he heard rumors of ancient treasures coming from island of Lesvos? Does he come searching for source? So when he climbs down, down the shaft, clicking his camera with flashes of light once, twice, five, six times, and I surprise him and he falls, I do not grieve, Katerina. It is for the best, I think, but awkward. Cannot throw him into the sea off the shore—here the dead swim for Petrá! Cannot leave him floating in the pool for old Sokrátis to find. Better to tuck into cemetery until can borrow *Poulâki Mou* once again. Bad luck old Voufounos die and want his grave before it is free—or maybe not so much bad luck as the gods test me, who knows?"

We are stumbling along the path by the little rill, Mike's body hanging limp and heavy between us. In the moonlight I catch the gleam of sweat on his forehead, and see his mouth set in a harsh line. I realize suddenly with a pang of horror that he is in pain. His legs—my God!—he can barely move them!

"He won't be able to do it, Kostas," I wail. For I see *Pouláki Mou* has drifted even farther. Could Kyriakos have lifted anchor? She's moving slowly, sluggishly, but she's certainly moving. "Look how far she is!"

For a split second Kostas checks his stride, and in that moment I feel Mike come to life. He jerks his right arm off my shoulder and topples his full weight against Kostas, throwing him off balance.

"Run, Kay! Run like hell!"

I can't leave you. The thought checks me for that one fatal moment, as I, torn between love for Mike that commands me to stay and love for Mike that tells me to obey, turn—too late!—to run, Kostas with one easy blow knocks Mike to the ground, leaps over his fallen body, and seizes me by the arm.

"No, Katerina, do not leave us." For the first time his voice has lost that undercurrent of laughter, or enjoyment. "All swim, or none—you understand? Make husband to walk, now, and quickly! *Pouláki Mou* must be well away before dawn." And he slips out that wicked snakelike knife and holds it to Mike's shoulders . . . between Mike's shoulderblades. "Choose, Katerina," he says softly. "You give me your promise, I help husband to swim. You not promise,

I finish him now, easier for to carry, nice and quiet, no rebellions." And his eyes—suddenly they are a stranger's, foreign, alien. Eyes with death in them— *my* death, I think: friendly Death, cooperative Death; Katerina, meet my loyal partner, Death . . .

"I promise, Kostas," I say in a voice I don't recognize: calm, steady, unemotional. "Put your knife away, you won't need it."

We lift Mike to his feet. He is a dead weight again—real? faked?—his arms once again slung around our shoulders, his feet dragging as we stagger up onto the road, and cross it, and begin the tricky descent to the rocky shore below.

Where the living hell are the soldiers? My God, the whole Turkish fleet could be landing here! Don't they care what goes on on land? Do they just sit there, watching the sea, and the hell with murder, rape, abduction, highway robbery—you name it? Or maybe we look like a trio of drunken tourists bent on drowning ourselves in our attempt to sober up!

We are making considerable noise, slipping and stumbling over those loose, rolling stones, when *"Adhélfeh mou!"* Yeoryios hurls the cry across the beach like a javelin, like a great stone, and he comes leaping down across the rocks, Damian well in the lead. *"Stamáta! Stamáta!* he cries in anguish. *"Trellós eéseh?"* But Kostas is deaf to his brother's plea. He flings Mike down as if he's so much dirty laundry, and slipping out his knife, whirls—toward me? toward Mike?

"Damian! He has a knife!" I cry, and I throw myself across Mike's body and cling with all my strength.

"Ókhi! Ókhi!" Damian screams, shrill as a rabbit in a trap. And he leaps between Kostas and me, and

that leap—that choosing—is enough to give Yeoryios time to reach us, to seize Kostas' arm, and
though older, to prove the stronger, for he spins
Kostas about to face him.

"*Atdhélfeh mou! Trellós eéseh?*"

They face each other down: the toil-worn, the
heavy-hearted, the life-embittered, and the young, the
proud, the beautiful. Yeoryios speaks slowly, harshly,
biting off his words, rage and grief infusing each
phrase. And Kostas laughs, and switches to English,
as much out of some instinct for drama, I suspect, as
to inform Mike and me.

"You are right, I cannot kill my brother's son. No
glory in killing a cub, only in killing the lion, I am
right? But if you worry so much about shame to the
family, then to keep the mouth shut for one little day,
hokay? By noon tomorrow I am safe away from Piraeus, and you need not to watch the trial, the
prison—I am gone, like hawk into the blue, like eagle—"

"You go nowhere!" Yeoryios retorts. "You have
no friends, no family. You are *anáthema!* You are accursed! Katerina, do not fear for your husband, he is
safe. Kostas who was my brother is a dead man!"

And Kostas leaps, his knife raised high. Yeoryios
parries but a fraction of a second slow; I hear the cloth
rip, and see in the moonlight the black rivulet where
the blood flows. And Kostas changes his grip, to hold
the knife blade upward.

"*Ókhi!*" Damian cries. "Run, my uncle—run, run!
Look there—Kyriakos deserts you!"

Kostas flicks a glance past, and sees what Damian has seen: *Pouláki Mou*'s sail is hoisted and she's
caught a slight breeze . . . She's some hundred yards

farther along toward Molibos . . . is now on a line aslant the beach where the *karpoí* signs gleam . . . gleam like animals' eyes . . . like the eyes of cats crouched in wait along the edge of the road . . .

"No need for long farewells," Kostas laughs, and leaping away from Yeoryios, from Damian, he turns and runs lightly, like a deer, like a Hermes, across the coarse stones toward the silver-dappled water.

The flare of the mine is a bursting star. Kostas flings up his arms like a sun-worshiper, topples backward, and lies still.

CHAPTER

27

Are we alone? I want to kiss you, Kay."

"Alone enough." I place a careful kiss on his cracked, blistered lips.

A mistake. No spark, no connection. Nothing.

We are at Zoë's, Mike, Nikos, Zoë, and I. Mike still has the tape over his eyes, still is haggard, bearded, exhausted, but no longer unwashed. Zoë and I have bathed him, and now he lies between her best linen sheets, slowly letting go, letting the warmth creep back into his hands and feet as I hold the cup for him and he sips hot tea well laced with brandy.

Nobody had to rout out the army or the police. Jeeps with searchlights and helmeted men cradling wicked-looking weapons clotted the road by the ΚΑΡΠοι beach so soon after the detonation of the mine I think now they must have been alerted by Damian's first frantic "*Ókhi!*" And of course the blast awakened all the village and most of Molibos. Nikos was among the first to come running. "Katerina! You are unhurt? I give thanks to God!" It was he who dealt with the mayor, the sergeant of police, the army lieutenant, he who sent word to Papa Andronikos, sent for the doctor, and urged Verek to take the stricken Damian home. And then he knelt beside me where I was cradling Mike in my arms, and: "You do not tell me you go to rescue your husband!" he said. "You do not wake me! I slept! I cannot believe I slept!"

My God, only a poet would in all innocence say such a thing at such a time.

Zoë brings warmed olive oil, and I begin to work at the top layer of the tape that encases Mike's face from his forehead to below his cheekbones. You'd think they'd been planning to mummify him.

As I crouched there on the beach, trying to comfort Mike when his arm or leg would be racked by cramp, I'd seen *Pouláki Mou* come about, no longer silently under sail but with motor chugging brazenly as she headed back toward Pyrgotafos. Then the mayor took Mike and me to Zoë's, so it isn't until now that I've been able to hear from Niko what happened when Kyriakos dropped anchor in the harbor and was met by the sergeant of police.

"I go with them, of course, Katerina. I want to hear what he has to say. His story is simple. Night after night Kyriakos hides in *Pouláki Mou,* he tells them, waiting for the pirate who took your husband to return. He knows someone has used his boat to take husband away, he says, and maybe will need boat to bring him back. He is there when this pirate comes—as we all know to our sorrow, it is Kostas— who threatens him, Kyriakos says, who makes him to agree he will sail *Pouláki Mou* near the tower, and there pretend to be fishing while he, Kostas, swims ashore after husband. But Kyriakos is not willing to wait patiently like burro, like donkey; he plans to pull

— 371 —

up anchor and let the boat to drift out in the channel. Alone, he says. He does not wish to ferry the American father of his dead friend's son one mile, two miles out to sea, and there help throw him overboard like spoiled fish . . ."

I have one layer off. I must go very slowly, very carefully, for where it adheres to the skin of his cheek there are welts like burns. Mike is being very stoic, giving no sign that anything I do causes him the slightest discomfort. Somehow this toughness, this apparent indifference to pain unnerves me. Or maybe it's his silence: as if he's pretending we aren't here, he isn't here, what's happening to him isn't happening. I suppose he's had lots of practice at it, this past week . . .

"Why did Kostas think he could force Kyriakos to help him?" I ask Nikos, my voice shaking. And answer my own question: "He must have had some sort of hold over him, obviously." *Steady, Kay. It's over. Mike's here, and he's alive.*

"Kyriakos tell police he is afraid of Kosta's knife." Nikos takes fresh oil from Zoë and begins work on another section of layer number two. "But I think the sharp point he fears most is on tip of Kostas' tongue. Kostas know something that Kyriakos fears for the police to know—oh, yes, I am sure of it."

"Are you saying Kyriakos let *Pouláki Mou* drift beyond the mines on *purpose?*" I can't help it, the notion horrifies me: it's an excess of treachery . . .

"He tells police he did not think about the mines," Nikos says slowly. "I think this is not truth, Katerina. Story he tells me—we go afterwards on board *Pouláki Mou* and he fix coffee—this story is not same

— 372 —

as he tells police. He has something to show me, he says . . ."

Nikos is silent for so long at last I prod him.

"Why didn't Kostas just hop in his taxi and take off for Mytilene without going near *Pouláki Mou* at all? Or to the tower, either, for that matter? He could have freed Mike by phoning Voula from Athens, as he told me he planned to—he'd have got away scot-free, then—"

"No, Katerina, he cannot soar free. Kyriakos has cut his wings. What he show me on *Pouláki Mou* is four million drachmas."

"On *Pouláki Mou!* And all along I thought—but why didn't he just leave it in his taxi? Under the seat, or something?"

"He did, Katerina." Grimly. "From there Kyriakos takes to even better hiding place, under torn nets in hold of his boat."

"So Kyriakos has been mixed up in this all along?"

"No, no, he comes in very late, and then on side of angels—if it is as he says." Nikos looks thoughtful. "The longer I think over what Kyriakos tell me, the more I believe him, *kyría.*"

At least two more layers under this one. Maybe three . . .

"Kay, who is this 'Katerina' guy?" Mike's voice is husky, as if his throat hurts. "I think I know his voice."

"We meet in Athens, *kýrie* Cunningham. I am Nikólas Paradéllis, godfather of Damian and friend to Katerina."

"Very good friend," I say, and manage a smile. "His friends call him Níko."

Mike extends his hand in the general direction of Níko's voice. "Mike to mine." Stronger now, though still hoarse. "Do me a favor, Níko—what the hell *did* Kyriakos tell you?" A hint—just a hint—of a grin.

"Is not easy for me. It is about my friend from all my life." His thin, ugly face is very tired. "This, then, is the story Kyriakos told me. When his boat is damaged, he knows somebody besides himself has sailed her. This is very strange happening, for no sailor here bother another man's boat. Also your husband has disappeared—another strange happening. It is Kyriakos' belief that two strange happenings occurring at same time are almost surely linked. His boat, then, is used when your husband is taken. He feels certain it is Kostas who has sailed his boat—Kostas knows how, though a very poor sailor. Also Kostas likes money and beautiful women. If husband dead, widow will be lonely."

Nikos does not look at me, but studies the edge of the tape as if it is a script in a foreign language.

"After old Voufounos's funeral, Kyriakos goes to *tavérna* in Molivos. Kostas stops on return from tourist trip to Eressos. They drink wine. Kostas' taxi is not parked on edge of *platéia* but right in front of *tavérna*, and he sits where he can look at it. He should have put sign on it, Kyriakos says to me in scorn: 'Ransom money is here!' So that evening—last night, Katerina—when it is dark but before moon is up, Kyriakos goes to where taxi waits by Yeoryio's house, and he very quiet like wood smoke blowing goes through the taxi, and finds the money—it is easy, it is indeed under rear seat, Kostas is too simple, he says. Kyriakos takes the money to *Pouláki Mou*, and sails to Molivos, where harbor is right by the road to

Mytilene, as you know. And there he waits. He is confident Kostas will drive to Mytilene as first step in his escape, but will he look to make sure money is safe before he starts? Kyriakos hopes no. 'My luck is in,' he tells me. 'Kostas does not look. He sneak out very quiet and drive to Molivos, I hear car coming. I get out in road and wave down taxi. Naturally he stops—what else?''

Nikos gets up abruptly, brings out a crushed package of cigarettes, selects one, and lights it. "I quit to smoke some other time, when my life not so full of drama." He takes a turn or two about the room. "Kyriakos tells me he has a plan. He will make Kosta show him is your husband alive or is he dead? If he is alive, somehow Kyriakos will give him back to you, but this will not be easy, because Kostas has knife to his throat—" Nikos looks at me uncertainly.

"A little matter of drug-running." I nod. "Kostas was kidding around one time, dropping a lot of heavy hints. Kyriakos was not amused, as I remember."

"Yes . . . What Kyriakos say to Kosta there in the empty road by the harbor is this: 'You are a murderer. You have killed Katerina's husband. I do not worry about me, I go to police.' Kosta says, 'No, no, I do not kill husband, he is safe, and when I, too, am safe, I say where he is, and everybody happy.' 'What you will use for travel?' Kyriakos asks. 'If you think ransom is in taxi, you are big fool. It is on *Pouláki Mou*. And I think you, Kosta Demetriou, will not go to police and complain I have robbed you of your ransom money. No, you will get Katerina's husband and bring alive to *Pouláki Mou*, and then I will give you your half the money.' " Nikos inhales deeply. "Because, you see, Katerina, Kyriakos knows Kostas will not believe him if he does not seem to want money, too. Just to take risk for you—for your husband—no, that is not believable, not to Kosta." The lines in his ugly face grow deeper.

"I see," I say slowly. "Kostas came after Mike in order to get the ransom back . . . get it back without attracting attention, I mean. He could hardly kill Kyriako right there in Molivos, after all. What did he think Kyriakos planned to do? He must have realized they could hardly—either of them—turn Mike loose. And Kyriakos wouldn't have a getaway plan—"

It's all too complicated . . . Byzantine . . . and I am very tired. Thank God only one layer more . . .

"Maybe Kostas think Kyriakos planning to kill him and your Mike, and take all the ransom, and sail away in *Pouláki Mou*. If that is his plan, he, Kostas, will be quicker—*he* will kill Kyriako, and husband, and take money, and so on and so forth. So Kostas goes on the boat. And Kyriakos say where shall I sail after husband? And Kostas say I tell you when you get there. And Kostas say where is the money? And Kyriakos say I show you when you bring husband. And so very trusting and friendly they sail to the tower, and Kostas swims to shore and so far all goes well. But then the gods mix in, Katerina. *You* are there. Everything is changed. Kyriakos, when he see you coming from the tower, knows never must you start to swim, Katerina, you will die. Kostas likes beautiful women, true, but money he love. Also he is now in too deep water. You will drown before you reach *Pouláki Mou*, easy to hold you under; or he will bring you and there before Kyriakos can kill him he will hold that knife to you and say where is ransom, tell me or I kill her—Kyriakos has very vivid imagination, being a sailor. And then—ah, here come Damian and Yeoryios, he can see them running, running up the road! He decide he must leave his seat and join the play, not just sit and watch the actors . . . So he moves *Pouláki Mou.*"

For a long moment Nikos is silent, studying the glowing tip of his cigarette. Then: "I think much of what he tells me is truth, Katerina. I think it is true Kyriakos does not wish to help kill your husband, that he try to think how to save him. But when he move his boat . . . perhaps he does not want Kosta to swim back, he does not want to have to kill him or be killed himself; perhaps he wants Kosta dead, silent, no danger to any man, but not by his knife. Or perhaps—and this is what I like to think, Katerina—perhaps Kyriakos in spite of all is still true friend of Kosta, and wants give him his chance. He move *Pouláki Mou* beyond the *karpói* to see if gods are friendly—why not? Who is to say which is better— to be free for a few days, a few weeks, then have shameful trial and rot many years in prison, or to have swift death on stony beach under starlit sky?"

I'm down to the last layer of tape. It's glued to the lids, to the fragile, delicate skin around the eyes. Slowly, slowly I coax up the edge, work the oil in gently . . . "Nearly there, Mike darling," I say, my voice shaking.

Mike gives a convulsive jerk, and his breath comes shallowly. "Damned . . . damned leg," he mutters. "Sorry."

Nikos' nicotine-stained fingers slide down Mike's

calf, find the cramp, the agonizingly knotted muscle, and begin to knead it, gently at first, then more and more strongly.

Gone . . . Gone . . . Gone . . . Gone . . .

Nikos looks up, his face white. "This time I do not need to run to ask who," he says, his voice tight with grief. "It is for my friend."

There is nothing I can think to say.

Zoë shuts the door against the noise, but still we can hear the strokes of the bell, we can count them, if we want.

. . . Sixteen: Seventeen: Eighteen: Nineteen: . . .

We have just got the last of the tape off, and I'm wiping Mike's lids and lashes (what's left of them) free of the oil when the door opens and Yeoryios steps in, ushering a reluctant Damian before him. Damian is clutching a stiff bouquet of carnations and roses.

"I have come to ask pardon for sins of my brother," Yeoryios says with heavy dignity. His hand on Damian's shoulder, he propels him forward.

Damian gives Mike a quick glance, then away. He thrusts out the flowers. "My aunt Verek wish for you soon good health," he mumbles, sends one burning glance at me, then drops his eyes.

Mike looks at him. I can't read his thoughts. (I don't want to.) He looks. He keeps looking. Then: "Thank you."

Damian studies the floor. "My aunt Verek say never say thank you for flowers, they will die," he mutters.

Gone . . . Gone . . . Gone . . .

Yeoryios casts a glance over his shoulder as if the sound of the bell is a hound at his heels. "It is for my brother," he blurts out harshly. "My brother who turns his knife against me, who plans to murder you, *kýrie* Cunningham, and not for honor or for freedom, but for money—for money! How can I grieve for such a one? Yet I do grieve."

So he does. So he did—as Damian and I know. He and I had watched in horror as Yeoryios raced across the beach, raced to where Kostas lay supine, face turned sightless toward the stars. Crouched to see if Death had claimed him. Begun to drag him back across the rocky beach, back along the path they'd come . . . thought better of it, and spread his jacket over Kostas' face (what was left of his face) but not before Damian had seen. And we'd watched Yeoryios sink to his knees, his face in his hands and blood dripping down his thigh, and kneeling there, mourn his brother.

Mike raises himself on an elbow. "Listen, Demetriou, your brother wasn't in this until I got off that plane, drugged out of my skull. He didn't plan it, he just got roped in—" Mike's voice cracks; it is clearly still painful for him to speak. Only his courage and his kindness, I think with stinging pride, drive him to offer Yeoryio whatever consolation he can scrape up. As I reach for the tea and hold the cup to his lips, he gives me one look—the first he has really *looked* at me since the blindfold is off—and the sudden blazing love that leaps across the space between us is almost tangible . . . I can almost hold it. *It's going to be all right: he loves me: in spite of everything, he loves me* . . . We are kissing though we do not touch.

"That fellow who doped me—the wine seller— he dreamed the whole deal up, Demetriou. I grant you your brother jumped at the chance to get in on it, but he didn't start it, remember that." Mike takes the cup from my hands and drains it. I give it to Zoë to refill. "They talked mostly in German, which they assumed I didn't know. Your brother wasn't in any position to say no, even if he'd wanted to." And he takes the cup again, smiles his thanks, and empties it.

I reach for his hand, and I hold it. *Alive, alive, he's alive!* He looks at me again, and again between us there leaps a current of such love . . . I turn as if to share this love with Damian, and I see the anguish on his face. How can I rejoice when my joy is bought by his grief? He *loved* Kostas, in spite of what he was—or because of what he was. Daring. Impudent. Cunning. Resourceful. He didn't see the greed, the ruthlessness, the consummate selfishness. Or perhaps he did—finally. Perhaps he grieves as much over the toppling of his idol as over his death.

How helpless we are to protect our children! And not only from bodily harm. We can only arm them, with knowledge, with prudence, with courage, and with stoicism if all else fails. But when we do this, what is left of their childhood? Childhood is not needing armor . . . I feel again the helplessness I felt as Damian and I watched the figure running in the moonlight, light and swift and full of life one moment, brought down like a deer in midleap the next. Freedom . . . leaping to freedom. *Kostas chose . . . I know he chose.* He snatched what gift he could from the gods, and they were kind. To die young, and free, and at the height of his powers.

Mike is smiling at Damian. "I am very glad to see you at last. For a while there I wasn't sure I ever would. And I thank you. I'm kind of hazy about a

— 380 —

lot that happened last night, but I do know I owe you my life."

"Don't say thank you," Damian says with difficulty, "you're my friend—" His voice breaks on the word.

"I tell you this, *pehthí mou*," Nikos says, "it is not you who have caused your uncle's death. Kostas is dead these eight days or more. When he choose to join in the capture of Katerina's husband—whatever the reason, whatever the threats that Sanzio used—that moment is the death of his *psikhí*—his soul."

"Yes, though I did not wish it, it was I," Damian says in a choked voice. "If I did not look to see who comes for the money—if I did not wait, hidden in the great olive, to watch—"

"Then your American father dies," Yeoryios says harshly. "But you, *mátia mou*, stop to take all the credit. Did I not ask him to sell for me my findings of treasure? Did I not cause him to meet this *poniró*, this seller of stolen goods, this outlook for bandits? I do not turn a knife on my brother, but I cause his death all the same!"

The detonation of the mine has been like the crash of the car against the tree: for no one who heard it will the world ever be the same.

"Kyriakos say for me to tell you this, Damiane," Nikos says gently, his hand on Damian's shoulder. "He knows you will grieve. The gods weave a net, he says, a tight, tight net, and our fish swam in freely and of his own wish. I say Kyriakos is right. Grieve for your uncle, but do not blame yourself. That is arrogance, and the gods punish all arrogance but their own."

Damian stares up at him angrily. "Then they will

punish me! I know what I know—I had *choice!*" His voice breaks. Tears are streaming down his face.

My God, what can I do, what can I do? He's going to blame himself, as I blamed myself about David. That's the worst grief: the stabbing, gnawing, unceasing guilt. And it was I he chose: it was against me Kostas turned his knife . . . against me, in whose eyes, Damian, you saw your mother's—and I can't have you for a son!

Mike gropes for the glass of water. "You are right, Damian, you had a choice," he says huskily. "When you saw your uncle had his knife out, you screamed *'oh-hee'*—no! A man can't go against his own soul, Damian, and you didn't." He sips, sips again. "Your godfather told me about your father, how he was a man to make the name of Demetriou much honored and respected. What your uncle did can't change what kind of a man your father was. And you're his son—look, we all make choices all the time, Damian, and you chose—you, your father's son—chose to say no to murder." He looks across at Yeoryio. "With such a son of your brother in your house, I don't think you need feel much shame."

"Mike," I say swiftly, "we—we can't have Damian. The law won't let us. We aren't Greek."

I'm sorry, Mike. Oh, God, I'm so very sorry.

Mike looks at me, his blue, blue eyes remote.

"I think you have Damian in spite of this law," Yeoryios says quietly. "He is my brother's son, he is my son, but he is *kyría* Katerina's too, Mr. Mike. You have problem: your woman has son in Greece. My wife want me be sure to say when you bring her to see him, at name days, at Christmas, at Easter, our house is your house."

Damian shakes his head. "I choose my American father, and so my uncle die!" he blurts again, his eyes dark as the pool beneath the tower. "*I* kill him, my uncle Kostas!"

And what can I say to ease his grief? Desperately I cast about in my mind . . . What was it Mike had read to me . . . that I'd been so mad at him for reading to me . . .

"Listen, Damian—listen to me. Before I came my husband read to me about your country, and one of the stories was this—do you know it? Zeūs sits at the gate of heaven, and he shakes feathers from two jugs—feathers of good and feathers of evil. A feather of good touched my husband, and feathers of evil covered Kosta, and it was not your fault, Damian . . ."

Thin comfort.

Damian says nothing.

Gone . . . Gone . . . Gone . . . Four: . . . Five: . . . It's starting over.

Yeoryios reaches to clasp Mike's hand. "I see you again before you leave for America. Now my friends come to my house, and I must be there with my wife." Then, to me: "If you do not come to the funeral, *kyría* Katerina, everyone understand and forgive. Your place is here, with your husband."

Damian follows him out without so much as a backward glance. Nikos, too, gathers up Zoë with a look, and at last—at last!—Mike and I are alone.

The ritual of apology, of atonement—whatever it is that Yeoryios and Damian have just done—has exhausted Mike. For a few moments he lies very still. When I kneel by the bed, he opens his eyes.

"I'm sorry, too, Kay." His voice is just above a whisper. "So now you lose another child you love. Damn it, it's not fair . . . Katharine, my Kay . . ."

I heard it. I heard him say it.

He puts his hand against my cheek, and I know it's true at last: *Mike is with me.* The past year still exists; it's part of the fabric of our lives—it always will be —but it's no longer the dominant, the only thread. David's death has been worse for me than for Mike because it was my fault. It was something Mike and I could not really share, not fully; he hadn't been at the core of it, as I was. So, too, his capture—his captivity—is something I cannot share completely. Our lives circle around and around each other like two atoms on a single pole, but never identical, never truly overlapping. And that is right, and as it should be . . .

"I love you, Mike. Oh, God, I love you, I love you! Don't ever stop loving me, because I won't be able to bear it. If you've already stopped—well, damn it, start up again, you hear?" And I don't know whether to laugh or cry, so I do neither.

"That's what I kept saying," Mike tells me. "Over and over and over, all the time. 'I love you, Kay,' I said. In spite of that gag. With every cell of my body. I kept hoping to hell you heard me. God, how I prayed I'd get the chance to tell you! That was the worst—when I realized they were bound to kill me— when the Greek made it plain he knew you, saw you every day, gave me bulletins about how you were doing. When he called Sanzio by name, I knew it was a sure thing—"

"*He* did? *Kostas?* You're sure?"

"Yeah. The other guy—was he American? I never

figured it out—he had some kind of standards, professional standards, I guess. He kept arguing they had to let me go if the ransom got paid and you didn't go to the police—it was the only way future snatches would come off. Anyway, that was the worst, when I knew I'd never have the chance to say what I didn't—what I was so damn stubborn and—and mad . . . too stupid to tell you . . ."

For a few minutes Mike drifts toward sleep, and I—I can't get enough of looking at him. *He breathes: he's here: he lives: he is, he is.*

"He won't be the same next year," Mike says suddenly.

"I know . . . But you don't have the same child come home that you send off in the morning. Or husband either, actually. It depends on what's happened that day."

"Or wife, Kay. You're not the same woman I put on the plane . . . What did *you* think about?"

"That I didn't see how I was going to get through the rest of my life without you."

"I thought about you. You and David. He was with me, I think, all the time. Was he with you?"

"No," I say, and face the truth of it. "Damian was."

But I have walked in Damian's shoes. I understand the unreasoning, the implacable guilt that gnaws him. The *if only . . . if only* he castigates himself with because he didn't tell Yeoryio, didn't tell Niko . . . there'd have been time, then, to persuade Kostas to turn back. But he came for me. Why? Because I, too, had said, "I only have you . . . I can trust only you."

Mike is deep in healing sleep. A most strange,

most unfamiliar feeling is creeping over me . . . of peace . . . of burdens laid down. I've buried David at last, not his death, but the circumstances of his death. I love him—I will always love him, always mourn him—but he is dead, and I'm alive, and so is Mike. It's true our lives are interwoven, entangled, but our threads are separate. David's was brief—a bright golden strand that played out early. I had not willfully snapped it off. It had been spun that way.

As had Kostas'.

Now I must write Damian. Somehow I must find the words, the healing words no one said to me when I needed them, that I had to find for myself.

I take a clean sheet, and very carefully, for these are important words I'm writing, perhaps the most important I've ever written, I begin:

Dear Damian, my Greek son—

Wrong. Start over.

Dear Damian, my beloved son—

And now my pen flows smoothly.